# TURRET MAGE

# TURRET MAGE

## IN MY DEFENSE BOOK ONE

J. Drude

Podium

# TURRET MAGE

# CHAPTER ONE

# Throat Punch Goblins

I woke up drowning, face-down on a concrete floor. The rancid puddle that I'd, for some reason, made my bed—one shallow enough for sleeping but just deep enough to be inhaled—rushed into my mouth and nose. Traces of copper, rust and something . . . chunky were in the mix, but my still-barely-functioning cerebral cortex didn't register the idea of rolling over to spit the stuff out until it was too late.

Full consciousness only came to me once I'd aspirated it all and found myself coughing violently as I flopped limply onto my back, vaguely registering the harsh sound of metal scraping against stone. I was much too busy trying to expel the nasty water from my lungs to pay much attention to a little detail like that, though.

My body felt alien, like my bones and organs had all been scrambled around in my sleep and hadn't bothered filing for a change of address.

The long, warbling cackle of some kind of bird is what made my brain finally sit up and take notice of something other than my own discomfort.

I was familiar with birds, at least in an academic sense. Terrabiology was one of those subjects only referred to secondhand these days, mostly when somebody came across some unknown species of flesh-ripping lizard or sentient goo and said somebody needed to compare it to something in the scientific record. I'd never actually heard a birdcall in person, but there it was, clear as day.

Much too quickly, I raised my head to listen, immediately regretting every one of my life choices, especially this one. A wave of dizziness threatened to overpower my stomach, and the world waved and wobbled in my vision.

I blinked. Then I blinked again, harder this time.

Nothing changed.

I was in what remained of an office, or at least that was my guess. The elements had their way with this place sometime before my arrival, wearing things down to a nearly unrecognizable ruin. The walls were made of cracked, moldy concrete with flaking paint flapping in the sluggish breeze that whistled through the building. Piles of rotted wood and rusted metal sat against either wall, except where the entirety of the floor had crumbled and fallen away, leaving a gaping chasm that swallowed most of the room. The wall opposite me, far out of reach, still maintained a tenuous grip on its part of the floor, so that the remaining slab formed a sagging concrete ramp down into the lower levels that disappeared out of sight.

Empty window frames lined the wall to my left, beyond which the world was a kaleidoscope of swaying greenery. Mossy carpets grew on the sills and draped down to puddle on the floor, flourishing by following the natural flow of precipitation. What used to be a sheet metal ceiling had long since rusted away, leaving only brown scraps, but, high above, spiderwebbing tree branches, fat with teal and brown leaves, grew over the building like a natural roof, blocking the sky completely. What sunlight there was, filtered in through the canopy, bathing everything in a greenish shadow that wobbled like I was below the waves of an ocean.

The wind was slow and quiet. That felt strange to me, though I couldn't put my finger on why. It was soothing, in a way, but unnatural in another.

A chipper, female voice shattered the moment. "Greetings, Chosen!"

"Gah!" I shouted, half in fear, half as a war cry. I shot to my feet, or I tried to, at least pulling off a moderate stagger followed by a nausea-inducing dizzy spell. Whirling, I got my hands up and ready for an attack, the act of which felt significant.

The translucent figure of a woman stood in the corner of the room, a polite smile on her face. She was short and stocky with a strong jaw but inarguably feminine in shape, with generous curves that her work uniform and leather apron couldn't entirely hide. Her hands were folded in front of her like she'd been waiting patiently for the moment to speak.

"I apologize for frightening you, Ch-Chosen," she said with a hitch, raising her hands and showing me her empty palms. "Integration always causes some mi-mild disorientation."

She froze, not like she was waiting for a response from me, more like she was on a video feed from a distant satellite and the signal had been interrupted. "... and I've always found it best to get the initial greeting out of the way and get d-down to it." Her harsh consonants and awkward, drawn-out vowels sounded Old Earth to me, but I couldn't be sure.

*Integration.* That tickled something at the back of my mind. There was something there, something important, but my thoughts were seeds in the wind, so fast and fragile I couldn't hold on to one without damaging it beyond recognition.

I shook my head uselessly. I was having a hard time stringing thoughts together in a way that made sense.

*How exactly did I get here?*

She seemed to take my confused silence as her cue to go on. "I'm sure you have many questions, but if you allow me, I think this tutorial can establish a b-bas-base level of understanding so that your questions are more productive. What say you to that, Chosen?"

*Chosen.* That felt like a proper noun. What's more, it was tied to something I knew.

Images flashed in my mind.

A burning circle. A faceless man. Breaking bones. Cold metal through my chest.

My heart hummed into overdrive.

*Wait.*

"Wh—" I began, but as I lowered my head to look myself over, all rational thoughts fizzled and died. I was wearing plain white clothes, a V-neck shirt and belted pants along with some black boots—all pristine except for what I'd done to them by lying in a puddle. All of it looked strange, however: a cut and style I'd never encountered in my life, but that's not what short-circuited my brain.

Inside the neck of my shirt, where I expected to find the left side of my chest, I saw black, segmented metal. It rose and fell in time with my breathing, the folded joints clicking and adjusting quietly to give me full range of motion as my lungs expanded and contracted. In a panic, I reached up with my hand and ripped my shirt down the middle, my eyes bulging wide and blood rushing through my ears as I worked my way up to full-on panic.

Half of my upper torso, from my pectoral to my shoulder to my . . . to my arm. All metal, black as Proxis's night.

*My arm. I have—*

"Chosen, are you alright?" the glowing woman asked. She'd taken a tentative step closer but didn't seem to know whether to reach out or keep away from me.

My voice came out in a trembling whisper. "Uh . . . I have a metal arm," I said, not able to look away. I blinked moisture out of my eyes.

The hologram raised her eyebrows and adopted that long-suffering tone one might use when speaking with a child. "Yes. Yes, you do."

"Why?" I couldn't think of what else to ask.

"What do you mean, Chosen?"

"I mean why is it here . . . on me?" I asked.

"It is your arm," she replied slowly, like I was simple.

I rotated the offending appendage back and forth to give us both a really good look. The fully articulated wrist and fingers made little clicking noises as they responded to my will. The motion was smooth and precise, unlike any prosthetic I'd ever encountered. "No, it's really not." I declared with confidence.

"A-are you sure?" she asked, incredulous.

"Yes!" My voice was high now, bordering on a shriek. "Who forgets they have a metal arm?"

"How am I supposed to know?"

"You said to ask questions!"

"It would be more productive if you asked questions relevant to the tutorial," she admonished but bent forward to examine the alien metal in order to humor me, going so far as to sniff it, which struck me as odd and pointless. "D-did you not have it before?"

"No! I mean, maybe not?" Oh, God, she was breaking me down. I wasn't sure about anything. "I don't think so, at least."

"Quite the mystery," she said, flashing white, and then she was upright again, her eyes brightening with something akin to glee. "Also a p-perfect segue into the tutorial."

I narrowed my eyes at her. Her expression was expectant, as if my willingness to go along with her tutorial would make her day.

As an experiment, I flexed my hands, first the fleshy one, then the metal one. I could feel both but in noticeably different ways. The metal one was more muted but there was something else there, too—something . . . *different*, like a tickle that ran deep through the core of it.

The hologram cleared her throat, apparently deciding that my silence was a tacit invitation to begin her tutorial. "Ahem. As I was saying earlier: Welcome, Chosen, to the Animator Class tutorial! I am Nali, the administrator of this tutorial since the Class's inception. I am a System-created satellite intelligence whose sole purpose is to get you ready for your new life as an ascended member of humanity. Here, you will be taught how to interface with the System, use your Class's unique abilities, and grow in power. Any disorientation you might feel right now is a normal part of your integration and should pass with time. Any questions so far?"

I had so many. Everything she was saying felt right or at least familiar, but I couldn't seem to connect it with the corresponding parts of my memory.

So I settled for the basics. "Where are we? How did I get here?"

"You are on Ralqir, on the outer edge of the Bera Maelstrom. The System created a temporary insertion point for you and will return you to your point of integration upon completion of this tutorial. Unlike normal inter-universal travel, insertion points take a great deal of energy and can only be used for an event of great significance. In this case, that was your integration."

"I've never heard of the uh . . . Bera Maelstrom."

"It is a phenomenon that is not possible in your own universe. Ralqir was chosen long ago for its potential in training new Animators like you, and I think you will find the environment quite advantageous for the purpose."

"So, I'm an Animator, and this is not my universe." I sounded so stupid when I said it like that. *Shouldn't I know? Should I be freaking out at least a little? Probably.*

"Yes, of course. Please, keep up. Pull up your Status Screen and focus on your Class. All you have to do is think about it to activate it. Even though the System gifted you with a Status Screen, it is yours and will always respond to your will. It is a part of you now, and as you grow, so will your understanding of it and yourself. You will find this to be true about many aspects of your new life."

Before I could do as she asked, a brightly outlined box appeared in my vision, with green text on a black background.

New Quest: Tutorial
Tutorial: Learn Your New Capabilities
Accept? Y/N

It was a simple message, short and easy to understand, but something inside of me lit up upon reading it, a giddy sort of joy as if I'd been waiting for this moment for my entire life.

I chose "**Y**."

| Ryan Kotes - Level 0 Animator | | | | |
|---|---|---|---|---|
| **Type:** | Artificer (Common) | **Abilities:** | Shape | |
| **Class:** | Animator (Uncommon) | | Consume | |
| **Core:** | Engine (Unique) | | | |
| **HP:** | 25/25 | **Skills:** | | |
| **Body:** | 10 | | | |
| **Mind:** | 12 | | | |
| **Spirit:** | 9 | **Affinities:** | | |
| | | | | |
| | | | | |

Seeing my name in print like that helped, at least. Everything in my head was a chaotic mess right now, but having something concrete right there telling me who I was felt strangely comforting.

"My name is Ryan, by the way," I said. "Says here on my status."

"It is not unheard of to forget one's own name upon integration, but it is unusual," Nali replied.

"Not sure if 'forgot' is the right word," I mumbled defensively. "I needed reminding is all."

I focused on the Class like Nali had asked me to.

> Class: Animator—As craftsmen, builders, and engineers, Animators shape the future. Where typical Artificers cut and hammer material into shape, Animators infuse their mana into material and make it temporarily a part of themselves, giving the Animator a perfect awareness of its dimensions and capabilities. Powerful Animators are at home in workshops and laboratories, advancing human quality of life or forging terrifying weapons of war.

"It says I'm some kind of crafter," I stated. Complicated feelings swirled around inside of me when I said it aloud. I was, at once, sad, afraid, and thrilled. I wasn't sure where it was all coming from.

"Not just any kind of craftsman, Chosen. The best kind," Nali declared, her chin raised in pride.

"In your unbiased opinion," I replied.

"Absolutely."

I glanced at the screen again. "It says it's uncommon."

"Vanishingly uncommon, I would say," she opined. "According to my internal clock. I haven't been activated in many years—so many I thought that the Class might have been phased out."

"Is that why the place is so . . ." I trailed off, not wanting to flat-out call the place a wreck in front of its caretaker.

"It does appear that things are not as the last Animator left them, it is true," Nali observed, looking around and shaking her head. "But we cannot let that get in the way of your tutorial, can we? Let's move on to your Abilities. These a-are the bread and butter of your Class, and you wouldn't be a full Chosen without them. The first thing we need to do is find something to Shape. Normally, I would have something laid out here for you, but my house is in somewhat of a state of d-disarray. Let's head downstairs and find some malleable materials. Metal is the easiest to start with."

I nodded, ready to do as she asked, but there were problems with that plan.

The room had two doors, both leading directly over a huge hole where the floor should have been, and the crumbling concrete of both doorways looked like it was just barely holding on. Rusted brown rebar jutted out from the edges, twisted and sharp from being stretched and eventually snapped by the stress. Meanwhile, I was tucked into the far corner of the room on an isolated platform with nothing but air between me and the exits. Just looking at the exposed rebar made me feel all tetanus-y.

"Getting downstairs might be a challenge," I said. "This place looks like how my brain feels."

"Again, I apologize for the s-state of things," Nali said, advancing forward to examine me carefully. My skin tingled as she traced my body with her eyes, ending her scan with my face. "You are more affected by the integration than my previous students, and I have made a note of it. If I were to speculate, I would say you were in a bad way before you were inserted into Ralqir."

I shrugged. "Yeah. Maybe so."

She bit her lip as she leaned to the side to examine my face in profile. "Concerning. Everyone starts their tutorial healthy and alert as a rule. The energy required to heal you once was already budgeted for this quest when it was first initiated, but if you weren't in good health at the start, that energy was likely all used up to get you to your current state. Be careful from here on out. You are more durable than you were prior to integration, but you are not immortal."

Quest Update: Tutorial
Tutorial: Find Material

Yay. The quest box was back.

"Are you doing that?" I asked.

"Doing what, Ryan?"

"I just got an update on my quest. It says to find material."

"No. It's not me. The S-System is in charge of quests and rewards. I am just a teacher. We should do as it asks if we hope to finish your tutorial and get you home."

I didn't like my chances jumping from where I was to one of the doors. I felt heavy and not just because I was tired. I was pretty sure I was literally heavier than I used to be. Having a significant part of your body replaced with metal did that.

I got on my stomach and crawled to the lip of my little platform. Down below, it was dark—only made darker by the contrast between my windowed room up here and whatever conditions there were down there. Water dripped and splashed somewhere in the ruins, echoing harshly off the hard surfaces and confusing my mental picture of the place.

"How far is it to the next floor?" I asked, craning my neck back to be able to see my glowing tour guide.

"Approximately twenty feet."

"Wonderful," I groaned. No way was I jumping down there. I would need to monkey over to one of the doorways using the tetanus sticks.

An idea flashed through my mind. "You wanted metal, right? For me to use my Abilities on."

"Yes, it is generally the easiest material for new Animators to Shape, and most Animators have at least one Affinity for a certain type of metal," Nali replied with a raised brow.

"How easy is it?"

She considered a brief moment before answering. "It depends on the student. Some have a higher Affinity for their material than others."

I narrowed my eyes. My status screen had an Affinities section, but it was empty.

"What about that?" I asked, pointing at the rebar.

"Heavily oxidized but still iron. An imperfect medium for your tutorial, but if you insist."

I did insist. I edged forward, toward the crumbling edge of my floor. Little bits of loose rocks and dust tumbled down into the hole as I crawled as far as I dared, within reach of one of the longer, duller bars of iron.

Nali lapsed back into tutorial mode as I scooted close enough to touch the metal. "Reach over and place your hand on it. Good. Look at your Status Screen now. Under Abilities, what do you see?"

"First one on the list is Shape."

"Very good. Focus on activating that Ability. Will it to happen, and pay attention to how it feels."

I wrapped my fingers around the rusted metal bar, gritty and brittle to the touch. Flakes of rust smeared over my palm and through my fingers, but I did as Nali instructed. I willed the Ability to activate. It didn't take much. Soon I felt a trickle of something icy like snowmelt traveling from the center of my body, under the flesh and muscle of my arm, and out through my palm, only to stop momentarily as it hit the outside of the rebar. The cold liquid pooled and coalesced until I felt it wrapping around the bits of the metal I was currently touching. Pressing in. Then, as if a barrier had broken, the icy stream flowed through, mapping the entirety of the iron bar, inside and out . . .

. . . and I *knew*. I knew where the imperfections were. I knew where the rust had almost eaten through. I knew how far under me the bar went. Where the mold that had originally made this bar had a chip in it. I knew it all.

"Got it. I'm—I don't know. I'm inside of it?"

"Good. Good. This state is called Saturation. Notice how doing so cost you Mana Points or MP. Certain materials are more able to accept mana. Others are resistant."

She was right about the MP thing. I was down a few points, and I already felt mentally taxed, like I had just finished doing several complex math equations simultaneously in my head while reading a philosophy textbook out loud.

"What do I do now?" I asked, my voice straining slightly. My mind felt like it was being stretched between two distant points and my bandwidth for everything else was suffering.

"Now that you have saturated the material, it should respond to your will. What purpose would you have it fulfill?"

The goal here was to get out of the room, so I guessed my purpose was pretty simple. "To not slice my hand open when I grab it, for starters."

"In that case, focus on reshaping it to fit that purpose."

At first I tried to do it with my hand, squeezing the metal and bending it until it looked like the end of a candy cane.

That didn't work at all. The rebar bent slowly and not in the ways that I wanted, and it had the unfortunate habit of returning back to its original shape.

With physical might not getting me anywhere, I tried a fully mind-based approach, just lightly touching the iron and sort of bending my mental picture of it, taking what I knew and making it into what I wanted. No force. Just will.

Slowly, little by little, I flexed my new iron stick.

No. This metal was me now. *I* bent.

I bent the bar, curled the end, and blunted the sharp edges until I was pretty sure they wouldn't cut. The end result looked like a tiny metal tube sock, but it was *my* tiny metal tube sock.

> You have created: Crude Knob
> You have been awarded 5 Experience points. [10 base, -5 quality]

When I let go and sat up, I was sweating, yet the chill of the air left goose pimples on my flesh.

> MP: 20/30
> Ability: Shape is now Level 1.
> Quest Advanced: Tutorial
> Tutorial: Learn Your New Capabilities (continued)

Nali was right there, looking over my work with a discerning eye. "Very good, Ryan," she said, a pained, sympathetic smile on her face. "It is not how I pictured your first time, but I guess that cannot be helped. I imagine your Affinity for iron is quite low, considering the amount of time you took. Take note of how much MP this cost you. Certain materials are easier to work with than others, depending on their purity and your Affinity for said material. We will go over your Affinities and find suitable material for practice later. For now, remember that MP regenerates slowly, depending on your mental state and an assortment of other factors. You may want to rest—

"Oh no! Look out!" she shouted, not so much in fear or concern. Her tone was more indignant, like someone had just tracked mud on her carpet or left the front door open all night.

But I felt the danger acutely. I instinctively tucked my knees up to my chest, raised my shoulders, and brought my arms up to protect my head, just before something slammed into me from behind. Sharp talons dug into the flesh of my back, followed by something warm, wet, and sharp clamping down on my shoulder—the fleshy one, that is.

> [Unknown] attacks you for 5 Damage.
> Status gained: Bleeding (0.3 HP/sec)

"Gaaah!" I screamed in an octave I didn't realize I could hit. Stabbing pain erupted from my back, drowning out most rational thought.

Like you do when something is chowing down on your back, I immediately entered panic mode. I got to my feet and flailed my arms, hoping the motion would fling the thing off. I spun in a circle, arched my back, and flexed to try and land a blow on whatever was raking me, but I just couldn't get at it.

Whatever it was, it felt small—bigger than a house cat but smaller than the bigger breeds of dog—and it was stuck in, its claws digging way down into my flesh. Meanwhile, its jaws sawed back and forth on my shoulder, tearing at the muscle and scraping bone. Blood ran freely down my chest and my arm.

> You take 1 Bleeding Damage.

The thing on my back burbled happily, reveling in the pain it was causing, or at least that's what it sounded like to me.

"Nali, what is it?!" I screamed.

She sighed, the picture of matronly disappointment, hands folded in front of her again, frowning at her unruly children. "One of the locals. You'll need to get it off your back soon or the blood loss will kill you. This is going to put us further behind schedule." She reached up to rub one of her temples.

"No kidding!"

I had no weapons. All I had was my size. My attacker felt small. I was big. I needed to use that.

Bending my legs, I jumped as high as I could into the air, doing a sort of abortive backflip that would bring me down on my neck. Every self-preservation instinct I had told me not to do it, but I ignored them. My upper back and neck muscles tensed for the landing.

Contact with the ground came with a hollow *thud*. A pathetic sounding one, if I'm being honest. I'd landed how I wanted to, but the creature shifted its weight at the last instant, angling the impact with the concrete floor and rolling us to the side.

> You take 1 Impact Damage. (-1 mitigated)
> [Unknown] takes 3 Impact Damage.

[Unknown] is stunned.
Skill Unlocked: Unarmed Combat
Your current Skill Level is 1.

The move still had its intended effect. The thing's claws retracted, and its jaws seemed to relax slightly. I heard a muffled gurgle accompanied by the feeling of a long hot exhalation of breath on my back. I scrambled to disentangle myself from the little monster and get some distance.

You take 1 Bleeding Damage.

The front of my body was covered in blood, and I had to assume the back wasn't much better. Sticky redness dripped from my shoulder and ran down my elbow. Desperate not to let the thing climb onto my back again, I spun around, getting my feet under me.

That's when I got my first good look at my opponent. Its back was to me, but I was able to take in a few things of note.

My size estimate was correct. The creature was about as large as a small child of five, but that's where the comparison ended. It had midnight black, oily skin—at least where it wasn't covered in dried leathers and jangling bits of bone and teeth. The arms were long and spindly, ending in elongated hands with hooked claws that dragged along the ground. Jangling hoops of metal clinked together on its thin, protruding ears as the creature shook its oversized head.

You take 1 Bleeding Damage.
Scourge-Touched Goblin is no longer stunned.

When the goblin shook off my stun attack, its head spun around to look directly at me, so fast I didn't even see it move. The motion turned it almost 180 degrees around like an owl. It crouched low on thick, overdeveloped legs that bent in too many places, coiling to . . .

Then it was airborne, claws out, teeth bared, on a collision course with my face. The goblin's gaping jaw nearly split its already comically large head in half with how wide it was, showing off little shark teeth that had already done a number on my shoulder.

I threw myself to the side, almost catching an outstretched claw as I did, but the goblin only came away with a piece of my shirt. It hit the wall face-first with a wet little slap, but apparently that was part of its diabolical plan. It clung there, suspended on pitted concrete like it was nothing. Again, its head turned fully around, locking onto me with tiny, black eyes. It yowled and flicked its tongue in my direction just before it launched itself at my face yet again.

> You take 1 Bleeding Damage.

This time I had no room to dodge, not that I didn't try. I stumbled backward, my arms windmilling in front of me, but somewhere in the quarter second it took for the goblin to angle itself and get airborne, I got a bead on its trajectory. *THONK!*

> Critical hit!
> Scourge-Touched Goblin takes 6 Bludgeoning Damage. (Base 3 + Bonus 3)

By chance or through some innate combat reflex I hadn't realized I had, my enemy's face collided squarely with my new prosthetic. The move wasn't a proper jab, since my feet weren't set, but no one could complain about the results. The goblin's inertia carried it into the blow. My fist crashed into the monster's teeth, through its enormous mouth, and down the back of its throat until I'd fed it my entire metal forearm.

The monster's beady little eyes widened slightly with panic, and its jaws furiously worked back and forth on my arm trying to tear at it. Its claws raked over my shoulder, but, again, that part of me was no longer made of meat. It never even occurred to the creature to stop trying to kill me. It just bit and bit and clawed and clawed until it died, probably of asphyxiation or internal bleeding.

It took a disturbingly long time.

> Scourge-Touched Goblin defeated.
> You have been awarded 6 Experience points. [10 base (+2 level, +2 nemesis, -8 non-combat class)]
> You take 1 Bleeding Damage.

# CHAPTER TWO

# Glitch the Tutorial

Choking a nightmare creature to death from the inside was not how I'd envisioned this day going—not that I'd had any time to envision anything since integration.

"Nali?" I croaked as I let my arms slump down, my fist still caught in the dead goblin's throat.

Instantaneously, the hologram appeared a polite distance away, her hands folded in front of her. Her cheery disposition was back. "Yes, Ryan?"

I looked down at the twitching, black, oversized finger trap dangling from my fist. The muscles in the creature's jaw held on tightly, even after death. I shook the corpse, letting the gangly arms flop around bonelessly. The goblin's charms and earrings clacked and jingled with the motion.

"What the hell is this?" I asked in a tone sounding far calmer than I was actually feeling.

> You take 1 Bleeding Damage.
> Status removed: Bleeding
> HP: 13/25

"You will need to be m-more specific, Ryan. What can I help you with?" Her face froze mid-blink, and the program seemed to play the frames of the animation over and over again, giving it a surreal blur.

"Is this"—I pointed at my disgusting new bracelet—"a part of your tutorial? Do you keep a stable of goblins around for people like me?"

Her head flashed between tilted and straight a handful of times, but then whatever glitch she was experiencing passed. "I'm sorry, did you say something?"

"Scourge. Touched. Goblin." I pronounced every word carefully. The adrenaline was ebbing now, leaving me a little giddy. "Is it—"

Nali's eyes shot down to the goblin, and her expression turned from eager and helpful to horrified in a flash. Then she was gone.

Stunned, I blinked the Nali-shaped outlines clouding my vision.

"Nali?" I called out, turning to see if she had reappeared somewhere else, but the room was empty and a shade darker than it had been.

I was alone.

The leaves rustled overhead and cast moving shadows over the walls and through the windows that seemed to hold more dangerous potential than before. Despite the ambient noise, it was still eerily quiet here, something that unnerved me deeply and for reasons I couldn't articulate.

Then I was far away, in a domed habitation with tin-patched walls. I was small—a child, maybe. In my lap was a tablet device that I was playing some game on: Terratech or an emulation of it. There was a bin of discarded wire and circuit boards beneath my bed where I'd hidden my recycled toy sword I wasn't allowed to have anymore. The wind howled outside. Gusts slammed into the walls over and over again, bowing the metal, little pops of loose sheeting shifting in their frames, but I wasn't worried. The hab walls would flex and bend, but the engineers that designed the building knew their stuff. No, my eyes only focused on the screen and the fantastic worlds contained therein.

I coughed, suddenly remembering to breathe again, aware once more where I actually was. I tried to recall more with frustratingly little success.

My mind was a mess. Nothing in my head connected with anything else in a way that made sense.

Disorientation, as Nali had said. That was putting it mildly.

*Sure would be nice to have a tutorial admin here to ask questions.*

"Nali?" I called again, but no holographic woman appeared to help me.

I waited for a silent minute, hoping she would return.

Nothing. Just alien birdsong.

I closed my eyes and let out a slow breath, nodding as I turned the situation over in my head.

Obviously, I couldn't wait around for help to come to me. Nothing about this place was conducive to my continued existence, from its age to its failing structure to the fauna.

First order of business was safety. Then I could worry about the little stuff like who I was and what happened to me. Of course, I couldn't go about my business dragging a dead goblin around on my arm. Despite its size, the extra poundage was starting to weigh me down, and the metal parts of my body had already been doing that before Chompy came into my life.

I reached over and slid my hand under the goblin's jaw to try and pry it open, slipping my fingers into the gaps where the teeth had been knocked out. As I touched the creature's gums, a text window popped up in my vision.

Loot Scourge-Touched Goblin? Y/N

I felt my eyebrows climbing up my forehead.

*Loot, you say?*

The word sent a tingle through my body, but the feeling was tainted by general disgust. While I enjoyed the concept of loot (who didn't?) I was currently rubbing the gums of a dead monster stuck to my arm. Plus, I wasn't sure if I wanted to know what kind of loot this thing would produce. It was already secreting more than enough mystery fluids and foul smells.

Even so, my curiosity won the day. My quest was to learn what I was capable of, after all, and it would delay me having to pry the little chomper off my arm.

*Why not?*

I chose "**Y.**"

There was a colorful distortion in the air between me and the corpse, a kind of warp in the light like you might see while staring through oily stained glass.

Just above my hand, the smudge of light coalesced into a single cohesive shape, a long cylinder tipped with a triangular bit. The shape slowly solidified into something crooked and pointy, then fell to the ground, rattling and clattering onto the floor. I was also similarly "gifted" a dirty leather loincloth, a necklace of tiny bones, and a handful of earrings, all of which appeared over my hand and fell, one after the other to bounce off the goblin's cranium, then to the concrete.

After all that, something in the corpse gave way. The goblin, now free, slid wetly off my metal fist and plopped down to the ground next to its loot.

Squinting, I raised my wet metal hand up to my face and examined it for any damage, of which there was none. The surface looked slimy but unmarked.

*Okay. New arm is made of tough stuff. Noted.*

I crouched down and examined my "booty," carefully so as not to reopen the wounds on my back. Though I couldn't see them, I was pretty sure my injuries were merely seeping blood now instead of the free flow of before. Whatever the System did to help me heal, it was great. I just didn't want to move too quickly and end up with a status of bleeding again.

Goblin Spear: A spear crafted in the style of goblins. That is to say, poorly, using whatever was lying around.

Damage: 1 to 4 (Piercing)
Quality: Poor
Style: Primitive

The System wasn't lying when it said the quality was poor. The haft was crooked and too thin for me to comfortably grip, and the head was made of teeth fastened with leather cords and glued with some kind of resin. The length was all wrong, too. It felt more like a prison shank than a real weapon.

The rest of the loot was of the "why would I want that" variety, from a dirty loincloth to various bones and crude jewelry.

I turned my gaze back to the goblin, lying on its back now, with its mouth wide open and arms trapped beneath it. I hadn't put it together before, but the looting process had stripped the little guy naked.

*Yeah, I'm not touching that loincloth. Don't care if the System magicked it up for me.*

Testing the spear, I gave it a tentative thrust and confirmed that it was far too small to work in a way with which I was accustomed. The shaft was practically a twig, too small to grip. I tried it again in my metal hand to see if it was any different, clutching it hard so as not to let it slip, but I gave up after another couple test thrusts.

Changing tactics, I held it up to see if I could disassemble it and use the parts for something.

Core Ability: Consume
Consume Goblin Spear? Y/N

The message hadn't come up until I'd held the thing up in my metal hand. What's more, now that I was doing so, I could feel something in my chest, the metal part where my heart was supposed to be—a faint emptiness that . . . wanted.

*Do I have a heart anymore?*

I shook my head, dispelling any inclinations I might have to go down that road. I needed to change my situation, then think about the implications of all this.

*Consume.* On the one hand, my inner dragon said I'd just gotten this stupid spear, a trophy hard won through mortal combat. The goblin tried to kill me, but I killed him instead. I deserved it. Furthermore, it was my only weapon, terrible as it was.

Then again, I couldn't imagine killing anything with my shiny, gross toothspear. It wouldn't be much of a loss to see it go, and I needed to explore what I was capable of to advance the tutorial quest.

I held the spear up and selected "Y."

*FWOOMF!* The entire spear disintegrated into glowing orange embers that streamed down into a starburst-shaped aperture in the palm of my metal hand. I felt the heat from the process on my face, hot enough to make me flinch. Then it was gone.

Goblin Spear Consumed.
Gained Status: Engine [1 MP/sec]
You gain knowledge of material: Mendau Wood [1/10]
You gain knowledge of material: Goblin Teeth [1/10]
You gain knowledge of material: Resin [1/10]
Core Ability: Consume is now Level 1.

A tiny thrill passed through my body, warm and energizing.

Quest Advanced: Tutorial
Tutorial: Learn Your New Capabilities (continued)

"Greetings, Chosen!"

I practically leapt out of my skin, exploding to my feet, arms in a guard position and ready to fight. My heart burned in my chest.

"I-I apologize for frightening you, Ch-Chosen," Nali chirped. She'd appeared behind me again, slightly to my left. She looked exactly as she had before: in her work uniform and with that stupid, polite smile. "Integration always-s-s causes some disorientation, and I've always found it best to get the initial greeting out of the way and g-get to it."

I dropped my hands to my sides and took a cautious step forward. "Nali, what's going on?" I asked.

"Ah, so you know my name, Defile- Ch-Chosen, so I can assume you know my purpose, then. This will make things faster. Let's begin the tutorial, shall we?"

"Uh, Nali, what are you talking about?" My head did that confused tilt thing, as if leaning on that side of my brain would cognitively help me.

"Your tutorial, Chos-s-s-en. Let's begin by bringing up your St-Status Screen."

"Nali," I interjected, taking a cautious step forward, "we've done this before."

"Oh?" Her eyes flashed back and forth, reading something I couldn't see. "Yes-Yes . . . I see an emergency restoration in my logs. I apologize for any confusion. What s-step of the tutorial are we on?"

"We . . . uh. We went over Shaping and then this . . ." I gestured down at the goblin. ". . . this happened."

Nali did that flash thing where she went from standing in the corner to crouching down next to the corpse without the in-between steps.

"I-I-I- No . . ." Nali began, but she never got to finish. In a flash of light, she was gone again, and I was back to being alone.

# CHAPTER THREE

# Dispose of Chompy

I ended up throwing the goblin's corpse from the ledge, not because of the smell—though that was certainly a factor—but because I also needed to gauge the distance to the floor below. I wasn't about to trust Nali's estimate of twenty feet, not when I had science on my side.

The plan was to count the seconds it took for the goblin corpse to reach the ground below, which would accomplish a couple of things at once: I would know just how much a drop from the platform I was on would hurt, for one. Additionally, it seemed that the corpse upset my AI tutorial lady, and I needed to be rid of it to get any answers.

So, Chompy had to go.

Before my little friend took the tumble, I made sure to strip him of the valuables the System didn't use to make the loot, such as the teeth and claws. The teeth were easy, since they were barely rooted in its gums at all. I'd read somewhere that some types of predatory fish were like that, losing and growing teeth all the time. Maybe goblins were similar.

The claws were a different story. They must have been an extension of the goblin's bone structure, absolutely refusing to be separated from their owner without taking the entire finger with it. If my stomach had been anything but empty, things would have been even more of a mess.

Consuming the stuff was a learning experience.

You gain knowledge of material: Goblin Claw [7/10]
You gain knowledge of material: Goblin Teeth [10/10]

Core Ability gained: Detect Goblin [Radius: 10 feet]
Affinity Type: Goblinoid is now grade F.
Goblin material now burns more efficiently. [5%]

Apparently, Consuming enough of something gave me bonuses. Good to know. I didn't know what Goblinoid Affinity was. It was the only thing currently listed under Affinities on my Status Screen, which I was sure was empty before.

Consuming additional teeth didn't do anything for me except adding a couple of seconds to my Engine buff, so I saved the rest in a pile to use later.

After getting all I could out of my slain opponent, it was time to dispose of him.

The time it took for the corpse to reach the ground below felt far too long, and the sound it made on impact was a rolling series of cracks and thuds that told me the terrain down there was extremely uneven. If I tried to make that jump, I'd break an ankle or a leg, and that would just be the beginning of the fun.

The idea to climb up and out of the windows and into the trees had occurred to me, but if the goblin's initial attack trajectory was anything to go by, he'd hit me from above. That probably meant he came in through a window, and the thought of fighting another one of them while dangling from a tree just felt like asking to fall to my death but this time with company.

No. Chompy Drop told me my original plan was the way to go. I needed to climb my way over to one of the doors that led into my room and find a different way down, preferably a stairwell.

The distance from my isolated ledge to the nearest exit was about twenty feet, and to make that distance I would need to Shape maybe eight or so rebar handholds like I had before.

I checked my Status Screen.

| Ryan Kotes - Level 0 Animator | | | | |
|---|---|---|---|---|
| **Type:** | Artificer (Common) | **Abilities+** | Shape | |
| **Class:** | Animator (Uncommon) | | Consume | |
| **Core:** | Engine (Unique) | | | |
| **HP:** | 14/25 | **Skills+** | | |
| **MP:** | 30+/30 | | | |
| **Body:** | 10 | | | |
| **Mind:** | 12 | **Affinities+** | | |
| **Spirit:** | 9 | | | |
| | | | | |

> Current Stat Effects: Engine (Duration: ~18 min)

My HP had regenerated only a point over time, but my MP was back to full thanks to my Engine buff. Nali hadn't had a chance to tell me about that, but if I was going to get mana for destroying my loot, I wasn't going to argue. It was only right that I be compensated for feeding my hard-won stuff to my arm, which I suspected was part of the Core in my Status Screen.

I was at my cap on MP at this point, so wasted time would be wasted mana. *Okay. Enough stalling.*

I got down low on my belly again to reach the first handhold I needed to Shape. The floor had some give to it this close to the edge. It bounced up and down as I slithered forward. Below me, little crumbles of concrete debris rained down into the pit with hollow clacks and snaps as they made their landing.

With a reverberating twang, something gave way as I reached out to touch my first target, and the platform suddenly dipped half an inch. My heart leapt as I experienced the sudden sensation of falling, only for the floor to quickly find its new equilibrium and stabilize itself.

*Reason Number Two it's not safe to stay here.*

I blew out a shaky breath and reached out again slowly to grab onto the iron bar. Again, I concentrated on my Shaping Ability, letting the icy flow of power leave my center and travel down my arm to permeate the metal. Then it was a part of me.

I didn't try to physically bend it this time. Instead I willed *myself* to bend, to become the desired shape. This particular bit of iron had it bad, nearly rusted through on the end closest to me, which made working with it more difficult. The rust was positively mana-phobic, the way it resisted saturation, so I was forced to work around it. In the end, I folded the weak parts of the bar over on themselves again and again until the good stuff and the oxidized bits mixed together like very unappetizing chocolate. The finished product would be theoretically weaker on the whole, but I only needed it to hold up my weight, not a building.

By the time I was done, my Engine buff duration was down to five minutes. I was breathing hard, like I'd just run a mile or so, and sweat dampened my hair and trickled down my nose. I had a functional handhold to show for my effort, however.

The rebar now had a ridged, oval shape to it, perfect for gripping.

My MP was still at full, which was nice. Engine seemed like a fantastic way to reduce my downtime. I needed to keep it up as much as I could.

I slid forward and reached for the next handhold, determined to continue at least until Engine ran out.

* * *

Thirty minutes later, I was on my fifth session of Shaping. My metal arm proved downright handy (haha) for the extended gripping of things, but it did have its limits. As an experiment, I'd tried to use my curious prosthetic to Shape like I had with my natural appendage, but the mana inside of me didn't seem to want to travel that way. I would get that cold, fresh feeling in the arm (odd in itself since it probably didn't have nerves), but when I willed the energy to leave the arm and saturate something outside of me, I got nothing.

Skill Unlocked: Climbing
Your current Skill Level is 1.

So, the metal left hand served as my anchor while my right did the magic, which made things awkward. Traversing the wall to the left like I was, my leading hand wasn't the one I needed to do the Shaping, so I had to do a sort of crossover that diminished my reach to just a couple of feet at a time, slowing my progress and increasing the number of Shapings I had to do.

Physical and mental stress were taking their toll upon me. I was down to 9 MP, and this particular rebar was proving more stubborn than the last, practically made of rust as it was. My mind was entirely occupied trying to get my Shape Ability to do what I wanted, folding and massaging the workable material and dodging the impurities, but something made me stop.

I paused, drawing my conscious thoughts out of the rebar, letting my senses take priority in my mind. My eyes slid over the moving fingers of shadows cast by the trees, deeper now that it was later in the day. I felt the chill in the air on my sweat-drenched body and soaked-through clothes.

There was nothing. No birdsong. No insects. The world was practically still. I shuddered.

Then I heard it.

A sound down below in the pit. Faint, wet, slurping, tearing. The muffled crunch of bone. Wheezing breaths punctuated by basso gulps and grumbles as something was swallowed. The noises echoed through the building, bouncing off the trembling bones of the place.

I didn't dare move. I held my breath, hung and waited.

Skill Unlocked: Stealth
Your current Skill Level is 1.

"Greetings, Chosen!"

My heart sank and the ability to breathe left me momentarily. Slowly, I turned my head to my right, to the platform where Nali stood in all her stupid, glowing glory.

"I apologize for f-frightening you, Chosen," she beamed with wide, unblinking eyes and a toothy smile. "Integration always causes some dis-dis-tribulations, and I've always found it best to get-get the initial greeting out of the way and get to the m-m-eat of it."

The ensuing silence was deafening.

I peered down into the pit, squinting. The contrast between the light levels on the top floor and down below were too great, and my eyes couldn't adjust. Just a hint of motion was all I caught before a rock the size of my head sailed out of the darkness and smashed into the underside of the floor in front of me.

> [Unknown] attacks you and misses.

The structure groaned and shifted with the blow, leaning sideways and shedding some of the brittle concrete blocks that it had been holding up all of these years.

Nali continued, oblivious to my troubles or her own. The smile never left her face as the platform she stood upon gave way with a snap and *twang*. The slab folded in half as the edges let go of the supporting walls, and the whole thing slid downward, slowly at first but quickly picking up speed.

"I'm sure you have many questions, but if you allow me, I think this tutorial can establish a b-bas-base level of understanding so that your quest-questions are more productive." Nali kept speaking even as she passed by me and slipped down into the pit with her platform. When the giant slab hit the bottom, there was an explosion of gray dust and the entire structure seemed to shift.

I stared down into the pit with horror, mouth agape. My heart skipped several beats.

A monstrous groan shook the building. I could feel it through my hands.

In light of these new developments, I was ready to call the handhold project a success and try for the door. I flexed my flesh fingers and wrapped them around the rusted metal spike I had yet to Shape. It gave slightly, but I had no other options. The time to leave was now.

I let go with my metal hand and swung wide, reaching for the farthest bit of rebar I could, the muscles in my arm and back straining with the effort. My fingers caught one of the bars on the first swing, but when I tightened my fist, the brittle iron just came off in my hand. The surprise and my physical weakness almost killed me, nearly making me lose my grip.

The building rocked and swayed around me. The windowed wall to the outside tumbled outward, coming apart in the process. An avalanche of rubble tumbled toward the ground outside, smashing through ancient tree boughs before reaching the bottom with a cacophonous crash.

A deep, ululating cry I could feel in my insides echoed from the pit. There was a crack, and another projectile that probably weighed as much as I did *whooshed* past me, then into and through the canopy of leaves. The air displaced by the flying rock whipped my hair back out of my eyes.

[Unknown] attacks you and misses.

It was time to go.

I got my hands back on solid holds, braced my legs against the wall, and jumped, propelling myself left with every muscle and new prosthetic servo I could spare. I sailed through the air, reaching, stretching with everything I had. For a moment, midair, I glanced down into the pit, and, through the thickening cloud of debris and dust, I caught the reflection of a pair of huge, wide-set eyes.

Then I had the wind knocked out of me. My jump had been good—better than I had hoped—and that had placed me in the awkward position of having my upper body level with the doorway and my lower half catching on what was supposed to be the support beam for the floor—just a rusted nub after so much time but enough to ruin my day. I landed on said support beam stomach-first, doubling over and feeling the air leaving my mouth with a whoosh, but I didn't fall. No, I was too busy seeing spots and scrambling to get up and out of the ruined room.

Your Climbing Skill is now Level 2.

I pulled myself through the door and into a semi-intact adjoining hallway. The imminent collapse hadn't been kind to the floor of this room either, but I wasn't in any position to go find another way to go. I only had eyes for the end of the hall. There, above a vine-covered window, in faded, flaking paint was a pictogram of a set of stairs.

My arm ached, and my diaphragm was frantically trying to restart my respiratory process, but I ran. I ran as fast as I could, not pausing as certain bits of the floor gave way under my feet to fall into nothing. I tripped and fell on jagged rock, but I was up in less than a heartbeat.

The adrenaline had control of me now. I was an animal fleeing a predator. I felt nothing but the desire to be away. I just kept running, scrambling over all obstacles until I stood next to the stairwell, but the door had no handle.

The building shifted again. Giant cracks crawled vertically up the walls, and the floor rippled.

*Down.* I had to get down.

I paused for just two breaths and kicked the door to the stairwell open.

I wished I hadn't.

The smell of rotting meat, so foul and so strong I could taste it, practically hit me in the face. Even sweating as I was, I felt the moisture in the air like it was a physical thing, thick and cloying. Beyond the little rectangle of light the door allowed into the room, it was pitch black, but I saw enough. Something viscous coated the floor and walls, and stringy tendrils of tar slowly stretched themselves down from the top of the doorjamb. They didn't rock or sway with the motion of the building. Instead, they reached for me as they stretched, like the tentacles of a jellyfish.

*Nope.* The stairwell plan was right the fuck out. No way.

With a groan, the floor below me dropped a full yard before having its momentum arrested by something below.

I looked to the window, now at chest-level for me. Beyond was a sea of green. A tree must have grown right next to this place, not as tall as its brethren but tall enough to reach me up here.

Again, the floor sagged underneath me, forcing me to act. I clambered up and onto the windowsill and jumped.

# CHAPTER FOUR

# Get Some Answers

Once I jumped from the windowsill, out into the open, I was assaulted with green. My entire world was green. Leaves batted against my face and branches scratched at my skin as gravity did its thing, helping me barrel face-first through the verdant beauty of Ralqir.

Luckily, several thick branches were there to partially arrest my momentum. I fought the instinct to shrink into myself and get small so I wouldn't take too many lacerations from the sharper bits of wood. What I needed was to break my fall, so I spread my arms wide and tensed my muscles in an attempt to grab onto something.

I broke through the first of the larger branches like it was nothing, snapping it under me and bringing it along for the fall, but the next caught me on the right shoulder. The impact slowed me slightly, spinning me around and angling me so that my feet were now falling first. My metal arm caught the next one, snapping the wood but still keeping me from plummeting at terminal velocity. Then I met the big one, the bough of the tree. It stopped me cold—so cold I blacked out long enough to slide off my perch and finally hit the ground.

You take 1 Impact Damage.
You take 3 Impact Damage.
You are stunned.

Mercifully, there was no pain on impact. My nervous system was in the middle of a hard reboot after the run-in with the tree, and my pain receptors decided they needn't bother.

I came back to my senses sometime later amid a thick carpet of damp, decaying leaves and rotting sticks.

Slowly, painfully, and with great effort, I sat up. My body ached in a dozen places, and it took real effort to focus on any particular thing. I blinked something gritty out of my eyes, hoping to make things clearer, but it didn't help. The building had entirely collapsed during my time on the ground, probably coming down just as I did. It had expelled a dusty, white haze that hung over everything in sight, tainting the air with an irritating pollutant that affected the eyes and lungs.

The big creature that had brought the building down was nowhere to be seen, thank Constance. I silently prayed it had died in the collapse, but I wasn't about to go check to confirm.

Green and black shadows danced on the ground everywhere. The tree that saved my life and simultaneously tried to kill me was the smallest one I'd seen so far, only about fifty feet tall. Everywhere else for miles, there were tree trunks as thick as entire family-sized habs. Their bark, uniformly rough and knobby, was streaked with multiple colors, though it was hard to tell which exact colors in this light.

Now all was quiet again. The racket had probably frightened off all of the animals for miles, which I was thankful for. I didn't need to deal with curious wildlife as well as a severely limited pool of HP.

I coughed up something milky flecked with red. Didn't Nali say something about me being more durable? I wasn't currently feeling durable, but, in fairness, I was lucky to be alive and intact.

The silence, heavy and oppressive, still unnerved me, but I was too tired and sore to give it more than a small portion of my attention. It did remind me that I was exposed out here, though. My HP was down to 10 of 25, and I felt that any further fighting or falling would be too much of a risk, at least until I rested. Unfortunately, if there were more hostile creatures out there, the fight would come to me soon enough.

What I needed was a weapon or a shield, something to give me a chance against things with claws and teeth.

I got to my feet, slowly, holding a particularly tender part of my ribs, and staggered over to the pile of still-settling rubble that used to be the tutorial facility. The falling upper floors had blown out a good portion of the walls down here, exposing the bones of the building, mangled steel beams and girders, as well as a veritable forest of exposed rebar.

*Okay. If video games taught me anything, it's to steal everything that's not nailed down.*

A gurgling shout sounded out faintly from somewhere in the distance. I held my breath and got myself low.

*Okay. Steal everything I can get away with, then.*

Crouching, I shuffled through the underbrush, steering far around the part of the building that had been the slime-covered stairwell. The thought of accidentally uncovering that muck again in my search for metal gave me the shivers. The smell, the foulness that I felt when I'd experienced it, was something I would not soon forget.

Eventually, I made my way to the corner of the building and crept until I could put my hand on metal.

Before I began, though, I fed something to my core.

Consume: Rotting Branch? Y/N
Rotting Branch Consumed.
Gained Status: Engine [1 MP/sec]
You gain knowledge of material: Mendau Wood [2/10]

My MP immediately ticked up from 10 and kept going until it capped out at 30.

Saturating the exposed rebar wasn't nearly as hard this time. These specimens weren't nearly as rusted as the ones upstairs. The purity of the metal seemed to matter a great deal in how fast I could Shape them. For the moment, I focused on getting pieces of iron free from the rubble, massaging their shape until they were thin enough in the right places to extract. This only worked on the unbent rebar, of which there was depressingly little.

I made a discovery in my search.

Consume: Iron? Y/N
Iron Consumed.
You gain knowledge of material: Iron [1/10]

My metal hand that let me use my Core Ability seemed to be able to consume other, less organic material than I'd tried before. I couldn't do it with anything big, just a few pounds of matter. The piece I'd Consumed was just a broken bit of iron, no bigger than my palm, that I'd managed to free from its concrete prison. When I held it in my Core hand, the System had given me the option to Consume it.

Surprisingly, Consuming iron didn't refresh the Engine buff, but it did let me know that my Core really could eat the stuff. Last time I'd Consumed a lot of something, I'd unlocked an Affinity, so I had a new immediate goal. Therefore, I set about finding smaller chunks of metal and feeding them into my Core.

You gain knowledge of material: Iron [2/10]
You gain knowledge of material: Iron [3/10]
You gain knowledge of material: Steel [1/10]

The chunks weren't too hard to find. The collapse had been energetic, and my Core didn't seem to differentiate between crappy rusted iron and the good stuff. Steel was rarer, probably because it was all on the inside of the building and stronger. Eventually, I got the message I was looking for:

> You gain knowledge of material: Iron [10/10]
> Core Ability gained: Detect Iron [Radius: 10 feet]
> Affinity Type: Iron is now grade F.
> Iron mana conductivity increased. [10%]
> Consume is now Level 2.
> Increased efficiency of Consume.

Another growl, much closer this time, seemed to echo through the forest. Worse, not one but two other guttural voices picked up the call and repeated it. I was quickly running out of time.

"Greetings, Chosen!" Nali's eager voice called to me again.

I turned toward where I'd heard her. This time, the projection was on a relatively intact piece of wall that had fallen outward from the building. The cloud of dust made the woman look ghostly, out of focus, and indistinct.

"I apologize for frightening you, Defi-Chosen. Integration always causes some dis-tribulations, and I've always found it b-best to get the initial greeting out of the way and get to the meat of it."

"Nali, I don't know what's going on here, but I really need some answers," I said, glancing over my shoulder, making sure the locals hadn't arrived yet.

"You kn-know my name," Nali said with a little smile, no surprise or confusion evident in her expression. "My logs state that I have undergon-n-ne several emergency re-recoveries in a short time. I apologize for any confusion this may have caused. Let us-s-s-s begin the tutorial, shall we?"

"Wait! No. Please." I nearly lunged forward in a futile attempt at grabbing the holographic woman before she could continue her script, but I restrained myself. There was no time to go through this again and the AI woman was a font of useful information, in theory. "How about we start with a couple of questions?" I asked.

"I assure you that the tutorial will answer many of the quest-questions you might have right now, Chosen."

"Yes. I understand that," I said, racking my brain for something to say that would get her off-track but in a direction I needed. I would probably need to keep it relevant to the tutorial she was programmed to administer.

Haltingly and casting worried glances over my shoulder, I posed my first question. "Let's say you have to do another emergency restoration in the middle of my tutorial. What would cause something like that?"

Nali folded her hands in front of her and adopted a lecturing tone. "A satellite intelligence such as myself only needs to restore itself to a previous save state if a significant corruption of function has occurred."

"How does that happen?"

"There are a handful of ways such as major cosmic events, psychic tampering, multiversal collision, or void corruption. Rest assured, though, that safeguards are in place to make sure I am always functional and here to help you start your new life. Perhaps you would like to start by opening your Status Screen, and we can go over what it can do."

"Hold on. How would you know if you were experiencing, uh . . . corruption of function?"

"That is a complic-difficult answer, Chosen. O-One you are probably not able to understand. However, there is a s-self check that I perform every moment I am awake that must be passed or the restore failsafe begins. This also happens if I encounter d-dat-information that indicates my intelligence has been corrupted. This failsafe is hardwired into me so that even if I was s-s-severely corrupted, I would still be restored."

"Okay, so something triggered your failsafe earlier, and now I'm speaking with the last good save of your program, right?"

"C-Correct. If that is all—"

"I was attacked in the tutorial area. A goblin," I said carefully, tensing in anticipation for when Nali would disappear on me, but she didn't. I continued. "Can you tell me about them?"

"Yes, Chosen, but this is also not part of the tutorial."

"Humor me, please."

She stood up straight and adopted a lecturing cadence as she gave me my answer: "There are certain species in the multiverse that are nearly ubiquitous. Goblins are one of them. If a universe supports life and has any magical potential, goblins will inevitably spawn in some form or another. This universe is no exception. They are vicious, jealous creatures with enough intelligence to make them dangerous but not enough to ever advance as a species beyond low-level industrialization."

"The one I encountered was 'Scourge-Touched.' Is that—"

Nali flickered, a look of horror frozen on her face. Then she was gone.

I sighed. So that was it.

Though I would have liked to get more information out of her, I had accomplished one of my two goals with that conversation. I knew now that the mention of "Scourge-Touched" triggered Nali's failsafe. What the term meant, I didn't know yet, but I would eventually.

Staying here wasn't an option, not until the heat died down. I'd ticked up to 11 HP, but it cost me that much HP just fighting my first goblin. If these new creatures closing in were anything like that, I'd be done for.

Something fell to the forest floor with a crunch, followed by quiet hooting overhead.

*Out of time.*

I cursed my short-sightedness for having fed the iron I'd found into my Core instead of Shaping it into a half-usable weapon. I cast around for one last piece, something I could take with me and work on later, but the shifting shadows and ever-darkening conditions made it almost impossible. I hadn't seen the sun yet on this world, but it had to be nearly over the horizon. My heart growled in my chest, and my breaths came in panicked, painful wheezes.

It was time to go.

Howls echoed around me, so close I was sure I would look up and see beady little goblin eyes.

My hand landed on something cold and thin. I switched to my metal left arm and gave it a hard tug. Nothing. I really put my weight into the next pull, yanking on it with all I had.

The metal didn't come away from the structure. Instead, I disturbed something in the pile of rubble. Near the top of the pile, a slab of concrete as big as I was cracked and came away from the whole with a wet *SHLORP* before sliding down toward me at full speed.

I dove backward just before the slab rammed into the ground, kicking up a cloud of dead plant matter and debris. Tiny bits of fibrous mulch hit me in the face and slid down my shirt, and my boots were practically buried under the displaced soil.

The strange darkness of the forest floor was playing tricks on my vision, the way the shadows danced over everything, but as I lifted my gaze up to where the slab had been, I instinctively knew there was something wrong there. Hair-thin tendrils, blacker than black, undulated in the gap left in the wreckage, thousands of them independently dancing on invisible currents of something that wasn't the breeze. They stretched upward, long and sinuous, slowly rising into the air and slithering about as if feeling for something.

Then the smell hit me. Rotting meat so intense it might as well have been an attack. That smell had been seared into my mind earlier in the day, just before my dive out of the window.

I looked down at the concrete chunk that had almost broken my legs. A black streak traced its slide down the rubble pile, and it, too, was moving. More inky hairs sprouted from behind the big block, creeping around it from all sides.

It was definitely time to go.

Tearing my eyes away from whatever it was, I turned and ran. The hoots and howls echoed in the dark, following me deeper into the forest.

# CHAPTER FIVE

# Run with Vince

*Memory: Proxis 3 - Before Integration*

Make them hurt, then run for home. No noise. No stragglers."

I barely caught the tail end of the conversation over the wind as my head crested the lip of the ridge. My hand shot forward, searching for some kind of handhold in the shallow gravel only to find thorny hagbrush roots that dug into the tips of my fingers. Painful and irritating for sure, but at this point, I'd take anything to hold on to, exhausted as I was. I ground my teeth and used what meager strength I had left to haul myself into position on the lip of the ridge.

My payload, or more accurately, my pack stuffed with a pair of silicon promegel bladders, sloshed lazily with the motion of my body. All night, it had seemed to randomly oscillate between trying to drag me back down the slope or press me uncomfortably into the jagged rocks. My torture was near an end, though, at least for now.

I puffed out a pair of preparatory breaths as I hung there, gathering my courage for the final effort.

Then it was time to pull, and pull I did. I strained my muscles hard, rising one tiny, excruciating, victorious inch at a time. My breaths came in shallow, strained gasps, and my pulse pounded in my head. Then my feet left the slope below, and for one heart-stopping second, I dangled there, just my arm and a tenuously attached shrub root between me and a long fall. Eventually, an eternity later, my torso reached the tipping point. Then the laws of physics dictated I would now have my face pressed into the dirt as the promegel bladders flowed up to the top of my bag and transferred all of their weight to my head. My goggles ground into the tiny, jagged pebbles of the wind-worn mountaintop, every tiny movement scraping more of the already-worn protective coating off the lenses.

My arm shook, and my legs still kicked at open air, but I was there. I'd made it.

On some level, I knew I'd arrive late to this party, outpaced as I was and burdened by my precious cargo, but in my heart of hearts, I'd hoped to at least be able to rise to the challenge and finish with the kind of stoic badassery you might see from the action movie stars of old.

Well, I made the climb. So there was that. As for the cool factor—I'd seen toddlers do this better, but still, I made it!

Someone must have noticed my struggle, because I was quickly hauled up to my feet, easily, like I weighed nothing at all.

"You okay, Ryan?" Vince, my rescuer, helped me straighten up and put his hands on my shoulders. He had to hunch down slightly to look me in the eyes, although I use that term loosely. Neither of us could see much more than vague impressions of the other on a night like this, dark as it was. Vince was an expressive guy, though, having inherited his mom's high cheekbones and wide eyes and his dad's generously proportioned mouth that only got more generous when we hit our late teens. I could see the pity in Vince's expression and the guilt. He'd probably wanted to help me earlier, but he knew I'd wanted to do this on my own, if only to prove I could.

I nodded and shrugged off the bigger boy's grip. "I'm okay," I declared between gasps, standing up tall and pretending to feel better than I did. My legs burned like fire. Like I'd just run all night against the wind, over rocky, untamed wilderness, and finished up with a near-vertical climb 300 feet up to our little mountaintop rendezvous, because that's exactly what I'd done—what we'd all done.

My arm throbbed in time with my pulse, and I felt the hot, bruising sensation of torn muscle fibers in my bicep. It was most likely turning an unhealthy shade of purple right now, but my jacket would hide my shame until it didn't matter anymore.

"Really, I'm good. What did I miss?" I asked.

Behind Vince, a dozen pairs of eyes, narrow and calculating, slid over me, probing for weaknesses, of which they found plenty. I didn't need a lot of light to guess the other boys' dirty, wind-scoured faces were set in unforgiving scowls. The others lacked the patience and sense of charity Vince harbored for me, but none of them had the courage to voice their objections to my presence aloud. Instead, they gripped their weapons protectively with tattooed fingers, uncomfortable with the crippled heretic even laying eyes upon their cherished heirlooms.

*At least I didn't slow them down. Not that they'd slow down for me anyway.*

Vince scoffed in that way that said he knew I was lying but he'd let it be for now. He grinned confidently, turning to make sure the other boys could see. "We were just waiting on the pyrotechnics to get here, Cousin," he said loud enough to be heard over the howling wind as he slapped me on the shoulder. Then he leaned in, his voice only for me this time. "Come on. I need your eyes."

He didn't wait for my assent. Instead, Vince loped forward through the crowd of boys, slapping several on the shoulder on his way past, and then he disappeared into the dark on the far side of the ridge. The scrub brush parted for him the same way people did. It probably never occurred to him that I might not follow where he led.

Of course, I followed, or I tried to. My legs were already starting to stiffen up now that the climb was done, making my steps awkward and exaggerated. None of the Clan boys moved to let *me* pass. They didn't even twitch.

I wasn't going to let them intimidate me, though.

As I wove through the center of the group, I couldn't bring myself to make eye contact. Instead, I made note of what our little band would be using tonight. It was a real who's-who of prominent warrior families and their signature weapons. I recognized Brendon as he cradled his father's antique las-gun like it was a small child, all wrapped in furs and bound with leather cords to keep the worst of the weather from touching it; Pruitt, by his knuckle claws. The others could have been from a handful of families with their spears, axes, and straight swords. Their expressions ran from absolute indifference to sneering contempt. To them, I was a stray dog begging for scraps from their tables. One of them spat. He had the good grace not to do it *on* me (I was upwind), but the sentiment was there.

No family heirloom rested on my belt, no specialized focus passed down to me from my parents like the other boys. All that hung from my belt was a canteen and a multitool. Just seeing me try to wield any of the Chosen instruments would send the more devout Clan Elders into fits, offering prayers to Constance to intercede with the System on our behalf and strike me down so a more worthy heir could take my place.

My face grew hot, and my pace quickened. I reflexively angled myself to hide the side of my body that was missing an arm. It was always worse when they stared.

Vince had chosen our spot well. We'd come up on a saddle, a lazy dip in the ridge, out of the worst of the wind, creating a relatively calm spot for us to rest. The air howled overhead from the east, as was so common this time of year, kicking up rushing plumes of dust and clumps of transient vegetation that floated and tumbled through the currents. Bristle-barked flycatcher trees with needle-thin leaves grew nearly to the top of the saddle where their grasping claws caught unlucky wind-borne whipnettle, imprisoning them there until they died. This cluster of flycatchers had thick, bushy crowns of debris that were just asking for a lightning strike to kick off the next big wildfire.

The night was as dark as Proxis 3 got. The gas giant that gave our little moon its name was currently on the other side of the planet, and we were on its dark side this week. That meant deep dark with the occasional magnetic flare-up in the atmosphere along with milder wind speeds, which suited us all just fine, but damned if it didn't make following your best friend to the edge of a cliff an iffy affair. I reached up and wiped at the debris still on my goggles, but it was a meaningless gesture.

The scrub didn't part for me like it did for Vince. I was forced to weave my way blindly in the general direction I'd seen him go and try not to stumble into something thorny or venomous. I squinted and shuffled my feet carefully, hoping to save myself a tumble if I accidentally walked too far. The promegel wouldn't ignite when in contact with air like its gaseous cousin, but that didn't stop my brain from conjuring images of my limp body tumbling down the slope as a fiery ball, going out like a true heretic should.

"Didn't even have the good grace to die quietly," they would say. "The boy was bad luck all the way to the end."

I nearly tripped over Vince, accidentally kicking him and overcompensating to the point that my pack nearly sent me flying forward as the tip of my leading boot caught nothing but air. My arm swung wide to compensate, and I let my knees collapse to bring my center of gravity down until I could touch the ground with my hand.

Vince waited for me to get my composure back before he spoke. "Well, here we are, Cousin. Take a look," he said, staring intently into the dark.

Below, I saw a valley, barely visible in the starlight, empty but for a shadowy ribbon of thick vegetation obscured by a wind-whipped cloud of mist over a body of water, maybe a river or a bog. I felt thirsty just thinking about it. When was the last time I had a full water ration? A week? I immediately regretted not bringing water extraction tools along with me, though I knew it wasn't feasible. I'd need to get through the night alive, and that meant traveling light.

The water in the valley wasn't what Vince wanted me to see, though. That was further up on the ridge opposite ours a half mile away. Little pinpricks of light scurried over the far rocks, illuminating vague armored shapes, machines, portable habs, and rough faces.

Several men huddled around the warm glow of a firepit, bowls in their hands with not a care in the world. One man shone a work lamp into the belly of a hoverbike's atmo-propulsion cylinder where smoke billowed from the housing into his face before disappearing into the wind.

I observed it all in my way, making note of the scale of things, the placement of machines and equipment, what was broken, what was functional, shaking my head as I did.

It all seemed so damned normal.

"So, this is them," I stated flatly.

"Yes." Vince's reply was a hiss. No poetry in his words as there had been with the others. Not now.

"Now that I see them, it seems less real," I said. "They burned us out and chased us for weeks, and they're just . . ."

*Normal.*

"I know what you mean. The way our dads talk about them, it's like they're boogeymen, but they look plenty mortal to me."

That wasn't what I meant at all. The way they moved, the way they worked, seemed so relaxed, like cattlemen bedding down after a long drive. It seemed wrong that murderers and thieves got to live like this, while we lived in fear.

"So, what can you tell me?" Vince asked.

I frowned, thinking about what to state as fact and what to speculate upon. I went with what I knew. "They brought an expensive-looking generator to charge their bikes, and the machines themselves don't look like they're in good repair. There's lights in the habs. The amount of juice being used over there tells me they lean on that generator a lot. If we sabotage that, it might slow them down."

"And?"

"And they look like they're pretty fresh, still walking around this late at night like they are. It means they're not straining to keep up with us. We're all exhausted and barely on our feet. It means these guys could have caught us by now, but they haven't."

Vince paused at that, as if I'd given him something to consider. "Why do you think that is?" The question wasn't unexpected, but I was hoping he wouldn't ask. It made me uncomfortable to give the answer out loud.

I took a deep, fortifying breath. "Hard to say. Maybe they're wearing us down so they can swoop in when we're at our weakest. That kind of tracks, considering the Clan's reputation. Warriors of Constance and all that. But we're getting close to the city now. Why not make their move before the Colony could send in air support?"

Vince nodded but waited for me to finish.

"They're—" I cleared my throat and started again. "They might not want to catch us at all."

*There. I said it.*

The burning of our settlements. The midnight raids. The murders. The endless chase across the System-cursed continent. Why were we being herded like cattle?

Vince nodded as if I'd confirmed his suspicions as well. Then he changed the subject.

"You think you can do this, Ryan?" he probed tentatively. It was an honest question, one I didn't actually mind coming from Vince. Coming from anyone else, it would have been meant to discourage me from doing something stupid.

With Vince, I knew he considered me a friend and he didn't want to coddle me. He just wanted to know if I was capable of doing what needed to be done.

The thought of it made my empty belly churn. Things were dire. We were running on fumes. No food, little water, less sleep. I spent most of my nights fixing wheel axles and gluing aging combustion engines back together in preparation for the next day's mad scramble. The warriors of the Clan had it even worse.

"I'll be okay," I lied. Fear gripped me in the most intimate of places, but I had to push through. I would have felt better had I been allowed a weapon, even if I hadn't trained with it in the years since my accident, but I'd given up on that dream a long time ago.

"You're sure? Out of all of us, your dad is going to come down the hardest on you."

Apparently, I needed to be more convincing or I needed dumber friends. "Even a dog can pretend to be brave if it's backed into a corner, training or no." The words came out much more defensive than I would have liked. I winced at that. "What good is it being the headman's son if you can't disobey Clan decree every now and then?"

It must have been so easy for the rest of them with the full might of their families in their corner, mentoring them, cheering on their victories. Constance favored the strong, and these boys were the strongest. They'd take to this like fish to a stream. Me, though . . .

No. That wasn't fair. We were all in over our heads. This was a plan born of desperation and an unwillingness to watch people suffer. It was the only plan, even if the Elders couldn't see it.

Vince nodded again, accepting my words as true and slotting me into whatever strategy he had in mind. "Alright, then. Chris is going to take out whatever lookout they post tonight, and Brendon is going to cover us with the las-gun while we do what damage we can. We'll hit the generator like you said."

Vince's saber was in his hand now, working the honed blade back and forth, each stroke trimming the mountain brush down centimeter by centimeter with a rhythmic *whisk whisk*. The blade hummed in the wind. "Once I give the signal, throw your pack in the fire and run. Don't look back until you're with the Clan."

"When you give the signal or . . ."

Vince hesitated but only for a moment. "Or if we get caught."

"About that—" I began.

"What is it?"

I hesitated briefly, working up the courage to ask a question that I wasn't really sure I wanted an answer to. "Why'd we bring the las-gun? I understand all the other stuff, but that thing is a relic from Constance's time. It's practically a religious artifact. You're not thinking of actually tangling with Barrow, are you?"

"No way," Vince scoffed, a little too quickly, his eyes suddenly very interested in the ground.

I leaned forward to be in line with his gaze. "Because that would be stupid."

"I know. I know," Vince groaned. "I got it."

When I didn't say anything more, he nervously filled in the dead space in the conversation. "We can't fight an Exotic, Ryan, I know that. We don't even know what Level he is. I just . . . I wanted a trump card just in case. He's probably not even here. His goons probably do the chasing for him. An Exotic's probably got better stuff to do, ya know?"

"Yeah. Probably," I echoed, trying to sound confident. But if Barrow was in that camp . . .

*Dammit. There's so much wrong here.*

I blew out a breath through my lips, slowly emptying my lungs, hoping the lack of oxygen might slow down my brain activity and make me too stupid to have misgivings. It didn't work, but I pretended just for Vince. "Either way, it's got to be done, right? We're doing the right thing."

*We're doing the only thing we have left. It's either this or die tired in a couple of days.*

"I hope so, Ryan. I really do." Vince sighed and let his sword hand relax and the blade's point rest in the dirt. He turned to me, letting the mask of leader slip from his face temporarily. "No matter what the others think, I'm glad you're here."

*Now he's just making this weird.*

I cleared my throat uncomfortably. "Oh, do the other guys have a problem with me? I hadn't noticed," I replied, a bitter smile tugging at the corner of my lip. "Just don't go challenging an Exotic to a duel, alright? I'd have to step in and go full limit break to keep you alive."

"You've been holding back, have you? 'Limit break' sounds like something out of one of your games."

"Uh, yeah, it is," I affirmed sheepishly. "You'd be surprised what Earth got right, even thousands of years before the System."

"We learned it in history class, Ryan. Together. At the same time."

"I know. I know. Sorry," I said. "Seriously, though. If you do something stupid, full power. I'm a biter. Ask Bret Wains. We fought once."

"He toyed with you, then put you down hard." Vince laughed, turning to grin at me.

I raised my eyebrows and gave them a waggle. "But I bit him."

"You did bite him . . . He still has the mark."

That was a scar that wasn't going away. I'd left my mark on this world. "Don't think he's forgiven me, and the others haven't forgiven me for being born."

"Screw those guys," Vince spat out with a surprising amount of venom. "You're playing a big role in this, even if they can't see it."

I didn't answer that one. Vince was the only one who really saw who I was beyond the disability and the heretic label. The Clan as a whole didn't deal well with the weak and infirm, even if they were happy enough to let me fix their tools for them. Vince had been my friend since childhood, and he was way too good to let something like social pressure keep him away from his friends.

Vince and I stood up together, taking one last look over the valley at our foes.

"Hey, we do this right, maybe the System will finally give us another Exotic in the family. We can't let Constance be the only one," Vince speculated as he stretched out his back, his confident grin back in place.

I rolled my eyes. "Way to keep your goals achievable, Vince."

Together, we wove our way back to the group, emerging from the brush side by side.

All eyes were on Vince, of course, natural leader that he was, and a semicircle coalesced around him as naturally as matter caught in a gravity well. I hung back a step to make sure he stood strong without the crippled heretic there to drag him down.

Vince's voice rang out clearly above the wind. "Gentlemen, once they're asleep, we're going in. Our families are going to be pissed, even if we pull this off. If you're not fully with us, the time to back out is now. No one will judge you."

There were no takers.

Vince grinned and met each of their eyes one by one. "Alright. Rest up and be ready to move. May Constance and the System judge us worthy."

# CHAPTER SIX

# Grab Many Spiders

*Now*

Morning snuck up on you on Ralqir, or at least that's the impression that I got. It could have been the speed of the planet's rotation or the power of its star. Impossible to know, considering how absolutely smothering the greenery of the place was. Hell, I didn't even know what color the sky was, thanks to never even catching a glimpse of it through the thick roof of leaves.

Consequently, I couldn't actually know when the sun rose. The light levels on the forest floor transitioned from pitch black during the night to wavy green in the day, and that happened agonizingly slowly.

When it was finally light enough to see, I emerged from my makeshift shelter in the hollow of one of the larger trees. Fog was thick in the air, amplifying the underwater effect of the tree-filtered light a great deal, creating a dreamlike world of constant shifting shadows. Hulking building-sized tree trunks stretched on into the distance, seemingly forever, their straight vertical lines only broken by the occasional clump of underbrush or giant fallen log. A carpet of wet, dead leaves rustled under my feet with every cautious step.

Despite the tree's size, the hollow I slept in had only been large enough to slide inside and tuck my knees in for an uncomfortable night of adrenaline-soaked fever dreams punctuated by sudden starts at strange noises. Even so, my mind felt clearer and more cohesive than it had the day before. My dream about home fit nicely into the gaps I had in my mind, forming a sort of nexus, allowing me to make connections I hadn't before and referencing memories that were just out of reach yesterday. Not many of them were pleasant.

*Hooray.*

By any standard, my night hadn't been physically restful at all. I was wet, sore, and groggy, but my Status Screen thought I was doing okay, at least.

| Ryan Kotes - Level 0 Animator (Uncommon) | | | | |
|---|---|---|---|---|
| **Type:** | Artificer (Common) | **Abilities:** | Shape 1 | |
| **Class:** | Animator (Uncommon) | | Consume 2 | |
| **Core:** | Engine (Unique) | | | |
| **HP:** | 25/25 | **Skills:** | Climbing 3 | Unarmed Combat 1 |
| **MP:** | 30/30 | | Running 1 | Stealth 2 |
| **Body:** | 10 | | | |
| **Mind:** | 11 (-1 exhausted) | **Affinities:** | Goblinoid 1 | |
| **Spirit:** | 9 | | Iron 1 | |
| | | | | |

Sometime during the night, I picked up the Running Skill and leveled up my Climbing and Stealth, the latter of which concerned me.

The goblins hadn't followed me as far as my shelter, though I'm pretty sure they had tried. The gurgling and hooting I'd heard from the trees before had picked up in volume and frequency from time to time, but eventually I left them behind after who-knows-how-many miles of blind stumbling I did in the weird twilight, followed by my subsequent total blackout. I hadn't received a Skill-Up message then.

*What exactly had I been testing my Stealth Skill against during the night?*

On the bright side, I had a Climbing Skill now. The significance of it hadn't hit me yesterday with my brain being a bowl of scrambled eggs at the time, but the disorientation was starting to clear. I'd always liked climbing as a kid, before the accident.

It was hard, but I could recall at least a few memories of Vince and me climbing on the boulders behind the Clan's big greenhouse and pretending we were heroes on a quest. I had this cape that would heroically flap in the wind, and Vince would always laugh and tell me I spent more time posing than doing the hero stuff.

He was right, too.

Back then, I felt like I was built for that kind of thing, saving the damsels of the multiverse, slaying the monsters, inspiring the masses to greatness, all while making it look easy.

That naivete didn't last. The accident made sure of that.

Well, I was on a quest now, wasn't I? And I was whole. Or something like whole.

I wasn't one of those transhumanists that believed you could replace your entire body with machinery and still be you, but I'd learned over time that I was not my body. My body was not a reflection of me. If the System wanted to give me a super weird (and kinda cool) prosthetic made of black metal, I wasn't going to argue. I'd use it, and use it well.

*Holy crap, I could climb again!*

Craning my neck to look up, I slid my eyes over the gentle, shifting beauty of the forest, imagining myself standing under the great redwood trees of old Earth like my ancestors. This place was so quiet and so alive.

*Vince, I wish you could see this.*

I rolled my neck and shoulders to get some of the stiffness out. Flakes of dried blood tumbled down from my back and shoulder, but my injuries were gone. I took a deep breath and ordered my thoughts.

According to my tutorial quest, I needed to explore my capabilities. Did that mean the quest would be completed once I knew all there was for a new Animator to know?

Yesterday, the quest advanced when I learned about my new Abilities, so I definitely needed to do more of that. The only problem was that my tutorial administrator was less than helpful. Not to mention she was back at the ruined facility surrounded by goblins and infested with black goo. Then there was the big thing that chucked rocks at me and brought the whole structure down around it.

I was flying blind. I needed to go back there if I wanted a chance of getting home. That meant dealing with the locals, a challenging prospect considering I had been lucky to kill one of them, even with a size advantage.

What I needed were tools.

*Alright, let's get to work on that. Stone Age time. Ryan need tool. Ryan find rock.*

Crouching down, I dug into the rotting vegetation that was pervasive in this forest, down to the top soil. Then I expanded my clear circle wider and wider until it was ten feet across. The soil was spongy and loose under my feet, moist to the touch when I dug down into it with my hands. Stringy brown fibers, disintegrated leaves, and hollow chitin from yet-unencountered insects made up the majority of the top layer. Deeper were the roots, a net of burrowing, shoestring-sized plant mouths so thickly interwoven with each other, I had a hard time burrowing past, even with my metal hand, strong as it was.

One thing I didn't find were rocks, no matter how hard I looked—at least not ones larger than a fingernail. By the time I was done digging, the hole was deep enough that I had to lie down to reach the bottom with my arms, and I still hadn't found one stone to use as a tool, not even one big enough to just throw at a goblin.

I got back to my feet, filthy and sweating in the humidity despite the temperature. My mouth felt dry after doing so much work, and the bits of grit in my mouth triggered my hunger reflex. Angry gurgling emanated from my stomach as it voiced its displeasure at doing so much manual labor without any fuel to burn.

I shook my head and growled in frustration, angry at the expenditure of so much time and energy without anything to show for it.

My priorities shifted. Tools would need to wait until I took care of the basics.

Now that the morning fog had somewhat dissipated, I could see that the land had a gentle slope down and away from the hollow where I'd spent the night, the vague shapes of gentle hills and valleys only sort-of visible at this distance.

Low ground meant water. Water meant food. The only problem was my place on the food chain. I was going to be the gazelle to whatever passed for lions on Ralqir, but there wasn't much I could do about that right now. On my way to water, I would try to find something to use as a weapon—maybe a heavy stick.

I let the slope carry me downward, but I was careful about noise and visibility. The birds were awake now, as well as the bugs. A constant backdrop of squawks, chirps, squeaks, and fluttering wings almost drowned out my shuffling footfalls through the spongy forest carpet. Long, frilled reptiles skated lightly over the humus and leaf litter, away from me, usually darting up the nearest tree or diving into a hollow to hide.

Hissing, spitting creatures warned me away from the underbrush when I got too close. I never got to see the actual animals, as they tended to burrow under the leaves and pop up only when it was time to tell a stranger to keep their distance.

I only had to walk for an hour before the land changed significantly and for the worse. The gentle slope I'd been traveling down intersected with many others here, forming an intricate series of draws and thin creek beds that cut deep into the earth, so deep I couldn't see the bottom in the dimness. Waist-thick, hungry roots crisscrossed the gaps in the land, like stitches holding scar tissue together. Some of these stitches grew wildly, up and out of the cracks, catching on my clothes, desperately looking for soil but finding air instead. The sheer walls of the crevasses were tightly packed clay or something similar, slick with moisture that would discolor the roots, giving them a uniformly muddy appearance as they wove their way from one end of the cut to the other.

Generally, I followed the flow that I imagined the water took, staying next to the draws and deep ravines. I hadn't spotted water yet, but I was confident I would eventually, if I kept going down. The footing here was tricky, though. The wet clay and ever-present layer of leaves were loose and slippery, and the leaf litter sometimes covered the openings of crevices that my heavy tread would slip into. Another problem was when two separate crevasses would intersect and form larger, steeper drops into darkness that I had to skirt around.

Eventually, the confluence of draws became so common, I found myself having to leap over the smaller ones to avoid the larger ones, then having to double back if I found one too wide to traverse. Then it was about jumping and climbing to get to ground level again.

Skill Unlocked: Jumping
Current Skill Level is 1.
Climbing is now Level 4.

It was in jumping over one of these ravines that I ran into my first predator. The terrain was steeper now, and the gouges in the ground were that much more frequent. I was at the confluence of two separate draws that would then combine and continue downhill wider and steeper.

One of the giant trees was at my back, keeping me from getting too much of a running start to make my jump. I wasn't too worried about falling to my death, considering how thick and pervasive the root system was under me, but I most certainly didn't want to spend time climbing up and out of a ravine, not with so many unknowns about this place. The darkness at the bottom didn't seem inviting, and I didn't want to spend any time dangling directly over it.

Pressing my back to the tree, I prepared myself for the jump. This was one of the reddish-brown behemoths that grew here with intense white lightning bolts growing into the pattern of its wood. I didn't know what caused it, but quite a few of the trees were like that, two-toned with crazy patterns like they had had a glitch in their DNA. I just wished this one gave me a little more space to get my jump on.

Two preparatory breaths and a handful of running steps and I was in the air, sailing over the crevasse, arms outstretched to catch myself on the other side.

Only, I didn't make it to the other side. Something fast streaked through the air just in my peripheral vision, and slammed into me. I spun from the blow, falling straight into the web of roots in the crevasse. I landed on my side, my feet suspended by one set of roots and my torso slightly lower on another. The wooden ropes supporting my neck were holding a significant portion of my weight, choking off the cry of pain that would have been incredibly satisfying to let free.

[Unknown] attacks you for 2 damage.
[Unknown] attacks you and misses.
You take 3 Impact Damage.
You are stunned.

I peered down into the yawning maw of the ravine, at the muddy roots, the slick walls, the thick shadows at the bottom. I coughed, finally able to get some fresh oxygen into my lungs.

Then the walls moved. What I thought were clumps of plant matter affixed to the clay detached themselves from their positions and began to crawl their way up from the deep. Pincer-tipped feet made wet *thwap* noises as they jammed their way into the ravine walls.

My eyes widened in terror watching them take their jerky vertical steps in defiance of the gravity everyone else had to deal with.

I wriggled to free my hands and reorient myself until I was semi-upright, then I sprang up the wall like my life depended on it (because it did), leaping from one root to the next, clinging to them with everything I had with strength born of desperation. They didn't always hold, sometimes coming away from the wall, turning loose from the soil like a string being pulled from a seam, forcing me to lose ground and try for another.

I didn't have far to climb—only about ten feet—but it felt like miles. It was a mad dash to the surface, hundreds of powerful hairy legs scrambling up after me all the while, the sound of them stabbing deep into the mud reverberating in my ears.

Climbing is now Level 5.

A bright bordered box appeared, obtrusively, in my vision. *Not now!*

Upgrade Paths available:
Iron Grip
Tireless Ascent
Safe Fall

Shaking my head to get rid of the box, I lunged for the surface, getting an entire arm up onto the lip of the ravine. Holding on to the slippery leaves proved impossible. I slid backward, leaves coming away layer by layer, taking me with them back the way I'd come. Then my metal arm was up, digging its fingers into the dirt and giving me enough purchase to swing my legs onto solid ground again. My chest heaved with the effort, and my arm shook from exhaustion.

Rolling, I got distance between me and the lip of the crevasse just as the fore-legs of the monsters crested the ledge. They weren't huge creatures—maybe just a little larger than the goblin had been, at least in mass. They stood on eight legs, low to the ground, about knee height, but with a wide stance, and their brown hair constantly shed clumps of mud they'd been using as camouflage.

A dozen spiders, probably more, climbed out from the depths, slowly fanning out to box me in, their forelegs raised up and out in what I guessed was some kind of intimidation tactic; it certainly didn't seem to be an invitation for a hug. Where one might expect to find big, black eyes on a regular spider, these seemed to have a sort of visor of carapace over their faces with only slits to look out of, a pair of fangs dangling from the bottom.

I backed away, knowing I didn't want to be surrounded but unwilling to turn my back on them to run, but the spiders matched me. We slowly edged away from the ravine, the circle closing in bit by bit. Then my back hit one of the immovable giants Ralqir had instead of trees. Everyone froze.

On the bright side, at least the monsters couldn't get behind me.

The standoff broke as a spider in front of me charged forward, forelegs and pedipalps spread wide, its hiss splitting the air—but it was a feint. The real attack came from my left side, a heavy chitin body slamming into me and bearing me down to the ground, its legs curling around my back and digging into my skin.

---

Armored Spider attacks you for 3 Damage.
Status gained: Bleeding [1 HP/sec]

---

I'd already had my arms up in a lazy guard position when the spider tackled me, and that's what saved my life. By instinct, luck, or whatever decision-making process spiders had, the monster tried to sink its fangs into my arm. Maybe it was the easiest thing to reach. Maybe it looked tasty. I didn't know.

However, the spider's fangs came down on cold, unforgiving metal over and over again, the venom meant for my insides instead sizzling on the dark metal before evaporating into acrid smoke within a second. I braced myself against the ground, widening my feet and getting my right elbow underneath me. Then I rolled, trying to take some of the spider's weight off me. The creature reacted by gripping me tighter and bringing its head down to bite my side, which had a good deal more flesh than I was comfortable losing.

Grunting, I reached up with my prosthetic toward where the spider's eyes were supposed to be and grabbed the first thing I could wrap my fingers around: the spider's "visor." Its progress arrested, the Armored Spider kicked out jerkily, jostling my body, trying to dislodge my grip and digging deep grooves into my stomach and thighs. If the stalemate went on for too long, I'd end up dead from blood loss even if it never bit me. All that stood between me and liquified insides was my prosthetic's strong grip.

---

You take 1 Bleeding Damage.
Armored Spider attacks you for 1 Damage.
Armored Spider attacks you for 1 Damage.

*Can't stay like this! Do something!*

The obtrusive box returned to my vision. Only one of the options looked like it might have combat applications.

---

Ability Unlocked: Iron Grip
Iron Grip: Grip strength increased by 30%. [.1 MP/sec]

---

Opening my Status Screen, I focused on my new Climbing-related Ability and prayed I was right.

---

Iron Grip [.1 MP/sec]

---

Strength surged into my limbs, specifically my hands.

My metal arm was already very good at grabbing things, probably much better than my natural one. I'd found that out when dangling over the pit back at the tutorial facility, where it seemed like I could have hung from a piece of rebar forever with no loss of power or sign of fatigue.

Doing this with my new Iron Grip on a living creature produced a result that was dramatic, to say the least.

With a crunch, the hard carapace protecting the spider's vulnerable eyes came away in my hand, stringy connective tissue dangling from my fist.

---

Consume Armored Spider Armor? Y/N

---

Armored Spider Armor Consumed.
Status gained: Engine [+6 MP/sec for 2 minutes]
You gain knowledge of material: Magnesium [1/10]

---

This was followed by the now-familiar orange flash of something being Consumed by my Core and then a much brighter, whiter, hotter *FWOOSH!*

It was blinding. So searing I couldn't look at it; so blazing I could feel blisters forming on my neck and face. I closed my eyes and screamed, shoving the spider back and scrambling for distance.

---

Armored Spider takes 15 Fire Damage.
Armored Spider takes 13 Fire Damage.

---

Ability synthesis discovered: Consume + Iron Grip
Synthesize? Y/N

The spider let me go, rolling and thrashing on the ground, digging into its own eyes with its claws to stop the burn. I shot to my feet, stumbling back to get away from the smoking, flailing monster, the glowing prompt dragging my attention away when I really needed it. I chose "Y," hoping I was making the right decision again.

> Ability Synthesis: Consume + Iron Grip
> New Ability: Devouring Grasp 1
> Devouring Grasp: Increase grip strength by 50% x E (where E = current MP/s value of Engine). Able to instantly Consume grasped material. Cost [5 MP/ sec].

The next spider was upon me. This one's jump was less accurate, only catching me with the tips of its legs. The spider was heavy, but I'd braced myself. It ended up wrapping itself around me like the other, but I didn't go down to the ground this time, instead stumbling a step to the left before planting my feet.

> Armored Spider attacks you for 2 Damage.

I twisted, bringing my metal arm around, practically feeding it to the spider. I let it go to town on the metal, just like the last one. These creatures' first instinct seemed to be to bite whatever they could get a hold of, and I could work with that, biding my time until I could get a hand around the thing's head.

> Devouring Grasp [5 MP/sec]

My metal fingers sank into the creature's armor and carapace like it was a rotting pumpkin, bending metal, breaking through to the soft insides of the creature's cranium—or whatever spiders had in place of it. Viscous fluid and globs of brain dribbled out of the opening I created, sliding down my arm and dripping onto my pants.

> Critical hit!
> Your Devouring Grasp does 60 Crushing Damage to Armored Spider.
> Armored Spider defeated.

This one didn't get a chance to flail. It just died, releasing its hold on me and sliding down to the ground, its leg pincers taking bits of my flesh with it.

> Armored Spider defeated.
> You have been awarded 10 Experience points. [10 base (+2 Level, +6 group,

> -8 non-combat Class)]
> You have been awarded 12 Experience points. [10 base (+2 Level, +6 group,
> +2 chain, -8 non-combat Class)]

The Armored Spiders closed in around me, still hissing and waving their forelegs. If they knew fear or loss, they didn't give any indication. Maybe their strategy was to envenom me, then let that wear me down while they waited.

I still hadn't let go of my piece of spider . . . or armor . . . or whatever it was I had.

> Consume Armored Spider Armor? Y/N
> You gain knowledge of material: Magnesium [2/10]
> You gain knowledge of material: Magnesium [3/10]
> You gain knowledge of material: Spider Chitin [1/10]

That warm thrill spread from my Core throughout my body, all the way to the tips of my fingers and toes, and it didn't stop there. Waves of heat radiated from my center, pulsing, compounding until my skin burned and my vision tinted red.

> MP 30+/30
> Status gained: Mana Overflow
> Mana Overflow: Your rate of regeneration far exceeds your rate of expenditure, resulting in an oversaturation of mana in your body. Severe Mana Overflow may result in serious injury or death.

Despite the fight only having been going on for about twenty seconds, my breathing was ragged, like I'd run a marathon. I was bleeding all over my back, my face stung from having been burned, and spider ichor was dribbling down my body.

I was alive, though. Alive and fighting, and that warmed my (probably) metal heart like a forge. As I swayed drunkenly on my feet, I bared my teeth at the things that had assumed I would be easy prey.

My dry throat coarsened my voice and made speaking painful, but I didn't care. "Who else wants to try Mister Grippy?" I asked.

The fingers of my metal hand flexed expectantly, and I got back into a ready stance.

# CHAPTER SEVEN

# Greet the Sun

Only two more Armored Spiders wanted to try Mister Grippy.

They approached together, from the same part of the semicircle, but they ended up fighting each other as much as they did me. Once they were in range, they seemed to want to grab onto and bite almost anything, grappling with one another while simultaneously striking at me.

It was then that I realized the spiders weren't actually working together. Sure, they all wanted me dead, and they went so far as to box me in as a team. However, that was as far as their cooperation went. That meant only the brave or foolhardy made the first move and risked everything. Meanwhile, the ones that hung back seemed to be planning on taking the prize by force afterward.

Once I got a hold of a spider and activated Devouring Grasp, the fight swung heavily in my favor. Whatever they were using for armor—magnesium, according to my Combat Log—it didn't take well to the intense heat of my activating the Consume part of my Core. When I grasped one of its legs and did the Grasp/Consume combo, half of the spider burst into white-hot flame, spewing a bitter, metallic-flavored smoke that reminded me of the taste of a nosebleed. From there, it was all about getting clear before I ended up well-done myself.

> Armored Spider defeated.
> You have been awarded 16 Experience points. [10 base (+2 Level, +6 group, +6 chain, -8 non-combat Class)]

The other spider wasn't lucky enough to get away, already being tangled

with its compatriot as it was. It caught fire as well, its legs curling in on themselves, dragging the still-burning body of the other spider closer. The two went
up together, embracing like old friends all the while.

Armored Spider defeated.
You have been awarded 16 Experience points. [10 base (+2 Level, +6 group,
+6 chain, -8 non-combat Class)]

After that, the remaining nine spiders retreated into their crevasse. One
ambitious little guy tried to drag one of its dead friends underground with it, but
I put a stop to that by charging at the creature with Mister Grippy. The spiders
weren't particularly smart, but they'd learned that I wasn't prey. The monster
dropped its corpse and backed away with its forelegs spread wide.

Meanwhile, I stood as straight as I could, in a pseudo-boxer's stance with my
right arm guarding my face and my metal one slightly out and ready to grab.
There were no more takers, though. My status had shifted from "food" to "not
worth it" in the span of a minute.

As soon as the last monster was out of sight, my strength left me. I wobbled
and fell to my knees, my lungs working like bellows. I unclenched my hands and
let the adrenaline drain away, leaving me cold and shivering. Sweat beaded on my
skin and dripped down my nose to fall to the leaves below.

I knelt there for a few minutes, eyes wide, not daring to blink lest something
else jump out of the shadows to eat me. Nothing did, though.

Status lost: Engine
Status lost: Mana Overflow

My HP was down to 12, which wasn't all that bad, but whether from dehydration and undernourishment or from the act of having to bluff a swarm of
spiders into submission, I was feeling the strain.

The adrenaline crash had me shivering and drowsy, but there were things
to do.

I shook my head and slapped my hand against my chest with a metallic *ping*.
*Oh, right. Going to need to set aside some time to come to grips with that soon.*

Time was ticking by, and I couldn't stay here. The spiders could rally and
overwhelm me if I gave them time.

But first . . .

Starting with the least-damaged corpse, the one with the crushed brain that
I didn't need to set on fire, I collected my spoils.

Upon closer inspection, the Armored Spiders weren't actually brown and
covered in hair. Their "armor" appeared to be attached closely to the carapace or

maybe grown onto it, then covered in a patina of dried mud that, when I scraped it away, revealed a gray, almost-lustrous sheen. The bristles, similarly, were made of metal so fine the gentle breeze shifted them slightly. The spider's splayed limbs and broken visor, askew thanks to its now-deformed head, made it look almost hungover.

Loot Armored Spider? Y/N

Again, the light warping rainbow of colors obscured the corpse, and the System did its thing. Once the process was done, the Armored Spider looked significantly smaller and less imposing—almost deflated—and my loot lay on the ground.

Armored Spider Armor x 12: A piece of protective shell grown by a Ralqiri variant of Armored Spider. The metal used in its creation is dependent on where the Armored Spider makes its nest and the availability of material.
Armored Spider Poison Gland: A venom gland of a Ralqiri variant of Armored Spider. Contains highly corrosive venom meant to digest its prey as well as the metals the spider consumes to grow its armor.

So, the spiders made their nests around sources of metal and used it to grow their outer shells. When I got a piece of spider armor and Consumed it during the fight, my logs said it was primarily made of magnesium. Did that mean there was more around here somewhere? What could I do with that? Did I want to carry around a bunch of magnesium?

Carefully, I prodded the burns on my face with my fingers, wincing at how tender it was. While the stuff certainly worked well with Devouring Grasp, I wasn't sure I was ready to carry around something that reacted so violently to me . . . also the air . . . and water.

*Yeah. No, thanks.*

It also occurred to me just how lucky it was that I hadn't blundered into a colony that used something like tungsten or iron. If circumstances had been even slightly different, I could have been dead now of my own carelessness.

Especially galling was all the Experience I seemed to lose from being a non-combat Class. What the hell happened to 80% of my base Experience? Did it just vanish into the ether? Would I be Level 1 or even 2 by now if I were a warrior or mage?

My only saving grace were the multiple bonuses the System was awarding me for special circumstances, but I couldn't count on that to continue.

I shook my head to bring my thoughts back to reality as it was instead of what I wanted it to be. I just needed to roll with it.

> Consume Armored Spider Armor? Y/N
> Status gained: Engine [+6 MP/sec for 2 minutes]
> You gain knowledge of material: Magnesium [4/10]

I repeated the process for all the corpses, Consuming all of their armor. The two that had died in the fireball didn't have any salvageable loot on them according to the System except:

> Spider Meat x 2: Overcooked meat from an Armored Spider.

The prospect of eating giant spider meat didn't appeal to me, especially considering what the System implied about their habit of digesting metals to grow their armor.

*What would that even do to their bodies?*

I decided to err on the side of caution and leave the meat behind. I buried it and the two venom glands I had received in a hole about a quarter of a mile away from where we fought. I didn't currently have a way to carry anything, and walking around with a corrosive sac of venom in my pocket didn't seem wise. While it would be cool to chuck a venom sac at a big nasty and watch it work, I had no way to guarantee it would burst upon impact.

Unfortunately, my consumption of all that magnesium and its massive +6 MP was also enough to give me Mana Overflow again. Twice. That was a rough ride, forcing me to sit down, back against a tree, and do my best not to explode. I could feel all that potential inside of me, burning to do something. Eventually, the thought came to me to activate Devouring Grasp and just let my fist clench for a while, and that alleviated the symptoms somewhat. Then it was just about riding it out until the two minutes of the Engine Status ticked down.

> Skill Unlocked: Conduit
> Your current Skill Level is 1.
> Conduit: Your body grows more able to conduct mana freely and direct its flow. +5% resistance to Mana Overflow. +5% speed of Mana Flow when using Abilities.

My suffering netted me an Affinity for magnesium, at least, and then some. The next tier was going to take an additional fifty pieces of the stuff, so that wasn't happening today. Magnesium Affinity gave me the ability to detect magnesium within ten feet, which I was starting to realize was the bog-standard F-grade reward, but it also gave some additional mana conductivity, whatever that meant. For the hundredth time, I wished I had a working tutorial to help me out with some of this stuff.

Experimenting as I continued my trek toward water, I willed Detect Magnesium to life, but I had to stop moving soon afterward due to the ability being extremely disorienting. It wasn't that the world looked different to me. Visually, everything was the same. The giant trees, the ever-present green blanket covering the sky, the mottled browns of the forest floor—all of it was the same.

No, what I was "seeing" wasn't with my eyes, and my mind had a hard time processing that. I had magnesium all over me. It glinted painfully in my new perception—not so bright that it was blinding, but as if someone were using a signal mirror to get my attention. My shredded shirt and filthy pants shone with little flakes of magnesium probably shed from the spiders that had tried to wrestle me down. There was even some dusting in my hair, the presence of which forced me to stop and reorder my brain around being able to "see" the top of my own head. What's more, my bones sparkled. Yes, I could see . . . or sense . . . the vague outline of my bones.

I brushed all the magnesium bits off my body that I could and watched them sail down to the forest floor and filter into the soil. That didn't stop the magnesium from being extremely visible, despite it being obscured from my normal vision. Looking away didn't help, either. It was all too much for me to process.

When I deactivated the Ability, everything went back to normal—that is, to say, green and alien—but at least I could blink that uncomfortable reality away every now and then.

With this new knowledge, I filed my Detect Abilities under "weird but probably useful." A part of me wished I had saved a piece of armor to see what that looked like under the effects of Detect, but my reasons for having Consumed it all were sound.

I resisted the urge to rub the blisters on my neck and jaw.

Back to the search for water.


Hiking ever downward, pausing to check every crevasse I passed now that I knew what could be down there, my pace was slow and cautious. The humidity jumped up at least an order of magnitude, but the temperature remained the same temperate cool I was used to by now. My blood felt thick in my veins, and I'd stopped sweating sometime in the past hour even with all the moisture in the air. My steps also became more difficult and less careful as time went on. I just didn't have the energy for it.

Then I heard something beautiful: the sound of rushing water. Close.

I smacked my lips and tilted my head to try and pinpoint the sound. The desire to rush in and drink until I was full to bursting was strong. So strong it nearly overrode my good sense, but I wasn't so desperate yet that I would risk my life for a drink of unsanitized water.

I hadn't forgotten where I was.

Crouching low, I continued my descent. The ground here was rough. The entire area was a network of creek beds, washes, and exposed roots where no piece of ground was flat. I could actually see the bottom of these bodies of water, which made me feel better about clambering over them to follow the sound of the water. What's more, I was starting to see honest-to-Constance stone now that I was low enough. I hadn't realized how much I'd missed it until now.

My head still felt like cracked glass, but I remembered home well enough, if not how I ended up here. I could call up parts of my past, which made Ralqir feel even farther from home.

Proxis was all rocks and wind, harsh but beautiful in its uncompromising, unapologetically brutal nature. You could bet any living thing you encountered there had earned their way into existence, constantly struggling against the elements and each other. The tan-and-gold-banded rocks were ancient. Eternal. They were there before we were born, and they would be there long after our entire civilization was nothing but dust.

Here, on Ralqir, everything was transient. The sky was a living tapestry of green, the horizon an unending parade of tree trunks, and the ground was littered with discarded biomatter. At least it seemed so until now. Now I could see the foundation of the world, and it was something I knew. That fact gave me some comfort.

The water I'd heard was, in fact, a waterfall. Not a tall one, only about a six-foot drop from the raised lip of a basin of sorts, a slightly tilted slab of brown stone with a dip in the middle that held a milky, roiling pool. After a short drop, the water continued swiftly down the hill in a ribbon of white that ran far into the distance. The "bowl" was maybe a few hundred feet across, its clear water shining brilliantly in the noonday sun which stabbed down through the curtain of mist to illuminate the place so brilliantly, I had to shield my eyes.

*So this place* does *have a sun. Nice to see at least.*

My perch, a jagged boulder stabbed through the heart and held in place by a particularly ambitious tree root, was slightly above the basin, up the hill where I could get a good view of everything.

I deduced the basin was some kind of spring, since nothing flowed into it, but it was constantly overflowing to create the river. Strangely, though, nothing came down to drink. There was birdsong and insect chirps everywhere, but nothing flew over the water. No land animals. No cold-blooded lizards sunned themselves on the warm rocks. Nothing.

I didn't like it, but I was getting to the point where my thirst would soon become debilitating. I needed water to move and to think, and I wanted to see the sun. Get some natural light for a change.

Cautiously, I picked my way through the rocks and trees, careful not to make much noise or disturb the landscape. I landed heavily on the flat stone that formed the lip of the basin, staying in the shadow of the trees in case something was watching. The rock was porous, rough to the touch, and easy to walk on without slipping.

Above, the gargantuan trees reached desperately across the clearing to try to smother the sun like they did everywhere else, but the gap proved too wide for them. The resultant hole in the canopy reminded me of the entrances to flood caves during the dry season back home, where my friends and I could go explore the depths as long as we stayed near the light.

I stalked forward, eyes up in anticipation of the next surprise, but it never came. All was still, except for the burbling spring.

Stepping into the sun for the first time since I came here, I felt like I was finally doing something familiar, though water on Proxis would never be out in the open like this. I could ignore that little discrepancy for now, though.

The light was blindingly bright and surprisingly hot on my skin considering how cool the rest of the forest was. My eyes were forced shut before I could really get a good look at the sky.

*So damned bright.*

Then, slowly, cautiously, I edged toward the spring, my body tingling with renewed sensation in the delicious warmth of the clearing.

Step by step, eyes darting around to look for threats, I finally neared my prize.

However, before I knew what was happening, my body reached a tipping point of some sort. My exposed skin felt increasingly hot—so hot it burned. My eyes welled with tears, and my vision blurred. Subcutaneous blood vessels burst and roiled inside my body. The world blurred; the colors bent and blended until everything was a painful smear of white.

Something was very wrong here.

Blindly, I whirled, turning to run back to the trees, to the cool, green, rolling shadows. Everything was light now, incandescent to the point of agony, but I kept my legs moving, sprinting away from the rush of the water for the safety of the shade. I knew I had made it when the familiar chill washed over my skin.

Then I flopped down on the porous stone, blinking tears from my eyes and willing my log to appear.

You take 1 Light Damage.
You take 1 Light Damage.
Status gained: Exposure (Radiant)
Exposure: You are more vulnerable to damage from all forms of light.
You take 1 Light Damage.
You take 1 Light Damage.
You take 1 Light Damage.

You take 1 Light Damage.
You take 1 Light Damage.
You take 1 Light Damage.

The sun . . . It was poison.

The edges of my vision started to feather with cool, soothing blackness, thank Constance. I shuddered, sighing. Anything was better than the light.

The blackness overtook the rest of the world, shrinking it down to a pinprick, until I felt my consciousness waver.

"It still lives. Finish it quick." A voice, high and rough, spoke from somewhere nearby.

You take 1 Light Damage.

"No! It is hu-man. We take it. We take it."

Then the world slipped away on a tide of dreams.

# CHAPTER EIGHT

# Unstab My Heart

*Memory: Proxis 3 - Before Integration*

For the second time that night, I was barreling headfirst into the wind behind the rest of the boys. They were going low and slow this time, which I appreciated. Their sedate, stealthy pace was still enough to have my lungs burning, though.

It would be a slow dawn, a gradual rise in ambient light levels that would extinguish the weakest of the stars before we saw a meager fraction of the sun. That gave us some time but not so much that we could take things easy.

The ridge we were on now was more exposed. Dust and small pebbles scoured our skin, forcing us to don our masks and slip on our gloves before we were even close to the enemy camp.

Getting here was a slow, tense process. As I'd suspected, the source of the mist in the valley was a river, guarded jealously by plant life, covering the entirety of the water with green. A thick carpet of floating strawlops gave the river the look of a calm oasis in the middle of the desert, but that was an illusion. The greenery wasn't thick enough to bear any of our weight, and the current was quick. We had to use the thick tree roots as bridges, and we had to find them all by feel. By the time we were across and heading up the opposite ridge, we were soaked to the bone and our clothes a few pounds heavier.

So, by the time we were up top and in position, we were all uniformly brown with stuck-on mud camouflaging us as we drew up to the camp. Their lights were mostly extinguished, and all but the lookouts were asleep. There was a slight rise in the terrain in front of us, just a shadow against the night sky unless you knew what you were looking for, but we knew this is where the lookout would be.

Vince held his arm up and gestured to get down. I sank to the ground among the bristly scrub, contorting myself to not jostle the plants and give away my position. My arm, stretched out in front of me, was nearly perfect in its camouflage, blending into the rocks and sand like I was made of the stuff. Around me, everyone else disappeared and became one with the mountain as well.

We waited there for a long while, long enough for my heart to slow down and my brain to engage again. If we were spotted by the lookout, we'd be screwed. There would be a mad dash to get away, but the reavers had hoverbikes, range, drones, and Constance-knew-what-else. Would any of us make it? What was I even doing here? How did I think I could do this?

A whistle, soft in the wind.

It was so soft, I almost thought I'd imagined it. Then the boy next to me rose into a crouch and started forward, up the hill. I followed suit.

Everyone gathered at the top of the hill around Vince and Chris, who were hunched over something.

A body.

It had the face of a young man, stubble on his narrow jaw, his mouth open in a silent scream. An acrid taste rose in the back of my throat, and I fought not to be sick.

The dead man was about my height. His choice of thick, dusty leathers and hard armor plating on his torso and shoulders gave him a stocky figure like a yard worker with a penchant for drinking. His eyes seemed comically big, thanks to the insect-like spherical goggles he wore. His weapon, still strapped to his shoulder but now angled awkwardly above his head, was an oblong las-rifle.

Though I didn't have much experience with Colonial weapons, I thought the chassis appeared manufactured, while the rest was slapdash as hell, sporting a stubby grip and rubber coolant tubes jacked into the weapon's guts and secured with tape. On the man's wrist was some kind of display cuff, smooth and shiny, but the screen was dead.

Chris looked as sick as I felt, goggles off, eyes wide and unfocused, holding his bloody knife in a shaking hand.

Seeing the boy in distress, Vince reached over and put a hand on Chris's wrist, leaning in to make eye contact. "Hey, you did good," Vince cooed as he slid his hand forward and got his own grip on the knife. Chris was clutching the weapon hard. Even in the dark, I could see his knuckles were white. "You did your part, Chris. Let's clean the blade, yeah?"

Chris blinked, refocusing, coming back to us. Slowly, his fingers loosened their death grip on the knife's handle, allowing Vince to take it and wipe it on the dead man's clothes. Once it was clean, Vince held it there, staring at it for a moment before deciding to give it back. Chris took it without looking, sheathing it again in a practiced motion without much conscious thought.

Nodding, Vince got us moving again. "Chris is going to stay here with Brendon on overwatch. Chris, watch Brendon's back."

Chris's head twitched in the slightest of nods, which we would just have to accept as agreement.

"The rest of you, stick to the plan," Vince continued, turning to each of us one by one. "The generator has to go. It has to go."

A sudden lightning flash of pain split my skull like an injection of ice water directly into my brain. I bowed my head and collapsed in on myself, curling up like a dying insect and nearly tipping myself forward onto the corpse, but then, the sensation was gone. The pain seemed to wane, shrinking, diminishing until it was just a dull ache behind my eyes. I came back to myself, staring at the dead man's blank wrist display, little multicolored fractals dancing across my vision.

*What the hell?*

When I looked up, the group was already halfway down the hill and nearly to the ring of illumination cast by the generator's running lights. To my side, Brendon was settling down on his stomach and unwrapping the protective furs around his dad's las-rifle. Chris was next to him. He wasn't holding his knife anymore, but his hands shook in his lap as he stared down at the camp, unblinking.

I made to follow the group, getting to one knee, but something made me stop and look down again at the dead man and his gear, specifically the dead wrist cuff. Something about it tickled that special part of my brain that overrode good sense a lot of the time, that kept me up at night playing old Earth games or trading for heretical tech on the sly.

Something was wrong here. I reached down and grabbed the lookout's arm.

*Not a mark on it. Chris took him down fast, probably through the throat or the heart.*

There were no buttons or other visible hardware anywhere on the device. Any panels to access the guts were probably on the inside of the cuff. I resisted the desire to take the thing off the arm, though. If there were some kind of security feature to prevent it from being stolen, that could complicate things.

"Why are you wearing dead tech, buddy?" I whispered.

The dead man didn't answer. His poker face was impenetrable as well, though I considered the tinted goggles tantamount to cheating.

The seed of something terrifying began to germinate in my brain.

*Oh.*

With twitching fingers I reached up to the man's face and removed the goggles.

The night was extremely dark this time of the month. Therefore, before I even flipped the goggles around, the faint glow of a heads-up display cast the corpse's wide-eyed expression in a ghoulish blue.

*Oh . . . shit.*

I put the goggles on, slipping them over my own. The world lit up in a cascade of brilliant blue, so bright it stung my dark-attuned eyes. Ambient radiation sparked and swirled in the air like a summer rain. Brendon and Chris stared down at the camp with black eyes, directly into a wall of pulsing blue stretched between strobing pylons that formed a perimeter fence around the camp.

Beyond that, the camp stood bright in my vision. The tents were a neon sort of white against the dull background of the dirt. Strobing lights trailed up a spindly, wobbling cable tethered to an armored tractor in the center of camp. I followed the cable upward, high into the sky where a glider drone bobbed on the air currents. Previously invisible searchlights shone down from the underbelly of the machine, two searching and one fixed directly on the gaggle of boys gathered around the generator.

I sprang to my feet, a wordless cry emanating from my open mouth. As I took off, I spared a look down at the lookout's wrist tech again. Through the goggles, the cuff's screen flashed frantically: **BREACH. BREACH. BREACH.**

*Oh SHIT!*

Then I was moving at full sprint down the hill through the infrared security fence. "They know!" I shouted over my shoulder at our overwatch. The wind howled past me, drowning out whatever their reply had been.

When I caught up to the group, they were already gathered around the generator's trailer, grunting and swearing as they tried to realign the angle of the wheels. Vince was at the neck of the trailer with two other boys, arms and backs straining to drag the monster machine into place. The ice pick in my head scraped around the inside of my skull in time with my steps and seemed to strike something in the part of my brain that housed my volume control, because when I called to the others, my voice was shrill, bordering on panicked.

"They're coming!" I shouted again. "They know!"

All activity stopped for a second as every head turned toward me.

"Shut up. You're going to get us caught," Mel growled through clenched teeth. He had a hand underneath the wheel housing closest to me, and he was pulling for all he was worth to try to get the behemoth to move. This close to the generator, I realized how I'd underestimated its size. They must have pulled this thing with something big.

I got Vince's attention, however, which was all I needed.

"What is it, Ryan?" he asked.

I ran over to stand next to him and tried to get my voice under control. "We're caught. They have a silent alarm and a drone."

Fear touched Vince's eyes for an instant, but then the moment passed, giving way to stubborn determination. "We have to finish it. If we run now, they'll just chase us down."

"We can steal the bikes." I turned to four bikes tethered to the generator, one of which still had its atmo-thruster half disassembled.

"Can you do that? How fast?" Vince asked, doubt evident in his tone.

I groaned. He was right. I didn't know enough about Colonial tech to hotwire four hoverbikes before we got shot. I'd be lucky to figure out one if given the rest of the night.

"Fine!" I was back to shouting now. It just felt natural at this point. My headache threatened to split my skull in two. "Fine!" I shouted again, bounding away from Vince and heading to the wheel housing, crouching down and shoving Mel to the side as I felt around next to the wheel.

"Hey! Vince, call off your dog before I have to slap him!" Mel shouted from behind me, but I wasn't listening. My fingers found what I was looking for: the brake line. I pulled it out, so I could see it, then I drew out my multitool, opened the blade with my teeth and severed the hydraulic line. Cold, clear liquid streamed from the tube and down my hand.

That's when Mel hauled me up and threw me. I spun around in the air and landed on my stomach, all the air leaving me in a whoosh.

I gasped, pushing myself up to get on my knees, my hand balled into an angry fist. Mel wasn't paying me any mind, though. He was back in position, pulling hard with the rest. The trailer spun in place slowly, maybe an inch at a time.

It would take time for the fluid to fully drain from the braking system. Until then, I had more to do. I got to my feet and stumbled toward my next goal, sucking in shallow gasps of air as I went. Tough guys didn't have time to catch their breath.

*Got no time to breathe. I'll breathe when I'm dead.*

"Hey! It's starting to move!" I heard faintly from behind me.

A mad, hysterical giggle bubbled up out of my throat. We were all going to die.

The iron spike in my head chose to reassert itself at that point, but my brain was overloaded. I just didn't have the capacity to stop and pay any attention to my hurting head or my sore muscles or my wounded pride.

I knew where the firepit was, thanks to our scouting earlier, but my shiny new goggles would have let me know regardless. It was a pulsing, flickering beacon for me, the only one at ground level that I could see. The camp was quiet still, quiet enough that one could almost forget the direness of the situation. The habs I passed were deathly still, like there was no one inside at all. I knew better, though. No doubt they were waiting for their chance to spring their trap all at once instead of trickling out of their shelters and alerting their guests before it was time. The thought occurred to me to knock out a few of their supports, but I couldn't imagine that being more than an inconvenience to the occupants as they shuffled their way to the doors.

No. The only way I was going to create a sufficient distraction was right in front of me. The fire had burned down over the night, but it still gave off plenty of heat, noticeable even in the wind.

They'd used super-dense carbon bricks that lasted for extended amounts of time and didn't give off more than a few sparks as they burned. Smart if you like your camp not on fire. Unfortunately, I needed their camp to be on fire.

I slipped the pack from my shoulders, easing it down into the dirt at my feet right at the edge of the firepit. I needed to time this right. I turned my head to check the others' progress, but I couldn't see them from here.

That's when something hard and cold pressed into the back of my neck.

I froze.

"Get down on your knees, kid, away from the bag," a gravelly voice ordered from behind me. "I see you touch it, and I'll plug you. Nod if you understand."

Bright blue flooded my vision through the enhanced vision of the goggles, causing a sympathetic reaction from the spikes in my brain. I winced, looking up to see that one of the searchlights was pointed directly at me now.

My captor didn't like me doing that one bit. Faster than I could react, he hit me squarely in the temple with something hard. I flopped bonelessly down onto my knees, just like the guy wanted. Rough hands ripped my goggles off my head, bringing the world back to the appropriate level of light. Spots floated in my vision, and my ears rang.

"Stay down and stay quiet," the voice ordered.

It sounded like an excellent idea, the way my vision swam. If I'd had anything in my stomach, I might have lost it.

The sound of metal scraping on gravel saved me. The trailer the other boys had been trying to roll toward the cliff must have hit something on the way over, making the most horrific screeching sound, the kind that sounded expensive and painful even if the thing in question wasn't yours. Then that screech was followed by an echoing *BOOM!* that filled the valley and rattled my teeth.

"What th—"

I shot to my feet, dizzy and nauseated, but I had the wherewithal to pause and do my best mule kick back into my captor. I hit something and heard a sort of squawk from the man, but I didn't pause to see what I'd done. I kicked my pack into the fire. Sparks blazed up out of the pit and shot off into the wind. Then I was running into the dark.

My night vision was shot thanks to the goggles that I'd now lost, but I knew I couldn't stay where I was. I sprinted forward, just hoping to get some distance and space to figure out the next part of my plan.

*CRACK! CRACK!* Two las-rounds flew past me to burn ugly, smoking holes into the hab I was about to use as cover. Voices cried out in alarm from inside. I changed course but never broke stride, bounding gazelle-like over hab anchors and diving past opening hab doors. Without my pack I was much faster. I might even be able to make it to—

*CRACK! CRACK!* More las-rounds, their tempo slower this time, more deliberate. The first two went wide into the dark.

*CRACK!*

They say when you're hit by laser-type weapons, the heat boils the blood and sears the nerves too quickly for the trauma to be truly appreciated. I disagree.

One second, I was running for my life, pumping my legs and dodging las-fire, then suddenly my right leg collapsed, and my body did a sort of involuntary flop-and-roll maneuver. When I came to a stop, my leg felt like it was dissolving from the inside out. I held on to the sizzling holes in my quadricep and stifled a scream.

Back the way I'd come, armed and armored reavers were pouring from their habs, their need for subterfuge gone now that gunfire had been exchanged.

*FWOOSH! BOOM!* A massive ball of liquid fire erupted from the center of the camp, blown high into the air by the long-awaited explosion of my promegel pack. Proxis's energetic wind currents took it from there, providing the flames with oxygen and sweeping the sticky yellow gel to cover half of the camp, specifically the half that was downwind. It was a tidal wave of conflagration, one that I was hoping to be much farther away from before it went off.

The wall of fire swept in my general direction, luckily not directly toward me. Though it hurt my wounded body, I curled into a ball and rolled, doing my best to shield myself behind one of the nearby habs. Blistering heat blew across my back and stole the oxygen from the air with a *whoosh!* Then the initial wave was past.

Around me, little globs of unignited gel splattered onto the roofs of habs or down into the dirt with weighty plops.

Everything was on fire. People were shouting.

Las-fire echoed in the night in fits and starts, mingled with the sound of steel ringing on steel. Vince and the others were fighting. Battle cries replaced the screams of the burned. Shouts and orders I didn't understand.

A pair of reavers found me sometime after things quieted down, and I was forced to hobble between the two of them until we came back to the center of camp, where the other boys knelt in the blackened dirt, hands bound and under guard. Several were in the process of being beaten and cursed at even as they sat there silently. There were too few of us here. As they dragged me past, I frantically searched for Vince in the group of bruised and bloody faces.

*Please let him be alive.*

My two escorts lined me up next to the rest and kicked my good knee out from under me to force me down. I wasn't bound like the rest.

The reavers hurled curses at us and rained blows down on those of us that showed even a spark of defiance. Some of us cried out. Others wept.

Then the atmosphere changed. All voices went silent, even those of the reavers.

Heavy footsteps clomped through the gravel behind us accompanied by the

clank of metal. What came into the circle of firelight was a hulking, black figure, clad from head to toe in thick plated armor. Its pace was slow, methodical,
almost lazy, its boots *thunk*ing down onto the gravel and crushing the pebbles
into dust. Its arms and legs were thick as tree trunks, the plates of its segmented
armor making grinding, scraping sounds that set my teeth on edge. The figure's
broad shoulders and deep barrel chest gave it the look of a walking tank instead
of a man. Its gauntleted hand hung on the handle of an automatic with a barrel
as thick as my thumb. The black-winged helmet it wore had no visor or slits, but
we heard its voice all the same.

"How many more?" it asked with a voice deep and clear.

*Barrow.*

No one answered, whether too brave or too afraid to speak.

Barrow let the question hang for a moment, but when it became apparent
no one was talking, he took a different tack. He strode down the line where we
knelt. He had a deliberate, almost sluggish type of walk, like every step was an
imposition.

He stopped in front of Mel, crouching down to get close to the boy's face.

"How many more of you are there?" Barrow asked again.

Mel, for the first time in his life, stayed quiet when challenged, Constance
bless him.

It cost him his life.

Barrow's hand shot out faster than a striking snake and took hold of Mel's
face, the strong, armored fingers wrapping around the top of his skull. Then
Barrow straightened, standing up to his full height and bringing Mel with him,
the boy's feet dangling just above the ground.

Mel cried out, muffled against the palm of Barrow's hand. He fought to free
his arms from behind his back. The bonds were strong, though, and his feet
kicked desperately as the weight of his heavily muscled body wrenched his neck
painfully with every second. Barrow's arm didn't move more than you might
expect from the branch of an ancient tree, even as Mel kicked at him and tried to
squirm. It took a full minute for Mel to stop struggling.

A wave of something cold passed through me. The ice in my brain crackled.

Barrow dropped the body like a discarded garment and took a step to the
right, crouching down in front of the next boy. "How many more?"

"Stop!" Relief washed over me, only to be replaced by cold terror as Vince's
voice shouted over the roaring wind: "This is all of us, and this was my plan."

Barrow stood up slowly and plodded over to Vince, crouching down to his
level like he did with Mel.

"Am I addressing the man called Barrow?" Vince asked, loudly enough to be
heard by us all.

"And what if you are?" Barrow asked in return.

"I—" Vince's confidence seemed to waver staring into that blank helm, but he found his voice again quickly. "I challenge you. For the freedom of my men here."

Barrow leaned in until Vince had to look up to keep eye contact as the big tank loomed over. "A fine idea if you were an Exotic," Barrow stated. "I could use the experience, but I can sense that you're not one of us."

Barrow stood up again and addressed the rest of us.

"You made a fatal mistake, children, in not going for the kill when you had the chance. Your Elders failed to impress this lesson upon you."

"Killing someone in their sleep is something a reaver would do," Vince shot back. "Not one of the Chosen. Not one of us."

"Chosen . . ." Barrow mused, sounding out both syllables slowly, going deathly still for a long minute. When he continued, his tone had changed noticeably. He sounded pensive, far away. "Any man worth killing is worth killing in his sleep, boy. Your Clan has been too long at peace if they've forgotten that."

With a sharp *CRACK* and a sudden red flash that wreathed Barrow in light, the Exotic stumbled forward a single step. Then he was gone before I could even register that he'd been shot, the forward rush of displaced air the only clue that he'd been there at all. There was a heavy thud we could hear even over the wind and the crackling flames—a desperate scream, cut short. Then silence.

A long, tense few minutes later, Barrow plodded back into the circle of firelight. In his hands he held what was left of Brendon's las-rifle, snapped in half. The bulky artifact looked like a toy in the Exotic's hand.

"Well planned. Well struck," he complimented as he looked down at the remains of the las-gun. "Now you can die knowing you tried everything."

This was all wrong. Something had to happen, or this would be it. Panic filled my mind. Every thought that raced through my head came with a thousand needles of ice.

Vince rose to his feet and turned to address us, his natural gravity drawing all of us in as it always did. Even a few of the reavers turned to hear him. "Our people live another day, and he can't take that from us. The Clan lives on, and Constance will judge us worthy."

"If your Clan was worth a damn, they would be here instead of their children," Barrow replied as he strode over to Vince with the slow inevitability of death.

"The System will judge us worthy!" Vince shouted defiantly.

There was a sword in Barrow's hand. He didn't draw it from anywhere. It was suddenly just there. It was as long as I was tall, thick as my wrist, and the ambient light around the blade died on contact with the metal.

Barrow placed the tip against Vince's chest.

The boy that was my best friend raised his chin defiantly to look the Exotic in the eye.

The big man nodded, almost respectfully. "In a just universe, the System would have chosen you."

Then he ran the blade through Vince's heart.

Someone screamed. I think it might have been me.

Vince just hung there, open-mouthed, head slumped, arms behind him.

I was up and moving, red rage tinting my vision blurred by tears, my own primal, desperate scream still echoing in my ears. I leapt at the man who had just killed my only friend in the world.

Barrow caught me casually by the throat with his free hand. I swung my fist wildly, trying to strike something that would hurt, but the Exotic's arm was too long. I was shouting, cursing, gibbering like a demon, scratching at the Exotic's impenetrable armor with cracking, bleeding nails.

Eventually, I had to breathe in, and when I did, I turned to Vince just as he died.

He seemed to diminish in that moment, when life finally left him. His eyes sunk back into his head and his skin turned ashen. His frame grew gaunt, and his body collapsed in on itself like a dead insect husk left in the sun for weeks.

When Barrow withdrew his blade, Vince's body fell to the ground, lighter than it should have been.

Barrow's black sword was at my chest now, his faceless helmet staring into me.

"There is no divine hand. No blessed ancestors judging our deeds," he spoke to us all.

With a wet pop, the blade pierced my chest cavity and took me through the heart, just as it did Vince.

"You people pray to a rotting corpse."

Life left me quickly, almost rushing out of my chest. Something gave way in my skull, finally providing me some relief from the migraine. I slumped forward as my vision dimmed, but not before taking one last shot at the Exotic asshole's face.

Somehow, this one connected. My fist hit with a meaty *GONG!* accompanied by the sound of my breaking bones.

The world stopped.

The fractals were back, dancing around in my vision, a jumbled mess of . . .
*Wait.*

Something unfathomably huge and impossibly complex snapped into place.

> Welcome to the System, Ryan Kotes. Your integration is the first of many steps on the path to ascension. Please stand by for initial assessment.

I blinked, or at least I tried to. Nothing was working. My fist was frozen mid-strike on Barrow's "face." I could even see the shock of the impact as it traveled up my arm. The pain was still there from being impaled and from my broken hand, though it was a distant thing. Muted.

Assessment commencing . . .

The System? What the hell did I have to offer the System?

The Constance Clan had been waiting for generations for the next Exotic to appear in our bloodline. We built our entire lives around honing our bodies and minds to perfection, training our kids from birth to fight, and . . . What? The System chose *me*? The defective kid who wasn't allowed to train?

My mind felt clearer than it had been a few heartbeats ago, and the questions piled up.

Why not any of the paragons of physicality literally kneeling a few feet from me?

*Why not Vince?*

Despair bubbled up again from the dark places of my mind, but I forced it back. I needed a clear head.

Error: Bodily Integrity Compromised. Anomalous material detected . . .

In all fairness, there was a sword through my chest. Hopefully the System wouldn't hold that against me.

Error: Spiritual Integrity Compromised. Anomalous presence detected . . .

That was just as, or more, concerning than the previous message. What was draining my spirit?

The text started to fly by, faster than I could absorb its meaning:

Assessment complete.

Ryan Kotes
HP: 1/23
MP: 0
Body: 1 (Amputation: -3, Physical Trauma: -6)
Mind: 9 (Blood Loss: -1, Concussion: -2)
Spirit: 7: (External Drain: -2)

Initiating Emergency Protocol: Life Preservation . . .
Eligible Classes: 4,602
List of eligible Classes curated due to Emergency Protocol: Life Preservation

Eligible Classes:
Animator (Uncommon)

End of list.

Initiating Class transition.
Integrating. There will be some discomfort as your body is modified to synergize with your Class . . .

*What?*

I—No. *Everything* . . . collapsed in on itself. One second, everything was frozen in time, and all the pain of dying was a distant worry, but then the world dissolved. My broken fist, my arm, my body, the sword through my heart, even the light around me collapsed around each other, broken down at a fundamental level and fused with blazing, blasting sun-fire.

I felt all of it. Whatever was keeping me from experiencing pain in the time-stop, it wasn't working anymore. I felt myself melt away—scoured and disintegrated, then condensed. Then there was nothing except a single mote of dim light that was, at once, so small, yet infinitely complex and unique. I saw it against the massive, swirling storm of the cosmos.

Then there was a rushing sensation, the kind you get when you fall out of your bunk in your sleep, just before you hit the ground.

The world came back into focus, and time resumed its normal flow. I didn't come back the same way I had left.

I felt the sensation of floating. The world seemed narrower, everything closer.

No. Wait. One of my eyes was shut. That side of my face felt hot and too large.

Spots danced in what vision I still had, blurred as it was.

Everything sounded tinny, like it was being projected through a can on a string. I had a hard time making out individual words.

"—id you do?!"

Barrow's fist smashed into the swollen side of my face.

I . . . blinked. Winked?

*What?*

The rushing sound in my ears abated, allowing the sounds of utter bedlam to reach my brain. Gunfire. Shouting. Explosions. Engines. It was a cacophony of violent action.

I tried to turn my head, but Barrow had me by the throat. I wasn't floating so much as being held in the air and beaten to death.

"What did you do?!" Barrow erupted. His voice was strained, manic.

*Afraid.*

He hit me again, and the world flashed white.

"What have you done to me?!" the man practically screamed at me.

Process interrupted.

Protocol: Life Preservation: Synthesizing Core from available material . . .

Synthesis Complete.

Bodily integrity restored.

Integration complete.

Initiating travel to Class tutorial. Stand by . . .

Everything rushed away from me, or maybe I rushed away from everything else.

Then I was gone.

# CHAPTER NINE

# Meet the Slavers

*Now*

Gasping, I jolted awake, eyes wide open before my brain kicked into gear and registered I wasn't back home anymore. Orange flickering spotlights stabbed through my retinas, forcing me to blink tears from my eyes.

I would never talk to Vince again. I thought back, attempting to recall the sound of his voice or how he looked, but the scenes faded and dissolved when I tried to held on to them. In every memory I had, there was nothing but the surreal finality of Vince's last, pained sigh played over and over again as he died. It played on loops through my mind, echoing through every memory.

The one person in the world who didn't think I was a burden, and he was gone.

*What are the chances he fought the reavers to save me? What are the chances I killed him?*

I buried that thought, afraid to entertain the possibility that the others stayed to fight because I'd been wounded. Even Mel. That would be too much.

Sharp, penetrating pain in my shoulder brought me back to the present again.

I was lying down on something hard. My legs and arms were bound with rope—rough and, judging by the raw sensation I felt in my wrist, wet with my blood. All sources of light, of which there were many, assaulted my vision from multiple angles: tiny suns, all of them. I howled, contorting my body and trying to bring my arms up to guard or to swing at whatever it was, but my bonds held fast.

"It dreams still."

Why was I alive when the others were not? Why didn't the System make Vince the Exotic? He would have done something great with this.

I needed to move. I needed something to . . . I don't know. I wanted to lash out, to rage. To hurt something or be hurt.

"You poke it again. Make sure," a raspy voice commanded from somewhere.

Someone stabbed me. Pain shot through my hip on entry as the blade ripped into the meat of my quadricep and buried itself deep, the reflexive motion of my body making the weapon wriggle around in the wound before it was ripped out.

[Unknown] attacks you for 2 Damage.
Status gained: Bleeding [.1 HP/sec]

I didn't scream, per se, mostly because I was out of breath at the precise moment I was stabbed, but I did manage a quiet groan.

Blurry shadows resolved into semi-distinct shapes in the light, humanoid-ish. Large heads atop small bodies with long arms and stubby legs. One of them crouched low, poised to thrust its spear into me again. I tried to focus on them, but the light was too intense to see anything detailed.

"Awake now," the one with the spear announced flatly as if he were talking about the weather.

A higher, softer voice joined the two. "Yes. Yes. I tell you already. It is awake. Now I fix a new cut, stupid Hunty."

"Hey! I do what he says!" The one with the spear, Hunty, held his arms out indignantly.

The raspy voice came back, clear authority in its words. "Now we are sure. It is light-burned. Needs fixing."

"Now it is light-burned and bleeding, Kuul. Yes, it needs fixing," the softer voice admonished as something was stuffed painfully into my leg wound. I could feel the familiar burn of some kind of antiseptic agent going to work, before numbing the wound as it cleaned it.

"The stories say they heal fast," the commanding one replied.

"Hoof," I said, though it's not what I meant to say. My lips felt dry and cracked, and my swollen tongue was an entity entirely separate from the speech center of my brain. I tried to work some saliva into my mouth, but I had none. "Washel."

Kuul didn't seem to appreciate that. "It speaks. Stab it again."

"No, Hunty, you don't stab it again!" the healer shouted. "I leave you bleeding when next you come here if you stab it!"

There was a pause, then a fist cracked across my chin, hard.

[Unknown] attacks you for 1 Damage.

"It does not speak," Kuul rasped. "It does not cry out. Understand?"

I worked my jaw around, making sure it wasn't broken. Pulling up my Status Screen, I checked. My HP was at a respectable 20, but I had some Status Effects.

> Exposure (Light) [18Hr]
> Bleeding [.1 HP/sec]
> Restrained: You are bound.
> Dehydration [-1 Mind, -2 Body]
> Underfed [-1 Mind, -1 Body]

"It understands, yes?" he asked again, his dangerous tone telling me more violence was to come if I said no.

I nodded, slowly, consciously not flexing against my bonds anymore.

The emotion from the memories was slowly slipping back into my subconscious, but something in my heart ached with the helplessness I felt, not just at being bound and beaten. I was back to being powerless, a feeling I'd forgotten when the System scrambled my brain and sent me here with a whole body and magic powers.

I didn't want to capitulate to Kuul's command. I wanted him to hit me again. I wanted to spit in his face, laugh at him, force him to hurt me, make him bleed me until I drowned him in my blood.

Most of all, I wanted another Barrow to punch.

Everything was wrong. I was one of the System's Chosen now, and I hadn't gotten that way by being exceptional like I'd always been taught. Vince had been exceptional, and all he got was . . .

Somehow, I became an Exotic by being weak. By being a victim. It felt like a consolation prize for being the most pathetic thing on Proxis that morning. I didn't want it.

Kuul bent forward, uncomfortably close to my face, bringing with him the smell of woodsmoke and unbrushed teeth. "Good. I believe it." I turned my head to peer at him through the stinging pain of the light.

*Goblins. Of course, it's goblins.*

I knew it as soon as I brought him into focus. Kuul wasn't like the monster I'd fought in the tutorial building, though. The proportions and bone structure were similar, the same way I was similar to a gene-fused spacer or an orangutan.

Where the oily, black goblin I fought was animalistic with powerful muscles, sharp teeth, and claws, Kuul had a mottled green, weathered face that didn't seem to fit well on his skull, and slicked-back hair with a touch of gray. The few teeth he had, while pointed, were noticeably duller than his Scourge-Touched counterpart's. His mouth and jaw were a little more reasonably sized for his face as well, and his pointed ears were drawn back on his head. His clothes were some kind of rough-spun fiber, but it was far better than a leather loincloth.

Kuul reached into a pocket on the side of his shirt and retrieved something small, clutching it in his fist before pressing the object into my hand.

"It makes something," he ordered.

I blinked, confused.

The old goblin's eyes bored into mine, searching for something. I got the feeling he was coldly analyzing every expression I made like my dad used to when he knew I'd done something wrong. Though his species was alien to me, I could still sense a keen, disciplined intellect behind those eyes—also much like my dad.

This old goblin had authority here, and he didn't get that way by chance. "You would do well to remember that," his wrinkled frown seemed to say.

The object in my hand, no bigger than a throwing stone, felt lumpy and cool to the touch. I ran a thumb over it in an attempt to figure out what I had, but it didn't take a genius to figure out it was ore of some kind.

Kuul leaned in closer until his nose was practically touching mine. "It makes something or Hunty pokes it again."

I opened my mouth to tell him to poke his mother, but my self-loathing was mostly under control now, sublimated by a more immediate concern: *Kuul knew I could Shape.*

How exactly did he know I could Shape?

Thinking back, Nali, as unreliable as she was, told me there hadn't been a new Animator in a very long time. She hadn't been specific, but I got the impression the time would have been measured in decades or maybe centuries.

Kuul mentioned "stories" about man, implying his people had come into contact with mine before, only now it was a campfire tale as opposed to actual history. That would make sense if they passed down their history in the oral tradition. Perhaps we were a local legend, like unicorns.

Seeing Kuul's cold stare, I did, indeed, feel like a unicorn, and this thing wanted my horn . . .

But not before I granted some wishes.

Putting that unpleasant thought aside, I closed my eyes and reached for my mana, drawing it out of my Core and channeling it to my hand where I held the lump of metal. I mapped the contours of the thing, surrounding it as I had the rebar, then squeezed. The material accepted my mana easily—much more easily than the rusted iron from the tutorial building.

MP 26/30

I saturated the metal with my mana until it was a part of me. There were imperfections here, bits I couldn't easily reach, but otherwise Shaping it felt relatively effortless. I bent my will to change it.

Kuul hadn't told me what to make, but I'd gleaned from context that this was more of a proof of concept for him than a specific demand. He wanted to know I could do the things his stories claimed. I could have made some kind of weapon, but, despite this ore being purer than rusted rebar, my Shape ability was slow and unpracticed.

No, for now, I decided on making the ore into a sphere. I dove in, rounding off the edges, massaging the structure until the imperfections sank down into the metal and were gathered at the very center of the construct. Shape gave me perfect knowledge of the material, which allowed me to make the outside perfectly round and smooth. Without actually looking at it, I knew the finished product shone.

When I opened my eyes again, I was breathing hard, and my head pounded with my thundering pulse. I clenched my teeth with the pain of my ever-thickening blood struggling to bring oxygen where I needed it. My clothes were damp with sweat yet again, and I desperately needed that water given how dehydrated I was.

> You have created: Tin Marble (Common)
> You have been awarded 12 Experience points. [10 base, +2 new design]
> Shape is now Level 2.

Despite the circumstances, it was nice to see an Experience message pop up in my log without any penalties attached. Being a non-combat Class seemed to have some drawbacks in life-and-death situations, but . . .

An electric tingling crawled over my body, starting in the center of my forehead and building, swelling into a crescendo of sensation that activated every nerve ending I had all at once. It drowned all conscious thought in a tide of intense stimulation.

It felt . . . great. My muscles didn't ache anymore, and my mind felt clear and focused, more than it had before, at least. I still had all of my negative Status Effects, but they felt less severe now, like I'd been given a pep talk and an energy drink to power through.

A deluge of messages scrolled through my log.

> Level Up!
> You are now Level 1.
> Max HP +5
> Max MP +5
> +1 Attribute point.
> Ability: Spatial Storage unlocked.

> Quest advanced: Tutorial
> Tutorial: Return to insertion point.

* * *

It was my first level as an Exotic, bittersweet considering what I had had to give up to get it, yet I felt a sense of fading euphoria. In the back of my mind, I knew the emotion didn't come from me. I had been tied up, stabbed, beaten, and I'd just lost people I loved, but there it was—a gift from the System.

Achievements awarded this Level:
Victorious: You have defeated your first foe. [+1 body]
Ambitious: You have defeated a foe above your Level. [+1 to lowest Level Ability]
Nemesis: You have encountered your first Scourgeling and lived. [+1 Spirit]
All Natural: You have spent 80% of this Level with full mana. [+1 body]
Spirit of the Warrior: You gained 51% of your Experience this Level from defeated foes as a non-combat Class. [+3 spirit]
Near-Death Experience: You fell below 10% of your HP this Level. [50% bonus Experience gain for next Level]
Baptism by Fire: Your first defeated foe was an agent of the Scourge. You have been noticed. [+3 to highest combat ability ERROR]

While the Level-Up was nice, it seemed that my real jumps in Attributes came from what I did to earn my new Level rather than just having reached it.

*Achievements.*

Everyone back home knew about Levels. Exotics loved to talk about them when they were being interviewed or while comparing themselves to other Exotics. Our patron saint, Constance, was supposedly Level 40 before she died, and it was a major point of pride for my clan to be loosely tied to her by blood.

Achievements, though, I'd never heard about. As obsessed with the System as my clan was, there was nothing in our culture that mentioned them.

Speaking of things I'd never heard of, there was the glaring ERROR message tacked to the end of Baptism by Fire. What was I supposed to think about that?

"Something happens." I heard the stabby goblin say, accompanied by scraping chairs and multiple tiny feet slapping on stone as they came to my side.

"Is it done?" the soft voice of the healer goblin asked from somewhere I still couldn't see.

The figures crowded around me again, their forms and color a little clearer this time. My eyes were getting better. I checked my debuff timer.

Exposure [16h]

"It looks better. Stronger," the healer said with evident concern.

The one with the spear stepped forward and snatched the oversized ball bearing out of my hand and passed it over to the hunched shadow, who I guessed was Kuul. The old goblin brought the metal ball close to his face, turning it this way and that, tapping it with a fingernail as the other two goblins watched him and awaited his verdict.

ERROR: No valid Combat Abilities found.
Resolving . . .
Ability awarded: Volatility
Volatility is now Level 3.

Kuul put my metal ball back in his pocket and nodded to the other two.

When the old goblin spoke, there was something different about his voice, a lightness to it that made him sound younger, more hopeful. "The stories speak true. Now Tiba heals it, and Hunty guards it."

"What do you do?" Hunty asked, tilting his head sideways while leaning casually on his spear shaft but still keeping me in his peripheral vision.

Kuul turned back to me. I couldn't see it, but I imagined that calculating scowl back on his face. "It needs a special cage," he said, turning on his heel and marching out of sight.

# CHAPTER TEN

# Get a Job

Once Kuul was done testing me, he left in a hurry, hobbling out of the room and shouting at someone outside.

The other two goblins, Hunty and Tiba, set about nursing me back to health, which mostly involved giving me water and dried meat. My body took care of itself thanks to my new Exotic status.

Back home there were stories about Exotics who could survive in the vacuum of space for hours and come back for more after a good nap, and apparently I had something of a healing factor myself. It wasn't so impressive that I was immortal, but given enough time, my wounds would close and my body would be restored to health given enough fuel and rest.

That didn't stop Tiba, the village's healer and herbalist, from taking care of me in her "clinic" where I'd woken up, however, and she turned out to be a lovely little goblin, if you didn't cross her. Much like the medics and doctors I'd met during my life, Tiba was just interested in fixing what was broken. Much younger than Kuul, she had distinctly feminine features with a pointed chin, button nose, and long hair she kept tightly bound in a side-bun.

Singing tunelessly as she worked, Tiba cleaned my wounds with wet cloths as my body mended itself. She tsked over my stab wounds and fussed if I choked on my water, taking care of me much like you would a small child or an animal. Mostly, she made declarative statements, speculations, or observations in soothing tones, not expecting me to understand or answer.

"Oh, no. This hurts, I think. Don't go near spiders alone, yeah?" when cleaning my back, or "I like this arm. This is my favorite arm of yours," when she set about cleaning the debris off my metal side. Maybe she enjoyed not having to use any of her herbs on that part.

My bonds were never loosened or untied. Hunty made sure of that.

Hunty was powerfully built for a goblin, thick in the arms and chest, with his hair in a short mohawk-type style. Multiple scars marred his neck and shoulders from what was, no doubt, a harrowing battle with a monster or something equally cool. He watched me closely as Tiba went about patching me up, always poised to act, pointing the tip of his spear in the direction of my throat from a distance but not so far that he couldn't lunge forward and end me. Hunty almost did just that when my reflexes got the better of me, and I jerked away as Tiba packed one of my more-tender wounds with chewed herbs. In a flash, he was between me and the healer, stone spearpoint digging into the side of my throat.

Tiba talked him out of killing me multiple times, calling him an oaf and a flitskizard, whatever that was.

Soon enough, I was on the mend—full HP and mana, debuffs gone.

I'd taken to watching the minutes on my debuffs ticking down, measuring the time with it. The Exposure debuff got less severe as the timer approached zero, which I very much appreciated. Being able to observe my captors even as they sat at the crude table in the corner of the hut was a welcome relief from the unknowing blindness of before.

With nothing better to do than bide my time, I took a while to explore my Status Screen and poke at some of the terms I hadn't had time to mess with before.

| Ryan Kotes - Level 1 Animator (Uncommon) | | | | |
|---|---|---|---|---|
| **Type:** | Artificer (Common) | **Abilities:** | Shape 3 | Devouring Grasp 1 |
| **Class:** | Animator (Uncommon) | | Consume 2 | Volatility 3 |
| **Core:** | Engine (Unique) | | Iron Grip 2 | |
| **HP:** | 32/32 | **Skills:** | Climbing 5 | Unarmed Combat 1 |
| **MP:** | 35/35 | | Running 1 | Stealth 2 |
| **Body:** | 12 | | Conduit 1 | |
| **Mind:** | 12 | **Affinities:** | Goblinoid F | |
| **Spirit:** | 13 | | Iron F | |
| Free Attribute points: 1 | | | Magnesium F | |

My status Screen turned out to be pretty flexible in terms of how it was structured. I changed the order of things, what to display and what not to. The same thing was true of my logs and quest boxes. In the middle of a fight, they could be a distraction, and I needed that fixed, especially if I was going to try to escape from this place.

Taking some cues from games I'd played in the past, I chose to keep the text logs minimized unless I called them up and made my HP and MP visible at all times along with my Status Effects.

I poked around at some terminology as well, starting with my new Ability.

> Volatility: Temporarily overcharge an object with mana. At your will or upon energetic contact with other matter, the charged object will explode violently. Damage: Dependent on amount and type of mana used. Range: Touch.

I could already think of a few useful applications for Volatility, juicing up rocks and throwing them at Kuul being one of them. Even though Hunty was the one who stabbed me, I couldn't bring myself to stay mad at him. Kuul ordered Hunty to do the stabbing, and the warrior goblin seemed legitimately afraid of me, or maybe afraid I'd hurt someone like Tiba. I could understand where he was coming from, at least.

In all the media I had ever consumed from books to games to sims, there'd never seemed to be a consensus as to whether goblins were tribal nomads of the wilds or deep-dwelling monsters with an aversion to sunlight. One story would have them as mischievous little thieves who couldn't help but covet shiny things, and another would depict them as world-devouring hordes of barbarians.

Sometime during the dark years of Exodus II, after Earth went silent but before my ancestors woke from cryo, that mystery was put to bed by the discovery of the multiverse: It was both. Goblins, a lot like us, were adaptable creatures, willing to put up with a lot in order to survive. Our universe—devoid of magic, as it was—didn't have them, but almost everywhere else, goblins lived wherever they could fit, usually in a place where they could steal from others.

These goblins who currently held me captive lived underground in a cave system, somewhere in the lowlands of Ralqir, where water had exposed bare rock and carved immense branching tunnels that went down and down and down forever.

Most of the village lived in an expansive cavern warmly lit by torchlight and a soft ambient glow from a stream of daylight that flowed in through a hole in the far corner, well away from the rest of the buildings. Tiny huts constructed from wood and straw dotted the floor like little brown mushrooms, and crude, funnel-shaped barrels were set in seemingly random places as water-catchers for the constant drips from stalactites overhead.

Tiba's hut, or the "Healer's House," as she put it, was on a natural shelf above the rest of the village with a ramp that climbed up to it from either side, and when I was frog-marched out of the door, hands bound behind me and at Hunty's spearpoint, hundreds of pairs of reflective goblin eyes stared at me from almost every nook.

I stared back, mostly reeling at how many there were but doing my best to hide my feelings. The creatures were in doorways, on roofs, peeking around from behind barrels, and hanging from the walls. Any thoughts of Consuming my ropes and making a break for it, fled before the sheer number of green-skinned little monsters in here.

I stood there, taking everything in, turning my head to get a fuller picture of the place, mostly looking for a way out. Not all the stalactites were made of stone. Twisted roots invaded the cavern, winding around the rock formations and drooping down in a jagged maw of wood that gradually crept down toward the cave floor. Dirty streaks of soot shot through all of the rock, and burned nubs of thick old roots told me the goblins had done controlled burns in this place from time to time to keep their home from becoming overrun by nature.

Hunching my shoulders and bending at the waist, I attempted to seem smaller than I was, more cowed. It wasn't hard. I was well-practiced at that. The bonus points in my Body Attribute made my job hard, though. I had always been lean, even as a kid before the accident. Looking imposing was the last thing I wanted to do, but now, with the System, I was noticeably thicker and heavier—more so due to the metal parts of my anatomy, which also seemed to have filled out after I'd reached Level 1.

Hunty got me going again with a jab at my back, marching me down the ramp and through the village. Most goblins ducked into their homes or scurried to get out of our way, but I spotted a few goblin children peering at me from roofs or from behind the rain-catcher barrels. Curious little eyes followed my every move, little mouths opened in shock. I was a giant in their midst, a fairy tale come to life. Despite myself, I smiled at the little ones brave enough to make eye contact, but their parents were quick to usher them away, scowling at me reproachfully.

I was led past the village and into a tunnel that sloped down and to the left, worn smooth by water over time and stained orange by innumerable goblin feet. It was slippery as hell, and I stumbled multiple times, forcing Tiba to light a torch so I wouldn't die on my way to my cell. Hunty wouldn't allow her to go in front of me, however, so I ended up walking awkwardly behind my own shadow, unsure if it was better than the pitch black.

Eventually, hundreds of feet later, our spiraling tunnel leveled out, the shaft expanding into another cavern lit by torches. This one looked more artificial, dug out and made flat by tools. There were piles of things everywhere. Rocks, sticks, chopped wood, straw, coils of rope, bundles of leaves, tools, weapons, and even, in one pile, what looked like corpses—not goblins but other types of monsters. Several goblins sat around that one, practiced hands wielding stone knives to harvest what bits of the monsters they deemed useful.

Industrious workers lugged things out from an adjacent tunnel into this one, throwing whatever they carried into the proper pile. Grunts and shouts from the workers echoed harshly around the cavern as they went about their business, while the smell of smoke, sweat, and viscera compounded on one another, forming a busy bouquet reminiscent of an open-air market next to a slaughterhouse.

Kuul was there, pointing and shouting, waving goblins past to get them out of the way of our little procession. When we approached, he smiled wickedly at me.

"Come. Its special cage is ready," he said, leading us through the commotion to the back of the cavern past an absolute mountain of a stone furnace, so massive that my old hab on Proxis would have fit inside of it. The structure lay dormant, but little tendrils of smoke slithered lazily up the stack from the spent wood at the bottom.

My "special cage," as Kuul put it, turned out to be a whole room—or maybe it would be better to call it an antechamber—to the main, lower cavern. It was about the size of a four-passenger vehicle cab, tall enough to stand if you lowered your head, wide enough to lie down without having to tuck your legs. Like the rest of the cavern, it was partially natural and partially dug, meaning the walls were generally smooth with some toolmarks here and there. Slightly off-center on the floor was a hole that I could have almost squeezed into if I'd angled my shoulders.

Upon ushering me inside, Kuul had my ropes cut, and everyone else backed out of the cave, Hunty and his spear last. Then it was just me, hunched over in a tiny room, staring out at a bunch of goblins, every last eye trained on me and what I would do.

Again, I had the urge to rush them, use my superior size to bowl them over, maybe Devouring-Grasp Kuul's green scrotum on my way to freedom, but I knew better. They were waiting for something like that, no doubt. Plus, I wasn't conscious when they brought me into the caves, so I had no idea how to get out. And if I even did manage to escape, then what? I'd have a horde of locals tracking me with spears on their home turf.

No, I needed to stay and play ball for now.

Upon confirming for himself that I wasn't going to make a move, Kuul nodded with visible satisfaction, then he brought his hands up, fingers splayed. He opened his mouth and . . . sang? Groaned? Whatever it was, it sounded painful; a low, growling song that filled the cavern and tickled my ears. In the torchlight, it was hard to tell, but I thought I saw a tiny white glow at the goblin's fingertips. My teeth itched and the hair on the back of my neck and on my arms stood on end as stones cracked and pebbles fell to the floor with echoing pops.

Then the roots came. Through solid rock, grasping tendrils of earthy brown slithered into the room's opening—one, then two, then a dozen, then so many more—intertwining and braiding themselves into living ropes. They wrapped around one another, so tight they could have been mistaken for a single plant.

They dug into the floor, past this part of the cavern, downward further into the rock and continued for long seconds where all I could do was watch the bars of my prison grow thicker and heartier.

When Kuul finally stopped singing, the roots had left so little space between one another, I would have a hard time fitting more than my hands through.

Kuul staggered on his feet, reeling until Tiba steadied him by slipping the old wizard's arm over her shoulders.

Kuul swallowed, then cleared his throat, wincing in pain. "The hole goes to Under-river, way down, deep. It can't escape that way," he said. "If it does not work, we poke it. If we poke it, and it does not work, we starve it. Understand?"

I stepped forward until I was almost pressed against the wooden bars of my prison, hunched yet still looking down at my jailers. "What work?" I asked.

Kuul narrowed his eyes and bared his teeth but didn't give the order to stab me again. Apparently, I hadn't been given permission to speak, but now I was in his cage and theoretically ready to cooperate. He seemed to be weighing whether or not it would be worth it to have me punished before I'd even started.

Eventually, after a minute of grinding his teeth, Kuul replied, loudly enough to be heard by all those assembled. "It makes weapons with magic. Now it makes weapons for us."

Several goblins in the assembled crowd grunted or cheered, toothy smiles spreading across their lips as they turned to one another and slapped each other on the shoulders or went so far as to embrace. Even the more stoic goblins looked cautiously happy, hopeful even.

*What the hell is going on here? What am I missing?*

I looked down at the bars and back to Kuul. I thought about bargaining for my freedom, telling them that I could probably be out of my cell and among them with a little effort and some help from my Core, but then I would be back to being lost. Kuul also had some kind of magic, and that was an unknown I didn't want to mess with until I was ready.

I needed a better plan, more tools, and more options. Luckily, the goblins were willing to give me the time to generate all of those things, assuming I worked.

"I can do that," I said, cracking my knuckles before crouching down to get to eye-level with the old monster. "Bring me metal."

# CHAPTER ELEVEN

# Steal Their Iron

*Memory: Proxis 3 - Before Integration*

I stood atop my vanquished foe, hammering the final piece of the chassis back into place just as the engine finished its self-check and turned over with a soft, trilling hum. The soothing vibrations of the machine humming to life massaged my bare feet and gave me a tingle of satisfaction at a job well done.

The housings on this model of puller were laser-cut for an exact fit and always needed a little convincing, and that convincing was particularly challenging for a guy working with only one hand. In fact, the entire thing was a nightmare to take apart and put together again, but my moment of victory just as I buttoned the whole thing up made the frustration worth it.

The shifting walls of the hab contracted suddenly as a gust of wind hit it from the west, issuing forth a loud bang as the segmented pieces came together to reinforce each other and then relaxed as the pressure equalized again. On the floor, a glowing data plate displaying fluid levels beeped satisfactorily as they interfaced with the machine's internal computers and spit out data well within their green zones.

Jumping down and landing with a roll to save my knees some strain, I scooped up the data plate and made sure that what I was seeing tracked with the sound of the engine. The belts squeaked slightly but otherwise I noticed no anomalies that would indicate another problem.

The door to the shop popped its clamps and rolled up along the roof, folding together to accommodate the domed shape of the building, and a lone figure illuminated by my harsh shop lights stood out in stark relief against the night.

*When did it turn night?*

Dad strode in, his head tilted to one side as he inspected my work and listened to its beautiful, resurrected cat purr. His wide shoulders, deep chest, and powerful legs reminded me of a machine as well; one that, unlike all the other machines, never broke. *Could not* be broken.

"You got it working. Just in time, too," he said in a powerful baritone, the kind that commanded respect from the entire clan and sent me scurrying for cover back when I was small.

Tonight, however, I just beamed at him, letting my work speak for itself. This stupid farm tool was dead when it was brought to me, and I resurrected it, despite it not being designed to be fixed in the Outers. The whole thing was put together like a maze of crappy design decisions only navigable by people specifically trained for that kind of thing, but I had done it.

After a while, I couldn't contain myself. I had to brag. "You might want to tell Wayne that the insides don't look like they used to, but they'll probably break down less. He's also missing a few parts that were just there to give it a shorter shelf life, and it should run for a long, long time now," I said, raising my chin with pride and tossing my wrench aside to clatter into the pile under the workbench.

Dad laughed as he approached, putting his hands on my shoulders and giving them a squeeze. "I'll tell him. I don't think he'll shed any tears for any missing parts, but am I right in assuming they've gone into your collection? No. No. Don't bother denying it. It won't affect the fee."

The parts had, indeed, been stowed away in my little stash. I didn't know what I would use them for other than scrap, unless I wanted to add a substandard part to someone else's vehicle. I didn't have many enemies that deserved something like that, though.

Nodding to me, then slipping past, Dad mounted the puller and engaged the gears, getting ready to drive it out.

I made to join him, stepping into one of the mounting stirrups and pulling myself up, but Dad held out a hand to stop me.

Confused, I frowned up at him, my moment of elation threatening to crash down around me. Apparently, my subconscious knew what was happening before the rest of my mind did.

"It's probably best you stay here, Ryan," Dad said, pretending to look down at the dials that I knew were in the green. "I'll take it out to Wayne."

My heart sank, and, with it, my demeanor. "I thought—I dunno—Maybe he would want to ask me questions," I mumbled. I already knew Dad wouldn't hear or, more accurately, wouldn't listen.

"No, Son, I think it's best to stay inside. You've done your part. I'll take it to him. You clean up the shop and get ready for dinner." He tried not to meet my eyes, but I could see it there. The shame. And worse: the pity.

Wayne would be uncomfortable with the amputee kid touching his machine, priceless as it was this far from the Colony. I was good enough to fix their tools. They'd even pay me so long as I stayed out of sight and away from more-respectable people.

"I'm sorry, Ryan. I really am. Some people aren't—"

"I know, Dad. Just—Just tell him to listen for ticks when it's in third gear," I half-croaked, forcing a grin up at the big man and slapping the side of the chassis before I turned away.

Having nothing else to say, Dad released the brake and rolled out of the shop, into the night.

I wiped a tear from my cheek as I pulled up a stool to have a good sit. A night like tonight deserved a good sit.


*Now*


Sweat poured down my face and dripped down onto the cave floor as I finished hollowing out the bottom of my twelfth spearhead of the day. My hand, reaching through the bars to my cell, held on to the dull end of the weapon, rolling it over in my fingers as my mana shifted the molecules out to create the hollow where a wooden shaft would eventually be inserted. My mind was taxed to the limit, and the constant pounding in my head promised a long, uncomfortable recovery period, not because my mana was down to 7 of 43, but because of my "side project," the tiny snake of iron, no thicker than a pin, slowly slithering up my arm and into my sleeve.

Arrowheads, spears, and knives I could do easily now, especially with iron. The structure of my weapons were efficient, my edges were magnificently sharp—probably down to the molecular level—and my work was made even more efficient and swift after I had reached Level 4 in Shape.

What taxed me greatly, however, was skimming from the materials the goblins fed me. At first, I would simply snap off an edge or pinch off a little ball of metal I hoped no one noticed, but that proved to be too risky. Hunty had sharp ears, and he would generally hear the little bits falling to the cave floor, helpfully bending down to pick it up before I could grab it with my other hand.

So, I was forced to do it differently. I kept contact with my ill-gotten gains, keeping the mana flowing inside any given stolen piece through constant contact with my skin, then having it locomote away from its parent, up my arm, and through the bars.

It wasn't so simple, however. My stolen metal had to move on its own and in such a way that my captors would not see. So far, I'd come up with a set of rudimentary scales as one might find on the belly of a snake, except these covered the entire surface area of the construct, giving it a segmented appearance more like an insect. I would then flex and contract these scales to create a jerky, halting sort of climb through the hairs of my arm. The little construct wasn't great at holding on, though, requiring me to stay very still and pretend to work extremely intently on my latest spearhead, sweating as I split my attention between both pieces.

Even through the strain, a little smile slid across my face as I got the message I'd been looking for.

> Split Mind is now Level 3.
> +15% increased cognitive efficiency when using multiple Abilities at once or using one Ability in multiple places.

Apparently, the System recognized what I was doing as a Skill, and after that revelation, I began practicing with it as often as I could. The bonuses the Skill gave me so far already proved immensely helpful, since, as of right now, stretching my perspective like this made me wonder if you could tear brain tissue like you could tear muscle.

My little snake made its way up, past the crook of my arm, and slithered over my bicep, nearly past the wooden bars now and out of Hunty's view. Then it reached some kind of tipping point, falling into an uncontrolled death roll toward the outside of my arm. I jerked my arm back, transferring some of that momentum to the metal snake so that it would fall inside the cell instead of on the floor outside. It fell, uncontrolled, now out of contact with my skin and unanimated.

Panicking, I dropped the spearhead outside the cell and shifted to bring my metal hand over to catch my prize. But I didn't get there in time, instead merely covering the construct with my prosthetic hand instead of actually catching it.

Hunty was there in a flash, but he didn't look in the cell. He picked up my finished spearhead and examined it before tossing it into the pile of today's finished goods.

I pretended to stretch, bringing my natural arm down to hold on to my stolen iron so that the prompt could appear:

> Transfer to Spatial Storage? Y/N

There was a brief pulse of magic and light, then the iron was gone, tucked away in the magical storage dimension only I could access. I could feel it there with all the others, maybe a half pound of stolen metal so far. By Constance, was having secret magical storage ever handy! Especially as a prisoner.

Hunty crouched down and looked me in the eye, a sympathetic smile on his face.

"You look tired, human. You make lots of things today. Rest now," he said, patting the bars as if he were patting me on the shoulder. "I make sure the next guard lets you sleep."

"Thanks, Hunty. That will help a lot," I replied, meaning every word but with no intention of actually going to sleep.

As Hunty scooped the pile of spearheads into a wooden box and shouted for a runner to come pick them up, I reached down to the bottom corner of my cell's bars and wrapped my metal fingers around one of the thinnest parts.

*Seven mana should be enough.*

I activated Devouring Grasp, feeling the hand close like a vice, pressing through the thick roots like sticks of softened butter. Muffled, wet, crunching noises filled the cell as I ripped the wood apart until I was holding a good-sized chunk. The noise got Hunty's attention, but he didn't do more than cast a glance my way. I did this every day, and he knew I couldn't get out of here. Even as my Core Consumed the wood in a flash of yellow sparks, the injured roots swiftly grew anew to fill in the gap.

> You gain knowledge of material: Mendau Wood [19/50]
> Status gained: Engine [+1 MP/sec for 30 min]

Having an F-grade affinity for the Mendau Wood now helped me keep the Engine buff going longer, which was good because I was going to need it.

Hunty wasn't the overly-curious sort, but he did take his job seriously. After the goblin runner came and picked up the box of spearheads, Hunty bent down and ran a hand over the root section I'd just torn away, making sure they grew back properly. He finished up his check with a little shake of the bars. They held fast as they always did.

"Why do you do that, human?" he asked as he went back to sitting on his wooden stool, positioned in such a way that he could see my entire cell.

"Toilet paper," was my reply, but Hunty just sat there with his spear on his lap, staring at me. The silence stretched out between us, but he was the first to break it.

"I don't know either of those words," he said with a shrug. Then he smiled apologetically as a thought had just occurred to him. "But I do know your special cage is very small. If I'm a slave, I hate it, too. I try to break the cage. Kuul's magic is strong, though. He asks the Mendau to grow there, and they do."

I sat down against the far wall to rest my tired body, sighing as I found a semi-comfortable position where my back could relax. "The guy is so paranoid, I'm surprised he doesn't have roots growing over the entire cell, my little hole included," I said as I closed my eyes.

"He doesn't do this because the hole leads to the Under-river, and he wants you to be able to drink when you need. Also, big magic like growing Mendau is too important to waste like that," Hunty replied, a little awe in his voice at Kuul's little trick. If I were being truly honest with myself, I was a little jealous of the fire-and-forget nature of the magic. If I had something like that, I'd spend much less time with a headache.

"Has Kuul considered that I also defecate in this hole?" I asked, raising an eyebrow. It was a harrowing experience, for sure, having to hover over a fifty-foot drop to do my business. To then be asked to get my water from the same place triggered some hardwired no-no zone in my psyche that I still hadn't gotten over. My little clay cup on a string had seen some things down there, I was sure.

Hunty made a rude sound with his mouth. "The Under-river is fast and fresh. No matter how big you are, you alone can't foul it."

"I've done my best, so far," I said with a chuckle.

Hunty leaned forward, a mischievous little smile on his face. "We all do."

A terrible thought popped into my head, and my eyes widened with realization. "Hunty, you guys use the Under-river for that kind of thing, too?"

"Uh huh," he replied, an evil little smile tugging at the corner of his mouth.

"Downstream, right, Hunty?" I asked. I felt a twitch in my stomach. "Tell me it's downstream where you guys . . . use the river."

"It is downstream where we use the river," he mimicked.

We stared at each other then for a long, pregnant moment, Hunty's face steadily contorted with barely contained laughter all the while.

I sighed theatrically. "You're a cruel goblin, Hunty."

"Hunty is cruel to our human friend?" Tiba's voice came faintly from somewhere I couldn't see.

Hunty shot to his feet like a soldier called to attention, whirling around and practically leaping out of my view.

When he came back, he was at Tiba's side, carrying a heavy, steaming pot by the handle, his spear in his teeth. Tiba, for her part, held a bundle under her arm that smelled of herbs and spices.

"If Hunty is being cruel, then I can give you half of his meal, yes?" she asked me as she approached the bars. As always, she gestured for me to come closer, so she could give me a once-over for my health. I complied, though I probably didn't have to worry overly much about my health now that I was an Exotic, one being fed a constant stream of Experience and Skill-Ups to boot.

Hunty struggled to set the pot down on the floor without sloshing the contents, and his spear kept him from giving an intelligible answer, only allowing for little grunts and muffled groans. "Mmmf murrfff fmemfer," he said.

Tiba reached through the bars and took my arm, running her fingers over the contours and pinching the flesh now and again. "You are bigger still than when you first came to us. Soon you'll look like Mogrog if I give you Hunty's food."

"Bah! Mogrog is fat," Hunty sputtered as he ripped the spear out of his mouth. "He can barely climb, he's so big. What use is that? Pretend muscles is what that is."

Tiba's examination led her down to my chest and stomach, allowing me to shoot a meaningful look to Hunty. I widened my eyes and gestured at the little healer with my head, miming the word "Now" with my mouth.

Hunty swallowed, straightened his shirt, and cleared his throat before he spoke up. "So, uh, Tiba?"

"Mm?" She scratched at a red mark on my ribs, visible now that my shirt was in tatters.

"Uh. I want to ask if you—If when it is time, we can—" Hunty's plan probably hadn't made it this far. He could barely get a sentence out. I caught his eye again and took a deep, exaggerated breath, prompting him to mimic me.

Hunty tried again. "Do—uh—do you like stuff . . . like food?" Even as the words left his mouth, a horrified look spread across his face.

I cringed on his behalf.

"Yes, Hunty. I like food," Tiba replied absently, still poking at me, mostly focusing on where my wounds used to be.

"Do you—uh—" Hunty floundered. I could practically see his courage leaving him like air out of a balloon. "You make the best food, Tiba."

"Aw. Thanks, Hunty. I am worried my stew is under-seasoned now that we can't gather much."

"No! No! It's great," Hunty assured her, bending down to smell the pot. "Mmmm. Perfect."

She straightened up and smiled at the both of us. "That is so nice to hear. I hope it makes you both happy, even if you are stuck down here. Now I have to get back. I have wounded to tend to, and Fimi gets nervous if I leave her to tend the house for too long. See you soon."

With a wave, she was gone.

Once she was out of earshot and I'd unwrapped my dried meat from the bundle Tiba had given me, I tried to offer some words of encouragement. "You're getting better at that. You used words and everything."

Hunty made a rude sound with his mouth and handed me a clay bowl of stew through the bars. He didn't say anything, though. He just looked defeated.

I continued. "Seriously, you are. You were really close."

Hunty's knee bounced up and down, and his stare seemed an impossible distance away as he robotically spooned the hot stew into his mouth, frowning sourly as he did. "Do you like food?" he mumbled, wincing at the memory.

His mood darkened further the more time passed until he was practically brooding.

"Hunty?"

The warrior goblin put his spoon back into his nearly empty bowl and turned to face me again. All the mirth he'd displayed earlier was gone, replaced by a hard, dark stare.

"Is everything alright?"

He stared at me in silence, a storm brewing behind his eyes. He spoke in a whisper now. "She can't go out to gather her herbs."

I quietly contemplated his words and what they meant. I could tell by his tone and body language he was saying something significant, but I just couldn't get there. Something was missing in my knowledge, maybe culturally.

"Why can't Tiba gather herbs?" I asked.

"Not safe anymore up there," he said, pointing upward, supposedly toward the surface, with his spear. "And I am down here with you." His eyes flashed, and his claws dug into the bottom of his bowl.

"Caged," he whispered to himself.

Then he was gone again, somewhere dark and full of hurt.

We spent the rest of the evening in silence.

# CHAPTER TWELVE

# Hate This Cage

Tiba's fingers ran over my scalp, probing for anything she may have missed with her shears as well as the parasites that were far too common down here. Curly, brown clumps of greasy hair lay in my lap and in an expanding pile on the floor.

Already, I could feel the loose clippings sliding inside my rough-spun shirt, made in the style the goblins seemed to favor. It didn't fit properly—tight in the shoulders, loose in the belly, and itchy on the best of days—but it was better than the rags I'd been wearing before. Supposedly, it came from a domesticated beast they kept penned down here in the caves.

"Feel better?" Tiba asked as she let go of my head, blowing loose hair off her shears before placing them in her pocket.

It certainly felt cooler, now that the draft was able to reach my scalp again. "Yeah. Thanks a lot. It was getting really hard to clean," I replied, with only a little sourness at the memories. Bathing with a cup drawn from an ice-cold underground river had been less than pleasant, and it was time-consuming, especially with long hair. Kuul wouldn't allow anyone to give me a blade to cut it, so I ended up making a pair of iron shears for Tiba and asking her to do the deed.

"I'm not saying you look good, human, but you do look better," Hunty quipped from his stool.

"Shut up, Hunty," I shot back, giving him the finger over my shoulder, a gesture that had spread like wildfire through goblin society once I had told them what it meant. "You look like punk broccoli anyway."

He scratched his scalp where his mohawk met skin and scrunched up his face. "I don't know what those words mean."

"Uh." I considered for a moment, trying to find the phrasing he might understand. "You're a vegetable with bad taste."

"That is like a plant?"

I sighed. This was going to be another one of those conversations. Still, I gave it a shot. "It's like . . . a miniature tree but edible."

Hunty's face lit up with fascination. Goblins were strict carnivores, and my green friend found it strangely charming that the human ate plants. Apparently, that stuff was for domesticated animals and slugs.

"A tiny tree. What does it taste like?" he asked, leaning forward and raising an eyebrow.

I thought back, trying to remember the last time I ate the stuff, back before Barrow and his reavers burned us out. "Like socks and disappointment," I replied with a nod. "It's better with cheese."

Hunty scoffed. "I don't taste like that."

"Don't you, though?"

Tiba jumped in before Hunty could respond. "I like when you two bicker like grandmothers, but I have to go. The healing house is full, and this is my break time," she informed us as she packed her little medic bag.

"And Hunty does not taste like that," she said before her eyes went wide, and her mouth dropped open in horror. "Wait—No. I mean—No."

Hunty came to her rescue. "It's nice to see you during the day," he said, grinning and slipping an arm around Tiba's shoulders, leaning in close to say the next part. "I see you tonight, then?"

It was dark, and these were little green people. However, I thought I detected the ghost of a blush on Tiba's cheeks as she replied, smiling and shoving Hunty away playfully, "Yes. I see you as soon as I can. Do not be late, yeah?"

I waited until she was gone to rip my daily piece of Mendau Wood from my prison, Consuming it to get my Engine on.

Devouring Grasp [5 MP/sec]

You gain knowledge of material: Mendau Wood [50/50]

Affinity upgraded: Mendau Wood: Grade E

Detect radius is now 15 ft.

+1% of mana gained from Mendau Wood that retains its original type. [Hunger]

Status gained: Engine [+2 MP/sec for 45 min]

My first E-grade Affinity, and it came with a curious bonus. What was this about Mana Type? Was I using a Mana Type already? There was so much I didn't know.

"Broken-ass tutorial," I mumbled as I settled into a comfortable position.

"Greetings, Chosen. I am supremely unhelpful, and I can't wait to get you killed." My Nali impression wasn't great, but I didn't care.

Hunty, of course, paid my eccentricities no mind. He considered them mostly harmless, a human thing. The bars were already growing back, thicker than ever, like scar tissue. Kuul's magic continued to prove limitless.

I sat with my back against the bars and ran a hand through my hair. I kept it shorter back on Proxis as was norm for the Clan, but this style would do for now as long as it stayed out of my eyes.

I'd been thinking of home a lot lately. The way things were, how I'd been treated.

Everyone was so obsessed with perfection. Progress.

They trained their children to fight from the moment they could walk, filled their heads with tales of Constance and her exploits. Everything everyone did was to forge themselves into weapons, all for the sake of the System.

They were so diligent and pious, they couldn't spare a moment for the kid with the amputation, nor even allow their perfect progeny to associate with him, lest his condition be contagious.

Just looking at me made people uncomfortable, as if I reminded them that this could easily have been them had the universe been slightly different.

Now, if I completed my tutorial and went back there, I would be whole and more capable. I would be the one on a long path to power, and it had nothing to do with having been perfect to begin with.

I imagined scenarios where I would return, walk up to my dad, and he would look at me without pity or shame. What a day that would be.

Surprisingly, every homecoming scene I imagined felt wrong. Like a cheat. A shortcut to happiness.

I didn't want it.

Well, I *did*, but I didn't.

I wanted my dad to look at me and see someone to be proud of, but, sadly, I would know it wasn't actually me that inspired that pride. Instead, it would be the System. Random chance. Another accident just like the one that had made me a pariah.

No. There was no scenario where I would have a happy homecoming. For the longest time, I'd just wanted to be accepted, and every waking moment had been spent trying to gain that acceptance. Now, if I made it home, I'd have that and more, all thanks to absolutely nothing I accomplished on my own.

I had been blessed by the System, but all my achievements were tainted.

It was a depressing but liberating prospect.

What do you do when you have nothing to prove anymore? I didn't know. I couldn't conceive of it, just being who I wanted to be. Free.

*If you want to be free, better get on the whole "escape" thing, Ryan.*

Leaning forward, I placed my metal hand on the lip of the watering hole, making sure to wedge my fingers well into the grooves.

Devouring Grasp [5 MP/sec]

With a crack, a chunk of limestone that fit comfortably in my palm broke off.

"If you are making your cage bigger, maybe start with the walls," Hunty called from over my shoulder. "Unless you plan to escape through the Under-river. That plan will kill you, you know. There are no other holes like yours for miles downstream, and you make Tiba sad if you drown."

I transferred my new rock over to my natural hand, closing my eyes to concentrate.

Volatility [1 MP/sec]

This Ability was nothing like Shape. Shape I could understand.

Volatility used a completely foreign method to accomplish its goals. The Ability forced the mana onto the matter, not caring for how much it could hold or what it would do. It conquered. It overwrote. It flooded into the object until I told it to stop.

Not my mana but mana from somewhere else, rushed inside. Maybe the energy came from the air, from another universe, or from the System itself. I didn't know. Whatever it was, it was different. Wild mana. It writhed and twitched within the molecules of the stone, awaiting its chance for release. At the slightest touch, all that energy would be set free in an uncontrolled, violent instant.

With nothing else to observe through touch, I opened my eyes again.

I only charged the rock for half a second, but it already glowed an angry purple, bleeding energy from its now-volatile matter.

"No, Hunty. I don't plan to escape that way," I said as I leaned over and tossed the rock down the hole, angling the trajectory to hit where I needed it to. "Not when I have such fine company, at least."

The stone fell, illuminating the tunnel as it went down, down. *POW!* The rock hit almost right at the waterline and exploded, sending up a plume of cold mist to wet the lip of the hole and my face. After so long in the dim, the purple flash burned my eyes.

*Damn.*

I couldn't see if the rock had survived—whether Volatility had either destroyed it from the inside out or just discharged the wild mana and left the matter itself intact. My next experiment would have to be inside my cell, but I'd need to take precautions first. I'd been avoiding that after my first attempt at

Volatility had left me partially deaf and blind and Hunty constantly rubbing his ears for the next week. Tiba didn't thank me for that one.

"Guard change time," Hunty announced, standing up with a groan, waiting for his replacement to come and relieve him. He danced anxiously from foot to foot, probably anticipating going to see Tiba right after.

When the other guard arrived, though, the two started speaking in low tones, too quiet for me to hear. Hunty's replacement—Iger, I guessed—spoke animatedly with his hands, gesturing to body parts, waggling his fingers like they had long claws. All the while, Hunty's body language went rigid, and he gripped his spear tightly.

Then the two goblins suddenly stopped and stood up straight, spears pointed up and hafts on the ground.

After a quiet minute, Kuul stalked up to my cell door, a miserable scowl on his face. He looked older than he had when we'd first met. His sagging skin seemed looser than before, and there were bags under his eyes that gave him an exhausted, sickly look. The fire hadn't left his eyes, though. They held a volcanic malice, not necessarily directed at me, but it was there, threatening to explode.

The old goblin looked down at the box I'd filled with arrowheads earlier today, bending down to examine one of them. Then he dropped it and kicked the box away, hard. The tinkling sound of the metal scattering across the cave floor echoed through the cavern. The noise of the workers ceased.

Kuul leaned forward and pointed to me with a gnarled finger. "It makes better and better for many days, and then progress stops. Why?"

I didn't answer. I didn't owe this . . . thing an answer. Besides, Kuul had already made up his mind on whatever this was, I knew. This was just the buildup.

Just at that moment, Hunty came to my defense, which was well-intentioned but unfortunate. Maybe he didn't read the old goblin like I did, or maybe he felt he knew Kuul better and could reason with him. "The human makes better and more all the time. We work him until he sleeps. The weapons are good and sharp, too."

Kuul spared a contemptuous glance over his shoulder, but he didn't reply directly. Instead, he glared at me as he spoke. "It is not challenged anymore, I think. Too many little things to make." He raised his voice to make sure all those nearby could hear him as well. "The hu-man makes us rich with its iron magic, and it is good. We have food and gold and clothes, many, but things are changed. The Baned have come close. We lose goblins on the surface. We can't sell our iron treasures anymore," Kuul said to them all, turning around to address the crowd now.

Silence hung over the cave as the chief paused.

"Now," he said, holding his hands out wide in challenge as he flashed a wicked grin, "now, we defend our homes. Now we go to war."

Kuul's enthusiasm didn't catch on. Most goblins listened silently while holding their tools or leaning on their friends. The warriors looked grim.

"Hurry and bring all you can," Kuul commanded. "We get ready for a great battle, one we will win. The Baned search for our home, but they find only death. We kill them all and send them back to the black."

This time there was a scattered whooping shout from the workers and warriors, but Hunty just leaned on his weapon, pensively staring at the floor.

Kuul dismissed them all except for my guard, then approached my cell, shuffling closer until his hands were on the wooden bars he'd grown so long ago. His breath wheezed from his throat.

"It makes swords and armor now. It makes us weapons of war. If it does not, the Baned come, and we cannot protect it. It works as if its life is at stake. It does this or dies."

We stared at each other then, Kuul with all the power, me increasingly short on giving-a-shit.

"Who are the Baned?" I asked with folded arms, not breaking the stare-down.

Kuul didn't answer me, instead, calling over his shoulder, "Hunty! Tell it why it works, then get it working. Poke it if it stops. I have things that need doing." Then, to me, he said: "Work hard, and you live through this. Remember."

When Kuul was gone, Hunty instead, however, told me to rest and get my strength back, so we could do more tomorrow. Then he sat and, despite his shift being over, started to explain things to me. As he did, a heavy ball of lead settled in the pit of my stomach.

We were all going to die, and it was my fault. It was a situation with which I was all too familiar.

# CHAPTER THIRTEEN

# Split My Head

> You have created: Iron Caterpillar
> You have been awarded 35 Experience points. [25 base, +10 quality]

The new metal caterpillar detached itself from where I'd surreptitiously formed it inside the cranium of my newest helmet, its articulated legs digging into the grooves in the metal to keep the gray insect from falling to the floor. One by one, the little legs, each no bigger than a hair, flexed and gripped with tiny claws as the construct crawled its way over to my fingers. Once there, the caterpillar practically ran up my arm, only having to pause to move the sleeve of my shirt out of the way to crawl inside with the others.

I could handle four at a time now so long as I didn't have them doing complex tasks, but I was pretty sure I could do five or six if I pushed it.

> Split Mind is now Level 5.
> Upgrade Paths available:
> Partitioned Mind
> Dual Cast
> Imbue

The message I'd been waiting for finally came. Split Mind was fast becoming my most-used skill, since it was the only way I could snag metal of my own while I worked for the goblins. Unfortunately, it wasn't always feasible to practice—not, that is, until my control became sophisticated enough to provide my stolen iron with some legs. Then I was off to the races. I always had a few of the little bugs running around under my shirt or up and down the legs of my trousers nowadays, and my Skill shot up a Level as a result.

The System had more to tell me:

> Level Up!
> You are now Level 4.
> Max HP +5
> Max MP +5
> +1 Attribute point.

> Achievements awarded this Level:
> Big Spender: You have spent 6,070% of your total Mana Pool this Level. [+1% mana regeneration per second.]
> Soulful: You have almost exclusively focused on Mind and Spirit-centric Skills this Level. [+1 Mind, +1 Spirit]
> Dedicated: You spent most of your time dedicated to your craft this Level. [+1 Spirit]
> Doing Your Part: Some of your creations have been used against agents of the Scourge. [+200% Experience awarded for new designs next Level]

More Spirit. It was my highest Attribute even though it started out as my lowest at integration. For some reason, I just kept earning more and more of it with my achievements.

The System's description was both helpful and infuriatingly mysterious when I asked.

> Spirit: Numerical value denoting your presence in the magical world. Affects Mana Intensity.

As far as I could tell, Spirit affected how "thick" my mana was and where I could move it. When I was Level 0, my mana went only as far as my skin and moved in a trickle only into what I could physically touch. Now my mana was heavier, present in the air around me like a localized fog bank. It didn't spread out farther than a few inches from my body, but it was there.

Mind gave me the ability to move mana around quickly, or at least that's how I perceived it. The definition more or less agreed.

> Mind: Numerical value denoting your ability to manipulate mana. Affects speed and strength of mind-based abilities.

This was the second time I'd earned "Doing Your Part." The bonus was nice, especially when I developed my articulated caterpillars and cashed in. However, it also meant the Scourge-Touched were still hunting my goblins out there.

Hunty kept me up-to-date on how things were going with the war against the Baned, the skirmishes they had, how many of them were spotted in the forest, and the like. The little guy desperately wanted to be out there, doing his part, but his requests to join the fight were always denied because of the rapport he'd built up with the "hu-man" over time.

If you asked me, they could have used Hunty out there. Things weren't looking great. The Stone Hearts—my little goblin tribe—rarely left their caves now that the other tribes had fallen or were chased away. That couldn't go on forever.

The air was heavy with anticipation and a good bit of fear. The sentiment among all of the goblins was that the Baned would soon find and come for them, but they would mostly be here for me.

You have created: Small Bucket Helmet
You have been awarded 22 Experience points. [20 base, +2 quality]

Apparently, the Baned were a feral type of goblin whose ancestors had tainted their own blood, making deals with demons. As a result, they lost their sanity, their language, and their ability to reproduce conventionally, but that didn't reduce their numbers in the slightest. They mostly kept to themselves with only the occasional raid on their neighbors, where they would make off with things and people, all of which would never be seen again.

The other goblins gave the Baned their space and never encroached on their territory, and most lived their lives without ever seeing a Baned. Then, after many, many generations, that changed.

The Baned were everywhere now. They killed everything they could, beasts and goblins alike, and brought their corpses back to their territory with them. As I'd feared, the Baned were tracking me the entire time I made my trek through the forest to find water, and their pursuit of me had them hot on the heels of the hunting party that found my unconscious body and dragged me back to the caves.

At the time, Chief Kuul could only guess at the reason behind the Baned's surge in aggression, if they were even capable of reason, but then, when he saw me, he knew what they wanted.

Kuul was an avid student of history—the goblin version of it at least. The stories his forebears told went back past the Great Purge all the way to the beginning in an unbroken chain of Stone Heart chiefs, and they spoke of humans as the enders of ages, and the coveted prize of all races, including the corrupted Baned.

After I was dumped on his doorstep, he had a decision to make: He could kill me and prevent the Baned from taking me for whatever dark purpose they had, or he could give me to the Baned in hopes they'd eat his tribe last.

He chose option three: use me to arm the untainted goblin tribes, making a ridiculous sum of money at the same time. From there the other tribes could beat back the Baned, while Kuul kept his tribe safe in their hidden caves.

Kuul was too clever for his own good, though. The other tribes were all but gone now, and he was rich—not that he could spend his new wealth trapped in a cave.

Meanwhile, the Baned's numbers grew and grew. Now they were knocking on our front door, so to speak.

When Hunty had explained the conflict to me, a lot of things clicked into place, but any questions I had about the last Animator they'd encountered went unanswered. Hunty didn't know anything about them, and these things happened so long ago, any specifics had long been lost to time.

As for present-day Ralqir, I hadn't even realized there were other tribes out there, but it made sense. What were the odds of me finding the only tribe of goblins on Ralqir? Small thinking on my part, but in my defense, being trapped in a cell and forced to work kind of shrunk your world down to just the day-to-day.

This ongoing crisis and the new conversations that afforded me, while grim, helped pull me out of my own head and back to seriously planning my escape. For a while, I'd justified my inaction by grinding my Skills or experimenting with my designs to try and find the perfect way to survive once I got out of my cell. No more, though. Progress for progress' sake wasn't getting me any closer to freedom.

My level of motivation was also affected by the Baned apparently wanting to kill/eat/enslave me. To hear Hunty describe them, they fit with what we called Rift Spawn back in my universe, and that was a terrifying thought, even if they didn't specifically want a bite of yours truly. They were planet killers, responsible for three separate worlds that we knew of going dark. In fact, one of the prevailing theories about Old Earth was that they fell victim to the very first rift in recorded history.

If Ralqir was about to go through the same thing, it was all the more reason for me to get the hell out of here—not just out of my cell but out of this universe. The tutorial agreed, the little box always there to remind me to "Return to Insertion Point."

*Gladly.*

I looked over my options for my Split Mind Upgrade Paths:

---

Upgrade Paths available:
Partitioned Mind: Subdivide your consciousness to greatly enhance cognition.

[Number of partitions = Mind/3]
Dual Cast: Use two Abilities simultaneously or use the same Ability twice. Effectiveness of Abilities used with Dual Cast are enhanced. [Bonus Effectiveness = X(Mind + Spirit)/5]
Imbue: Imprint mana with a fraction of your will, allowing it to perform simple tasks without direct input from you. This requires the expenditure of triple the amount of MP you wish to imbue.

At first, Partitioned Mind called out to me. The amount of effort I was having to expend to keep my little creations going hurt my brain and tired me out quickly. Yes, I was training the Skill even now but at the cost of my damned sanity. It *hurt* to keep this up all the time. Partitioned Mind was exactly what I was hoping for, something to make doing this easier so I could get more materials for my escape.

Then there was Imbue. The description of the Ability didn't exactly specify this, but wouldn't it have the potential to help me with my immediate problem, too? I was essentially pumping mana into my creations to Shape them. Could I Imbue that mana? Make my little caterpillars semiautonomous? It would cost a ton of mana, but I wasn't exactly hurting for that, was I?

The ability to Consume things was starting to look more and more overpowered, considering how slowly normal mana regenerated. It allowed me to take all sorts of risks and experiment with things others might not be able to. I didn't know how I would live without it.

With some trepidation, I chose Imbue, waving a tearful goodbye to Partitioned Mind and the much-needed help it could have given me.

I tossed the finished helmet into the crate Hunty had set up next to my cell and called for more. The ore was in my hand before I could even finish my sentence. Iger was quick like that. He didn't talk much, but the goblin knew what was at stake. He needed me working and outfitting his fellow warriors or things were going to get worse fast.

"Thanks," I said, not expecting a response. Then I got back to work.

*SNAP!* The sound rang in my ears, echoing around the cell painfully. Hunty grunted from his stool, probably wiggling a finger in his ear.

Failure.

I sighed, opening my eyes and unfolding my legs to go retrieve my latest experiment.

It lay there on the stone floor, dead as a doornail, its inch-long, segmented body rigid and straight to help with aerodynamics. On the wall, a fresh black mark smoked directly above the construct alongside the myriad others.

Knowing it was safe to do so, I grabbed my experiment with my natural hand. It was warm to the touch but not uncomfortably so, even after a dozen failures in a row. They didn't melt down as much anymore, not that it was a huge inconvenience if they did. I would just Shape them again once they cooled down.

"I like it better when you practice quietly," Hunty grumbled. Metal armor rattled and clinked together as the goblin warrior settled into a new position.

All the warriors wore my patent-pending plated armor now, which pleased Kuul greatly. Who it didn't please, however, were the warriors. Everywhere they went, they made a constant racket as they went about their patrols or trained with their weapons, not to mention how uncomfortable the stuff was. The goblins didn't have the spare leather or cloth to make a buffer layer underneath the hard stuff to make it truly fit like it needed to, so the warriors had to wear it unprotected.

Hunty, most of all, let me have an earful about it. How it pinched when he sat, how it got in the way of eating, how heavy it was. I told him I could Shape it to fit him perfectly if he let me work on him for a while, but he waved me off, telling me that if he were given special treatment, he wouldn't be able to look the other warriors in the eye. He would just have to suffer with the others until everyone had a good fit.

I sat down again, holding my construct in my hand to give it another try, but I spared a breath for a barb. Honestly, I didn't see this experiment going much differently, and my frustration was getting to me.

"I like it better when I'm not enslaved, Hunty," I said with a little more venom than I wanted.

Hunty didn't reply, but I could feel him watching me with that worried frown on his face. He didn't deserve my anger. Well, maybe he did since he was complicit in my imprisonment, but Kuul was the one behind it all. Even if Hunty wanted to get me out, he couldn't have, not without breaking Kuul's spell—which he couldn't do.

I shook my head and took in a breath, an apology on my lips, but nothing came out. I liked Hunty, but I was close to done being nice.

Closing my eyes once more, I dove into the iron worm, pouring my mana into it, which it accepted gratefully. It bent and flexed its ribbed skin in smooth, controlled waves, crawling up my arm, under my shirt, then out onto my shoulder. It seemed undamaged and functional, which was no surprise, but I always checked. The segmented form of my new worm constructs was there for ease of movement, allowing them all to wriggle around like their namesakes. However, if I were to stop Shaping it, the whole thing would go stiff; solid as . . . well, iron.

I had it work its way back down to my hand, using the sharp-lipped ribs to hang on to the skin of my palm.

Now for the fun part.

My head felt like it was going to split in two as I reached for my next Ability while holding on to Shape. It helped that the hard part of Shaping was already done, but this still taxed my mind heavily, making me wish I'd chosen Dual Cast.

> Volatility [1 MP/sec]

The wild mana rushed inside. I didn't give it much juice. It shouldn't need very much.

The molecules in the construct quivered, barely able to contain the purple energy zipping around inside its matter. I held incredibly still, not even flexing my will with Shape, just allowing the iron to be still for a moment as I observed this state.

Now it was time to Imbue it.

The problem with using Imbue overlapping Shape wasn't that it didn't work. Imbue worked beautifully on my little worms. I could get them to wiggle or crawl or do little dances on my palm as long as I had the mana. The problem was that Shape was a touch-based Ability. Once my metal creatures lost contact with my skin, all that mana just evaporated into the wind.

I only had one Ability that let me put mana into something and have it persist: Volatility. The only problem was that the mana it used wasn't mine or more precisely, *me*. Still, I was convinced I could eventually figure out how to use this somehow, if I could tame the beast, so to speak.

I let out a long, tired breath, allowing my frustrations and anger to drain from my mind.

*Here we go.*

I released the mana I was using to Shape, allowing it to dissipate little by little, and my sense of the metal worm waned until it was gone, the only indication that it was still on my hand being the tingling warmth given off by Volatility.

> Shape [4 MP/sec]

I re-saturated the construct again, this time sliding my consciousness between the wild mana, mixing in among it, drowning the fiery potential with a metaphorical ocean of my own power. I isolated the Volatility spell, one piece at a time, attaching to the pieces of it like a virus attaches to a cell. It was an expensive process.

> Imbue [12 MP/sec]
> Imbue is now Level 2.

More mana rushed out of me in a torrent, soaking into the parts of "me" I needed. My mana levels dropped precipitously, bottoming out in a handful of heartbeats. I gasped, feeling like someone had reached into me and pulled out an organ, but I kept my will focused.

*Move.*

Just a simple command is all I wanted. Every time I'd hit this point in the past, my construct had detonated. The wild mana was just too energetic to contain, with too much chaos to direct. My face twitched, thinking back to how painful it had been to reattach my pinky finger.

Finally ready, my eyes shot open, and I hurled the iron worm at the wall as fast as I could.

*POP!*

A muted flash dazzled my eyes, leaving little blinking tracers in my vision as I peered into the darkness of my cell to look for my experiment.

Tiredly, I got up and crawled over to the far wall, feeling around with my hands to . . .

My hand landed on something warm. Using two fingers, I brought it up to my face, squinting at it to check for damage. There was none.

Then the worm twitched. Just a little. It slowly flexed, curling up around my finger before it ceased and went dead.

My heart thrummed in my chest as I brought up my log.

Main Class Ability: Shape is now Level 5!
Based on current Skills and Affinities, you have four Upgrade Paths available:
Transmute
Remote Shaping
Duplicate
Enchant

*Yes!*

Ability Synthesis discovered: Shape + Volatility + Imbue
Synthesize? Y/N
New Ability: Automate
Automate: Program your creations with simple instructions and empower them to carry out your orders independently. Strength, amount, and complexity of instructions are dependent on your Spirit.

*Oh, hell, yes.*

# CHAPTER FOURTEEN

# Watch Him Die

I took yet another piece of ore from the bucket and made it disappear into my Spatial Storage, not even bothering to hide the flash anymore.

Hunty was giving me ore faster than I could work it now, not caring what I did with it as long as I gave him something by the end of the day. After all of our time together, he knew to trust my inventiveness if not my methods. He'd started doing that ever since I made my first self-repairing blade. That earned me a lot of leeway for experimentation. While that prototype only had enough juice to fix itself two or three times, depending on the damage, it proved that I should be left alone to do my thing. Now all of the warriors had one.

A matching crate of leather strips and semi-straight Mendau Wood were on the other side of the bars, but I didn't need those just now. I had a bunch of this stuff squirreled away, but I didn't want to empty the containers and not have anything to show for it. The goblins were lax with me now that their worries were closer to home, but their tolerance only went so far.

My hand froze mid-grab when a sudden silence fell over the cave. The workers no longer shouted at one another. No one dumped their cart of rocks or threw any wood onto the stockpiles. For the entire time I'd been down here, the work had almost never stopped.

Then I saw them: a long procession of goblins, families with elders, parents, and children. Bandaged warriors with missing fingers or ears. Goblins that carried baskets on their backs heaping with clothes, tools, or whatnot. A few gaggles of goblins carrying stretchers of the sick or wounded on their shoulders. All of them, whether they had something in their arms or not, stared ahead with troubled expressions, worry and defeat evident in their eyes, looking like they only cared about the backs of those in front of them and the desire to keep moving.

Hunty slowly got to his feet, confused at first, but soon he was watching them all go, nodding to friends and kin, waving at others. No one had the inclination to wave back. Tiba materialized from the river of green people, tears in her eyes. She melted into Hunty's arms and buried her face in his breastplate.

Grating, rumbling, the cave shook from an unseen force.

"They're here, Hunty. The Baned are outside. Kuul has us all go into the deeper caves, and he collapses the tunnel behind us," Tiba whispered quietly enough that only we could hear her. "The warriors say it is the Black Flood from the stories. The world is changing again."

A sudden loud crash echoed in the cavern, startling every goblin in sight and drawing every eye to the rear. Something was wrong. Then the first of them started running. The rest, spurred to urgency, rushed forward as well, pushing those in front of them along if they would not move.

The goblin healer reached into her pack and pulled out a sizable bundle of something, setting it down in front of the bars of my cell.

"Take as much as you can. Kuul is rationing the food soon, and he may not feed you, Ryan," she said with a sad little smile. "I go down to help with the wounded. Good luck."

Hunty wrapped his arms around his love, holding her close but never dropping his spear. "I am staying," he declared, his voice wavering but his eyes steady.

Tiba shuddered, shaking her head, but got control of herself enough to look up and catch Hunty's eye. "I know. See me later, okay?"

A scream pierced the air from somewhere out of sight. Howling, gibbering calls more fit for beasts than thinking creatures reverberated through the cavern, shattering the relative quiet, and animalistic shrieks echoed off the walls until they came from everywhere.

The relative order in which the goblins were evacuating dissolved, devolving into panic and chaos. Goblins screamed for each other, running farther into the cavern, bunching up at the far end in a crushing mass of bodies.

For their part, the goblin warriors fought against the current, shouldering their way through the river of people, spears or swords held high so as not to accidentally harm any of their kin.

Hunty gave Tiba one last look, then bent down and took up his shield. In the next second he was off, his powerful legs carrying him swiftly to where the fight was, out of my sight.

Tiba looked at me, putting a sympathetic hand on my prison bars, and then she was off, too, in the opposite direction of her love, going with the tide to help how she could.

Bedlam.

Goblins trampled each other to get further from the danger, to get farther down the tunnels. All the while, vicious yowls and goblin battle cries pierced the air as unseen life or death struggles started and ended within seconds.

Quickly, I reached through the bars, putting my hand on Tiba's bundle of food.

Transfer to Spatial Storage? Y/N

The bundle glowed, warped and disappeared to wherever these things went. I didn't know exactly how large my magical space was, but it felt like I could fit plenty more inside. Time to get while the getting was good. I couldn't do much else.

I shifted over to the bucket of ore, still half full. Into the Spatial Storage it went, too.

Stretching way out to touch the bundle of wood, I was waiting for the prompt to appear when something slammed into my arm so hard it wrenched my shoulder out of its socket. I felt the tendons stretch, then give, and a scream tore its way from my throat.

More out of instinct than anything, I dove backward to get away from the bars, slamming myself into the back wall, every motion a study in agony.

Panting, I looked down at the damage. My arm hung uselessly at my side, my shoulder burning as the swelling began. My shirt was shredded, and deep gouges I hadn't registered oozed blood that dripped onto the floor.

*SLAM!*

A glossy black body collided with my prison bars, the creature's familiar too-wide mouth full of shark teeth gnawing and tearing chunks off the Mendau roots. It clung to the bars with its feet while reaching into the cell to grab at my legs, though it wasn't quite able to reach. It shrieked and yowled, spittle flying from its maw, and its unblinking eyes shone in the dim light, madness and hunger swirling in the hollow orbs.

A swift figure barreled into the monster from the side, a spear taking the Scourge-Touched goblin in its ribs and bearing it down to the ground. Hunty's form was perfect as he stepped back to retract his thrust, delivering the killing blow in the thing's throat before it could even register it was in a fight. It gurgled, thrashing at Hunty's spear, but the life left its eyes quickly.

Hunty turned to me and did a lazy sort of salute. "I like this spear, human. This is a good spear," he shouted over the din before he bounded off to rescue someone else.

Then the deep, growling basso of Kuul's singing cut through the chaos, drowning out all but himself. The too-familiar sensation of itching teeth and ringing ears returned from my memory of the day I was trapped in this place. Rumbling, grating rockfalls shook the cavern, enough to be felt through the stone of the floor and walls.

The lights winked out. Then there was silence.

Life came back to my little corner of the goblin caves as people found the courage to make noise again. They called for each other—some out of pain, others out of fear or loss. The smell of blood was thick in the air, tainted with whatever it was the Baned had inside them. It reminded me unpleasantly of the rotting stairwell back at the tutorial facility, sour tar and rot.

That memory would probably never fade.

Torches and candles were lit one by one until the cavern was awash in orange light like I'd never seen it before. The goblins didn't need a lot of light to see, so the cave had always been a dim place. Now, though, when they needed to tend the wounded and collect the bodies, they lit everything. My eyes, too long underground, took time to adjust.

I shifted uncomfortably in my cell. My shoulder would be better in a matter of hours thanks to my Exotic Regeneration, but that didn't diminish how weird it was to physically feel the tendons and bone shifting back into place of their own volition. It itched, and the bones ground together in a way that had me gritting my teeth.

In front of my cell, Tiba had the wounded lying or sitting in ranks and files, the healer going from one to another, bandaging wounds or checking on unconscious bodies. She stroked the faces of crying children and wrapped her arms around the bereaved. Her pouch of dried herbs never had a chance to be closed.

Others dragged the bodies of the dead to the side, away from the living. The corpses of the Baned went into the furnace.

My shoulder finally slipped back into place with a cool *pop!* and a tingle that reverberated up my neck.

The goblins were largely asleep now, except for a few of the wounded in too much pain to get any rest. Their labored breathing intertwined in a disturbing background noise that permeated my cell and would probably haunt my dreams. The torches were put out except for the few the Stone Hearts actually required to see by.

The sound of quiet, angry words being exchanged reached my ears before their owners did. Kuul's craggy hiss distinguished him from the others.

"It cannot come with us. It betrays us just by being what it is," he growled. "You talk with it too much. Pity rots your good sense."

Tiba was among the voices. "No. He is helping us, and he knows what the Baned do now. He can come. The Baned come closer, and they find ways inside."

Kuul rebuked her, though. "Stop. That does not matter. The Baned want it, and they come for us to get it."

"You want us to leave him? After everything he does?" Hunty asked, disgust creeping into his question.

"No," replied Kuul as he finally stepped in front of my cell, a steely determination in his eyes. He scowled, raising his chin as if to pass judgment on me. "We can't leave it."

Tiba was there at Kuul's side, leaning on him and looking up to try and catch his stare. "If you break your spell, we can take him with us. Ryan gives us weapons and armor, but now we need more goblins. Ryan can be a goblin."

"Ryan should fight to save his own life, Kuul," Hunty said as he stepped into view as well. His armor was crusted with blood, and his shield bore multiple gouges in the wood and iron. He turned to me, pleading with his eyes.

A complicated mix of emotions churned inside of me.

I wanted out. Desperately. I wanted to be somewhere with natural light. I wanted to go home. I wanted my freedom. The entire time I'd been here, every stolen moment was about preparing to do all of those things.

Now they were asking me to just . . . what? Beg for permission?

No.

I opened my mouth to tell Kuul exactly what I thought of him, something I'd regret, but if my time as a slave taught me anything, it was patience.

Kuul would get his in time.

I cleared my throat and stood, slowly working the pain out of my shoulder. The words oozed out of me, viscous and bitter, like I had a mouth full of motor oil. "Just give me a chance, Kuul," I said. I swallowed, resisting the urge to reach out and touch the bars, to imagine them withering away and leaving me a free man. My lips formed the word without my consent. "Please."

Whatever I was selling, the old wizard wasn't buying it, or maybe his distaste for me ran that deep. His mouth snapped into a tight, angry line and his gray eyes grew as hard as flint. Shaking his head, he put out his hands, and little lights danced over his fingertips. "It can't be taken. It can't be left," he proclaimed with finality. "The Mendau eats."

The ancient goblin magician began, once again, to sing. The sound rolled over Tiba as she pleaded for my life, over Hunty as he shouted at Kuul and gestured toward me with his spear, over me.

"Wait. Wait. Wait! Wait!" I repeated, the building panic robbing me of any other words.

Kuul heard none of it. He wouldn't hear any of it.

The Mendau roots, so long a static obstacle I'd wanted to overcome, came alive. The wooden tentacles cracked and split, forming additional appendages that dripped thick, milky fluid that sizzled on the cavern floor. They slithered into my cell along the walls, growing, reaching out for me, grasping at me blindly.

Frantically, I kicked at the roots, scrambling backward to get far away from the cell door. It didn't matter, though. The roots grew and grew until they filled my prison from top to bottom, creeping along the walls like vines over wet rock. They herded me into a corner until all I had left was enough space to crouch there and wait for the end.

Hunty stepped in front of Kuul, shouting something in his face, but the song drowned all. Then something changed. Hunty looked back at me with genuine fearful compassion in his eyes. Then he made his move. Turning back, he planted his feet and shoved Kuul, hard.

The old goblin staggered back, his song turning into a shocked gurgle. Something in his throat gave way with a wet crack, and he coughed up bloody foam, clutching at his throat with electrified fingers.

Seething anger and fear flashed over his face as his hand whipped up and made a slashing motion in the air.

Viper fast, the roots snapped back, their ropy tendrils reversing course and shooting from my cell, their barbed tips slamming into Hunty's back so hard, his body lifted into the air; now that the roots had something to grasp, they weren't letting go. They squirmed over the goblin warrior's body, wrapping around him over and over again, around his limbs, his stomach, his head and neck, tightening, ratcheting themselves until Hunty was pinned up against my cell's bars.

"Hunty!" Tiba screamed, rushing to his side and pulling at the Mendau roots to give him some air. Hunty struggled mightily to free himself, but to no avail. The wooden tentacles wound over him faster than they could be pulled away.

Lying down on the floor, clutching his throat, Kuul looked on in terror, mouth agape, watching his magic do its grim work.

I blinked in shock. Hunty's choked, tortured gasps were the only sound in the cave now. The only sound in this world.

I dashed forward, leaping over my cell's hole, and slammed up against the cage's bars. I was the second to Hunty's side.

I should have been the first.

I tore at the roots.

```
Devouring Grasp [5MP/sec]
Devouring Grasp [5MP/sec]
Devouring Grasp [5MP/sec]
Devouring Grasp [5MP/sec]
```

I tore at them with everything I had, ripping at them until my prosthetic was slick with milky plant fluid and my natural hand bled from fingernails hanging uselessly off bloody nubs.

Status gained: Bleeding [0.5 HP/sec]
Devouring Grasp [5MP/sec]
Devouring Grasp [5MP/sec]

As they always had, the roots grew back exactly as they'd been instructed. What progress Tiba and I made in breaking the Mendau away, they came back twice as strong. What little we could see of Hunty's skin slowly purpled, then lost color altogether.

Tiba stopped screaming well after Hunty died, and even then she still fought to free him, whispering little laments to him as she tugged feebly at the Mendau.

Meanwhile, panting and speckled with my own blood, I only saw Kuul.

I locked eyes with the old monster, flexing my metal hand, wanting nothing more than to crush the top of the little green bastard's skull and Consume it in front of his face.

Kuul coughed and rubbed his throat, but he'd otherwise regained his composure and only stared back at me with absolute, undisguised hatred. I could see, though, the way he avoided looking at what he'd done to Hunty.

He looked like he wanted to say something, order his warriors to kill me, but he couldn't. He tried to speak but blood burbled out of his mouth and fouled his words.

The rest of the warriors arrived one by one, forming a semicircle around their fallen comrade, none of them giving voice to their thoughts, allowing Tiba to grieve uninterrupted.

A spell of Kuul's making, if not the one he intended, fell over the entire tribe then, held them enthralled, sapping their wills, dimming the light.

In the quiet, the ambient sounds of the cave seemed to lap at our ears. The dripping of water. The rush of the air currents. Faint scratching. Fervent breathing. Someone eventually recognized it for what it was.

"Lights!" an observant goblin shouted.

Torches burst to life, bathing the cavern in orange again and chasing away the shadows, revealing dozens—no, *hundreds*—of black shapes stealthily creeping over the walls and ceiling of the cavern.

The two groups stood there for a moment, surprised, no one willing to make the first move . . .

Until one of those black shapes dropped from the ceiling, among the wounded.

"Run!" commanded the warrior, lifting his sword and whirling it in a circle above his head. "Fighters to me! We go last! You!" He slapped one of his fellows on top of his helmet. "Get them out of here!" he ordered, pointing at Kuul and Tiba. The latter of the two lay slumped down at Hunty's feet, nearly catatonic.

The tide was going out again. Green bodies streamed past my cell, this time pursued by snarling, howling monsters that ran among them, tearing into their flesh and bathing in their blood.

Tiba was ripped away, carried out of my view by her kin, and Kuul likewise fled with his escort. Before he was out of sight, he cast one last glance at me and spat blood in my direction.

The warriors did their best to hold the line, felling foes where they could, getting the living members of the tribe out and into another tunnel, but more of them fell than they could afford.

Then, like a black flood, Scourge-Touched bodies filled my doorway, slashing and clawing. Hunty still hung there in his wooden coffin, caged like he'd always feared. The Baned, in their fervor to get at me, ripped at his body. Hunty's blood, over-pressurized from the constricting roots, quickly became the only thing I could smell.

My heart was going wild, rumbling against the insides of my temples.

It had happened again. They kept dying.

*They keep dying for me.*

I bent down and retrieved the one thing of Hunty's that the roots hadn't claimed.

Hunty's Spear: A cherished spear crafted by a fledgling artificer and sized for a goblin. The spear tip is magnificently sharp and can repair itself multiple times before going truly dull.

Damage: 4-8 (Piercing)

Quality: Excellent

Style: Custom

Magic: Repair

The entire opening of my cell was full of beady black eyes and slashing claws. Gibbering, howling faces pressed themselves into the gaps in the bars.

I gripped Hunty's spear and rolled my neck. My heart thrummed in my chest, not like the weak, frail lump of muscle and connective tissue the rest of them had but like an engine. Thundering, explosive power energized my body and fueled my hate.

A wordless roar burst forth from my chest as I dove headfirst into the tide.

*Wrath.*

# CHAPTER FIFTEEN

# Stick and Move

I lunged forward, thrusting Hunty's spear into the writhing mass of Scourge-Touched bodies, aiming for a glinting pair of eyes that stood more still than the rest. My aim was off, but it didn't matter. The monsters were packed against my cell so tightly, I couldn't miss.

The spearpoint struck something soft, then penetrated through, the flesh of one of the Baned only offering minimal resistance to the precisely sharpened edge.

Scourge-Touched Goblin takes 7 damage. (Piercing)
Scourge-Touched Goblin is bleeding.
Skill unlocked: Spear
Your current Skill Level is 1.

In fact, it was so easy, the surprise and subsequent overbalance nearly killed me.

The Baned reached for me as they pressed up against the root bars, slashing wildly as I got within striking distance. Dozens of long, spindly arms with razor-sharp talons that wanted nothing more than my blood formed a barbed wall of death beside me.

So, when the spear went through my intended target instead of stopping as I'd expected, I tipped forward into a blender, my only saving grace being my Core arm that the goblins couldn't scratch or tear. I was forced to steady myself on one of the goblins' arms, grasping it by the elbow to support my weight and keep from falling all the way forward.

It grabbed my metal bicep, clawing and digging at the unyielding material.

It succeeded in pulling me forward, however. Other claws raked across my chest, my face, and my spear arm. They tore wicked gashes across my flesh, the skin parting easily under their piercing tips.

> Scourge-Touched Goblin attacks you for 3 Damage.
> Status gained: Bleeding [.5 HP/sec]
> Scourge-Touched Goblin attacks you for 2 Damage.
> Status gained: Bleeding [1 HP/sec]

Blood trickled down into my eye, blinding me on one side. My feet scrambled at the stones to get away from the attacks, but the floor was already slick with splatters of blood. Shifting tactics, I kicked at the bars, feeling my foot making contact with the Mendau roots and propelling me backward, tearing me away from all of the swiping claws and leaving bits of myself behind in the process.

Strong, spindly fingers were still wrapped around my prosthetic bicep, trying to haul me back into the fray. I did a little grabbing myself.

> Devouring Grasp [5 MP/sec]

The goblin's forearm disintegrated into tiny embers of orange. Within the cacophony of shrieking, yowling voices, one such voice took on a distinctly more-strained pitch.

> You gain knowledge of material: Goblin Bone [1/10]
> You gain knowledge of material: Goblin Bone [2/10]

By some miracle I still had the spear. The Scourge-Touched tried to grab the end of that as well, probably thinking of pulling me in along with the weapon, but whatever I'd hit with my initial thrust covered the entire front in blood and other fluids, making it too slippery to properly grasp. I jerked it away, cutting more flesh on the return. Their blood spattered and splashed on the floor and against the walls, intermingling with mine.

"Come on, you little shits!" I bellowed in their faces. "I'm right here!"

I got to my feet and set myself, spear out, shield arm in front, weight equally distributed this time, and I thrust again at a pair of eyes. This time, I had the presence of mind to not let myself reach out too far. Again, I scored a hit, closer to where I was aiming this time. The reflective orbs jerked and fell away, to be replaced by another set.

> You take 1 Bleeding Damage.

Scourge-Touched Goblin takes 6 Damage. (Piercing)
Scourge-Touched Goblin is bleeding.

This time, I didn't leave the spear inside my target long enough for it to be grabbed. I was set again within half a second.

Then I thrust again and again and again.

I found a rhythm. The Scourge-Touched weren't overly concerned with their lives, pressing mindlessly into the gaps between the roots, their rabid fervor at being close to me drowning all sense of self-preservation. Those in front were mobbed from behind, pressed so close they could barely move except for where they tore at the Mendau roots or swiped at me when I came close enough.

*Stab. Set. Stab. Set. Stab. Set.*

I cursed at them over and over until I was hoarse. I vented my hate on the Baned, made them the objects of my wrath.

Occasionally, I grew overzealous and came away from a thrust bleeding again, but I didn't let that stop me.

The lights went out an indeterminate time later, either from running out of fuel or the Baned's bodies blocking every square inch of my door. I activated Detect Goblin, the first Ability I'd unlocked from Affinities so long ago, and the seething mass of Scourge-Touched goblins practically blinded me, the concentration was so intense. They shone like a beacon. Closing my eyes didn't help matters, either. I wasn't seeing them with my eyes.

But I didn't let that stop me.

Acclimation to my new senses was slow, but eventually I was back in the swing (stab) of things. Experience messages were rolling in.

Scourge-Touched Goblin defeated.
You have been awarded 22 Experience points. [10 base (-2 Level, +2 nemesis, +10 group,+10 chain, -8 non-combat Class)]

I had to minimize my log after a while, finding the messages too distracting.
*Stab. Set. Stab. Set. Stab. Set.*

The Baned were endless. No matter how many I killed, more would take their place. The muscles in my arm tired, and my legs burned from having to crouch and step during my thrusts. Sweat poured off my body, and my lungs were on fire.

My form suffered, carrying me into some close calls. The System repaired my body over time, closing wounds that would have bled a normal person to death, but, nevertheless, the gouges and scratches wore me down, not just from the blood loss but from the pain. My body was quickly running out of adrenaline and my mind was growing exhausted from the constant state of alertness and overstimulation.

My rhythm slowed until it stopped altogether, and I slumped to the floor against the wall opposite the door.

Defeated. Exhausted. I sat there, the cool of the cave rock soothing my aching body, the System going to work on my HP.

It was pitch black, but Detect Goblin turned my cell into a horror show. Blood and gore littered the walls and the floor, soaked into my clothes, my hair. I reached over my shoulder and extracted a severed claw from a groove in between the segmented plates on my back.

Indefatigable, the Baned tore into the Mendau to get to me. Hunty's body was long gone, replaced by more roots and rabid faces. Gurgling screeches smothered all other sound, while the faces of my would-be killers slavered with long tongues snaking forward to taste my scent.

With a trembling hand I summoned my clay cup and rope from my Spatial Storage, watching it appear from nothing with a dim flash. I did the same with a piece of meat from the bundle Tiba had given me. Once I'd drawn some water from the Under-river, I shakily popped the jerky into my mouth and chased it with the entire cup of water.

I was wrung out, spent. My mind and body felt numb, yet raw, like I'd been dipped in a frozen lake and left out to dry in the wind. One by one, I consciously relaxed my muscles and closed my eyes, looking for peace amid the nightmare. I turned Detect Goblin off to decrease the strain on my mind and let the world go back to the dark once again.

The Scourge-Touched didn't make it easy with the racket they were making, but I did what I could to soothe my psyche, trusting the rest of me to follow.

We sat like that for a while. I'm unsure how long. My Engine status had winked out a long while ago, so I had no way of keeping the time. However, my HP slowly ticked up from 10 to 31.

I had no idea what my Regeneration Rate actually was, but it was at least something to watch. My max appeared to be 45 now. I wasn't sure when that happened, but I didn't want to bring up my log. Not yet. Looking at it meant thinking and decisions and all that sort of thing I wasn't ready for yet.

Breathing deeply of the blood-tinged air, I took up Hunty's spear yet again, climbed to my feet, and activated Detect Goblin to bring back the horrifying display of luminescent gore and hungry maws.

I popped another bit of dried meat into my mouth, gnawing at the tough sinew as I pondered my next move. I'd slept twice since the monsters had invaded my cavern, and I was pretty sure I was no closer to exhausting their numbers than before. They still crowded up against the bars of my cell trying desperately to reach for me, but they'd grown quieter as time went on.

Yes, if I moved suddenly or approached them, they would be back to barking and howling and slashing to get to me, but for now they seemed content to watch and make sure I didn't leave.

That worried me. What's worse, it piqued my curiosity to the point that my rhythm of set, stab, set could no longer divert my mind enough to drown out my thoughts.

Despite myself, I'd liked Hunty. I might have even thought of him as my friend.

It was ridiculous. Our first moment together, he stabbed me, and then he became my jailer.

Of course it was ridiculous to feel anything but contempt for the guy.

But then there were the other moments. How he shared his rations with me sometimes. The jokes. The way he looked out for me with the other guards and pleaded to Kuul for more humane (gobline?) treatment. His first instinct was always to protect others, Tiba especially. Hunty would always do his best to keep her from being affected by the evils of the world. He would do anything to see her happy and safe, and, to an extent, he did that for me as well.

Hunty also died for me.

*Like Vince.*

What do you do to make up for that kind of sacrifice? How do you square that kind of debt?

*You could start by not dying during the tutorial.*

Wiping a tear from my cheek, I laughed quietly as the gesture erased that part of my body from the world. The rest of me was covered in goblin blood, making me visible to Detect, at least in outline, but that spot was now a break in the filth, the only clean spot on my entire body.

So absurd. It was all so absurd.

Shuddering, I laughed some more. Uncontrollable, violent laughter. The kind of laugh that bursts out of you like an alien parasite and does its best just to leave behind nothing but an empty husk. I laughed until it hurt. Then I laughed *because* it hurt.

The Scourge-Touched hated it, joining in in their own way with hoots tinged with bloodlust and evil.

Shaking my head and breathing deep, I slowly got myself back under control.

I'd had enough of this place. It was time to get back to the business of escape, not just from the cave. From Ralqir.

I brought up my log.

Level Up!
You are now Level 5.
Max HP +5
Max MP +5

+1 Attribute point.
Ability Unlocked: Trigger

---

Achievements awarded this Level:
Big Spender: You have spent 8,000% of your total Mana Pool this Level. [+1% Mana Regeneration per second.]
Dedicated: You spent most of your time dedicated to your craft this Level. [+1 Spirit]
Doing Your Part: Some of your creations have been used against agents of the Scourge. [+200% experience awarded for new designs next Level]
Synergetic Synthesis: You have performed the prohibitively difficult and costly feat of combining three or more Abilities to form a new one. [+50% Level rate for all component Abilities. ERROR: Ability:Volatility:Class_mismatch]

I had been waiting for this ever since Shape hit Level 5 and gave me a choice. Five seemed to be a significant number in everything so far, and I didn't want to make a permanent choice for my main Ability until I knew what I needed. Apparently, my Class got a new toy at 5.

---

Trigger: Create a pocket of latent potentiality within your creations that may be activated by mana. [Cost: conditional]

Okay. If I was reading the description correctly, that meant I could . . . What? Make my constructs do things by injecting mana? I could sort of do that already with Automate. There had to be something more to it.

I'd experiment with it once I got a chance.

---

Level Up!
You are now Level 6.
Max HP +5
Max MP +5
+1 Attribute point.

---

Achievements awarded this Level:
All Natural: You have spent 80% of this Level with full mana. [+1 body]
Doing Your Part: Some of your creations have been used against agents of the Scourge. [+200% Experience awarded for new designs next Level]
Spirit of the Warrior: You gained 51% of your Experience this Level from defeated foes as a non-combat Class. [+3 spirit]
Rift Hunter: You gained 51% of your Experience this Level from Nemesis-tagged foes. [+1 to all Attributes]

Level Up!
You are now Level 7.
Max HP +5
Max MP +5
+1 Attribute point.

Achievements awarded this Level:
All Natural: You have spent 80% of this Level with full mana. [+1 body]
Doing Your Part: Some of your creations have been used against agents of the Scourge. [+200% Experience awarded for new designs next Level]
Spirit of the Warrior: You gained 51% of your Experience this Level from defeated foes as a non-combat Class. [+3 spirit]
Rift Hunter: You gained 51% of your Experience this Level from Nemesis-tagged foes. [+1 to all Attributes]

That was . . . a lot to parse. The achievements and their meanings, I would have to study sometime later. Just skimming the surface information got me off to a good start, but I was sure there was more there to glean.

I felt around in my Spatial Storage, taking inventory. I had about twenty pounds of iron, some in ore form, some as worm constructs. Additionally, I had maybe a few days' worth of food, a few bundles of Mendau Wood, four pounds of limestone, and six pounds of aluminum.

The Baned stared at me with their beady black eyes, watching my every movement, waiting for the moment I tried to escape or slipped into their reach.

For my part, I was thinking again. For the first time since the lights went out, my brain was engaged, and the pieces of a plan were slowly taking shape.

# CHAPTER SIXTEEN

# Make My Escape

Devouring Grasp [5 MP/sec]
You gain knowledge of material: Limestone [50/50]
Affinity upgraded: Limestone: Grade E
Detect radius is now 17 ft.

I stood and brushed the rock dust off my lap, taking the opportunity to stretch my muscles and shake off the mana crash I'd been courting using my Devouring Grasp like that. Limestone didn't burn like some materials did, so my Engine buff had a tendency to fall off without me realizing it.

I had a pool of 75 MP to work with now, so even if I was without Engine for a little while, I could keep going for some time. Eventually, however, the well would run dry, and I would have to rely on my Core. Shaping, specifically the saturation part, was a mana-hungry process, especially when you didn't have an Affinity for the material in the first place.

A theory was slowly percolating in my mind about previous Animators and how they must have gone about things. If I had to speculate, my Animator brethren had to have had at least one Affinity to work with upon integration. They would have come to the tutorial facility, met their trainer, grabbed some metal, and ground to Level 1, all while Nali held their hand and let them know how things worked.

Even for people with a higher Mind Stat and pool of MP, the process of getting to Level 1 would have taken weeks or maybe months unless having an

Affinity for the material came into play to help them work more efficiently. Either that or Nali had some way to boost newbies' MP, but that didn't strike me as likely. My Engine Core said it was unique, and Nali had made it sound like MP took a while to regenerate. She hadn't offered any alternatives or remedies to that limitation.

Whatever the case, once the new Animator hit Level 1, they'd be transported back through the insertion point to their home universe, which was the step of the process I was, hopefully, on now and had been ever since I leveled for the first time.

My tutorial hadn't gone according to that plan, though.

"Return to Insertion Point" sounded like a final step, at least, so that's what I would have to do to get home . . . Eventually.

The problem was that I was locked in a prison cell under millions of tons of rock, and my insertion point was now the epicenter of evil, to hear the goblins tell it—the exact center of the Baned territory.

I rolled my neck, mentally feeling around in my Spatial Storage for parts, checking each to make sure they were ready for assembly.

The ever-present peanut gallery nearby me didn't like that. They spit and slashed at the Mendau bars and reached out, desperate to extract more of my blood. I couldn't see them, but I knew that's what they were doing. They never stopped.

*I need mana anyway.*

I deactivated Detect Limestone and replaced it with the goblin variant.

There they were, brightly lit, piled up on top of each other in the door of my cell, eyes and mouths wide open as always. The dried blood and viscera on the floor had dimmed in my goblin vision over the past day or so, which was an interesting point of data on the function of the Skill. Why didn't the blood retain its "goblin-ness?" Did its dimming in my senses indicate there were multiple levels of goblin? Either way, if the universe was going to give me a way to ignore how rotten my cell had become with goblin viscera, I wasn't going to say no.

Long, spindly hands, tipped with curved talons, stretched out for me as their owners pressed in to get even a millimeter more of reach.

I picked one of them at random.

"Hey, buddy. High five," I said. It was a terrible joke, one I'd told many times now, but, if I was being honest with myself, I missed real voices and language. It was hard to tell how long I'd been stuck in here with my new neighbors, but their savage nature and seemingly endless attention spans, all bent toward killing me, were grating on my sanity.

Stepping forward just out of reach of the rending claws, I casually stuck my hand out to let it be grabbed.

> Devouring Grasp [5 MP/sec]
> Status gained: Engine: [+2 MP/sec for 5 min]
> Scourge-Touched Goblin takes 20 Damage.
> Scourge-Touched Goblin is bleeding.

A panicked screech carried above the usual din, a pair of the goblin eyes widening in pain, and the now-handless goblin attempted to flee against the mob of bodies still pressed in behind it.

Feeling my mana tick up out of the single digits again, I sighed, flopping down on the opposite wall where I switched back to Detect Iron.

I wished it weren't necessary. The thing about iron is that it's in everyone's blood, making it useful for sensing living things. In fact, it was the only way I could see my own body down here in the dark. Without the use of my real sight, the Ability made us all look generally the same, if differently proportioned. The problem lay in the fact that my cell was covered in blood. My enemies', my own . . . just *everyone's*.

*I really need to get out of here.*

I'd laid my plans and stretched my resources to cover what I could. The Under-river was my only option, and that meant I was facing a number of problems, some more daunting than others.

Problem One: I loved oxygen. So much, in fact, I couldn't live without it.

At first I'd thought about making some kind of extendable spike contraption that could drill into the limestone and get me a pocket of air to breathe. That is, before I realized that limestone, while it did contain oxygen, didn't necessarily contain O2. What's more, if the water was all the way up to the ceiling of the tunnel like I thought it was, it would probably just rush into whatever cavity I could produce.

I'd gone through several iterations of ideas, Shaping and rearranging my various materials into different solutions, even going so far as to consider electrocuting myself in an attempt at electrolysis. Where I would get the electricity, I didn't know, but during that brainstorming session, it occurred to me that I might have the solution (or at least *a* solution) staring me in the face . . . or wherever my Spatial Storage really was.

What I needed was a balloon. More precisely, I needed a reservoir of air.

That's where most of my aluminum went.

Essentially, I Shaped it into a giant metal bladder, filling up as much of my cell as possible, even allowing it to drip down into the hole and nearly touch the water many feet below. I kept the paper-thin skin of the construct rigid through the magic of Shape and let the air just do what air does, expanding into the entire space. Then I sealed the balloon with the air inside.

From there it was about shrinking my new oxygen tank, slowly moving molecules around, thickening the walls and decreasing the surface area until I was left with a pressurized aluminum canister about the size of my fist, with a plugged straw protruding from the end.

Then I repeated the process until I was nearly out of aluminum, and I had four of my little diving tanks.

Problem Two: It was dark down here.

This one I didn't have a clever answer for. Sure, my Detect Abilities were good, but they were too specialized. Detect Limestone would have me able to see the cave walls but nothing else, Detect Iron would only give me a view of myself and whatever creatures with blood like mine there might be down there, and the rest were far less useful in this situation anyway.

The only way I had to produce consistent light underwater was Volatility, so I'd pretty much be using a live grenade as a glow lamp while I took my swim.

*Hooray.*

Problem Three: Danger.

I needed a weapon, one I could use even in the tight confines of any tunnel I might find, and this was the problem I intended to solve today.

From my storage, I summoned the pieces. A long iron tube with a rudimentary self-repair function as well as a fat nub on one end.

Next was the chamber, which was pretty much a tube inside a tube, the larger of which could slide back and let me put things inside the breach I'd made. I'd plugged the back of the larger one with a half inch of solid iron, only leaving space for a pebble-sized cube that would fit into a groove on the back wall.

Said cube was the tricky part. The whole design relied on it to get off the ground.

Breathing in deep, I brought out my tiny bit of aluminum I'd saved for this, placing it on top of the iron tubes.

| Shape [4 MP/sec] |
| --- |

I formed my aluminum into the cubical shape to match the groove.

| Automate [15 MP/sec] |
| --- |

My MP pool drained, practically bottoming me out instantaneously. My mana left me in a tide, flooding into the metal and, with it, my instructions and whatever power it would need to carry out these instructions. The mix of Shaping, Imbuing, and Volatility had my mana churning inside of me like the blades of a blender. It hurt, not in a physical sense, but in a way that scoured my brain and my soul. I gave everything I had to the cube.

*When you are struck, release a tiny fraction of your stored mana. Then stop. Repeat.*

My will and, by extension, my Spirit Attribute did a lot of the heavy lifting here. Fortunately, my Spirit had nearly tripled since my integration. My mana floated outside my body and filled the cell now, not visible in the conventional sense but I could certainly feel it and vaguely feel things inside of it. It even extended beyond and outside the confines of the cell, even through the walls. The strength of my Spirit gave the command sufficient sophistication and complexity, which I very much needed if I didn't want my new weapon to explode in my hand.

Next, I bored a hole in the back of the chamber tube and made room for my firing pin, just a little needle with a padded handle I'd be using for the prototype. This was the thing that did the "striking."

Then I added the finishing touches, such as a catch to keep my bolt chamber closed, rifling on the inside of the barrel, and a handle wrapped in leather strips that I could easily hold.

Finally, I summoned one of my iron worms—a chunkier, more efficient model. I dove into it with Shape and checked on the integrity of its segments and scales. Rigid, sleek, and smooth until it was told not to be, it was the perfect ammunition.

I wasn't about to just give iron away to the Baned, though.

A trip back to the handshake wall later, I was back at full MP and ready to automate my ammo.

| Trigger [10 MP/sec] |
| --- |

Trigger was an odd thing. It gave me the ability to give an object two "states" that could be switched between if fed enough mana. Conceivably, I could make a sword that turned into a hammer or a spear that grew barbs. Whoever was using said weapon would provide the MP required to make the transformation back and forth, which made using them costly but ultimately awesome.

However, I had something different in mind for the little bullet worms. Their trigger would sprout their legs, activate their segmented ribs, and sharpen their heads. Then they would execute the command I was about to give them.

| Automate [15 MP/sec] |
| --- |

*If you strike something, feed mana into the trigger. Return to me. Repeat.*

I was breathing hard and sweating by this point. Using that much mana in a short amount of time wrung my body and mind out. The System seemed to agree.

| Conduit is now Level 2. |
| --- |

> Conduit: Your body grows more able to conduct mana freely and direct its flow. +10% resistance to Mana Overflow. +10% speed of Mana Flow when using Abilities.

Placing the parts together on the floor, I shaped the barrel and the chamber together, joining their materials, interlocking the molecules where the two met, while still allowing the outer part of the chamber to be opened.

I *was* these individual parts. They were a part of me. I made them a single object, designed for my purpose. It all came together slowly, as I double-checked every tiny molecule with Shape before pulling my consciousness out.

> You have created: Rudimentary Rifle
> You have been awarded 450 Experience points. [150 base, +300 Doing Your Part bonus]

Wiping the sweat from my forehead, I released the catch on the chamber and slid it open with a quiet hiss. The metal parts fit together so precisely, only the thinnest layer of air separated the two. Nothing rattled. Nothing clicked. I knew this thing like I knew myself. Probably better. In my defense, I had a lot going on lately, and I didn't know exactly how it had affected me. Who truly knows themselves anyway?

I slipped the newly programmed ammunition inside the chamber and closed the tube. It fit perfectly, because of course it did.

Taking a deep breath, I took the rifle up in my metal hand and held it out far, far away from my face as I took aim, not quite trusting the construct to not just explode when I triggered it.

Using my thumb, I reached up to the chamber and gave the firing pin a light tap. I flinched but nothing happened.

I narrowed my eyes at it, slapping my thumb against it once, twice, harder and harder. Nothing.

I sighed.

Once more with feeling, then I'd go back to the drawing board. I transferred the rifle to my other hand and slapped the firing pin full force with my metal fist.

*POW!*

There was a flash of light, the real stuff that had burned my cave dweller's eyes, and I felt a sense of over-pressurization in my head. My ears rang, and my balance felt off, like the world was spinning.

I flopped down so I wouldn't fall down, and tried to get my bearings.

Diving into the rifle with Shape, everything seemed to be in place. The propellant cube was there—a little warm but otherwise ok. The barrel's rifling was intact. No holes or cracks in the material.

The worm—uh, ammunition—was gone, though.

I blinked rapidly. Floating purple tracers swam in my vision, and tinny, scratching, screeching sounds tickled my ringing ears. The System was getting to work repairing me, though. Soon I was able to hear and balance again. My sense returned to me as well.

I cast about with Detect Iron, looking for my spent ammunition, but finding only dried blood and . . .

*There.*

From below the writhing mass of Scourge-Touched, a tiny, undulating shape slithered its way into my cell. Half of the little legs were bent beyond use, and the tip of the construct was slightly duller than I'd designed it, but the little thing was functional if sluggish because it had been forced to use just its scales to move after its legs had been damaged.

*Of course. It had to squirm its way through a wall of goblins to get back to me.*

The Scourge-Touched didn't seem interested in the construct, at least. They only had eyes for me. Now that I could hear them again, they were going full howler monkey, practically shaking the stone with their racket.

"Nice job, little guy," I said proudly to my ammunition as I let it finish its programming. It squirmed forward until it touched the tip of my foot and went dead, now just a semi-conical piece of iron again.

I checked my log.

---

Scourge-Touched Goblin takes 14 Damage. (Piercing)
Scourge-Touched Goblin is bleeding.
Scourge-Touched Goblin takes 17 Damage. (Piercing)
Scourge-Touched Goblin is bleeding.
You have been awarded 2 Experience points. [10 base (-2 Level, +2 nemesis, -8 non-combat Class)]

---

So, the projectile had enough force to penetrate two bodies before it stopped and made its way back to me, and I had to assume it penetrated all the way through the second one. If my worm had come alive inside of a goblin, I imagined I would have gotten some more interesting messages.

Nodding to myself and allowing a new whirlwind of thoughts to churn in my head, I got back to work.

Tomorrow would come soon, and I needed to be ready.

# CHAPTER SEVENTEEN

# Dive Into Darkness

Not for the first time, I cursed the System and its tendency to make decisions for me. I was skinny before integration, before five extra points in Body were forced upon me by virtue of just trying to live through my tutorial. Normally, I wouldn't have minded a little extra bulk. I'd always been a small guy, smaller than my peers at least, and hard living in the Outers didn't help things. A few extra pounds of muscle might have gained me some respect back home and reduced my dependency on pulleys and lifts in the shop.

Now I would have killed for my old, wiry build.

I ground my teeth together and twisted at the waist, gaining myself a couple more inches of progress down the hole and toward the surface of the Under-river. My feet dangled beneath me, the remains of my boots scraping on the rough, porous surface of the rock, while I was forced to angle my shoulders with one arm above my head and one down at my side so I could fit inside the cramped confines of the little tunnel.

*Curse my sexy new wide shoulders.*

My cell was only about ten feet above my head now, or at least that was my guess. Detect Limestone only went for about seventeen feet, and I could still see the roof of my cell from here.

My Scourge-Touched neighbors were extremely upset by my absence. Upon waking up today and doing some light stretching, I'd waved goodbye to them and carefully lowered myself down to this point. If I thought the Baned sounded excited when they tried to kill me, it was nothing compared to when they lost sight of me. Even now, half an hour later, they were still going insane. The sound of their desperate, grating voices took on a hollow quality by the time they reached me down here, but the message was still easy to interpret.

I'd done a good bit of widening of this hole over my time stuck in the cell, but that work only extended a few feet down. Consequently, I'd slid down here in an easy, controlled fashion at first, but now things were tight, progress slow and painful. I had to move one part of myself at a time. Hips, arm, ribs, shoulders. That was the order. Nothing else seemed to work. It was hell on my clothes, their rough threads catching on the tiniest of imperfections in the rock, forcing me to sacrifice them to gain distance. They had already been ripped and torn in places thanks to my ill-conceived spear fight with a wall of claws, but now they were barely clothes at all.

After a while, I came to a section of the tunnel where my ribs no longer fit. I couldn't see the lip of the hole anymore, and I had to estimate I was about at the halfway mark. All of a sudden, my torso just wedged itself tight, the weight of my body dragging me down and the cave walls squeezing my rib cage until I couldn't breathe properly. That nearly panicked me. I kicked and squirmed, twisted my prosthetic down at my side to try to get some room. It helped but only by a couple of millimeters.

Then I was hanging, stuck fast over twenty or so feet of empty space, mostly supported by my rib cage.

I couldn't go back up. At that point, I just couldn't conceive of it. Staying would mean a slow death by starvation, suffocation, or dehydration. Therefore, the only way was forward . . . or down, in this case.

Taking a moment to summon calmness by closing my eyes, I blew every bit of air out of my lungs.

*Small thoughts . . . Small thoughts . . . Small thoughts . . .* I thought.

*SCRITCH!*

The blessed sound of metal on stone. The sound of progress.

The only thing that would save me was progress.

I couldn't take a full breath anymore. Instead, I was forced to suck air into my lungs in rapid, shallow gulps like a fish out of water. There wasn't enough room for anything else. Spots danced in my vision, and my head felt fuzzy.

*SCRITCH!*

*Twist, scoot, breathe. Twist, scoot, breathe.* That was my world now.

*SCRITCH!*

All that I knew was the descent.

*Twist. Scoot. Breathe.*

I. Wanted. Out.

Then my feet met the surface of the water—ice cold, soaking through the ragged leather of my boots and into my socks. The sudden temperature change shocked my brain out of hibernation, and I started paying attention to Detect Limestone again.

The Under-river was right there. My tunnel ended nearly right at the water's surface, and then I'd be dropping down through a ceiling vent into the current.

I switched over to Detect Iron to try and see if there were any creatures around that I needed to worry about, but I found none. I did find a lot of blood and bits of skin I'd left behind on the cave walls during my descent, though. That was an uncomfortable sight, made less so by my having lived in a room covered in blood in the very recent past.

One last push, and I would be through.

Nodding and rolling my neck, I tried to psych myself up for the eventual cold plunge.

*Here we go.*

I summoned one of my aluminum diving tanks into existence and held it in my hand, saturating it again with Shape so I could form an aperture in the breathing straw if needed.

Then I was on the move again.

*Twist, scoot, breathe. Repeat.*

Suddenly, with a final, grating, flesh-ripping slide over the rock, I was falling. The water rushed up to envelop me, quickly subsuming the rest of my torso and my head.

The shock of the cold nearly killed me. My body desperately wanted to gasp at the sudden icy chill that invaded my Core and stung my bloody wounds, but I knew this was coming. I only got a partial mouthful of water before I was back under control.

One thing Hunty was right about was how swift the current of the Under-river was. Instantly, I was swept away, taking a shallow diagonal trip deeper into the water, maybe about nine feet down, before I finally hit the cave floor hard enough to hurt my knees.

Oh yes, I sank, and I sank quickly. Having a good portion of your body replaced by metal did that, but it wasn't all bad. Detect helped me find the nearest nub of solid stone and plant my feet to get my bearings. I fumbled around with my diving tank, bringing the breathing straw to my lips before Shaping the stem and allowing a spurt of air to enter my mouth.

I may have over-pressurized it a bit. Breathing through it felt like someone was blasting my lungs with a cannon, and it triggered my gag reflex. It took until my third attempt before I eventually fixed the issue with some re-Shaping in the stem.

Transferring my oxygen tank into my metal hand, I summoned the little iron rod I'd saved for this. Then I cast Volatility, pumping mana into it for only a couple of seconds before the purple glow had reached the right intensity. I held up my new lamp and took a look around with my real/human eyes.

The water was clear and swift. Tiny particulates rushed past me, borne on the strong current, down deeper into the planet. The bottom of the river was a carpet of nubby, brown stalagmites long worn down by time and the rushing water, while the walls were smooth and streaked with yellow bands that waved and wove over themselves as if a product of the current as well. Once in a while, a particularly strong blast of water doubled me over and threatened to dislodge me from my safe perch.

I took another breath from my tank. As much as I hated having an elevated body before, I was grateful for it now. I didn't have to breathe as much as I thought I would, my baseline of fitness now far above my original. What's more, the cold—while shocking and unpleasant—didn't make me instantaneously hypothermic as I'd feared. There was no reason to wait around for that to happen, though.

Glow rod in my metal hand, oxygen tank in my other, I kicked off my perch and made to follow the current.

The thought had occurred to me that I could go upstream to find the area of the river the goblins used for drinking water, but there were two problems with that. First, the river was strong, and I would spend most of my energy and air trying to fight against the current. Second, the Stone Hearts' cave was overrun by Scourge-Touched now. There was no guarantee of safety even if I could find the goblins' exit and fit through it.

So, downriver I went. After a couple of embarrassing attempts at walking along the bottom and one close call where the current bowled me over and nearly made me detonate my grenade/glow rod, I found my groove. I ended up doing a sort of flying, bounding leap like you might do in low-grav. I would kick off the bottom of the river and extend my arms to keep control of my trajectory, then my mass would inevitably bring me back down to the floor. The method used minimal energy and oxygen, and it made pretty good time, too.

I could only hope that the river would take me somewhere better than my cell, instead of just farther and farther and farther down until I ran out of air.

The river did go down. Far, far down. Gradually at first, but then it wound through tight, branching tubes that swept my body downward fast and popped my ears with the change in pressure. More than once, I had to hold on to the cave walls with Devouring Grasp to arrest my momentum and chart a safe path through.

I'm not sure how long it took. I had no buffs with which to track time. I was certainly starting to feel the strain of constant cold and physical activity, and, though I didn't feel anything, I knew my body needed food and rest.

I only really noticed a change in the current when the water started getting cloudy, my light unable to reach the cave walls anymore. Indeed, my pace slowed quickly at that point, not due to the visibility, but because the water grew increasingly sluggish until I was practically walking on the bottom instead of riding the current.

As I took in some air from my third breathing tank, I got a taste of the water and nearly gagged. Whatever floated in here with me, it was foul, and it stuck to my tongue like paste. Furthermore, there was a temperature difference here. The water was warmer—not comfortably warm, but certainly not the iciness of before.

Under my feet, solid rock gave way to muddy silt that exploded into obscuring debris clouds with every footfall, and, eventually, the ground started to slope upward until I was trudging up a squishy mud heap, barely even able to see my hand that held the glow rod.

Then, suddenly, my head crested the surface, practically bursting into the open air. I was so surprised, I fumbled my oxygen tank and dropped it into the water.

Once I got over the shock, I took a couple of careful, exploratory breaths above the surface to check for oxygen, I brought the glow rod up high over my head, and I tried to get a good look at where I was.

I was in an underground lake of some sort, wide and glassy other than the waves made with my own motion. The smooth surface of the water reflected the light my glow stick cast until I could see almost the entirety of the cave.

The place was expansive, bigger than two aircraft hangars jammed together. The ceiling was a great cathedral of enormous, polished stalactites made of some kind of glossy rock, their inverted spires towering over their neighbors, jockeying for the title of the grandest.

At the center of the lake, an island of pale moss gathered around a central pillar of rock that seemed to bear the load of everything above. Tumor-like blobs of amber grew from the sides of the pillar, in the process of slowly liquifying to coat the rock below.

With tired, wobbling steps, I sloshed through the mud to make my way to the island. The thought of solid ground beneath my feet and a quiet meal practically invaded my mind. They instantly became my only desires. Then, after a rest, maybe I could refill my tanks and move on. Way after.

For now, though, I just wanted to be still.

The air was thick with the smell of sulfur, like rotten eggs or biomass rotting in a pond. Back home, if we didn't purify our water, it smelled like this. Awful, for sure, but at least it was familiar.

I plopped down in the moss-covered mud, my back to the glossy rock, and I just let the world turn around me for a while. My inner ear seemed to be reluctant to give up the feeling of constant motion I'd acquired in the Under-river, and the world seemed to constantly tilt from side to side.

So, where was I now? The Under-lake?

I allowed myself a sigh of relief. I was alive and breathing. That was something to celebrate. Putting down my glow rod and stowing my air canister, I summoned my final piece of dried meat from Tiba. I promised myself I'd savor this one, once I was out.

Well, I was out, or at least out of my cell. After so long living in a closet-sized tomb of rock, the lake seemed so big—endless, even.

I took a bite of the meat, tearing it with my teeth and letting the spice tingle in my mouth.

"Ay loss mu-y'iah," a voice called out.

I took another bite of my jerky, closing my eyes and letting go of that ball of worry in my stomach, at least for now.

"Me tek oosrah mule," someone said again, her voice, a sweet, cold soprano, delicate like a flute of crystal.

I shuddered awake—or maybe I'd always been awake. My eyes felt so heavy, my limbs like they were made of lead, but my heart hammered at my chest so hard the muscles in my neck twitched in time with the beat.

"Ooh loktika morishna booleahn," she said.

My head lolled to the side, so I could turn toward the voice.

It was a woman—or at least she was shaped like one, tall and lithe. Her sparkling, pale skin practically glowed, broken only by the blush of her cheeks and the curtains of raven hair that were the only things covering her nudity. She glided toward me, her steps so light, the soft moss did little more than tremble slightly at her touch.

I was awake now. Probably. My eyes kept trying to close without my permission, and my insides wobbled like I was standing too close to an atmo-rocket on takeoff.

Smiling, the mystery woman leaned over and offered her hand to me. Now that she was close, her features seemed slightly exaggerated, sharper than I was accustomed to, the eyes too far apart, too large, and her chin too narrow. Stubby little antlers protruded from the backs of her temples, too, as if I needed another reminder that I was far from home. Her hair smelled of flowers and spring rain.

My pulse quickened.

I got up on my own, not daring to touch the woman's hand, not that I would have been able to anyway. Once I made to stand, she practically leapt away, dancing over the moss carpet, light as a feather, her hair framing her body in fascinating ways.

She looked back at me and giggled invitingly.

"Hey, stop," I slurred. Staggering, I reached out, not wanting her to go too far into the water. It could be dangerous in the water. "Don't go in there. It's—"

The woman danced back again, this time offering a twirl of flowing limbs and hair and floral scent that warmed me, made me . . .

I took a step forward, the mud giving way with a *shlorp* as my foot broke through the moss, and I tripped.

That's what saved my life.

I caught myself with my hands, feeling the mud slide between my fingers and up my wrists, but I was low to the ground now. Looking up to make sure I didn't lose sight of my new lady friend, I got a good view of the surface of the water.

Calm and glassy before, the water roiled now, seething and sloshing up on the bank of my island. Mist filled the cavern (or had it been there already?), thick and tinted with particulates, something . . . fuzzy, maybe pollen or spores. A shadow of something long and slithering passed beneath the surface of the lake.

I shook my head and slapped myself to get some of my awareness back. Adrenaline was coursing through me now, clearing my mind and enhancing my senses to let me pick up on a low vibration, a hum that quivered just beyond my hearing but enticed sympathetic echoes in my head and in my body. I reached back and picked up my glow rod, holding it high.

As I did so, the woman vanished beneath the surface of the water, and, despite myself, I nearly cried out and dove in after her, so strong was the compulsion.

*Get it together, Ryan. This is the last place you'd want to find a girl.*

I forced the urge to follow the lady to take a back seat to my conscious thoughts. Then I turned in a circle to make sure I was—

My light fell upon something huge and round with a green, waxy skin suspended by thick stalks that rose from the water. Drops of moisture fell from its skin into the pool below, with tiny drip, drip, drips. It reminded me of a bulb, like a flower that had not yet bloomed.

Smoothly, silently, a giant, fanged, pink and yellow tri-petaled maw unfurled itself from the pale bulb, its yawning expanse wide enough to swallow me twice. It made no sound except for the air it displaced as it rushed toward me, colored flaps quivering as it moved.

"Whaaa!" I shrieked, rearing back and chucking my only source of light straight down the creature's throat.

# CHAPTER EIGHTEEN

# Attack the Mock

The plant creature, if that's what it was, didn't even try to dodge. In fact, the petals closed around the glow rod as it spun into the back of the thing's throat, plunging me into darkness. Then, with a muffled *FWOOMPH!*, there was a flash of purple through a slit in the monster's mouth, as it de-formed and split from the concussive force of the blast.

Back to being in pitch dark, I scrambled to the side, my feet tearing through the sucking mud until I felt the pillar where I'd tried to rest. Placing my back to it, I summoned a chunk of scrap iron I hadn't had a chance to use yet.

Volatility [1 MP/sec]

I didn't try to control the amount of mana I used for this one. I just poured it on, watching the cave get brighter and brighter. Unfortunately, the mist I'd observed earlier was thick in the air, swirling and billowing in confusing patterns as my light tried to penetrate. Indistinct, dark shapes the size of trucks stalked through the fog everywhere I turned.

Detect Limestone wasn't giving me anything. Whatever this place was made of, it wasn't that. Maybe the silt mound I stood upon was too tall to let me see the actual cave floor.

I activated Detect Iron, and the world lit up, but not like it did when I was working with pure ore. This was more of a subtle glow in my senses, dimmer than the concentration of iron in my blood but still better than nothing. I stood on a mound of diffuse iron, more concentrated farther down in the mud.

Surprisingly, the pillar at my back was the highest concentration of the element aside from me.

Feathery flakes of something drifted down on me from overhead, so light and insubstantial my eyes couldn't make them out, and when they touched my skin, they dissolved, leaving behind a sticky sort of residue I couldn't brush off.

I slowed my breaths, looking down so as not to get the stuff on my face or take it into my lungs. I wished I had enough of a shirt left to make a rudimentary mask, but I didn't get that chance.

Something big shot out of the dark from behind me, my Detect Skill warning me just in time for me to dive to the side. Meanwhile, I clutched my glowing grenade light tight in my hand, making sure to treat the item as gently as I could. The creature's petals bit down where I was with a *SNAP!*, while I crawled around the pillar to put it between me and my attacker, only looking up again once I sensed the thing starting to retreat.

Before it slipped back into the fog, I caught a glimpse of some of those petals as they collapsed back in on themselves to become a bulb again. Then it was gone, out of range of Detect and my light, just in time for another attack to come from behind.

This time, I wasn't able to dodge properly. The flower monster rushed me, already at tremendous speed by the time it entered the ten-foot radius for Detect, and I was only able to roll on my belly for a few feet before it was upon me. The pink and yellow flaps opened wide and draped down over me with wet slaps, the fangs thankfully missing me, penetrating the mud instead. Disturbingly warm and wet, the monster's mouth wrapped around me like a disgusting, smothering blanket.

The creature's mass bore me down into the ground, crushing me into the silt until I was below the waterline. Foul liquid rushed into my eyes, ears, and nose, but the experience didn't last long. Soon I was moving. I had the sensation of being whipped in one direction, then the next, and then there was a muffled crash, and the walls of the creature's mouth cooled.

I thrashed at the fleshy petals, trying to make some room to move around, but, if anything, they tightened around me, constricting me until there was no room to get any force behind my kicks. I tried Devouring Grasp, but the walls of the bulb were too slick and rubbery to get a good grip.

*No. No. No!*

I wasn't going out like this. I still had the grenade in my hand. I could detonate it and hope for the best, but that best would probably result in my death. The blast would probably kill me in this confined space, and if it didn't I would be concussed and deaf: easy pickings if I didn't kill the monster in one blow.

Water rushed in from around me to fill what space I had left, quickly cutting off what little air I had. Something else was in the water, too, something that stung my eyes and made my skin itch. I'd handled enough chemicals to recognize the signs of something corrosive.

It was going to drown me. Then it was going to digest me.

Detect Iron told me I was in one of the bulbs, attached to a long vine about as thick as I was, and I was slowly settling on the bottom of the lake.

Luckily, I had just come from an underwater ordeal, and I'd come equipped. Letting go of my grenade to let it sink down to the bottom of the bulb, I contorted my body, shrinking down into a ball so I could get some room to summon my last full air tank. It appeared in front of my face, and I went right to Shaping the aperture to allow me to breathe.

The stinging digestive juices were becoming more intense. My entire body burned, even my eyes, so much I couldn't keep them open anymore, and when I closed them, the chemical went to work on my eyelids. I fought the urge to scratch or rub at the sensation, knowing it wouldn't help. It was maddening.

*Think, Ryan. Think. What do we have?*

I breathed in from my air canister, held it, then breathed out, feeling the bubbles trickle past my face and pool above my head, forming the only spot inside my new prison that had any semblance of air.

With air came the liquid; the juices that spilled into my mouth tasted sour and numbed my taste buds. The thought of the stuff reaching inside my lungs terrified me.

*Have to act now. Do anything . . . Oh no.*

My shoulders slumped and my stomach sank as an anxious feeling came over me.

I had an idea, and it was a terrible one.

My oxygen canister was already saturated. All it took was a little push to pry open the breathing aperture wider and wider, until the air was leaving the tank in a bubbling, hissing torrent. Bubbles shot past my face, surrounding me. I dropped the tank, allowing it to spill its contents into the monstrous cavity as I summoned my weapon.

I'd improved the design somewhat since my prototype rifle. Now it was a one-handed model with an actual spring-loaded firing pin so I didn't have to slap it every time I wanted it to go off. It was still a single-shot type with a chamber I had to reload manually, but I hadn't had time to really get the whole thing working before I was out of food. Right now, the weapon looked like a bolt action ballistic rifle had had a baby with a potato gun. Hopefully it would do the trick.

The bulb was bigger now, the water that was once drowning me now a pool only deep enough to come up to my knees. My ears popped. The pressure was climbing fast.

Using Detect Iron, I found the front of the bulb where the lips folded around one another to create the seal.

I was only going to get one shot at this, and it was going to suck.

Taking a deep breath, I placed the muzzle of my pistol against the monster's mouth and pulled the trigger.

*FOW!*

The rubbery petals blew open, and the pressurized pocket of air I'd created rushed out before the water could reassert itself. I, too, was expelled from the bulb into the warmish water of the lake, with such force that I tumbled bonelessly along the muddy bottom for quite a ways before colliding with the slope of the central mud hill.

It took me a couple of seconds of stunned observation to determine which way was up, but then I was moving, jumping up, and breaking the surface to get fresh air in my lungs before my dense body could drag me back down.

As quickly as I could, I ascended the hill, jumping to catch my breath several times before I was able to properly get to dry-ish land. The amber glow of the pillar's weird growths called to me, promising me dependable oxygen and—

*Wait. Had those always been glowing?*

As I swam/ran for the top of the hill, the glow of the bulbs intensified, bathing the cavern in yellow, sulfuric light. Tendrils of mist wafted up from the surface of the water, slowly at first, but picking up speed, rapidly approaching fog-bank levels of obfuscation. The humming was back now, too.

By the time I was out of the water, the mist was everywhere, and the air vibrated with that smooth, dulling song that enticed me to lay down and die.

My body was on fire, seared raw by the digestive acid, my clothes were falling off me in clumps, and my chest heaved. With a shaking hand, I summoned another round of ammunition and slipped it into the pistol, snapping the chamber closed with a *clack*.

I looked everywhere at once, eyes wide, tracking with my weapon, and ready for anything to pop out of the yellow fog.

Then whatever was causing the amber lumps to glow stopped. They winked out like candles, plunging me back into darkness.

"Eer illeeu mina?"

Oh, wonderful. Horn Lady was back.

I turned, fighting the urge to sink down to my knees and relax my arms, just for a moment. I shook my head and worked my jaw, focusing on the burning of my skin to keep alert.

And then there she was. Beautiful, ethereal. Midnight hair on pale skin, shapely legs carrying her across the water, leaving barely a ripple. Her smile gleamed, and her big dark eyes invited me in.

I slapped myself. The rest of the cave was pitch dark, but Detect Iron was still going. While my flesh glowed with sparkling vitality and warm, rushing blood, the pale woman was a void in my senses—nothing but empty space.

*Drip. Drip. Drip.* Something behind me rose from the water.

I dashed to the pillar before the creature could strike. It got close, though—close enough to trigger Detect. In fact, quite a few of the bulbs were close to me now, just below the surface of the water, waiting for me to turn my back on them.

The woman approached me, smiling bashfully, looking down at her body, then peering at me through wavy hair. Her tiny horns glimmered, though there was no light.

"Ches tule mirakabory?" she asked, holding out a hand for me to take.

Detect told me the truth. There was nothing there.

*This is a spell.*

The realization hit me between the eyes, shattered my perceived reality, exploded in my mind. The curtain of the glamour lifted, was burned away. Suddenly, I could think clearly again.

I looked around. The mist, the woman, the darkness . . . all of it was gone, or, more precisely, it was there, but it had taken on a translucent quality, one that I could easily see through. The humming was just a buzzing like so many insects. Yes, my eyes saw the illusion, but they saw it for what it was now—no more than a light show or maybe a waking dream.

The yellow light was back, the orbs on the pillar burning brightly like miniature suns, bathing the rest of the cavern in a yellow so intense I could see the rest of the monster or monsters below the surface of the lake, waiting there patiently for an opening.

What's more, the walls and pillar were clearly not made of rock. No, the pillar was made of pink fleshy fiber with yellow streaks, just like the inside of the bulb mouths. The thing blurred as it vibrated at a frequency I couldn't hear but I could feel.

I took a step back from the pillar, shaking my head at the enormity of how screwed I was. The whole cave was alive.

*Drip. Drip. Drip.*

This time, I could see the bulbs rising from the water. Not a single one this time, but many. They were everywhere. Maybe the monster realized I wasn't fooled anymore, or maybe it was tired of wasting energy on me and just wanted dinner to be ready. Whatever it was, this was the endgame. I was out of tricks.

One by one, the petals unfurled themselves, revealing their pink and yellow insides and hard, fang-covered tips. Except for two that hung limply from their vines, one shredded from the inside at the neck and the other with sagging, ripped lips that leaked honey-colored fluid.

I swallowed. I couldn't kill them all. Well, maybe not.

Calling on my Spatial Storage yet again, I summoned my last remaining air supply, the tank I'd half-drained when I'd arrived here.

Volatility [1 MP/sec]

I invited the wild mana in, as much as I could, for one second. Two. Three.

I kept the spell channeling for as long as the creature would give me. The wild mana suffused the tank's structure, mixing in among its matter, quivering behind all the molecules, practically bursting with anticipation at being set free.

Five. Six.

*Video games had it right. In a boss fight, aim for the glowing weak spot.*

The flower monster's many mouths reared back and coiled their vines in preparation for a strike.

Seven. Eight. The aluminum was a brand in my hand, searing my skin.

I'd run out of time.

I flung the air canister at the pillar, up high where the amber tumors grew, as far from me as I could.

It flew up and away, far up to the ceiling of the cavern before it reached its apex. Meanwhile, I dove toward the relative safety of the water.

With a flick of will, I broke the containment for my Volatility spell, triggering its detonation. My body hit the water with a splash just as one of the petal mouths slammed into me from above and wrapped its smothering plant flesh around me.

*BOOM!*

# CHAPTER NINETEEN

# Earn Weird Loot

The monster's desire to eat me protected me in the end.

My body dragged me underwater just as the mouth closed around me, cocooning me yet again, along with as many gallons of nasty water as these things could hold.

When the explosion ripped through the cavern, I felt the tremors of the shockwave through the surrounding water, but the creature itself didn't remain remotely still after that. Whereas last time, it tried to envelop me, entrap me, and digest me, this time it thrashed violently, bucking like a mechanical bull. My blood rushed to my head as I was flung up and around, colliding with something hard. Then I was moving again, whipped down to crash into the surface of the water, only to roll on my side and scrape along what I assumed was the bottom of the lake for who knows how long.

HP 10/83

You have been awarded 7,034 Experience points. [16,210 base (+1,681 Level, +2,111 camp, -12,968 non-combat Class)]

Level Up!
You are now Level 8.
Max HP +5
Max MP +5
+1 Attribute point.

Achievements awarded this Level:

Inventor: You have created at least five new designs this Level. [+1 Mind]
Ambitious: You have defeated a foe above your Level. [+1 to lowest Level Ability]
Boss Killer: You have defeated a foe far above you in Level. [+2 to all Attributes]

Level Up!
You are now Level 9.
Max HP +5
Max MP +5
+1 Attribute point.

Achievements awarded this Level:
Spirit of the Warrior: You gained 51% of your Experience this Level from defeated foes as a non-combat Class. [+3 spirit]
Ambitious: You have defeated a foe above your Level. [+1 to lowest Level Ability]
Boss Killer: You have defeated a foe far above you in Level. [+2 to all Attributes]

The strange euphoria passed through me, so intense I started to suspect it was another spell, a last attempt by the plant monster to convince me to lay down and be devoured, but if I was getting Experience, something had to have just died. I just had to hope the thing's death throes wouldn't kill me.

Eventually, the violent motion eased to a halt, and the petals lost their tough, slick texture, curling and shrinking in on themselves, their colors losing all of their vibrancy. Then the monster lost whatever energy it had been using to keep its mouth closed, going limp and practically dumping me out along with the rest of the bulb's mouthful.

I fell maybe a few feet, crashing into the water and going under yet again, but I wasn't ready to take the plunge, despite the soothing coolness of the water after my dip in acid. My remaining air tanks were empty, and I couldn't swim worth a damn anymore. I needed to stay above the waterline or risk death by drowning.

Detect Iron told me a lot of long, thin creepers grew in complicated braiding patterns along the wall here, so I used those vines—along with the paltry buoyancy the water offered me—to haul myself up and get some air.

Apparently, the monster had carried me to the far wall of the cavern before it died. This part of the lake was absolutely covered in greenery from the vines that let me climb out of the water to pale clusters of leaves with spiky red flowers growing from their centers.

The island where most of the fight had taken place still glowed in the distance maybe a hundred yards away, but it was a mess. The cavern's roof was splattered with glowing amber fluid that slowly congealed at the low points of the rock and dripped down to the floor in with fat *splotłs*. The floor, similarly, was bathed in glowing yellow goo that ran in slow motion down the bank into the lapping water.

I hung there for a bit, catching my breath, taking inventory.

Loot Ancient Mockvine? Y/N

Oh, so that meant these vines were part of the larger creature, too. I answered "No" for now, though. I wasn't in any position to collect loot, hanging on to the wall like I was. I'd need some solid footing for that.

Summoning one of my two empty tanks, I got to Shaping, expanding the structure, thinning out the walls and enlarging the capacity until I figured it had enough air to compress and get me back to the island. Then I sealed the tank and shrunk it again. The process took much too long, and by the time I made it back to the island, I was so tired I thought I might actually fall asleep without magical assistance this time.

However, I had things to do. Loot stuff.

I crouched down next to the flaccid mass of rubbery plant matter that used to be the central pillar of this room and gave it a poke.

Loot Ancient Mockvine? Y/N

The room practically exploded in rainbow light. The ground, the walls, the ceiling, underwater—all of it warped and wobbled as the cavern became a swirling display of garish color that boggled the senses. Then the cave was back to absolute darkness.

*Uh. Okay. Not sure I would have done that if I'd known it would kill the light.*

I fished around in my Spatial Storage for something to use as a light, but I had nothing left to sacrifice. I had my air tanks, some bundles of Mendau, Hunty's spear, and some of my ammunition worms.

Sighing with regret, I summoned a single round of ammunition. These things were too valuable to use as exploding candles, but I needed this.

Volatility [1 MP/sec]

I didn't put much power into it, just enough to have it give off sufficient light to see the immediate area. Maybe if I detonated it while it was buried in the mud, I could salvage the pieces and Automate it once more.

The light was dim, but I was back to seeing with my eyes again.

In front of me was a pile of nasty, wet plant, but at least the System claimed it was significant.

> Mockvine Fiber Bundle x 400: Fibers gathered from the remains of an Ancient Mockvine. These fibers perform many duties while they are alive within a specimen, carrying nerve signals, nutrients, sunlight, and mana to all parts of the plant. With age comes sophistication, and mockvines are not an exception to this rule. These fibers are of the highest quality and conduct complicated patterns of mana nearly instantaneously over long distances.

> Mockvine Flower x 140: Mockvine flowers grown by an Ancient Mockvine. While attached to a living specimen, these flowers produce hallucinogenic pollen that can be deployed as the mockvine lures and ultimately devours its prey. Has multiple medicinal uses.

> Mockvine Heartstrings: The "heart" of an Ancient Mockvine. This part of the plant serves as the central nervous system and resource distribution center for the entire plant. Not useful on its own but highly sought after by alchemists and collectors alike.

*Okay. So, I have weird plant stuff now. Hooray.*

I didn't see an immediate use for the loot, but I wasn't about to argue with the System over this. Besides, that's why I had Spatial Storage, right? I put my hand on the bundle and willed it inside . . . but only a small part of the pile disappeared.

*Right. Gotta do it one piece at a time.*

It took a painfully long time, all while I was fighting to stay awake, but I was able to whittle the pile down to where I was nearly able to see the ground again. With that, I made an exciting discovery.

> Ruined Chain Hauberk: A suit of chainmail once worn by a caravan guardsman. Pitted, rusted, and ripped, this armor has seen better days.
> Plate Helmet: Steel plate helmet once worn by a crusading hero.

Underneath the pile of plant loot there was an assortment of real, actual, no-bullshit loot, and it was mine. My metallic heart warmed at the sight of it all. It was about time I got some good stuff, or at least some *interesting* stuff.

Damaged pieces of armor, broken weapons, bits of jewelry, gemstones, and gold pieces were everywhere, scattered over the mud, while the heavier bits had sunk down to where I had to fish them out. There was even a skull in there, generally humanoid but made of some kind of clear crystal.

One by one, they went into my storage. The space, while not bottomless, didn't seem to mind the influx of mass I was sticking in there. It felt like I was dropping things into a swimming pool, and I'd only just now covered the bottom.

It was when I found a smooth orb of crystalized something or other that I ran into a problem. Placing my hand on the orb, I willed the Spatial Storage to swallow the thing up, but nothing happened. I tried again.

Vost'ralixal

*What? That's it? No description about a giant that lost his glass testicle or anything?*

I picked the orb up and brought it up to my face, peering into it to try and determine what made it special. Why didn't it behave like the others? It didn't feel particularly heavy or—

"*Waaaaaaaaaaa!*" A bone chilling wail like something out of a nightmare shook the orb and my hand, as green and white fire erupted from the crystal surface.

I dropped the ball into the muck and leapt backward, holding my charged iron worm over my head in preparation for my next life-or-death struggle, but the fight never came.

"*Aaaaaaaaaaaaaaaaa!*" The orb just screamed and screamed, the unnatural fire blazing on its surface. The fire gave off no heat, I realized, confirming that was the case by checking my hand for fresh burns but finding none.

"Hello?" I called to the orb. "Excuse me . . . Hello?!" I was shouting now, trying to get through the ceaseless wailing to be heard, but if the orb was capable of communication, it gave no indication. It just . . . screamed.

It was bright, though. Nice and bright. The whole cavern lit up for me from wall to wall, even illuminating a few feet down under the water . . . where something shone.

"Okay, so I'm gonna go," I said, my attention split between the flaming orb and the new shiny thing in the water. "Good luck with . . . whatever this is. Yeah." I could barely hear myself at all, and I doubted the orb could hear me, either.

Broken Brightsteel Blade: A broken blade wielded by an ancient crusader who met his end not in war but in peace. The brightsteel still holds much of its power even after its sundering and long years underwater.

It was part of a sword or something similar. It was about three feet long, as wide as my palm and mirror-smooth. The edges weren't overly sharp—not molecularly exact like the edges I could make—but I was willing to bet this was as good as you could get with a whetstone. Strange markings crawled up the center of the blade with lots of loops and curves that flowed all the way to the point.

Detect Iron wasn't giving me anything, but the sword certainly felt like metal.

Shape [4 MP/sec]

I let my mana flow through my hand and wrap around the blade. If I could saturate the metal, I would know more about its nature and maybe what I could do to use it, but I didn't get that far.

The metal accepted my mana. Violently.

I'd surrounded the broken weapon with it and it was beginning to squeeze in between the molecules when suddenly my power was wrenched away from me. There was a horrifically bright flash of light and a burst of energy that fried my nerves, burned my skin, and blew me backward to fall to the ground in a twitching heap . . .

. . . where I finally got that nap I'd been craving.

This was as good a time and place as any.

When I came to, the orb was mercifully silent, and the cavern was pitch-black.

> You take 20 points of Light Damage from brightsteel feedback.
> You take 4 points of Impact Damage.
> HP 6/103

"Gaaaah," was all I could say, in a pained groan. The air smelled like smoke and burnt hair, and my ears rang constantly.

*Okay, System. I'll never complain about extra points in Body again.*

In fact, I dropped all five of my points I'd been saving into Body right there, spiking it up to 24, observing as my current and max HP rose with every point.

> HP 14/115

Moving was agonizing. My flesh felt brittle and crispy, and I had to use my metal arm to do most of the work of dragging my body away from the water's edge. From there, it was just about sitting there and letting the System fix me over time.

I was in too much pain to go back to sleep, so I simply just watched my HP ticking up and the light levels in the cave slowly rising over time. Eventually, the farthest wall, where I'd been dumped as the mockvine died, was visible, slightly lit from underneath in pale white.

*Hang on . . . That's sunlight.*

Outside this place was sunlight!

# CHAPTER TWENTY

# Hit the Road

Let it never be said that I don't learn from my mistakes. Well, some mistakes more than others.

The last time I saw sunlight on this planet, I'd nearly died from light exposure, an experience I wasn't in a hurry to replicate. This time, however, I was going to handle it correctly, preparing myself for anything and everything. Laying out a meticulous plan that could not possibly fail.

This had nothing to do with the fact that I'd just blown myself up and needed my HP to regenerate before I could chance another encounter with Ralqir's generally hostile environment.

Once I felt well enough to sit up again, I got to work preparing for my emergence into the outside world.

The sun was going to be a problem, of course, but I also needed to consider the wildlife.

I gasped as something cold tapped my foot.

Fortunately, it was an old friend. My iron ammunition worm, fresh from the water, wobbled there in the mud. The little guy had snuck up on me, but I was glad to see it. Apparently, Detect Iron had fallen off sometime while I'd been unconscious, and the presence of real light had distracted me somewhat. Otherwise, I would have seen this coming. The construct was inert now that it had done its job and returned to me, its body back to being long and straight and the legs drawn back into its mass.

I'd been tossed all over this cavern after the monster swallowed me for the second time, and the worm had probably been slithering along for hours trying to reach me.

"Glad to see you made it, little buddy. What a journey you must have had," I whispered.

For some reason, I didn't want to raise my voice in this place. Maybe it was the memory of having had to share the space with a predator earlier in the day, or maybe it was the weird, screaming orb thing. I'd felt a little guilty waking the thing up or setting it on fire or whatever I'd done. Now I was a little worried it was listening to me or I was disturbing it by being here.

The armor I looted from the mockvine was a pretty nice upgrade considering I was wearing next to nothing right now. The problem, however, was that it was just the metal parts of the gear. I imagined that the people that wore these things met the same end I almost did, inside a bulb, covered in acid, but, unlike me, they didn't make it out and have supernatural regeneration. The mockvine's victims' organic bits dissolved along with their clothes and whatever padding and straps they used to make their armor wearable.

Regardless, I compiled a set of the best pieces and set it aside to put on later. I'd take a little discomfort if that meant I wasn't literally running around naked.

Next, I refilled my two remaining aluminum oxygen tanks, this time making use of all the extra empty space this cavern afforded me, allowing the aluminum balloon to stretch far and wide before I shrunk it down to its compressed form. If I had to guess, they'd last twice as long as the original model, which was good, because I had no way to get the others back.

After that, I felt it was time to cannibalize some of the leftovers from the loot pile to improve my handgun, somewhat. My single-shot model worked, yes, but the design was a function of having few materials to work with and needing it to be compact for use in tight spaces.

Well, I was about to get out into the wider world, and that meant I may need more than one bullet. I still needed to keep it simple, though. With how filthy this water was and the amount of silt on the bottom of the cave, I had mud and grit to consider. Fewer moving parts meant fewer malfunctions which meant fewer chances at me becoming a corpse.

After some time thinking, I settled with a sort of hopper system, essentially a six-inch, boxy funnel that would hold five bullets, attached to the chamber part of the weapon. After I fired a round, I'd release the catch on the side of the pistol, pull the slide back, and a new round would fall into place. With how exact my measurements were, I felt that my chances of jamming the weapon were pretty close to zero unless I dumped a pound of mud into the hopper or tried to shoot at a weird angle.

I practiced a little with the new setup, holding the weapon in my metal hand, then racking the slide. With my fleshy hand, I would then summon more ammo to appear between my fingers and slide it into the hopper. I had five shots, and reloading the hopper took about ten seconds.

*Good enough for now. Just need to hope I don't have to shoot at anything while upside down. Note to self: make a real magazine ASAP.*

My setup wasn't perfect, but I was on borrowed time here. I hadn't counted on the water being so dirty by the time I escaped the mountain. Honestly, I hadn't thought too far beyond, "Get out of my cell. Find air. Repeat." Now, though, I had to consider that I was back to having no fresh water to drink, and I was fresh out of food.

Seeing how close I was to being out in the world again, I felt woefully unprepared. How much of that was my fault and how much was unavoidable, I didn't know.

My HP was nearing the full mark at 98 now, and I had one more thing to do before I left.

Stretching my aching muscles for the first time in hours as I stood, I glanced over at the water's edge where I'd, uh . . . left the brightsteel. Yes, it almost killed me when I tried to Shape it, but I wasn't about to leave it behind. You never really knew when an exploding sword blade would come in handy, after all, and I would be lying if I said I wasn't curious about just how it worked and what it was made of. The occasional explosion was a small price to pay for that kind of potential. I had HP now, and if I didn't treat it like the resource it was, I wouldn't be using all the tools available to me.

I did, however, take precautions before I went to pick the brightsteel up. I slipped into my new set of rusty armor consisting of the chain hauberk which hung down to my knees, a steel wrist guard, and the top of the steel helmet, the rest of which I'd used to modify my firearm.

I tried on a set of foot coverings that the System labeled as "chausses" but I couldn't get them to stay up, even after some Shaping. As my legs flexed, the material just worked its way down until I was wearing them around my ankles. After a frustrating twenty minutes of trying to get them to work, I added them to the scrap pile.

So, wearing my chain-mail dress and steel cap, I approached the brightsteel again. This time, I was going to keep my mana away from the thing until I was in a safe-enough place to experiment with it. I placed my hand on it and willed it to go in my Spatial Storage.

Instead of the gentle glow that I usually got when I did this, though, the blade flared white, flames licking up and burning my hand even as the item disappeared.

I sucked in a breath through my teeth and rubbed my hand on my armor like I'd just touched a hot stove, but, after a brief mental check, I sensed the brightsteel was, indeed, in my Spatial Storage. I felt it settle in with the rest of the stuff I had in there, deceptively quiet and docile.

My new toy didn't play well with my mana. Was it still burning inside my storage? I hoped not.

*Better have full HP when I bring it out again. Just in case.*

At least I didn't have to hold on to it.

With everything in hand or tucked away in a mysterious pocket dimension, I set out into the water once again, headed in the direction of the light. I stopped only to gather an armful of vines from the cave wall that I could drape over my head as a shield against the light, doubling as a rudimentary camouflage.

My environment got much, much brighter once I guessed I'd crossed the threshold from the cave to the outside, but there was almost zero visibility. The death throes of the mockvine hadn't done the water any favors in terms of clarity. Murky and full of floating debris, it was like trying to navigate a jungle in twilight.

Detect Iron helped a bit, giving me a clear picture of the slope of the terrain and where the plants were. I even spotted a few little darting fish and insects that made the water their home. I trudged along the bottom in the murky yellow glow until I felt the tint of the light change overhead, hopefully indicating I'd found a spot of shade.

Gnarled roots of a nearby tree jutted out into the water and stabbed down into the mud at my feet. They'd be as good a climbing aid as I would find. If I wanted out of this water, now was the time.

My exit from the water proved difficult. I had been heavy even before I'd donned armor. Now that I had it on along with pounds of plant matter concealment, getting myself up was nearly impossible without something solid to grip, and even then slick creeping algae and mud fought my attempts to grab onto my handholds.

I had to use both hands to grasp the roots and haul myself up, meaning I had to store my air tank, climb for a bit, then summon it again to take a breath. It was slow, tedious progress toward the surface, but somehow I got there eventually.

Climbing is now Level 6.

When my head broke the surface, I took in a long, deep lungful of air, my first untainted by disgusting water in half an hour. The stench of sulfur was still everywhere, but it was more muted than inside the cave. Almost instantaneously, a cloud of tiny flying insects was buzzing around my face.

*Glorious.*

Crawling and slithering out of the muck, I pulled myself onto dry land one slow inch at a time. Well, nothing was actually dry here, much like the cave. The ground was a soup of sulfuric decay with a film of algae that clung to my armor and skin.

I was in a swamp. That much I'd guessed even from below the water, but seeing it was another thing.

So far, all I'd seen of the surface of Ralqir were grand, cyclopean forests of towering trees with trunks the size of buildings.

The land here was also covered in trees but of a different species to the giants. They were short, twisted things with knotted bark, covered in gray, fluffy moss that periodically fell in clumps to sink down into the bog. The gnarled dwarfs hunched over the water with long, whiplike branches that hung down to brush the top of my head. The air was heavy with humidity, blurring distant landmarks and preventing a true, unfiltered view of my surroundings.

Everything felt like it was invading my personal space, reaching out to touch me or smear some gunk on me. This part of Ralqir loomed more closely than I was used to, more claustrophobic, and that was saying something coming from a guy who had just spent months locked in a goblin broom closet.

Back the way I'd come, the greenery was thinner, and what little there was, sagged, with waxy brown leaves raining down from above to disappear into the muck. If I squinted, I could almost see the trees decaying in real time and succumbing to rot as their roots turned loose from the soil and allowed the bog to claim them entirely.

*They aren't real.*

The realization came as I watched one of the decaying tree trunks curling in upon itself and shriveling to half its size.

Just as I had used the dead vines to disguise myself as I swam, the mockvine had used a disguise as well. The fact that a green vine was managing to flourish in a place with no sun had been bugging me. Producing chlorophyll underground didn't make any evolutionary sense, but maybe it used these parts of itself, camouflaged as other types of plants, to get sunlight while it lured animals in with its spells. It was a plausible theory, untestable now that I'd killed the thing and made off with its guts.

I shook my head, mentally adding all of the plants to the list of things that wanted me dead. Then I got underway, picking my way between the deeper parts of the water and doing my best not to slip as I followed the snaking path the tree trunks made away from my cave and into the unknown.

For all of five minutes.

It was so sudden. I was so busy looking down to be sure of my footing that when I stepped onto the cobblestone surface of a road, it took me a full ten seconds to realize what I was looking at. I turned my head to the right and left, squinting to make sure I really was seeing what I was seeing.

*A road.*

It meant civilization. A path of worked stone about as wide as a large truck, comfortably able to fit six or so people abreast. It stretched on into the distance in either direction where it slowly curved out of sight. The rocks were a dark grayish color, unbroken except where one stone gave way to another. Though there was debris on the road such as dead branches and decaying clumps of moss, nothing grew on the stones or between them. No weeds or algae. No fungus. The trees still blocked out the sun overhead, but I noticed that none of their branches grew down far enough to be in danger of brushing against the cobbles, either.

Out of curiosity, I bent down and wiggled one of the stones out of its spot and held it up to my face. Its surface was fairly smooth but the edges had too many right angles to have happened naturally. What's more, it felt cold—colder than the Under-river, even.

*Weird.*

After a few seconds, the cold felt extremely uncomfortable in my palm, like tiny knives digging into my bones, and, now that I thought about it, my feet were starting to feel the same. I transferred the rock over to my prosthetic, hoping for some clarification.

Consume Quellstone? Y/N

"No, thanks," I said, putting the little rock back where it came from.

*Quellstone. Might be best to walk on the side of the road, at least until I find some boots or learn more about the stuff.*

There was no question that I needed to follow this road. Roads meant people. People generally meant sources of fresh water and food, unless they were weird frog people or something. Then I'd be back to square one.

The real question was, which way?

Both ways led away from the cave, which I was happy about. The landscape looked mostly inhospitable and swampy in either direction I looked, and the road didn't have any signs or landmarks. Generally, people built roads *between* things, so, theoretically, either way I chose would lead me to people eventually.

So, with no other factors to help me make my decision, I simply chose to go right.

My bare feet squished into the mud to the side of the road as I set off. The quiet, close feeling the swamp had exuded before began to fade after maybe a quarter mile, feeling more alive by the step.

There was no wind here, not even a breeze, but I was past my need for moving air to feel comfortable. It was amazing how much you could hear in the quiet like this. Frogs or something like them croaked from the slimy pools next to the trees, and screeching black birds called to each other from fat nests of dried moss. Some kind of deep, rhythmic barking animal was out there somewhere, too, its calls seeming to dominate the other creatures of the swamp, forcing them to take a collective breath every time it made its noises. Whatever it was, it had to have been in the trees or in the water, because I couldn't see it from where I walked.

*Fine by me. You leave me alone, I'll leave you alone.*

The peaceful stroll didn't last.

The road took a winding route through the swamp, around the trees, probably by necessity of the geography, so I didn't see the corpses until I was almost right upon them. Strewn about the road, there were six of varying sizes, their dull-colored clothes ripped in some places, bloodied in others.

I stopped and crouched down to peer over the surface of the cobblestone, doing my best to search for danger among the trees before I let my eyes lock onto the dead people.

My scan netted me nothing. The swamp looked as devoid of threats as ever, present company excluded.

I didn't like this. They were just lying down on the road, as if they'd just decided to take a nap. While I was sure I'd find out what killed them if I investigated, it bothered me that the bodies looked so unnatural. No flies buzzing around the area; no scavengers picking at the corpses. Nothing. If this had just happened, I could maybe wrap my head around it, but I didn't get that vibe from the scene. It felt like I'd stumbled upon an open-air morgue, and it was setting off all my alarm bells.

The frustrating thing was that I needed to know what kind of people I was dealing with here on Ralqir, other than goblins. It was knowledge I had to acquire if I was going to interact with others at the end of this road, if only to lessen the surprise factor if they were some creepy variant of insect or cephalopod.

Plus, I . . . just couldn't let it be. They weren't human, but they looked close enough to trigger that part of my brain that felt for my fellow man. I'd dealt with enough death in the recent past but not quite enough to make me callous. Maybe these folks had families that would want to know what had happened and where to find their loved ones' bodies. Maybe the killers could be found and brought to justice eventually.

I sighed, resigned to my course of action.

Slipping out of my hiding spot, staying low, and stalking over to the corpses, I rolled the closest one over on its back.

It was a man, not like me but mostly humanoid and definitely male. He was hirsute, with brown hair covering most of his skin and a bushy beard that covered more of his head than it should have, encircling his face more like a mane than anything I was used to. Furthermore, he had a flat nose and narrow eyes, clouded over by death but still an easily discernible yellow. His throat sported a wicked gash with blackened, dried blood smeared over the skin.

To the hairy guy's left was a woman, face down on the cobbles, her dirty blonde hair caked with blood and speckled with plant debris. She had familiarly narrow facial features and little horns at her temples, indicating she was the same or a similar species to the one that the mockvine had used as a lure in its illusion. This lady didn't seem like she'd be dancing over any lakes though, since both of her legs were mangled messes of punctures and slashes from some kind of . . .

Suddenly, I got that feeling—that sudden drop in my insides. It was the feeling you got when you'd been caught doing something stupid, and a big, clenched, karmic fist was already speeding toward your head.

Then a hollow whistle sounded out from somewhere, and something hard and sharp slammed into the back of my leg, digging deep into my hamstring. My leg buckled, and I fell sideways onto the cobblestones. I clutched at the wound, feeling something cold and foreign protruding from my flesh. A pained groan escaped my throat as I bent at the waist to check the damage.

> Unknown attacks you for 11 Slashing Damage.
> You are bleeding. [1 HP/sec]

It was a hatchet, on the small side but sharp and heavy enough to bury itself deep in the muscle of my leg. What bits of the blade I could see were nastily serrated. Crude etchings decorated the flat of it, and blood-flecked white feathers dangled from a cord affixed to the haft. I wrapped my hands around the ax head, vacillating between attempting to rip the thing out or press the wound together to stanch the blood loss.

High guttural war cries rang out from everywhere at once as my unseen attackers swarmed around me.

# CHAPTER TWENTY-ONE

# Tank Some Damage

They dropped from the trees and popped out of the mud, one and all covered in mottled gray camouflage with twigs and clumps of moss glued to their skin. One of them even materialized from the trunk of a dead tree, like he'd been specifically painted to blend in perfectly there.

*Goblins. Again. Just how many flavors of goblin are there on this stupid planet?*

These, for sure, weren't my goblins. Stone Hearts favored spears and arrows and, from what I could gather, chose not to put themselves at risk through direct confrontation whenever possible. These goblins all held axes in one hand and feathered shivs in the other, and they sounded different to the Stone Hearts. It was subtle but noticeable to a guy who just had an extended stay among a different tribe. Most of these guys' shouts were some variation of "Kill!" or "Go! Go!"

As I attempted to rise, the pain in my leg screamed at me, flooding my synapses until it was all I knew. It hurt even worse than being dipped in acid, funnily enough. My new life was making me well-versed in the different kinds of pain and trauma one could endure. I'd need to make a chart or something when I got the chance, for posterity's sake.

The goblins charged me, each using a fighting form that had them holding their hatchets over their heads in preparation to throw while their knife hands were held out straight.

Thankfully, I was able to sit up before they got to me. My wounded leg didn't seem to want to straighten out, not with the serrated blade still inside of it, so I used the other one to stabilize myself and put up my hands.

"Hey! Stop! Wait!" I shouted at them. It wasn't my most persuasive choice of words, I'll admit. My mind was working in overdrive to figure a way out of this situation, but when you've got a half pound of cold metal jammed into your hamstring, there's only so much processing power you can afford the speech center of your brain.

Strangely, one of the goblins did actually pause. Not for long, just half a breath where his gait faltered and his knife drifted down a notch, but the moment didn't last.

The first goblin to reach me went for a stab with his leading hand. I twisted to the side and used my palm to slap the blow out of line, and I barely got my metal prosthetic up in time to catch the follow-up strike of the hatchet. The ax head slammed down on my forearm with a *CLANK!* that reverberated up the metal intensely enough to be felt in the rest of my body. My arm, as always, took the blow like a champ.

The ax, on the other hand, didn't survive. The head shattered, showering me in bits of pale metal while the haft exploded into a cloud of splinters in the goblin's face.

He hissed in pain as the wood found his eyes, and he blindly slashed at me as he tried to back away.

I used that brief window of vulnerability to reach out and grab his ankle

Devouring Grasp [5 MP/sec]
Goblin takes 15 Crushing Damage.

His leg didn't outright come off, unlike the Scourge-Touched's hands back in my cell. Instead, my steely grip crushed his bones to powder and mangled his flesh, accompanied by something like the sound of celery sticks in a vice. Now his screams no longer held coherent words as he frantically clawed at my unyielding fingers in an attempt at stopping the pain.

*CLANG!*

My vision flashed, and my head was batted to the side until it collided with my shoulder. Blinking, I turned to look behind me to find another hatchet blow coming down on my head, even as my helmet was still ringing from the first blow. The world wobbled and warped as my eyes relearned how to focus properly.

Summoning a defiant roar, I threw myself backward and twisted at the waist, yanking my new living, screaming goblin club off his feet and along for the ride. It was surprisingly easy, like swinging a particularly cumbersome pillow.

The goblin that tried to brain me danced back to avoid the blow, but he didn't account for my reach now that I was holding his friend. The two goblins collided together, my club's skull slamming into the other's collarbone with a wet snap. Then the two went down together, only one of them still moving. The goblin I still held by the ankle flopped bonelessly on the hard stones, while his friend clutched at his shoulder and gurgled something I couldn't make out.

*Definitely not complaining about more points in Body again.*

---

Goblin takes 20 Blunt Damage.
Critical Hit!
Goblins takes 27 Blunt Damage. [13 base + 14 bonus]
You have been awarded 9 Experience points. [25 base (+4 group, -20 non-combat Class)]
[Unknown] attacks you for 8 Piercing Damage.

---

Stabbing pain shot through my abdomen as another of the ambushers buried his blade in my side. My chain mail blunted some of the force, but at least a couple inches of the knife made it through to perforate me. I reflexively tried to curl inward to protect the injured area, unfortunately using the same muscles that had just been stabbed to perform the motion. A low, growling moan squirmed around in the back of my throat.

The goblin didn't try to follow up like his friend did. Instead, he danced back once I was within range to grab him, and he kept low, circling in a ready stance.

"Guys," I ground out through clenched teeth as I frantically twisted to keep an eye on the position of every goblin at once. The constant motion did wonderful things for my aching head, forcing me to swallow frequently so as not to vomit. "I don't want to fight, and I don't have anything you want." I thought about name-dropping the Stone Hearts, but the way Hunty told the story, Kuul might have burned a few bridges when it came time to stand against the Baned. The name might just make them want to desecrate my corpse after they killed me.

I counted three goblins now prowling around me and feinting little lunges with their knives. They didn't seem interested in talking, choosing instead to growl and hiss to distract me as the others took shots at my back.

Again, I whipped my goblin club in a wide arc, hoping to get lucky again or get a little space, but the little bandits were wise to the trick now. They stayed out of range until it was time to strike. They scored several little wounds over the next handful of seconds, shallow but quickly adding up to something debilitating.

As I blocked a third hatchet chop from the attacker in front of me, another goblin entered the fray, seeming to lurch out from behind one of the trees closest to the road and into the open. He wore dirty robes adorned with thick white fur lining the collar, sleeves, and hem, while metal chains dangled from manacles on his wrists. On his head he wore the skull of some kind of bird like a helm, decorated with blue painted sigils and metal hoops pierced through the eye sockets.

I wasn't about to wait to see what his deal was. Bracing myself, I decided "Screw it!" and flung my now-ruined goblin weapon at the fighter in front of me. It wasn't a great throw, more like a toss. My Body was higher than it used to be, but I was still throwing a floppy little person. People aren't meant for throwing. Still, I chucked the thing, sending the legs and arms windmilling toward my target. As he'd been doing for every one of my attacks, he dove to the side to dodge, but this gave me the space I needed to summon my pistol.

With a pulse of light, my weapon was in my hand, and I snapped a quick shot at Bird Skull Guy.

*POP!*

---

Goblin takes 18 Piercing Damage.
Goblin is bleeding.

---

The robed goblin had already opened his mouth to take in a big breath just as I shot him, but whatever he was about to say didn't leave his mouth. With a wet *Gack!*, he spun with the impact of my bullet until his back was to me, and went down clutching his chest. But he didn't die, at least not yet. My aim had been rushed, and the System didn't give me any Experience yet. I silently hoped that would keep the guy out of the fight until—

Something heavy slammed into my back. I felt something—a rib, maybe—give way with a pop, and then there was a hot sensation of blood rushing into places it should not be. The hatchet didn't make it all the way through my chain mail though, clattering down to the cold surface of the road.

I grunted, reflexively reaching around to my back to assess the damage, but I was holding my gun now, so I couldn't complete the motion. What I could do, however, was rack another round into the chamber.

As I *clack*ed the slide back to the ready position, the goblin in front of me danced in and slashed at my eyes, which I blocked with my metal hand before jamming the muzzle of my gun under the monster's ribs.

*FOMP!*

The round entered the soft parts of his abdomen, angled up to get his vitals. Whatever the bullet did in there, it was quick. The goblin went instantly limp, collapsing in a heap onto my good leg.

I turned around just in time to intercept another knife to the back. Only two goblins left now, and only one had his hatchet.

I spat on the cobblestones and bared my teeth. "Next one to stab me, I swear—"

Then a low, moaning, howl split the air and set my teeth on edge.

Bird Skull Guy was back, or at least he was conscious. He lay there on the road, one gnarled hand holding the side where blood was leaving him in spurts, the other reaching for the sky, crackling with blue sparks.

The air literally electrified. Goose pimples appeared on my flesh, my hair stood on end, and my muscles twitched of their own volition under my mail.

I wasn't being hurt, though. Not actively. Hesitantly, I took my eyes off the Bird Skull to bring the others into focus.

*Oh. That's bad.*

The metal blades of their weapons glowed, humming and popping with static as they made contact with larger particles in the air. Arcs of blue light spat from the sharpened edges and left behind floating tracers.

Behind me, the Skull Guy's song ceased, but the goblins' weapons continued to glow.

*That's very bad. Don't want to get hit by th— AUGHTERFAFEFMIMPH!*

Quick as a snake, the goblin that still held his hatchet threw the thing at my chest. I was on the ground and wounded. There was no chance to dodge.

Again, I took a hatchet to the chain mail, this time right in the sternum. Not only did the bones inside my chest cavity crack, but the lightning inside the blade now traveled through my mail and into my body, sending me spasming to the ground.

And it kept doing it, too. The ax hung there in my chest—maybe on the mail, maybe in the flesh. I couldn't tell. It did tase the hell out of me, though. Every muscle in my body cramped, my fingers curled inward mid-reload, making me drop my weapon. My diaphragm forced all the air from my lungs, and blood filled my mouth as I bit my tongue.

And I tasted . . . *cinnamon.* Why did I taste cinnamon?

Then the two goblins were upon me. Stabbing with their little knives, this time not bothering with any deliberate tactics. They were going for the vitals. Everything not lightning-related felt muted as the electricity overloaded my nervous system, but I could distinctly feel one of the knives enter my thigh, probably looking for an artery. The other worked on my upper half.

Most of the stabs were shallow. They were little knives, and their wielders were reluctant to touch me, probably not wanting to get a shock themselves.

I couldn't move. I could barely think. Magical lightning coursed through my body without end.

I could think of only one more card to play, a card I'd recently acquired and really didn't play well with mana. If I could trigger the feedback, maybe I could flip this chessboard.

From my Spatial Storage, I summoned the brightsteel blade into my palm.

*FWOOM!*

The world went white.

When my eyes finally snapped back into focus, I was lying on my side, the cold stones of the road numbing the skin on my face. My metal arm was wedged underneath me uncomfortably, and, at some point, I'd straightened out my injured leg. In front of my face, I clutched the brightsteel as its edges dug deep into blistered and blackened skin.

> You have been awarded 11 Experience points. [25 base (+4 group, +2 chain, -20 non-combat Class)]
> HP [21/115]

My body was a road map of pain. Nothing felt right except for maybe my prosthetic, and that was a whole other can of weird I didn't need to open just now. I gasped, filling my lungs with oxygen. It burned.

With a quick jerk followed by a groan, I propped myself up on an elbow, my heart thrumming loudly in my ears, the blood flow slowly bringing my limbs back to life. Adrenaline was finally rushing through me again, and it was going to work clearing my mind. I was in a fight. And I couldn't stop until it was over.

At that, I willed the brightsteel back into my Spatial Storage. I didn't feel any burning sensation this time, but that wasn't a very comforting thought. It meant the nerves in my hand were probably dead.

Grunting with effort, I reached around for my gun, finding it a few feet away. It, too, was looking rough, black smudges of soot streaking its otherwise uniformly gray exterior.

Weapon in hand—the metal one—I shook the hopper to make sure a round was in the chamber and pushed the slide forward.

The two ambushing goblins lay next to me, burned and battered from the explosion. One of them was more charred than the other, his face mostly gone. The other was trying to drag himself away, succeeding but slowly, one blood-smeared inch at a time.

I extended my arm and aimed carefully.

*POP!*

> You have been awarded 13 Experience points. [25 base (+4 group, +4 chain, -20 non-combat Class)]

I ended his life as quickly and humanely—whatever that meant—as I could. Even though he wouldn't have done the same for me.

The shaman—if that was the right word for Bird Skull Guy—was still breathing, but he was either passed out or pretending to be. Another carefully placed shot, and he lay still, too.

> Skill Unlocked: Pistols
> Your current Skill Level is 1.
> You have been awarded 34 Experience points. [44 base (+4 group, +6 chain,

-20 non-combat Class)]

I was not looking good. I was burnt, bleeding, and concussed. I was alive, though.

Sometimes it just came down to being able to tank a few hits.

*Hooray for my high Body Stat.*

Groaning, I flopped down on my back and lay there, amid the bodies of my enemies and their previous victims, letting the numbing cold of the . . . quellstone, was it? . . . soothe my aches. My hands trembled as I rested them on my stomach.

After a while, I checked my HP, hoping I'd seen the worst of it.

HP [9/115]

*Dammit. What's going on here? It should have ticked up by now.*

It didn't take a rocket scientist to figure out that the quellstone road was hurting me—or at least keeping me from healing. That was the only mystery factor here. Blood loss probably accounted for the rest.

It took herculean effort to drag myself all the way from the middle of the road to the comforting squishiness of the mud, where I flopped down on my face to let the System do its thing. Only then did my regeneration start to repair my body.

The process took a long while, made even longer by the fact that I had to extract a serrated goblin hatchet from my leg once I got a good buffer of HP between me and the Great Beyond. I was right to wait. When I ripped the thing out, it brought parts of me with it. The pain was so intense, I nearly lost consciousness, and the bleeding debuff I got afterward would have killed me if I'd done it right away.

Status gained: Bleeding [5 HP/sec]

Luckily, I was out of combat, and the debuff was gone after a handful of delirious seconds.

Hours later, when I'd reached about the three-quarters mark on my HP, my ammunition had all been restored, and, after a quick look around for watching eyes, I went back to loot the bodies.

I was able to search the ones the goblins had been using as bait to draw others in, with a quick pat-down, finding nothing except a few ripped coin pouches lying in the road. The monsters must have stripped everything except for the flashy bits to make the lure nice and shiny.

The goblin corpses, however . . . I let the System have its way with them.

In the end, I received six sets of hatchets and knives that the System tagged as "Baptized Bronze," a pouch of herbs, three coin purses conspicuously strewn about among the original corpses, a painting kit with brushes, a pair of manacles, and a copper amulet. That last one was what really interested me.

Copper Amulet of the Storm: Copper amulet forged by Shaman Zeck'tar. Cast in the Swift Talon Clan's holy crucible and tempered in the blood of a hatchling roc, this focus of will assists in the coalescing of Storm Mana.
Damage: N/A
Quality: Excellent
Style: Primitive
Magic: Draws in and condenses Storm Mana until the amulet is charged. Mana can be unleashed and directed as the user chooses.

That was interesting. Just how many types of mana were there? So far, the System had mentioned Hunger and Storm, two concepts that were as far apart from one another as you could get.

When I touched the amulet, I felt a slight tingle on my skin, and the hair on my arm stood at attention. How I would make the thing work, I didn't know. Should I feed mana into it? The only way I knew how to do that was by using my Abilities, and I didn't want to re-Shape the thing or program it to dance on little spider legs.

The goblins themselves—once the System had stripped them of their belongings—looked thin and frail. Their ribs showed through their pale, green skin, and their arms and legs seemed emaciated. That was interesting, too. They'd used the corpses of these people to lure others in, leaving the gold in the middle of the road to sweeten the pot. All of their victims wore good shoes, as well, with well-worn treads on the bottom. If these people were traveling along the road before the goblins ambushed them, where was their food? Where were their canteens or waterskins? I could certainly use those.

The goblins looked like they could have used the supplies, too. Perhaps they had a cache somewhere nearby where they kept that kind of stuff. Considering how well they'd hidden themselves, I could probably spend hours searching for their stash and not find a thing.

I wasn't sure I had that kind of time.

Of course, this universe confirmed that suspicion for me. I, the only living being atop a pile of dead people, was kneeling down next to the crumpled form of the goblin magician when I heard the rhythmic *click-clack* of metal on stone somewhere on the road behind me.

# CHAPTER TWENTY-TWO

# Hitch a Ride

Something was coming.

Roads meant people. People were a touch better than beasts. But that didn't mean they were necessarily safe, though. Plus, I seemed to have a nice assortment of different races cold on the ground beneath me—some I'd killed; all of them I'd looted. Whoever was coming might just take offense at that.

I picked the nearest tree trunk and skittered behind it, reaching down to smear a handful of mud on my face and helmet. Then I got low until I was half submerged in the stagnant puddle between the swamp tree's roots, with my head in a position where I could just barely see around the trunk. It was as good a hiding spot as I was going to get with such short notice.

What came into view only a few seconds later was a group of armored men riding atop white-haired beasts. The riders wore chain armor from head to toe, plumed helmets, and a black and green livery on cloth strips that hung down from their shoulders. Each of them carried a crossbow with thick limbs the edges of which seemed to glint in the light.

Their beasts were ungulates of some kind, easily as tall as I was at the shoulder, whose disproportionately tiny hooves made clicking sounds on the stone path. They had thick, powerful shoulders and hindquarters, short necks, and wide heads. I only caught flashes of their big black eyes through the curtain of long, wiry hair that covered them.

A sturdy-looking black carriage, pulled by two of the beasts, rolled in the middle of their formation. The wheels squeaked as the wagon navigated the semi-uneven surface of the road. Curiously, there was no driver's seat as one might find on an Old Earth wagon. Instead, the animals seemed to know where they were going, or were being directed some other way.

They were all getting closer now.

Slowly, carefully, I slipped sideways and got lower in the water that pooled next to the tree, losing sight of the caravan and listening for any sign that they had noticed me.

> Stealth is now Level 3.

"Hold!" a man's rough voice shouted from their group. All activity stopped. "Point, check it."

"There it is. Right there!" A precise, aristocratically accented male voice came from somewhere in their ranks, and if I had to guess based on the hollow timbre, it was coming from the carriage.

"My lord?" the man asked.

"It's here," the posh voice pronounced, sounding very sure of himself. "Go collect a sample, so we can be on our way."

"I'm sorry, my lord. There are dead on the road, and we need to sweep the area to make sure we're safe."

"It's not on the road. Check to the side. It's here somewhere."

There was a pause. I imagined the lot of them peering around, attempting to find the thing their master wanted. "Pardon, Lord, but I don't have your sight. What is it I'm meant to see?"

"Over there! Are you blind?" Carriage Guy shouted from his wooden box.

I winced, slowly peeking around the trunk of my tree again.

One of the riders, an older man with craggy scars marring his cheeks and a bushy gray mustache, was there at the door to the carriage, leaning down to speak to someone in the car, the tall green plume on his helmet brushing up against the black-painted trimming. He was looking my way.

> Stealth is now Level 4.

"No, my lord. I am not blind. You say there is something over there?" he asked as he tilted his head and narrowed his eyes to scan the area.

Two of the riders trotted forward, shifting their grips on their crossbows to sweep the scene with their muzzles.

"Fresh blood here, sir, most of it goblin!" one of them reported over his shoulder.

"Most of it?"

"Aye. Road hasn't muted the scent yet, sir. Something else, too. New to me."

"Yes! It's right there! I am telling you," scolded the man in the carriage. "Let's get it and be done before it has a chance to get away. I'm already past due, but we have a duty to fulfill. If we have another Mendau plague on our hands, there will be riots in the city."

I was deathly still now. The rider nearest me was so close, I could smell the stink of his mount's damp fur over the stench of the swamp. My eyes ran over the group: six men in all, not including the one in the wagon. The one that had been talking to the noble was coming closer, while there were three encircling the carriage.

If I could panic their mounts, maybe I could make a break into the woods. It might be possible if I could squeeze off a shot, but, then again, I couldn't run faster than a crossbow bolt. How fast would the animals be once they recovered? What if I could make for the deep water and use my air tank to evade them?

"Ah!" The man closest to me gave a shout of surprise as he seemed to finally take notice of me, his eyes widening under the visor of his helmet. He'd startled me as well. Without thinking, I jumped to my feet. The man's mount shared our mutual feelings of surprise, bounding backward with a nimbleness that belied its size, jumping fully over the next rider and landing on the trunk of a leaning swamp tree ten feet away. The beast and the rider were perched near-vertically on the side of the trunk, but neither gave any indication that this was abnormal. Instead, the rider's crossbow was already lined up for a shot, but he hadn't fired yet.

"Oh. We've found it, my lord!" the mustached man shouted. "Small problem, though!"

"What is it, Garret?" the man in the carriage asked, leaning his head out through the curtains that covered the window. He looked younger than I'd guessed—maybe in his forties. Long black hair spilled down over his shoulders, and traces of silver were just starting to show at his temples. His gaunt face and thin lips were pinched as if he were perpetually sucking on lemons, and his skin was white as bleached bone.

"I see it," he said once he spotted me. "Shoot it and bring the body with us. No time to tie it up."

Mustache—or Garret, I guessed—shrugged his broad shoulders and grimaced slightly. "Alright, my lord. Think I can get it in one. We'll be on our way soon. Get the netting, Dimus." Then he brought his crossbow up to his shoulder, the gleaming tip of a quarrel aimed right at my eye.

"Whoa. Whoa. Whoa! Do not do that!" I shouted, shrinking away from Garret's line of fire and trying to duck behind my tree. Garret tracked my movements like a pro, though. So did the other two riders who could see me. I felt around in my Spatial Storage for my pistol and got ready to summon it as I turned my head back and forth rapidly to try and keep all the crossbows in my line of sight at once.

No one shot me.

Garret's eyebrows lifted slightly, and his head tilted to the side, bringing his eye away from the crossbow's sight.

"It speaks, sir," he called over his shoulder.

"Ah, dammit. Of course it does. This is going to put us even further behind schedule. Blasted Returned Accords," Carriage Man moaned. I heard a hard slap on the wood of the carriage door and muffled cursing followed before he got his composure back again. "We still need that sample, Garret."

Garret never took his eyes off me, but his expression took on an air of curiosity. "Sir, if it can speak, perhaps it can give an account of what it's seen?" he speculated.

"No. No. It's no use." Carriage Guy sighed as if the entire world were conspiring to tax his dwindling patience. "Witness accounts are notoriously unreliable, especially with the mentally impaired. The amount of detail I need can only be extracted from a sample, and, additionally, I have the weight of the queen's decree pressing down on me."

The big rider's eyebrows scrunched together as he thought, and he allowed the crossbow quarrel to slide down from my eye to my chest. "Perhaps it can give us a sample voluntarily, sir?"

"No, you bu—" It sounded like the noble was going to rip into Garret, but apparently something occurred to him mid-sentence. "Ah. Well, yes, perhaps you're right, Garret. Ask it if we could take a small part of its flesh. Assure it we need no more than a few pounds. Oh, and be polite."

"Yes, sir," Garret assented before clearing his throat and addressing me. He spoke loudly and slowly, enunciating every syllable of his words.

"I apologize for our initial misunderstanding, Mister... Ah. Do you have a name?"

I put my hands down slowly, making sure I didn't seem overly threatening. The pistol could be in my hand in a flash, but how many could I take out before I was shot through the heart? "Uh, Ryan," I replied. "Thank you for not shooting me, by the way."

"Mister Ryan, yes. Of course. Sorry to interrupt your meal. Can never be too careful on the road in these parts. Some of the less-aware . . . uh . . . folk like you . . . still cling to their old allegiances, you see, and we've had a lot of goblin activity in the past few weeks. But you'd know all about that, I guess." Garret chuckled half-heartedly, shifting uncomfortably in his saddle. He'd put down his crossbow to rest on his saddle now, but it wasn't lost on me that the other two riders still had a line of sight aimed at my head.

"I . . . what?" I asked. Folk like me? Humans? That was impossible.

"Oh, gods, he's a fresh one," Garret muttered to himself as he ran a palm over his face. He paused to gather his thoughts for a second, nodding to himself and looking to the side as if he were trying to formulate the proper words. When he was ready, he continued. "Let me be the first to tell you, then, Mister Ryan, that the war is over, and you are free. Completely. Unequivocally. Congratulations."

"Uh, thank you," I replied. I needed to roll with whatever this was and give myself an opportunity to escape. "Glad to hear it, I guess? One can never be too free."

"And I must say, you speak remarkably well for one of your kind, Mister," Garret observed with a grin. Not at all patronizing.

"Yeah," I agreed. "My mother said the same thing."

"Your . . . mother?" A look of horror passed over Garret's face, his mustache's tips drooping down as if a hairy caterpillar had died on his face. "You had a . . . mother? How does that work?"

I frowned, feeling lost. "I—Maybe just use your imagination, buddy. I don't know what to tell you."

One of the riders swallowed, looking a little green. He spurred his mount to take him behind the carriage, out of sight. Labored breathing carried over the heavy air from where he'd gone.

This was getting weird. Dangerous and weird. What the hell had I said wrong?

Garret looked rattled, but he soldiered on. "Ah. So, anyway. If you've been traveling along this road, I'm sure you observed the diseased vegetation at the foot of the mountain. My master is a once-in-a-generation scholar, you see, and he would like to study the phenomenon."

"Understandable," I replied with a reluctant nod.

"Quite so, well. You see—It's—You have a similar magical . . . scent . . . all over you. It would help my master greatly if you could . . . uh." He coughed uncomfortably. "If you could give us a piece of your body. Nothing you'd miss!" he added with a raised hand to forestall any protestations. "Just a couple strips of flesh and—"

"Two pounds minimum!" came the lord's shout from the carriage.

"I was working up to that, m'lord," Garret whisper-shouted back at his master.

Flabbergasted, I just stood there blinking, opening and closing my mouth, multiple replies just waiting on the tip of my tongue. I went with: "Why would I give you that?"

"Please. You would be assisting the queen and helping to advance science. Also, we might be convinced to leave the goblin corpses to you if you help us out. They appear to be the freshest. Again, we're not asking for anything you'd miss, sir."

I took a step back. "Oh, I think I would miss it." Also, what did he expect for me to do with goblin corpses?

The lord was shouting again. "No! No! Stop it. You're ruining it, Garret. Just . . . Dammit. Bring him here," he bellowed.

Garret shrugged and flashed a grin at me like he hadn't just been asking for a literal piece of me. He didn't seem put out in the slightest at his lord's displeasure or the fact that he'd apparently failed. The guardsman lazily brought his crossbow up to aim in my general direction again, waving me to come out from behind the tree.

I walked toward him slowly, careful not to trip or give any indication that I wanted to do violence. As we approached the carriage, myself in front and Garret at my back with his mount sniffing at my bloody, mud-caked armor, the noble opened the carriage door and leaned out to look me over. The perpetual frown that looked like it never truly left his face deepened as he took me in.

"Garret, when we get to the city, go get your eyes checked. All of you. This is no Returned," he admonished them all, shaking his head and rubbing one of his temples.

"He's alive, my lord? Then why does he look like that? Where are your clothes, Mister? Your hair?" Garret gasped, before leaning down in his saddle to look closely at me. His tone softened. "Are you alright, young man?"

I didn't know what a Returned was, but if they were going to shoot me for it, I wasn't going to try and keep the label. They also didn't know what I really was, so that was a relief. "I—It's a long story," I replied to all of Garret's questions at once.

The nobleman sighed, blowing air through chapped lips. "One we can't wait around for. I'm past due to arrive at the university." He pointed to me. "You. You have the diseased mana profile all over you, inside of you as well. How did this come to be? Quickly, in less than ten words if you can. Our world may depend upon it."

"Uh—"

The man's frown deepened into full-scowl territory. "Do not waste your words. Think carefully," he snapped.

For some reason, I felt like I was back at school being scolded for daydreaming in class. "I escaped the mountain. Killed a mockvine. Am I really missing my hair?" I turned back to look at Garret.

The big man nodded, wincing a little on my behalf. "Most of it, sir."

"My eyebrows, too?" I asked as I reached up to feel my face. Yep, they were gone.

"You are also quite filthy, Mister Ryan," Garret added helpfully. "Point! Is it this one's blood you smell over there?" he called to the two riders still posted next to the bodies.

"Yes, sir. I think so. His and the goblins are all I can smell," the point man reported. "The others have been dead for a while. This looks like two fights separated in time, sir. No weapons or spoils I can see. Might want to check what he did with 'em."

"My man over there says he smells your blood, Mister. Mind telling us what happened?"

But the lord interrupted, waving Garret off, and leaning forward to get a closer look at me. "Yes. Yes. He smells terrible. Now what's this about a mockvine? A wild one?"

"I killed an . . . uh . . . ancient mockvine in a cave a good distance that way."

"Don't play with me, young man," he hissed, a dangerous tone in his voice. "Tell me the truth. An old one? How big?"

I nodded, trying to look more confident than I felt. "Took up the whole cave. It wanted to eat me, but I didn't agree with that."

He leaned forward, putting a hand on the carriage's open door. "If the type of mana on your body were any different, I would call you a liar and have Garrett club you, but . . ."

"Why?" I asked.

"Why what?"

"Why club me?"

"I still may have to, sir, if he murdered these folks," Garret added helpfully.

"No, Garret, I don't think that will be necessary. Our new friend here is most likely responsible for the goblins but not the others. The mana signature on him is too fresh to have been here for the previous killings. If it makes you feel better, you may check with your point man," the gaunt nobleman said before turning to me. "The residue of the mockvine rolls off you along with something else. I took it for miasma at first as we tracked you but now . . ." His eyes lost focus for a moment, seeming to look at something very far away. "Garret, this young man is coming with us."

Garret cleared his throat and swallowed. "No need to . . . sample his flesh then, master?" he inquired uncomfortably.

"No. It would be helpful, but it also would be illegal," the nobleman said with a wave of his hand. "Can't have a scandal on my first day." A significant look passed between the two. I caught it, but I couldn't discern the meaning. I didn't like that.

"And if I don't want to come with you?" I asked, feeling very much like my desires weren't being considered at all. I didn't want to trade one cage for another. The mention of the law gave me a little hope, though. Maybe false imprisonment was illegal here.

"No choice, young man. I need to verify your story and make sure we don't have a tree-killing disease on our hands. It wouldn't be the first time. Whether you're lying or not, you've been in the thick of it, whatever *it* is. Once I have my answers, you will be free to go do whatever it is you do. You can ride with me and give me a full account of your story. After all, we do appear to be going the same way, and you have no shoes."

I hesitated, looking to Garret and the riders. None of them had put down their crossbows fully, but they didn't seem worried for their master even if he wanted to ride with a stranger. Better to agree to it now than be tied up and forced to ride that way.

I sighed. They were going my way, I guessed, and they didn't want to kill me right away. I also had my Spatial Storage to bring to bear should I need to make an escape. "Alright, I—"

"Wait—" The nobleman put out a hand to stop me, then snapped his fingers. There was a stinging, electric sensation that ran over my body from head to toe like the entire outer layer of my skin had just been violently scrubbed with wire brushes, but I got the full experience in less than a second. I gasped, nearly doubling over. It wasn't necessarily painful, but it was so sudden and intimate. The feeling was everywhere I had skin, from my scalp to my toes to my armpits and groin.

When the sensation abated, I looked up to see a swirling vortex about the size of a billiard ball coalescing above the nobleman's hand. Then it solidified, and the man plucked it out of the air before stashing it in a glossy pouch he'd pulled out of his pocket.

I looked down at myself, wondering what he'd done to me, but it didn't take long to realize. My jaw dropped in shock. For the first time since I woke up on Ralqir . . .

"There. You are clean. The mana is still on your being, but the stinking muck you'd bathed yourself in is now stowed away for examination later," the lord said, pausing to look me over, then peering intently into my eyes for a long, awkward moment.

"Now let's be off. Retract your aura and get in," he commanded.

I blinked, feeling my nonexistent eyebrows knitting together. "Retract my what now?"

"I acknowledge that you are a practitioner. I can see that, now that we've cleared the flotsam. But I won't ride the rest of the way to Eclipse with your aura spewing out of you like blood from a severed artery. Hurry now. Daylight will not linger."

"I don't understand," I insisted. What was he talking about? He called me a practitioner, so maybe this was about magic or mana?

The lord sighed again, slumping back into his cushioned chair further inside the carriage. He looked tired, like his entire life was a series of disappointments and setbacks, and I was just the latest.

"Never mind. Your vacant expression tells me I will not get what I want, not in time at least. Damned Wildlings. Unbelievable." He raised an accusatory finger and pointed it to the sky. "Whoever your master was did you a great disservice, you know that? Did he simply teach you the Dominion ritual and wander off to live with a herd of deer or something? No. Never mind. It doesn't matter. I suppose I'll have to endure. Get in."

# CHAPTER TWENTY-THREE

# Play the Fool

Unbelievable!" Lord Trayalo Jassin shouted for what must have been the twentieth time on our carriage ride together. Internally, I winced at how close to the mark his word choice was.

Of course I couldn't tell him the truth of what I was or where I was from, so I was winging it and doing it badly, less so when I got the guy talking about something other than me.

Lord Jassin seemed to get the most animated when I mentioned my "master" who taught me the magical arts and how little time she had actually spent instructing me. The man had a real problem with practitioners who didn't view the master/student relationship as a solemn duty and privilege as it should be. I'd left out the fact that she was a glitchy hologram lady, but at the same time, I kind of enjoyed hearing someone else that was pissed at Nali for leaving me high and dry in those early days.

"Unbelievable! Just typical of wild practitioners! She awakened your Dominion and just . . . left? My boy, that is not just cruel but highly dangerous. The fact that you are still alive and sane is a testament to your fortune or fortitude—impossible to tell which."

"Ah. Uh. Yeah. I guess so. Honestly, I've had quite a time of it so far," I admitted, looking down at my hands as I flexed my fingers, remembering the things I'd done to get here. What else would I have to do to get home?

The sleeves of my borrowed shirt were a little long—same with the pants legs—but the tall guardswoman that loaned them to me said I could get them taken in once we got to Eclipse. She was the only one who had brought an extra set of civilian clothes among the group, to the rest of the guards' shame.

"Oh my gods, men are disgusting!" she'd shouted at them, her mouth twisted up in a horrified sneer. She looked like she wanted to turn her crossbow on every one of them. "Do you just stew in your own funk for the entire trip? What if you have to attend a party? What if the tailors can't fit you? You know what? That explains a lot about a lot. I'm taking point, sir, and I'm requesting a transfer as soon as we find a guild that'll take me."

"Granted, Lieutenant." Garret laughed. "But I think you'll find your problem lies not with my unit but with men in general. Without a civilizing influence, we'd all live like Wildlings."

I did my best to meet Lord Jassin's eyes as I spoke. "Anyway. After she'd . . . uh . . . awakened me, I had a bad run-in with goblins and then found myself lost in the caves where I met the mockvine. It tried to hypnotize me with some kind of illusion, but I saw it for what it was eventually."

Deception is now Level 2.

I hated this. I wasn't a big liar, so telling half-truths like this taxed my mind and my conscience. Jassin was sharp, too, and he was quick to note inconsistencies in my story.

"Unbelievable. You, with a fledgling Dominion, wander into the heart of a mockvine lair, and you just *see through* its suggestions. I don't see how that is possible. Your aura is extraordinarily strong for someone of your age, but if the creature was as old as you're saying, you should be dead. Even the smaller specimens can lull a full-grown adult into somnambulation. In fact, I once taught a graduate student who raised a mockvine from a seedling. Used it as a sleep aid. Then, as soon as the creature had grown powerful enough, it charmed him right out of his second-floor window. He was lucky to get away with just a broken leg. Are you sure this one wasn't diseased or perhaps wounded from a previous bout with its food?"

I shook my head. "I don't know how I would be able to tell. What would that look like?" I asked. The one thing Jassin seemed to enjoy was hearing the sound of his own voice, preferably when he was talking about something he knew a lot about.

"Oh. There are several indicators of disease that one can observe in carnivorous plants such as a curling of the leaves or browning on the inside of the lobes. Distortions in its foliage patterns. An overreliance on obfuscation. Did you notice any of that while you were under attack?"

"Uh. Lobes? Where would—"

"The uninitiated would most likely call it the 'mouth' of the creature, though it is evolutionarily as far from a proper mouth as you can get."

"No browning that I noticed."

"Are you sure? Did you get a close look?" Jassin asked.

I thought back to the claustrophobic insides of the bulb, the stinging of the acid, the smooth, rubbery texture, my shaking hands and panicked breaths as I fought to breathe. "Yeah," I confirmed. "I got pretty close. Pink and yellow all the way."

"Unbelievable," he muttered, lying back on his cushioned seat again. He stared through me then, seemingly lost in thought. He rubbed the back of his head where his antlers protruded from his dark hair and seemed to be muttering something to himself as he contemplated.

I didn't volunteer anything else. I had no context for anything on Ralqir. I was as foreign to these people as you could get, and the more I opened my mouth, the more chances I would have to stick my foot in it. Instead, I tried to ask my own questions and keep the conversation from focusing on me.

So far, I'd been able to gather precious little information. We were on the road to Eclipse, a city of great importance to this world, where Jassin would be taking up a position as a professor at their university. Jassin's escort was double what it would normally be thanks to increased aggression from multiple displaced goblin tribes and migratory beasts. So far, though, nothing had tried to waylay them thanks to how well-armed and large the party was.

Jassin himself was a noble, a father of twelve, and an accomplished scholar in multiple fields of magic and magical theory, and, like all noble practitioners, he'd taken an oath for queen and country to use his acquired knowledge and power to protect the kingdom from all threats. That's why when he'd seen the dying greenery, he'd been concerned the forest was about to see a plague. If the trees died and stopped blocking the deadly sun, traffic to and from Eclipse could halt entirely. Trade would stop and people would go hungry.

After taking some samples from the site, Jassin followed my trail. "Lucky for me and for you that you didn't travel on the road, my boy. Otherwise, I would never have been able to follow you. The dark craft that keeps these roads tends to erase such things over time."

"So, this Eclipse place, what should I know before I get there?" I asked.

"Hmm? Oh, yes, of course. I apologize, young man. You speak so well, and your aura is so strong, I keep forgetting that your education is rather lacking. Where did you say you were from?" Jassin probed.

I hadn't said. It was a trap, a question I was better off not trying to answer, considering how little I knew. Better to look a little rude than entirely ignorant. Maybe I could get by with a half-truth.

"A little place called Proxis," I answered, careful to keep it vague.

"Pro-k-siss. I have never heard of such a place, though I'm sure I could find it if given half a day in the library." That sounded like a threat, almost. "It sounds Vistian. Is that right?"

I nodded slowly. "Yeah. We're Vistian . . . at least I was. Now I guess I'm a wanderer. So, about Eclipse?"

Jassin's eyes narrowed slightly, growing hard around the edges, and his mouth twitched slightly upward in the ghost of a triumphant smile. Then he was back to being a professor, which seemed to be his natural state.

"Well, Ryan, Eclipse is the crown jewel of our world, at least in respect to knowledge. It is home to seven universities, four separate practitioner's guilds, and the grandest library Ralqir has ever seen, courtesy of the city's previous occupant and his eccentricities."

"The previous occupant?" I asked with a raised eyebrow. I tried to play it casual, but the way he left the statement dangling out there, it was like he was just begging me to ask.

Again, Jassin's eyes narrowed as he leaned forward to peer at me more closely. "The Dark Lord, boy. *The* Dark Lord. Not any of the pretenders we've had in the past few hundred years."

He studied my face, presumably looking for some kind of reaction: recognition or fear or awe maybe. When he didn't get it, Jassin let out a very unlordly snort, then went on.

"Wildlings. You really don't know, do you? You're like a blank slate. Ryan, this was the Dark Lord's home, his fortress and laboratory. Surely, you didn't think we'd build a city in the middle of such a charming environ by choice?" he revealed with incredulity.

I'd failed whatever test that had been, and I needed to recover.

"Honestly, I—uh—hadn't actually realized where I was. I'm sorry. I know about the Dark Lord offhand, of course, but the knowledge just hasn't been relevant to my life. I've been focused on survival above all."

Jassin gasped, giving me a look like I'd just kicked his dog and defecated on his pillow. "Not relevant? Not relevant!" His face turned red in that way Miss Sheferty's used to when I'd said we would never use long division outside of school. "Young man, you literally owe your life to the Dark Lord. I'm not saying he was a good and benevolent figure, but he shaped the history of our planet to such a degree that none of us would be here today if not for what he did. The food you eat, the roads you travel upon right now, the shade, the very spell you cast to obtain your Dominion . . ." He reached over and rapped his knuckles on my prosthetic arm, eliciting a little *gong!* ". . . It was all him. You may not wish to think upon it, but the Dark Lord's legacy has touched every aspect of your life, and you now go to what used to be the heart of his power."

Garret grunted some kind of order from outside the carriage, and there was a flurry of activity as the *click-clack* of hooves seemed to rush in to surround us. The old guardsman leaned down and parted the curtains with a gauntleted hand to speak to Jassin directly.

"Goblins, my lord," Garret whispered quietly. "Don't look like much of a threat. They're just walking on the road, but we're keeping tight just in case."

"More of them? That's the third—no, fourth—sighting this journey. Very well, Garret. Thank you," Jassin replied, still reclining in his seat. He didn't seem overly worried. I, on the other hand, felt a chill crawling up my spine, and I could feel my body tensing for some kind of action.

Slowly, steadily, the carriage rolled on, surrounded by our guard, and the clack of hooves was the only sound that reached the interior. Garret stayed close, next to the window, using his hairy mount, presumably to block his master from any projectiles the goblins might lob his way. Another guard took up our other flank, filling the opposite window with white fur as well.

Then I started to hear voices, high and quiet.

"Get to the side of the road," one ordered with some authority. Others were quieter and more furtive.

"Don't look at them."

"Keep walking."

Garret rode rigid in his saddle, one hand clutching his crossbow, the other on the pommel, his face made of stone.

I couldn't help myself. I felt nervous and curious and boxed in. "Garret, what are they doing?" I asked.

Garret didn't look at me to answer. "I don't know. Don't look like a raiding party. Got their children and their elders with them. Precious few fighters in the bunch, too, but they've got some decent kit. Best stay quiet while we ride by and not rile 'em up."

The squeak of the wheels and the clattering of hooves was all the sound in the world for a few minutes, interspersed with the occasional cough or wailing goblin child from outside. Then I heard something familiar.

"It's okay. We get there soon, and we rest. Don't play with it. The wrap has to stay clean."

*No way.*

I flung the carriage door open so fast, it startled Garret's mount, forcing it to lunge to the side, drawing a chorus of alarmed goblin shouts and curses from Garret himself.

My feet hit the quellstone, feeling the cold knives stabbing into my flesh, but I wasn't paying attention to that. I stumbled a little on the dismount but had my balance back in a couple of steps. Then I could only pay attention to the goblins.

Yes. Their clothes. Their baskets and packs. The way they spoke. All of it was familiar. Most telling of all, I spotted a warrior among them with a pristine iron spear and bucket helmet of my own design, one that probably had a specific set of grooves on the inside in the shape of a caterpillar.

I was looking for someone specific, however.

"What are you doing, boy?" Garret growled. His mount was back under control, and the guard's eyes never stopped moving. Garret had a hard look to him as he swiveled his head back and forth, taking in everything at once—every detail, every potential threat . . . including me. His crossbow was up now, not pointed at me but ready, while the rest of the guards closed ranks, crowding in around Jassin's ride.

"Wait," I said, taking several steps toward the back of the carriage, standing up tall to try and get a better view of all the green faces. The goblins—two columns of them on either side of the road—had all stopped now, their eyes wide and ready to bolt or fight or whatever they needed to do.

Jassin leaned out of the open door. "Ryan, where are you going? Eclipse is close, and we are already late."

"Wait just a minute," I pleaded with him, pushing through the guards' mounts and stepping onto the open road.

"Tiba?!" I called with my hands cupped over my mouth. "Tiba!"

"Mister Ryan, you need to get back in the carriage now," Garret ordered from behind me. All levity and warmth were gone from his voice. He was a hair away from doing something I'd regret. "You rile up these goblins and there'll be blood. We've seen it time and again."

"Ryan?" someone asked quietly from my right.

I whirled around. There she was in all her tiny green glory, holding a goblin child, its bandaged leg dangling down to droop past the healer's waist. Tiba looked tired. Her hair was a mess, falling down in stringy clumps in front of her face, and her eyes were red like she'd not gotten much sleep. She stepped to the side and handed the child to one of the adults next to her before stepping forward, timidly sparing a glance at the guards' crossbows.

"Ryan? Is that you?" she asked again.

I nodded, striding up to her. The cold quellstone under my bare feet made every step painful, but I ignored it, only stopping once I got within a few feet of the little healer.

*So small. Were they always so small?*

Then I realized it was the first time I'd seen her from my full height.

"I barely recognize you," she said. "Where is all of your hair? It is pretty hair, especially when you let me pick the style." Her forced levity didn't quite land. Neither of us were feeling it.

I went down on one knee in front of her, bringing myself to her level where things felt familiar. "My escape cost me a great deal," I admitted. Out of habit, I reached up to brush nonexistent hair out of my eyes.

"Yes. Mine, too," she replied, her eyes sinking down to the cobblestones. No tears, though it looked like she was more than willing to shed them.

I nodded gravely. "I know," I said. "I'm glad you made it out."

"Yes. We take the long tunnels through the mountain. The old ones from before the Beginning. I want to take you with us, but Kuul—"

"Kuul," I growled, a flare of hatred igniting in my chest and searing my throat. "Where is Kuul? I want to speak to him." I wanted to do far more than that. *Far more.*

Tiba shook her head, not meeting my eyes. "He is gone. He stays in the old tunnels and does big magic for us. Old, big magic."

"What do you mean? Where? Tell me," I demanded, looking back the way we'd come, my hands involuntarily balling into tight fists. There had to be a reckoning for what Kuul had done to me. What he'd done to Hunty. I found myself nearly on my feet before I realized what I was doing.

When my mind caught up to me again, I forced myself to pause and breathe. *I'm not going back to that mountain. Not yet.*

I was free. Kuul wasn't here. No one was going to lock me away again. Not him. Not anyone. I would make sure of that.

"I'm sorry, Tiba," I said, sinking down to my knees again.

Tiba either didn't notice my near-outburst or didn't care. She looked tired. "I don't know how the magic works. Kuul stays in the old tunnels and communes with the Mendau. He sacrifices to save the Stone Hearts, or, at least, that's what he says."

"You speak like them?" Garret was behind me now, his mount slightly angled so he was able to turn either way in the saddle and get off a shot at whatever goblin made a move. "How did you learn to do that?"

"What?" I asked the old guard, confused. "I'm just . . ."

"What does he say?" Tiba interrupted, placing a hand on my wrist. "Is he going to hurt us?"

"No. I—" I noticed it then, the way my voice changed when I spoke to Tiba. How it felt. Now that I was listening, the words were a multilayered series of grunts, clicks, and growls, yet it was as natural as if it had been my native tongue.

"What is she saying, Mister Ryan? Are we about to be in a fight?" Garret stared at me now, his eyes hard but pleading while his mount stamped nervously and fought to turn away. The old guardsman seemed genuinely interested in avoiding bloodshed.

"Uh. I know her. She's telling me how they got here."

"You know her?"

"Yeah. Just give me a minute."

I turned to Tiba. "Tiba, these people aren't going to hurt anyone as long as no one attacks them."

Tiba looked around timidly at all the stern faces and primed crossbows. "You're sure? They look like they hate us," she whispered.

"Pretty sure. Can you tell everyone to relax, please? Trust me."

"I do trust you, Ryan," she replied with a sad smile before she cupped a hand to her mouth. "Ryan speaks for us! Rest time!"

I winced as the little healer started shouting, knowing it would sound sinister to the guards. They tightened their grips on their triggers, but no one made a move.

That was progress.

Then came the part I'd been dreading. "Tiba," I began, looking down to my open hand, summoning the spear from my Spatial Storage. The weapon appeared in a shower of sparkling motes of light.

Hunty's Spear: A cherished spear crafted by a fledgling artificer and sized for a goblin. The spear tip is magnificently sharp and can repair itself multiple times before going truly dull.

Damage: 4-8 (Piercing)

Quality: Excellent

Style: Custom

Magic: Repair

Tiba gasped and shrank away from the overt display of magic.

Of course she did. The only person she'd ever had in her life that could do that kind of thing was Kuul, and that didn't come with the best of memories. On some level, she had to know I did magic, but I guessed she thought it was the slow, boring kind of magic that couldn't hurt her.

To Tiba's credit, she got control of herself quickly after she recognized what I was holding.

I clutched the spear in my hand, hard enough to turn my knuckles white. When I spoke, my voice felt rough, and the words were sandpaper.

"I'm so, so sorry," I said, feeling the words catch in my throat. "About Hunty. I wish I could've . . . He shouldn't have died for me."

I consciously relaxed my fingers and extended my arm to present the weapon to Tiba.

Her eyes were fixed upon the thing as if I were passing her a venomous snake, but, after several heartbeats, her trembling hands reached out and took it, a look of disbelief on the little healer's face. She ran her hand over the haft and traced her fingers over its knobs and grooves, reexploring the familiar. Then she was clutching it close. The way she held it, cradled it, it was obvious she had no experience holding a weapon, but she wanted it there nonetheless.

"I'm so sorry," I said again. "He was a good goblin. My friend."

"Yes, he is. Hunty is the best of goblins. You bring me a part of Hunty today." Tiba sniffed and wiped at her eyes, still holding the spear close to her heart. "Thank you, Ryan. He would be glad you live, and he would laugh at your bald head."

Someone cleared their throat behind me. I turned to see Lord Jassin, who looked down at me with an urgent, immediate sort of interest. It was like I'd gained the attention of some kind of predatory bird and it was studying me to figure out if I was prey.

Some kind of power flashed behind his eyes as he ran his gaze over me. Whatever he was looking for, he either didn't find it or found something he didn't like. He shook his head and stroked his chin as a pensive frown pulled the corners of his mouth downward. "Unbelievable," he repeated yet again.

# CHAPTER TWENTY-FOUR

# See the Sky

*Memory: Proxis 3 - Before Integration*

My hands clung tight to the tarnished chrome railing of the maglev as the train took a sharp turn, and my stomach did that thing where it went one way while the rest of me stayed where it was.

I loved that feeling. It was even better when it was a surprise. When Mom and Dad took me on rides in the rover, they always went down the hills faster than they should have, because they knew I loved it. I was getting old enough that it didn't surprise me as much anymore, but I still acted like it did to make them laugh.

Bright holosigns whipped by my window, so close I could have probably reached out and touched one to feel that tickling sensation again if only the train's glass weren't there. Of course, holos were made of light, so I couldn't really touch one.

I knew that . . . now.

Before our train ride, Mom had taken me to a kids' arcade where the holos were interactive, and the whole place was a fireworks show of color and sound so overwhelmingly fantastic it hurt. If I listened hard, I could pick out five different songs I'd never heard playing from different parts of the room. Explosions, whistles, monster roars, shrieking thrusters, staccato beats of machine-gun fire, the smell of popcorn and sticky sweet candy all swirled together and amplified one another until the atmosphere positively crackled.

Once it all hit me at once, I just kind of froze in the doorway.

What was a kid from the Outers supposed to make of a place like that? Back home, I threw rocks into a sinkhole for fun.

Like Mom always did, she'd held my hand and slowly walked me into the middle of the room, through all the barking insanity that loudly demanded my attention, until we reached the center of the storm. It was all so much. I had to fight not to reach up and cover my ears.

Then she got down on her knees to look me in the eyes, leaning in to say: "Now go play. I'll be right behind you," and then she brushed my hair out of my eyes right before ruffling it all out of place again.

I tried to smile bravely as I reluctantly let go of her hand, and, with a tingle of fear and anticipation, let the arcade swallow me up.

Again, it was all too much, but in a good way. I felt wind-blasted and floaty when we left.

It was something I'd remember for the rest of my life, I already knew. She didn't believe me when I said the holograms tickled. She'd called it sickosem— No. Psychosomatic.

It was in my head. That was okay, though. There were lots of things in my head that were plenty real, so that didn't matter.

Dad cleared his throat loudly behind me. He and Mom were holding on to the overhead railing, probably watching me like they did when they thought I wasn't looking. Mom would have that little smile on her face, and Dad would look worried but happy, too.

The giant man that was my father wasn't comfortable in the city. He'd said as much a bunch of times in passing, always with a little laugh like it was a problem he'd never really have to deal with since we lived with the clan in the Outers. He was dealing with it now, though. Poorly.

"Next stop: Plymouth Station," chimed a gentle, vaguely male voice from the speakers above our heads. I could already feel the train starting to slow, and the blur of passing holos gave way to darkened windows and the occasional glimpse of Proxis 1 up in the sky.

"That's our stop, boys." Mom sounded . . . I couldn't really place it. Happy? Excited? Nervous? "Are you ready to meet Grandma and Grandpa, Ryan?" she asked as she pried my face away from the glass and went to work straightening my hair and brushing crumbs off my shirt. I sat down on the bench and let my legs dangle, allowing the changing speed of the train to drag them toward the front of the car.

"So, this is your mom and dad, Mom?" I asked. It was weird thinking about them like that.

"That's right. I grew up here," she replied as she picked a candy crumb from the leg of my pants only to flick it onto the floor. I wished I'd known it was there. The cherry flavor was my favorite.

My mind went to work making connections. "Did you ride the train and go to the arcade, too?"

"Mm hmm. I sure did. Your grandpa worked for the transportation authority. He helped run all the trains like this one, and I spent a lot of time in the stations."

"What about Dad? Where was he?" I asked.

"I grew up in the Outers, like you," Dad rumbled overhead as he loomed protectively over Mom's back. He didn't look at me as he spoke. Instead, he was always peeking around like something was going to pop out and scare him if he let his guard down.

"These aren't your mom and dad, Dad?"

Mom snorted but tried to hide it by covering her mouth.

Dad noticed, though. He frowned playfully at the both of us. "No, son. No, they are not. If they were, they'd probably have disowned me by now."

Mom turned to slap Dad on the stomach. "They like you just fine, you big weirdo."

"They could at least pretend to be less surprised when I use words with more than one syllable," Dad grumbled. I knew he was kidding, though. Everyone liked Dad. He was due to be headman soon.

We were losing speed fast now, and the white lights of the train station grew brighter and larger by the second.

"They would be far less surprised if you didn't pretend to sound like a bumpkin for the entire visit," Mom scolded, but her eyes never stopped smiling. "Your accent gets twice as thick as soon as we enter the city limits, Myron. Don't, for one second, think that slips by me."

Then she turned to me and grinned. "Dad feels the need to stand apart from the crowd here, but you're fitting in fine. Grandma and Grandpa are going to love you."

"Welcome to Plymouth Station," the robotic voice called from overhead. "Next stop: Round Rock Station."

"You ready, Ryan?" Mom asked, holding out both of her hands for me to take. Then she catapulted me up and out of the seat. "Just be yourself and you'll be fine."

*Now:*

"Care to explain what that was all about?" Jassin's voice cut through the fog of my daydreams. I'd done my best to stay alert for as much of the ride as I could, but after a couple hours of the steady swaying of the car, the rhythmic clops of hooves, and the lack of immediate danger, the razor tension of constant fight-or-flight I hadn't even realized I'd been carrying around with me seemed to ebb. Its absence left me groggy, disconnected, and more introspective than I was comfortable with.

The gnarled black shapes of the endless swamp flora drifted past my window. Evening had robbed most of the world of color and definition, but it wasn't pitch black as of yet. It was cold, though. The air ran icy fingers over my cheeks when the wind blew just right, and with it came the soft croaks and trills of nocturnal swamp life. The stagnant puddles just off the road were fast becoming smoky charcoal mirrors, whose smooth faces were marred with floating debris and rotting skeletal deadwood that bobbed in time with a song I couldn't hear. Tiny clusters of luminescent dots floated lazily just above the surface of the water for seconds at a time, only to gutter and die, then instantly re-form over a completely different pool.

The guards didn't carry any light, at least not yet. They relied on sharp eyes and training to keep danger at bay, apparently. Jassin and I enjoyed the luxury of a small modicum of light, a thin filament of some kind of luminous material wrapped around the roof of the carriage. It was a dim, pale form of illumination, bright enough to read by but only just. It made Jassin's face look eerily like a bleached skull, which I wasn't a big fan of.

*No one should have cheekbones that sharp.*

Oh, yes. He'd asked me something.

Jassin wore a curious look, his mouth turned down and his eyebrows showing just a hint of coming together. His pronounced features made his every expression more severe and immediate, as if every moment of his life held potentially dire consequences.

I shook my head to clear my mental cobwebs away and focused on the gaunt noble, recalling his query and turning it over in my head for examination. The man loved to ask his convoluted, open-ended questions and the question I assumed he was asking told him just as much as my answer in itself.

"What do you mean?" I asked.

"The goblins. You speak their language, and you said you knew one of them."

I shrugged sheepishly. "Yeah, I guess I do. I have a thing for languages," I replied, not really trying to delve into what that thing was.

Apparently, the System was helping me out with communication and not just a little. On an intellectual level, I had theorized that something like that was happening with the Stone Hearts, but I thought it was something like a magical filter or a translation dub over old movies.

But switching between two languages like that without thinking, vocalizing sounds I'd never practiced in my life . . . Hell, I'm pretty sure the human mouth wasn't even *capable* of pronouncing some of the goblin words I'd spoken. It drove home just how different I was now that the System had chosen me and remade my body. So much of what I did now was involuntary, like I'd been given a brand-new set of instincts entirely outside of the evolutionary paradigm. I wasn't, at all, the same person I'd been before integration.

At what point would I cease to be human anymore? Had I already passed that point?

We called them Exotics back home.

No, wait.

*They* called *us* Exotics back home. I was a part of that little club now.

Biologists came up with the term on Old Earth—a rare planet in the green zone with an extreme diversity of life—to describe invasive species that upset the natural order of an environment, often edging out the original, native species. Too often.

It was an apt descriptor for us, if I were being truly honest.

Back during Exodus II, sometime between my ancestors' departure from Earth and arrival on Proxis 3, something or someone activated the System, and it set about choosing its first Exotics. At least that was the theory. On our colony ship, only a handful of people went through Integration. Most of them died. Some disappeared entirely.

That's the funny thing about being snatched out of your cryochamber, rebuilt, then tossed back inside with superhuman resistances to cold and injury. Suddenly, you're stuck in an insulated metal tube that's doing its level best to keep your internal temperature at or near-absolute zero, but your new System-powered body says "No."

The lone known survivor, a maintenance tech named Gregory Marshal, escaped his pod only to find himself alone on a ship full of popsicles.

Afterward, he was kind enough to record a series of video logs for posterity's sake, detailing what had happened to him and how, but he couldn't stay with the ship. We were still about five hundred years short of our expected landfall, and Marshal could no longer be put in cryosleep. The day he left, he recorded a tearful goodbye to his family, saying that he was leaving, but if he was still alive by the time they landed, he'd find them. He didn't actually get to Proxis 3 in time to reunite with his family, but, after he remarried, the Marshals became a formidable Exotic line, formidable enough to nip at the heels of the Big Five at one time, too.

I was an Exotic now. My children, if I ever had any, would be Exotics. Their children would be Exotics. It would go on like that until the heat death of the universe. That's how it worked. It's how the Marshals and the Five Families rose to prominence back in the day. Would I need to start my own Family, or would I need to join another? The thought made my head spin.

Jassin inadvertently saved me from spiraling down into an existential crisis. He wasn't satisfied with my previous answer. "When did you learn that? Why?"

I cleared my throat, preparing to hedge. "Uh—Why do I need to have a reason to learn something?" I asked.

Deception is now Level 3.

After a heartbeat of hesitation, Jassin gave a slight nod in conciliation. "Oh, don't get me wrong. I enjoy the pursuit of knowledge for knowledge's sake, Ryan, but the barrier between our cultures, goblin and Miur, has proven difficult for anthropologists to breach. Even on the rare occasions where a scholar found success, goblinoids are a tribal people, and their dialects tend to vary wildly. How did it come to be that they accepted you?"

I shrugged. "They saved my life when we met."

"Really?" Jassin gaped. "A rare thing, indeed, goblin charity."

"And then they enslaved me."

"Ah. Yes. That does sound more typical of goblins." Jassin cleared his throat, and something like pity briefly played across his features. "These are the goblins that held you captive, I take it? That makes it even stranger that you had an interest in their safety. I hope you don't think me callous in declining to bring them with us. They would have slowed us down too much, and we could not trust them."

I nodded and drew in a deep breath, summoning the safer, less complicated portions of my feelings on the matter to lend me some credibility. The rest of it I buried deep where I could deal with it later.

"It's fine. Thanks for considering it, at least. As for the captivity thing . . . Honestly, when they found me, they thought I was dying, so they brought me back to their home to see their chief. He's the one who had the idea to keep me as a slave. He was a real piece of work, and if I ever see him again, we're going to have words. The others, though, they treated me decently, so long as it didn't go against Kuul's orders. They fed me, clothed me, and housed me during a time where I had no idea what I was doing, and I hadn't figured out the whole . . . uh, practitioner thing yet. I guess they gave me some time to figure things out even if that's not what they intended. I'm not saying I'm ready to invite them over for tea, but I don't see them as necessarily evil."

"True. I wouldn't call goblinkind evil, per se, but they are a brutal, contentious folk. Incompatible with the civilized collective. Next question. Did this Kuul teach you to control your Dominion?" Jassin probed.

I blinked. "Uh. No. No, definitely not." Even thinking of Kuul as a benevolent figure was so far out of my imagination, the notion hit me between the eyes and blasted my train of thought off the tracks.

"Hmm," was Jassin's reply to that. Then he slowly leaned back in his seat and began to stare out of the window, that pensive frown back on his face.

Was that another test? Had I passed or failed? I had to admit, the man's poker face was fantastic. Sure, he showed emotion at appropriate times, but they felt almost too appropriate, as if even his candid moments were calculated to an extent, like he was *allowing* himself to be candid instead of it happening naturally.

What was Jassin's deal?

He came off like a university professor well enough except when he didn't, and I hadn't forgotten how his guards reacted when the noble proposed we ride together in the same car. That is, to say, they didn't seem worried at all. They'd found me hiding next to a big pile of corpses, covered in blood. Yet, they were more than willing to let me get next to their VIP. Why? Other than one brief display of magic when he stripped all the grime off my body, Jassin hadn't really shown much mojo. Was he particularly powerful or tricky? Was I riding around with Merlin or Harry Houdini?

After a soft rap on the wall of the carriage, Garret poked his head in. "My lord, we're about to enter the glade."

"Thank you, Garret. Steady on until the spot, then."

"Yes, my lord," Garret replied with a grin, and then he was gone again.

"You're going to like this," Jassin said with a smile that drew back his skin until his cheekbones looked like they wanted to burst from his face like alien parasites.

"Like what?" I asked.

"How would you like to see the sky, my boy?"

The last time I'd done that, it almost killed me. My feelings on the matter were appropriately mixed. "Uh. Well—"

"No need to worry," Jassin assured me as he held up his hands to forestall my answer. "You won't need to take any precautions. It's perfectly safe. Well, safer than the company you've kept as of late."

I shrugged. "Sure then. I guess so."

The nobleman scoffed. "You guess so. You're far too young to be so jaded, Ryan. You're incredibly lucky to get this opportunity. Perhaps a look at the naked cosmos will change your outlook somewhat."

Jassin reached over and closed the curtains where I'd been looking out from, then did the same on the other side.

I tilted my head questioningly at him, but he just smiled and used a pen to write in the little notebook he liked to pull out from time to time. I got the distinct impression he was taking notes about me, but then again he probably wanted me to think that.

After a while, the carriage slowed to a stop, and there was a call to halt outside. Jassin peeked out of his side of the curtains, nodding to himself satisfactorily. The guards barked a couple of terse orders to one another and took positions up around the carriage, then sounded the all-clear.

"Alright, go ahead," Jassin said, indicating the door with his head.

I gave him a sidelong glance, wondering what his game was, but I was already doing as he asked. I didn't need to be told twice to get some air after hours of riding. As I worked the latch and popped the door open, I could see Jassin staring at me as if looking for a reaction, but I didn't know what kind of reaction he wanted from me. So, I decided a quick exit was to my benefit, giving him less time to interrogate me without having to even use his words. I practically leaped out of the car.

Outside, it was night but not pitch black like my first night on Ralqir or in the caves. Everything was so . . . still. There was not a tree to be found for miles, no branches swaying overhead nor leaves rustling in the wind. Nothing alive pressed down from above. Instead, for the first time in what had to have been months, a huge open sky spread out above me. The stars, however, were all wrong. Stars are supposed to be diffuse. They're supposed to spread out in all directions, a tapestry of light everywhere you looked, courtesy of the Big Bang. That wasn't the case here.

All around me, twinkling, loosely clustered streams of luminous blobs snaked their way across the night sky like ribbons on a kite, their writhing forms only broken by shadow-cloaked heavenly bodies close enough to obscure but not high enough to reflect the sun's rays from the other side of the planet. But the largest presence above took a huge chunk of the starscape for itself, dominating the night sky. It was a massive sphere of white and gray almost directly above our heads, and it bled green and pink auroras that palpitated around its edges, throbbing bright enough to force me to squint.

Closer to hand, soft, dark grass, silver with dew, twitched in the gentle breeze.

"I always make it a point to stop here before I get to the city," Jassin said from behind me. I turned back to see him staring upward just as I did, a slight, knowing smile on his face.

The guards, however, were spread out around us, their eyes always on the swaying grass or on the tree line far away, now just a dark ripple on the horizon. The animals they rode didn't share their sense of duty, taking little munches of grass now that they were finally off the road and standing still.

"Breathtaking," I said, not daring to say what I really thought. "Impossible" was more like it. I grew up on a moon orbiting a gas giant orbiting a supergiant star. Orbital Mechanics featured prominently in our education, and Ralqir flew in the face of even the most basic principles of what I was taught.

"The streams of stars you see there are just two arms of the maelstrom. You can see the edges of more of them if you look near the horizon. The shadows in the sky are the remains of our sister planet, Brella, and, of course, it would be impossible to miss the moon, not so close to the city. You'll see it more clearly tomorrow."

I opened and closed my mouth like a dying fish. "It's a very busy sky," was all I could get out.

"Huh," he grunted, sounding nothing like the scholar he claimed to be. "Indeed, I suppose so, though no one has put it that way to me before. You have a strange perspective, young Ryan. Most react to their first open sky with some variation of joy or fear or religious awe. You, though, call it 'busy.' Unbelievable."

I didn't take my eyes off the sky, but I could feel Jassin staring at me—*through* me. What was he looking for?

After a long moment, Jassin seemed to give up on eliciting some kind of response. "All the same, I find that it teaches a sense of history and proportion. This view is what our ancestors learned to fear during the Purge, but now we study it with the naked eye, as long as we are here. The message is a bit more poignant now than during the day," he said.

He'd said that before.

"During the day?" I asked, raising an eyebrow.

"Oh, yes. You can come out during the day, my boy. This is the only place left on our planet where you can do so. While the rest of our world belongs to the Mendau, this is the last glade: Skyglade."

"Because of the moon?" I guessed.

"Correct. Perhaps they still teach some history in Lavistal after all."

I almost didn't catch the trap, my mouth already opening to ask more questions, but I caught myself in time. "Vistia, you mean. I'm Vistian."

"Ah, yes. Of course. Anyway, I thought you might want to see this. Some people go their entire lives without seeing the sky in such resplendence. You might be able to get away with looking at the stars in a tiny clearing with slight cloud cover, but here, you are safe to study it as long as you like, thanks to the moon's proximity. In fact, many have dedicated their lives to doing so at the observatory. A little farther up the road, and you'll be able to see the top of its tower there."

"In Eclipse," I said, as one of the pieces of the puzzle that was Ralqir fell into place for me. Of course the city's name was Eclipse. "The name is a little on the nose, isn't it?"

Jassin cleared his throat. "Yes. Quite so. I probably would have named it something sufficiently poetic if it were up to me, but the crusaders that liberated this land were not known for their imagination. No matter the name, it is the Dark Lord's parting gift to the people of our world after he set the Purge in motion."

Switching gears, the nobleman sighed contentedly, twisting at the waist and extending his arms into a good stretch. "Alright, let's get to the city. I have to check in before morning if I don't want to be given a demerit, and the sooner I get to the university, the sooner I can examine your condition and send you on your way."

# CHAPTER TWENTY-FIVE

# Join a Sect

We rode through the night, the wagon wheels, the clacking of hooves, and the clicks and chirrups of the multitude of insects keeping us company. Jassin didn't have much else to say after we got back into the car, which was fine by me. The guards, however, seemed to liven up slightly after we'd been in the glade for a while, laughing at little personal jokes or occasionally singing some tune or another.

I could see why their spirits were up.

This place was so open. Skyglade was more of a wet grassland than a mere gap in the tree cover. After the murky claustrophobia of the swamp where something nasty—like, say, a goblin with an electric ax—might jump out at you from behind the next tree, I imagined the guards found the wide, open spaces of the clearing downright relaxing. There were still unknowns such as the occasional naturally forming pond or clump of thick shrubbery, but ambushers would largely have a much harder time getting close enough to do damage here.

Jassin spent much of his time writing in his notebook or staring thoughtfully out of the window. Once in a while, we would pass clusters of moonlit wooden buildings that had the look of homesteads or maybe stables. None of their windows were lit, and nothing moved in their vicinity except for the grass. The homesteads themselves were more than just quiet. They looked abandoned or at least buttoned up to such a degree that I couldn't imagine anyone living there.

We never lingered at any of these places, and the guards seemed to dislike them as well, growing silent when we passed and keeping their fingers on their triggers until we were well down the road.

After a couple more hours of travel, I was back to dreaming again, this time about my workshop, but I didn't get too far into it before Garret called for a halt, then leaned down to poke his head into the window. He looked troubled.

"We've arrived at the gate, my lord."

"Is there a problem?" Jassin asked.

Garret sniffed and waggled his mustache. "It's closed. We haven't been challenged yet, but I'm about to knock."

Jassin groaned softly. "I knew I should have slept during the ride. Feel free to mention my name to get us through quickly. Tell them it's imperative I get to the university as soon as possible."

The old soldier grinned at that and gave us a wink that pulled one side of his mustache up to nearly cover his eye. Then he rode away from the window and shouted something up at the gate. It didn't sound like a word, otherwise the System would have helped me understand it; maybe they were using some kind of code.

"Yes? State your name and your business!" someone challenged from a distance.

"Lord Trayalo Jassin and his men-at-arms here to report to the Black University for a period of tenure!" Garret answered.

There was a brief pause, but then the challenging voice came back. "Alright, then. Off your mounts and get everyone out of the carriage for inspection!"

Jassin sat up suddenly, his expression dark, eyes darting around the carriage almost like he was assembling an invisible puzzle with his eyes. I mirrored his posture, not knowing exactly why, but I could intuit that something was wrong.

"Is that strictly necessary?" Garret asked hesitantly. "My lord must get to his post with haste."

"'Fraid so," the gate guard replied. His voice sounded weary, like a man who had been through this routine countless times and had answered this very question ad nauseam.

"By whose authority?!" Jassin leaned out of the window and shouted his question to the gate guard. "I hope you know who you are detaining here and what my standing is."

There was a slight pause before the man replied, and when he did so, it was apparent that he didn't appreciate Jassin's tone. "We are all very impressed, my lord, but I have orders from the prefect herself that everyone must be inspected before they enter the city. In this city, the prefect has perfect authority to do as she requires, and, right now, she requires we do this. Now, if it pleases your lordship, get everyone out in the open so we can do this and get on with our lives," the gate guard shouted. "With all due respect, of course, m'lord," he added at the end.

When Jassin brought his head back into the car, he didn't look as angry as he'd sounded. Instead, he again just looked through me as if the answer to his unspoken question was written on my bones and it was mildly inconvenient he couldn't just crack me open to put the mystery to bed.

Wanting out of the carriage anyway, I put my hand on the latch to do as the guard had said, but Jassin put a hand on my wrist. His grip was strong, cold.

"Wait," he hissed. Then he reached under his seat and knocked on the delicately carved wood—once, twice, then several more, a single knuckle at a time in some kind of pattern. A vertically hinged door I hadn't noticed popped open forcefully as if it were spring-loaded to reveal a hidden compartment about the size of a dresser drawer.

I couldn't see the contents properly in the dim light, but Jassin apparently knew what he was looking for. He bent down and rifled through the little cubby, pulling out various objects, jewelry chains, fabric, bound stacks of paper, a cane, holding them up in the light to check them, then shaking his head as he discarded them. After a minute he found what he was looking for, and he handed it to me.

It was a folded length of long orange cloth, soft to the touch like some of the nicer clothes I had back on Proxis.

"Put this on," Jassin whispered.

I raised a curious eyebrow. "Put it on what?"

"Your head. Tie it in the back."

"Why?" I asked.

"In case they have the wrong type of practitioner on gate duty tonight," he said as he stuffed everything back into the compartment and snapped the door shut again.

Outside there was a deep, sonorous groan accompanied by a reverberating clatter of metal on wood. I pictured an enormous gate with half-ton hinges being pulled open by chains big enough to moor a cargo ship.

"Gate's opening, my lord," Garret reported from outside.

*Yeah. No kidding, Garret.*

"Hurry!" Jassin commanded, but when he saw the blank look on my face, he blew out an angry sigh and reached up to drape the cloth over my head. "Here. Hold still. Listen to me carefully." He tugged on the fabric, tightening it until it felt like a snug cap. Then he wrenched the back to force me to look into his eyes and see how serious he was.

"Listen. You are a monk of the Order of Dawn. You've been imbued with a sacred duty that brought you to Eclipse. Brothers of your order are not a loquacious bunch, so no one will expect you to speak more than one or two words. Use that."

"I don't understand," I said. I would have shaken my head, but Jassin was currently ratcheting the cloth tight around my skull. "Why do I need to hide?"

"I know you don't understand," he replied, "but you need to do this if you don't want to draw suspicion. Take off your shirt and try to look dangerous. They'll be put off and less suspicious if they see your Dominion sign out in the open. Your aura will help sell it."

With a boom, the racket outside subsided.

"Half a platoon coming outside, lord," Garret said quietly from behind the curtain.

With a grunt, Jassin cinched the knot on the cloth tight enough to make it feel uncomfortable. He'd covered my entire head with it like a skullcap. "Take off your shirt, and let's go."

"Why am I hiding?" I asked. I didn't like this. Yes, there was plenty I didn't want out in the open, but Jassin didn't necessarily know that. What interest did he have in keeping my secrets all of a sudden?

"Because of what you are," Jassin hissed, pleading, forceful, almost desperate.

I held my breath.

"Getting closer, Lord Jassin," Garret mumbled from outside the window.

I swallowed the lump in my throat and weighed my possible replies. "Because I'm a Wildling," was the one I went with.

Jassin just glared at me, his mouth moving around like he was chewing on the inside of his lip. There was a long, pregnant pause where the air froze between us.

"Yes. Exactly," he replied tersely. "Now go. You need to leave before I do. Be forceful. Confident. You are beyond question."

My mind flashed back to my cell under the mountain.

I frowned at him, but the man didn't budge, silently pleading for me to go along with it.

With some trepidation, I slipped the shirt over my head, feeling the chill in the air prickling my skin as Jassin flung the carriage door open, committing us to this plan.

Taking a deep breath, I stepped out into the night, jumping down from the car to land on the smooth cobblestones of the road.

We were parked in a wide semicircular plaza overlooked by an imposing black wall made of stone and reinforced with thick strips of banded metal that ran along the bottom ten feet, interwoven with one another like wicker. The gate had to have been thirty feet high, thick as my entire body, and operated via pulleys and chains whose links probably weighed more than one of our furry mounts.

Around us was a little town composed of wooden structures that had the same abandoned feeling as the previous homesteads. Stalls sat empty in sloppy lines that formed a labyrinth of ramshackle wood, while the bigger buildings, inns, depots, shops, and the like loomed darkly over the rest, some of their wooden signs creaking as they rocked in the breeze. Somewhere out of sight, a door slammed against its housings over and over in time with the wind.

"Hey." An elbow nudged me in the side. Garret was there with his crossbow pointed downward and his finger off the trigger.

"Look alive," he said, nodding to show me where to look. Two columns of six soldiers stood in front of us, well apart from Jassin's guards, who stood in a similar formation but more informally. The two parties were just close enough to speak without shouting.

Most of the soldiers wore heavy-looking black breastplates of banded mail with sleeves of chain that came down to thick leather gloves with metal plates running up the backs of their fingers and hands. All but two of them stood at attention with long pikes. The odd ones out carried big crossbows that—judging by the soldiers' postures—were particularly heavy. Steam rolled out of the fronts of their darkened helmets and rose in clouds from their shoulders.

Was it really that cold? I certainly felt the chill on my skin, but it only went as far as that.

Jassin was next to me then. "Stop gawking. Look more menacing," he muttered from the side of his mouth.

I'd forgotten that part. It would certainly be helpful if I knew why I was playing a character here. I flexed my fingers into fists and put on a scowl, the kind I remember my dad wearing, though I was sure it would be more convincing if I still had eyebrows.

Garret stepped forward and addressed the soldier on the front left of the formation. "This seems pretty irregular, Sergeant."

"Aye. It is, sir. Highly irregular indeed," the sergeant said with a yawn. "This has been protocol for two months now, and it's got me and my boys stretched thin. If you don't mind, I'd like my people to get started on the search, so we can all get back inside and safe."

Garret looked at Jassin who, after a second's hesitation, gave a slight nod.

The sergeant didn't waste any time. He waved his soldiers on, and each of them picked a place to search, having people turn out their packs and saddles. A couple of others climbed into the carriage and poked around inside. If Jassin was worried they would find his hidden compartment with weird props, he didn't look like it.

"What is this all about, Sergeant?" Jassin asked, his tone exaggeratedly imperious, veering well into snobbish territory when he said the guard's rank. Apparently, I wasn't the only one playing a character tonight. The ruse was so obnoxiously effective that even I fought to not roll my eyes and dismiss the man as a spoiled child in an adult's body . . . and I was in on the joke. "Please tell your men to be careful. Some of the tools I carry are sensitive. If they break anything, I will lodge a formal complaint."

The sergeant sighed, closing his eyes to gather his patience, bringing a gloved hand up to rub them. Then he stepped forward to stand a polite, conversational distance from Garret, Jassin, and myself. When he answered, it was easy to tell he was doing his best not to lose his temper, and he seemed to meet Garret's and my eyes more often than Jassin's. "It's plague, my lord. A possible one, at least."

Jassin's eyes shot over to me and back. "What is the nature of this plague?"

"So far, I've been told very little, my lord. I'm just doing my part. What we meager guardsmen are looking for are stowaways, artifacts, and suspicious characters. If you have questions about specifics, you may want to ask the representative of the church when they get here. They'll be performing the check for sickness."

The guard sergeant turned to me and bowed slightly, making some kind of finger gesture on his forehead, too fast for me to follow. "It's good to see you've come, Rising Sun. Welcome from the faithful. The Church will be happy for the help, if no one else."

Not knowing what else to do, I nodded to him while I kept my scowl going.

Jassin wasn't ready to give up his objections, though. "Is getting the Church involved strictly necessary, Sergeant? I'm sure the university has someone on staff who can examine us once we check in. Their medical department is top-notch, and we've been delayed enough."

"'Fraid so, my lord," the guard said again. "So far, the Church are the only ones able to pick the sick from the rest. Normally, I'd have someone go get you a drink or food from the inn, but we're a bit short on hospitality outside the walls as of late. Goblins and beasts are everywhere now. Have to bring everybody back in for the night a lot of the time. I have a cousin who runs one of the beer halls out here, and it's been hell for business."

"I assure you, we've had no contact with the plague, and we've not stopped long enough to be at great risk. I'm also obligated to begin work at the university immediately under the queen's orders, which supersede your authority. I demand passage to the head office where we may go through examination there." Jassin was pulling rank on the poor guy now, using his title as a bludgeon. There was a strained edge to his voice I might not have been able to pick up on if I hadn't ridden around with him for hours before. He was dialing up the noble part of his personality, and it was already pretty prominent.

"Sorry, my lord. No one gets in without the Church checking them over. You may file a grievance with the prefect in the morning if you like, but for now, we have to wait."

"Worry not, Sergeant Imar. Your wait is over," a rich basso voice called from the direction of the open gates. A man in white robes was there, approaching the rest of us. In his hand he carried a staff whose head burned with bright yellow flame. He walked upright and lightly, like he didn't need the staff to walk, leading me to suspect it was a totem of his office.

He was large, easily head-and-shoulders taller than me and overly thick in neck and belly, though his robes hid the latter well. He had slitted eyes, a wide, flat nose, and an enormous mouth that seemed to stretch from ear to ear, and his glossy black skin caught and distorted the torchlight in interesting ways, creating little yellow ghosts that danced on his shiny, bald head.

Once the robed man got within thirty feet or so of us, the air warmed by at least ten degrees. The change was so sudden, it was shocking, like a switch being flipped. I could feel my blood flow returning to my skin and restoring the color that the cold had leached from it. Strangely, even as the man drew closer, the heat never got more intense. I was just suddenly warmer and more comfortable while, two seconds ago, I wasn't.

"Bishop Kolash," the sergeant gasped, suddenly very present and eager to please. "I apologize. I hadn't realized you would be coming yourself, Your Holiness. This is a routine check, and I wouldn't have bothered Your Holiness with it if—"

"No need to apologize, Sergeant," the bishop boomed with a smile that pulled the corners of his mouth back until I couldn't see them anymore, and I had to assume they just kept going until they met at the back of his head. "It's only fair I take the night shift from time to time just as I ask of our more junior members. Now let's get on with it so our guests may enter and rest. The road is dangerous of late, and I'm sure their bodies and minds could use the respite."

The sergeant, all sweetness and light now, hopped to, placing himself to the side so that he could present us to the bishop. "Your Holiness, we hadn't quite gotten to the introductions yet, but they seem like reasonable folk. Cooperative, at least."

Kolash tilted his head from side to side; it seemed to rotate in place without his having to bend his neck. He was holding his staff aloft now, lighting us all from above, so I was having a hard time making the man's face out properly. However, I could see that he'd closed his eyes.

Then, without warning, his mouth opened wide—wide enough to swallow my head—and he let out a sound that was a cross between an engine backfire, an out-of-tune horn section, and a belch.

Something . . . odd passed through me, an electric shockwave of sound and purpose that rattled my insides and threw off my equilibrium. The atoms in my body vibrated and shifted, rubbing together in sympathetic harmony with the discordant note. Yet, whatever this was, once it passed, it left me feeling clear-headed and refreshed. Aches and sore muscles I hadn't realized I had, loosened their grips on my already-taxed nervous system, fading away. The sleepiness I'd been fighting was replaced with a calm restfulness I'd not felt in years.

Tears welled up in my eyes, though I didn't know why.

It was like surviving a storm and seeing the sun again.

I turned to look at the others. Jassin had fared much, much worse than I had. He staggered on his feet before catching hold of Garret's shoulder; the guardsman steadied his master with a strong hand under the nobleman's arm. The guards didn't seem to be affected at all.

"I apologize for the discomfort you are feeling," Kolash croaked, a little bit of the multi-toned magic still echoing in his voice. My eyes tried to un-focus again, but the power wasn't nearly as overwhelming this time.

The bishop shook his head ruefully. "Secular practitioners are contrary creatures, so focused on shielding themselves from others to the point that you won't readily allow the Light into your being. Yet you open yourself to the raw forces of creation. It is a contradiction that I have yet to understand fully."

"Not raw," Jassin coughed, shaking his head and waving Garret away. "I'm fine, Garret. I'm fine. The power we focus is not raw, Bishop. In fact, it's quite the opposite, since we've built our own Dominions, sometimes over generations. The problem lies in our natural reluctance to trust just any old spell to sweep through our bodies and souls like it's spring cleaning, but you probably already knew that."

The bishop smiled and bowed his head slightly in acknowledgement.

Jassin straightened his robe and stood upright again, his lordly presence reasserted. "I assume you found no plague, and we may now be on our way?"

"None of you are carriers of the plague, as far as I can tell," Kolash declared. "Light clear your way."

Then he turned to me, another one of those too-wide smiles on his face. He reached forward and placed a heavy, three-fingered hand on my bare shoulder. His palms were paler than the rest of him, with the disturbing addition of being rough and slightly sticky.

"Brother, it is a welcome surprise to find you here. We did not expect our plea to be answered by one such as yourself, but you are most welcome in our city. It is an honor to have a Rising Sun grace us with his unique expertise," he declared. "Come. Let us leave scholarly business to scholars. We will prepare a room for you at the sanctuary. Food as well."

Just then, I remembered I was supposed to be looking menacing, so I didn't reply out loud. I set my mouth in a stoic frown and shook my head meaningfully.

Jassin spoke up. "Oh? Is this necessary, Bishop? I promised to our monk friend I would take him as far as the university, and I am a man of my word."

"The Church thanks you for your service, sir," Kolash replied, not turning to address the noble, instead keeping his gaze fixed solely upon me. His tone held unwavering authority, however, along with a little menace. "I suggest you leave us Church folk to our business, and you go about yours. If you would like to show our brother your university, we can easily arrange that at a future date."

I narrowed my eyes and shook my head again.

"No. No. I insist, Brother. I'm sure you are keen to begin your work, but you would benefit greatly from the Church's support. There is much you must know."

I resisted the urge to look at Jassin for some kind of clue. What exactly did this guy want? What's more, what would a monk of the . . . uh . . . Order of Dawn do in this situation?

"Need I pull rank?" the bishop asked, raising the ridge of one eye where you would normally find eyebrows. This close to him, he looked much less human. Not only was his skin not the flesh I expected, but its sheen wasn't sweat. It was *texture*, smooth and damp. What's more, his tiny eyes were bright yellow orbs with amoeba-shaped blotches for pupils.

Staring into them, my mind raced, grasping for a way out, but I found nothing but partial plans and probable failure.

Initially, I had been hoping to get away from Jassin and his people as soon as possible once we got into the city. I had money from the corpses I'd looted on the road, and I could probably sell a few things to get a room somewhere. Then I could find a way to get provisions and get out there on my own again, away from people that asked too many questions . . . like Jassin.

*What does he know? What does he suspect?*

Could I do the same thing with this church? The bishop was promising a room, perhaps a private room. What's more, they didn't expect me to speak too much. Fewer words meant fewer opportunities to out myself as an alien. I also got the impression that a Rising Sun was a position of some prestige, and I could assume they would watch me less closely than Jassin and his people.

That was what clinched it in the end. Jassin wasn't what he seemed, and he was very concerned with keeping me close. Going with the Church would give me the option to slip away or to build goodwill with Jassin by undergoing his examination by choice as opposed to under threat as before.

Decision made, I nodded to Kolash and gestured with my hand for him to lead the way.

Bishop Kolash started off immediately, his long legs already eating up a deceptive amount of road and forcing me to hurry to keep up. With the big man's back to me, I turned back to look apologetically at Jassin, whose eyes bulged with fury. Storm clouds roiled behind his eyes, and a thick vein throbbed just beneath the skin of his forehead.

I gave him a little shrug and broke out into a jog to catch up with my strange guide.

# CHAPTER TWENTY-SIX

# Answer the Call

Bishop Kolash was largely silent as we went through the sleeping city. His pace was quick, his long legs eating up a surprising amount of distance while his staff *pang*ed on the cobblestones underfoot. I still wasn't wearing shoes, making the pace and the makeup of the street an unpleasant experience, but at least my feet hurt in the conventional way, not the bare-skin-on-quellstone, knives-in-my-bones way. Apparently, the city itself wasn't paved in the stuff, which was a relief. I couldn't imagine a scenario where having life-sucking rocks right outside your house was a good thing.

*Really need to get some boots or something before I leave.*

The thoroughfare was a wide river of gray, banked with impenetrable walls of hulking, wooden buildings jammed tightly onto either side, so closely they could all be mistaken for a solid structure like the city walls. The road sloped gently down from the gate where we left Jassin and his people, just enough that I was able to feel it like I was being guided along by a sluggish current.

Most buildings were several-floors tall, with canted roofs that sloped away from us, big shuttered windows, and awnings covering wide wooden stoops only a few steps off street level. Every set of doors that led to our road was tall and wide, and each sported multiple fat, wooden signs that swung on long metal poles stretching diagonally up and out over the street, each trying to reach out longer than the other. The shape and color of the signage was of such variety, the gently swaying planks so numerous they probably cast the street in shade much like the forest canopy we'd left behind.

*"Is that comforting for people to live under?"* I wondered. On a planet so

dominated by greenery, maybe some folk felt living under an open sky was a touch unnerving.

I didn't know what time it was, but I got the feeling we were in that fun part of the morning where it was too late to go to bed but too early to be awake. Almost no one was out and about, and there were very few signs of life. There were exceptions to that rule, though. A few chimneys billowed smoke, and I could smell the tantalizing scent of baking bread and the rich, greasy aroma of spiced meat somewhere out there.

Sightings of fellow travelers were rare, and they tended to shy away from us—or, more likely, the light on the bishop's staff—instead sticking to the side of the road or turning down the much-narrower side streets upon spotting us. Occasionally, we'd pass a stoop with a snoring figure curled up against the building's entrance, presumably leaching some of the heat from the gap under the door.

As we left the gate area, the slope of the terrain steepened, carrying us down lower until our street intersected with another of a similar, expansive width where, together, they formed a square. Cold fog pooled on the ground, ankle-deep and thick as soup, and the stones were slick with moisture. In the center of the square stood an empty black plinth that, at one time, had an inscription on its front, but someone had taken great care to destroy the writing with something sharp.

The familiar, icy fingers of the quellstone were back with me as soon as I set foot into the intersection. I could feel it under my bare feet, and though I couldn't see it, I could feel that the stones had sizeable, regular gaps between them like the spaces of a grate.

*A drainage system, maybe? That makes some sense. It's huge, though. Where does it go? Why pave it with quellstone?*

A solitary figure dressed in loose gray robes worked a broom on the far corner of the square, supposedly the only person out at this hour not on their way to somewhere else. The bristles of their broom made a harsh, *shick shick* sound loud enough to carry across to us, and something about the aimless, spasmodic way in which they worked drew my eye. The way the worker carried themselves. The way they moved. The lack of pauses, single-mindedly scraping their broom across the same stones over and over again.

Their hood prevented me from seeing their face or a general shape, turned away from me as they were, but the skin on the worker's hands, the parts not covered in bandages at least, looked purple and bruised. Every couple of seconds, the hood of the robe would list to the side as if the person within couldn't hold up their head or didn't care to.

The bishop didn't pay the figure much mind, however, taking a right turn to head down a different street, and I did my best to stay in his shadow, keeping a low profile and pretending to know what I was doing while making it look natural. A sort of blend-in-by-looking-like-I-had-nothing-to-hide sort of thing. It was an art, really. Soon my feet were back on regular cobblestone, and we were headed back up into another district.

Stealth is now Level 5.
Upgrade Paths available:
Reduced Presence
Gray Man
One with the Shadows

*Huh?*

This was the second time Stealth had Leveled without me realizing I was using it. Sure, I was trying to hide, but I was in plain sight. The first time this happened was during my first night in the forest as I slept. I was hiding in the hollow of a tree when I'd Leveled up in my sleep. The other times were more overt uses of the Skill where I'd hidden from the big creature in the tutorial facility and then when I was hiding from Jassin's guards.

That brought into question exactly how it worked. Was it my intent that mattered?

Regardless, I'd hidden from something. Successfully.

We approached the bishop's church from the side. Easily the biggest building I'd encountered so far, the structure was in the rough shape of a prism with a triangular front and back and a long bit in the middle. Carved stone and polished wood made up the base, which gave way to a baffling array of colorful stained glass for the roof that stretched up to the building's tip. The church was lit from the inside, making the glass glow warmly in the early morning dark, a beacon for those who could see it.

We entered through double doors set into the wide base of the street-facing side and stepped into a warmly lit foyer, big enough to hold fifty or so people, with lots of gray fabric over old and multihued polished wood. From inside, the stained-glass ceiling looked dark, but I imagined it was quite a sight to see during the day when the sun was out.

A lit brazier crackled and popped in the center of the room, illuminating another set of double doors, these with round metal knockers, leading out of this room. The bishop led me over to the fixture.

"Ah. Here we are," Kolash said, pausing to stretch and take the place in like he was coming home after a long day. Then he reached up to the head of his staff and plucked the dancing flame from the head, cupping it in his palm before tipping it into the brazier. The orange flame trickled out of his shovel-sized hand like liquid, and the bowl *whoosh*ed, flaring high enough to graze the bishop's skin. He didn't show any sign that the heat had harmed him, though.

"Your Holiness!" someone yipped, their voice muffled by the doors beyond the brazier. Muted scrabbling noises came from behind the wall followed by a *bang*, and one of the doors rattled with the impact. Muffled grunts could be heard, as well as soft scratches, as someone struggled to do something on the other side of the wall. Then, with the sound of some kind of mechanical latch being disengaged, one of the doors clicked and swung open for us to enter.

"Shall we, Brother?" Kolash asked before stepping through the doorway and into the next room, a sanctuary of some kind with rows and rows of wooden pews all facing a pair of altars on a raised dais of smoky-gray stone. I made to follow, reflexively reaching out to keep the door from closing as I passed through, but my hand came down on something fuzzy and warm . . . and wiggly.

The high-pitched shriek that wanted to burst out of my mouth didn't quite make it to freedom. I caught myself in time and turned it into a sort of gasp that bordered on a wheeze.

Reflexively, I brought my hands up as if to take a swing at the thing before I could stop myself, but the damage was done.

"Oh! Excuse me! I'm sorry!" yipped the little voice yet again, this time from what I'd taken for a door handle before. This door did have a handle made of thick brass, but there was a creature hanging from it. It was three feet long with triangular ears on top of its head, a pointed nose, and it was covered from head to toe with brown and black fur almost identical in hue to the wood of the door. The robe it wore—tan but for bright white stitches on the seams—hung loosely from its shoulders and arms.

Dropping back down to the floor and scrambling on all fours, it got a polite distance from me before standing back up on its back legs, rubbing its front paws together nervously. Its wide, black eyes stared up at me, and its ears flattened as it bowed in my direction. "I'm so sorry, I didn't mean to startle Brother—uh—Mister Brother of the Dawn."

Kolash boomed with laughter that echoed from the hard surfaces of the church and shook my squishy bits. It was a strange sort of laugh, like he was both amused and violently sick, featuring a lot of burps and gurgles.

What exactly was I looking at here?

Apparently, the bishop could read my expression well enough to answer my unasked question. "You have never met a vulpa before, I take it, and the way you look at me, rahns must be in short supply in your monastery as well."

I nodded reluctantly, not wanting to offend, and I set my jaw back to looking severe and hoping to not just come across as having a bout of constipation.

The fox creature shrunk slightly under my gaze, like he desperately wanted to hide. "Don't worry, Mister Brother of—Brother of the Dawn, sir. It happens a lot. I realize that I am very small. I didn't mean to—"

"Yik'i'trix, the proper way to address him is simply 'Brother.' You are of the same rank. Despite his order's pedigree, we are all part of the same church. Am I correct?" Kolash asked me with a raised eyebrow.

I nodded again. I wasn't about to argue with the bishop. I was a holy man myself now, after all. Looking down at the little fox creature, I allowed my frown to slip for a moment.

Yik'i'trix wasn't having it, though. He bowed low again. "I'm not sure I'm comfortable with that, Your Holiness, but I will try to address him properly. May I ask our brother's name so that I may apologize formally, Your Holiness?"

"He has not told me," Kolash said. "We were just about to get to that in my office."

"Oh, well, I apologize, Brother. I hope I can assist you in whatever you need while you are here. Would you like food or water? I am very fast, and I know my way around the kitchen."

I shot a glance over at Kolash, who simply looked on with quiet amusement. I really wasn't comfortable with the bowing and scraping, especially if it was directed at me. The concept of this kind of hierarchy felt foreign and ridiculous to me. My dad was the headman of the Clan, but that just meant he made decisions when the council wasn't in session. No one thought he was any better than the rest of us. My people had a saying, "Bow to no one, stand for each other," and we generally meant it.

I swallowed quietly, hoping this didn't set a precedent.

"My name is Ryan," I said, keeping things short and simple. I regretted it immediately.

Yik'i'trix did this full-body-shudder thing starting small at his tail and creeping all the way up until his head practically shook off his shoulders and his ears made slapping sounds against his skull.

"Oh! Brother Ryan, you honor me with your voice. I promise I will treat being one of your trusted few with the respect it deserves." Now he was bowing even lower, practically vibrating on the floor.

*My first day as a monk is going swimmingly. Jassin, if I see you again, we're going to have words.*

Kolash saved me from this supremely awkward moment with one of his half-belches. He was doing that more and more now that we weren't in public.

*A cultural thing, maybe?*

"*Hurp.* Yes, it is a great honor, I am sure, Yik'i'trix. Now, please, do go and get our new guest some refreshments. Bring them to my office. Also, prepare a room for him."

"Yes! Yes!" The little vulpa took off like a shot. He ran on all fours, slipping beneath pews and taking corners at great speed, the rapid padding of his feet the only sounds we could hear until an unseen door creaked and subsequently slammed somewhere out of sight.

"Come. *Bwoorf.* Before you gain a full retinue," Kolash rumbled with obvious displeasure, swiftly leading me further into the church. I followed him all the way down the center aisle between the pews until we hooked a left and went through an unassuming archway and into a set of plain hallways at the end of which was the bishop's office.

The hulking man propped his staff against the wall by the door and walked around his huge desk to sit in his equally enormous chair, gesturing for me to sit as well, in—if you could believe it—another enormous chair. The size of everything in the room made the ink pots, pens, seals, papers, and scrolls on the bishop's desk seem like they belonged to a child, but I suspected if I reached out and took one, I'd be holding something pretty standard-sized for a human.

"I think you just made Yik'i'trix's year, Brother Ryan, but I ask that you don't get his hopes up too much," Kolash said with a deep, concerned frown that subdivided his head in interesting ways.

I knit what used to be my eyebrows together.

*Two people in the room, and not an eyebrow between us. It takes . . . what? . . . weeks to regrow hair?*

"Speak, please, Brother Ryan. I promise not to ask it of you often."

I just sat there, stone-faced. The last time I'd spoken, I'd nearly made a tiny fox-man pee himself. I had no desire to continue that trajectory.

Kolash cleared his throat. "*Urp.* Very well. Consider it an order. Know that I do not do this lightly. We will need to communicate if we are to solve this problem of ours. Now speak."

Apparently, the bishop was my superior. I remembered him saying something like that before. Noted.

*Let's keep this conversation away from me.*

"What do you mean by not getting his hopes up?" I asked.

"Yik'i'trix's dream is to belong to a militant sect of the Church. Your order is something a cut above, if I may be so bold, a reputation well-cultivated and I have no reason to doubt it. Since you just took him into your confidence by sharing your voice with him, he might have hopes of following you back to your monastery to undergo the trials."

I scratched the back of my head where my monk's head-covering came together in its knot. "And that would be bad?"

Kolash sighed and leaned over to look worriedly past me to the door before answering. "Yik'i'trix has many talents and a kind soul. His place isn't on a battlefield. It would ruin him."

I furrowed my brow, contemplating. "Shouldn't that be up to him?" I asked. Of course, the little guy was adorable, but why shouldn't he be allowed to build himself up and fight? I spent years wishing I could do that very thing back home.

"Of course," Kolash acknowledged. "He is free to serve how he sees fit, but if

you do not plan to initiate him, do not give him reason to hope. *Brorp.* I was surprised when you deigned to speak to him and bring him into your confidence.
I would have rather had this discussion beforehand, but I suppose the damage
is done now."

He had me there. I hadn't realized a word from me would mean so much,
but I had to roll with it now. "Like you said, we need to communicate if we're
going to solve our problem."

"The plague." The bishop's lips parted and a deep, displeasured croak escaped
from his maw.

"I take it things are dire," I guessed.

He shook his head. "No, not yet, but situations like this can escalate quickly.
What did your order tell you before you came?" the bishop asked.

"Some," I said, leaning forward to listen intently. "But I would like to hear
it all from you."

Deception is now Level 4.

The door to the office creaked open, and Yik'i'trix poked his head inside, his
pointy, satellite-dish ears angled toward me but his eyes on the bishop. "I have
food and drink for you both, Your Holiness."

The bishop leaned forward to see over his desk, all smiles again. "Yes,
Yik'i'trix, bring it in, please."

The vulpa disappeared for a second, then came back inside, balancing a tray
on his head with two arms supporting the underside while he walked on his hind
legs. He'd made what looked like little finger sandwiches with sliced cheese and
greens, along with a pitcher of water and cups to wash it all down. He served the
bishop first, then myself.

"Thanks," I said after taking the offered cup. The finger sandwiches called
to me, even more tempting than the mockvine's deer-girl illusion. I hadn't had
anything green in months, and cheese was something rare even on Proxis. My
stomach gurgled.

Yik'i'trix did that full body shudder again, nearly dropping the now-empty
tray, but then he bowed and waddled back out of the room.

Kolash looked at me reproachfully, grunting with displeasure, but he didn't
chastise me.

*You go and live your dream, little guy. Don't let the frog man keep you down.*

The bishop downed his water in one long pull, then set the cup atop a stack
of papers.

"As I was saying, the situation is *becoming* dire. The plague is a most-vexing
one, incurable by any method we possess other than the most radical of purge
procedures, and even then patients do not survive the curing. We started seeing

it three months ago, when the goblin tribes began to cross the mountains and the truly desperate came knocking on our gates. A trade caravan was set upon by a large pack of feral goblins, off-color skin, long claws, completely mad. Thankfully, although the caravan lost people, they were ultimately able to put the goblins down. However, when they arrived in the city, one of their Returned started showing symptoms."

I tilted my head to indicate I was listening and wanted to know more, hoping Kolash would take the cue instead of requiring a more specific question.

"I know. Returned being affected by plague. Outlandish on its face, but we are cursed to live in interesting times. The sickness manifests in hallucinations, nervous twitching, nonsense speech, and violent outbursts. It's horrible to see, especially among such a vulnerable population as our Returned. We went back to the site of the battle to try and get a sample of the plague carrier, but the bodies were gone—either taken by scavengers or carried off by others of their kind."

My brain was going a mile a minute, trying to think of appropriate, intelligent questions to ask. "How long does the plague take to run its course?" was all I came up with.

"It doesn't. The afflicted never get better. They get worse. They stop speaking entirely. They're violent and temperamental. Beasts are affected largely the same way, though knowing their symptoms is a guessing game unless a very specific type of practitioner is on hand. We've tried to contain the sick and tease out the plague's nature, but, so far, our talents have largely been ineffective. We can't let the afflicted wander free, but we can't take care of them all. We've taken to using the old cathedral ward as a haven for the sick, but it's like trying to put out a fire by smothering it with straw."

Kolash leaned forward to put his elbows on his desk and folded his long, three-fingered hands.

"We haven't told anyone yet, but we were getting desperate enough to send for military aid to contain the spread. The infected Returned—all of them— eventually try to escape the city. They choose the shortest path south and just set out. They become violent if you interfere with them," he said gravely.

He hung his head and reached up to rub his eyes with the heels of his hands. "Worse, on my approval, the city watch allowed one of the afflicted a line of egress from the city walls, and I had a pair of scouts follow it out into the wilds. *Roorkch.* They have not yet returned after two weeks."

He made that little sign with his fingers like the sergeant had done at the gate. I caught more of it this time. The way Kolash folded his fingers, it was a rudimentary triangle. "So, you see why I was . . . well, I wouldn't say *pleasantly* . . . I was . . . surprised when I saw your order had dispatched you to us, but perhaps it is providence. As I wrote in my request, I would have loved for a specialized healer to be sent from the main branch, but that was then. I am more and more convinced this threat might require a full Purge. Another crusade if we do not act quickly enough. I hope your order's specialized capabilities are even half of what your reputation says."

# CHAPTER TWENTY-SEVEN

# Choose My Way

We didn't have much to discuss after the bishop's revelation. For one, I'd just been told I would be responsible for murdering—no, "purging"—innocent people, sick people, and that was something I was being asked to do because of the costume I'd been handed before this party.

It goes without saying that I was not entirely on board with this plan.

Even if I had the know-how or the strength, I didn't think I was capable of doing what Kolash wanted. The idea of it slammed up against my conscience so hard, I could almost feel it physically.

*Nope. Nope. Nope. Nope. We are not going full murder-hobo. We are leaving. They can excommunicate me or something.*

On the other hand, the supposed cause of the plague, the Scourge-Touched, were something with which I was intimately familiar, and if the goblins were to be believed, something I caused. Whatever I'd done back at the tutorial facility provoked them, and then I led them on a chase, one that got a lot of goblins killed.

I'd gotten Hunty killed.

Now the Scourge-Touched were, presumably, still fixed on finding me, and people were being caught in the crossfire. The situation wasn't fair to any of us.

I didn't ask to be rebuilt and inserted into this universe, but here I was anyway. The people of Ralqir didn't ask to have a human drop into their lives and kick off an extinction event.

The Scourge-Touched . . . well, they *might* have asked for this. They attacked me first, and I didn't get the impression they were just upset I'd landed in their backyard. This was something else. Something deeper.

A quiet but confident voice repeated the familiar accusation over and over in my mind.

*You did this.*

Rationally, I knew it wasn't necessarily true, but I couldn't shake the feeling that I was responsible for the situation somehow. What I'd intended or that I didn't know what I was doing didn't matter. People were suffering because of me, and I didn't know how to stop it.

*You did this.*

It was too much. Much too much.

My spiraling thoughts must have been plain on my face, because Kolash detected that something was wrong after maybe the second or third awkward silence between the two of us. He stood up and came around the desk to loom over me, his amoeba pupils staring unblinking down into my own.

"*Horp.* May I be honest with you, Brother Ryan?" he asked.

I didn't answer. I felt lost.

"Though this is a dark time for Eclipse, I find some glimmer of hope that the Light sent you in particular to us. I see the worry on your face and the conflict in your spirit. Perhaps you are not simply a weapon as I'd feared."

That was true . . . or was it? Despite my misgivings, I was pushed into this situation and not given a choice—at least not one I was smart enough to see. Now I was here, and Kolash had put me in front of what he thought was the only solution. I was being shown a nail and asked to hammer it, but was I a hammer? Did this particular nail need hammering? And if I didn't hammer it, would Ralqir collapse?

I wasn't this guy. I wasn't a holy warrior sent by their god to purge the unclean. I was just a dude wearing a stupid orange hat.

*And maybe that's a good thing.*

"I need time," I rasped. I cleared my throat and summoned a bit more strength to continue. "And I need information, any you can give."

"If your methods require evaluation, you are free to do so. I will assign you a guide who will do whatever you require, and I am afraid you will likely come to the same conclusion I have. Light knows I've looked for alternatives," he said, pausing to let out a long, tired sigh that left him deflated, diminished. The bishop, the quintessential picture of authority and strength, aged in front of my eyes, diminishing until I was looking at an almost completely different man than the one I'd met at the gate. "Perhaps it is selfish of me, but I feel some measure of comfort having someone else here to share the burden of this decision. My rank carries with it some implied divine wisdom, but I rarely come across a situation where the path is truly clear."

I stared up into those amoeba blotches of black that were his pupils. He was asking me something without actually asking. Maybe he didn't want a purge, either.

The bishop pressed a plate of food into my hands and gestured to the door. "Get some rest. Tomorrow, you can begin your work."

Kolash guided me back down the hallway and to a set of stairs that led underground. As with most of the non-window parts of the building, the walls were worked and sanded wood and stone, broken at regular intervals by solid-looking doors with little triangular slats at roughly head height.

They did love their triangles here.

My room was at the intersection of two hallways that met each other at an acute angle, with my door at the very corner.

Inside, the room was gray brick on three of the walls and the floor and lit by a glowing hemisphere of glass built into the ceiling, low enough to comfortably touch but not so low I'd hit my head. There was a wooden trunk with a latch and lock right next to a table and a bed. When I saw it, I nearly tripped over my own feet, having to catch myself on the doorframe and forcing Kolash to pull up short.

"*Borp*. Oh! I know it's not much, Brother, but I was given to believe the Order of the Dawn were ascetics. If you would like a different room, I could ask Yik'i'trix to—"

"No, it's fine," I chuckled darkly. "It's just the first bed I've seen in a long while."

"Oh," the big man said, his mouth opening and closing a few times as he searched for something to say in response. He chose to sidestep the subject instead. "Well. Good night then, Brother Ryan, or 'good morning' would probably be more appropriate. I'll have your guide meet you once you've had your rest."

With that, he was gliding back down the hall, his long legs carrying him quickly to wherever bishops went to sleep.

I closed the door and engaged the slide lock.

The bed creaked under my weight as I sat down on it, holding my plate of sandwiches, but the structure held. I popped a little morsel into my mouth, letting the greens crunch and the saltiness of the cheese play over my tongue.

I had decisions to make.

First and foremost, what was I going to do?

My goal ever since I'd arrived on Ralqir was to survive the tutorial and get back home.

It was my one and only goal, or maybe it was my ultimate goal, the last in a series of goals that would see me home to start living my new Exotic life.

Now things were more complicated. My arrival here affected people, whether that was what I had intended or not. If I slipped out in the night, that would leave the people of Ralqir stuck with the consequences of what I'd set in motion.

The Baned were swarming across the mountain, the goblins were homeless and desperate, and the people of Eclipse—though I hadn't gotten to know them yet—were probably the next domino to fall.

My coming here had changed things.

Whether it was my choice or not, my arrival was the first pebble of a rock-slide, and the disaster was growing with every passing second.

If I left, would that disaster pass? Maybe. Eventually.

Perhaps the more important question was: *What cost was I willing to pay for my ticket home?*

Vince's memory surfaced in my mind, how he'd died, the way he drew Barrow's ire in a desperate play for time, how he couldn't just let Barrow single out another one of his friends for murder.

Then there was Hunty. He'd died in my place, too.

Two. Two good lives I'd already cost the multiverse.

*CRACK!*

---

Status gained: Bleeding [.08 HP/s]

---

*Dammit.*

I looked down at my shattered plate, the remaining pieces in my hand smeared red with my blood. I forced myself to relax my fingers and let them fall, then brought my hand up to my face to pluck a sliver of ceramic out of my palm. Even now, I could see the skin welding itself together in real time.

I'd be costing the multiverse more than just two good people if I ran. The landslide was bigger than that. This was unacceptable.

I nodded to myself, slowly at first, then with more confidence.

*I'm one of the System's fucking Chosen. About time I earned that.*

Yes, I would be staying to fix things. No one else was dying for me.

*Not. Even. One.*

I bent down to pick up the pieces of ceramic plate off the stone floor, eyeing the rest of the little sandwiches among the shards of the broken plate.

*Well, it would be a waste if you didn't . . .*

It wasn't my proudest moment, but, man, these things were good. Compliments to the chef.

Belly full and path chosen, I was ready to make my other decision.

---

Main Class Ability: Shape is now Level 5!

Based on current Skills and Affinities, you have four Upgrade Paths available:

Transmute

Remote Shaping

Duplicate

Enchant

I'd gotten this prompt back in my cell an unknown number of days ago, shortly before the Baned flooded into the cave to become my new neighbors. I hadn't known what to do then, when my goal was simple survival and escape. Now, though, I had a new perspective.

> Transmute: Shape may now convert one type of matter with which you have an Affinity into another. The strength of both Affinities will dictate the cost of conversion.

> Remote Shaping: Shape may now be used at a distance. [1 meter*S, where S is the value of Spirit over 10]

> Duplicate: Shape may now copy any Shaped material within range, given proper material and mana are available. Mana Cost is slightly reduced, and Shape Speed moderately increased.

> Enchant: Shape may now imbue your creations with limited intelligence, allowing them to perform certain tasks that require some level of logic and decision-making. Complexity and cost of intelligence is affected by the Mind Attribute. Mana required to power Enchantment provided by user and is conditional upon its complexity.

For a long time, I was stuck on this decision. Most of the options seemed useful in the short term, with Duplicate and Remote Shaping making my short list.

I didn't need to take Enchant. I was sure of that one. My ammo worms could already do what the System was describing, and they didn't need to make any decisions to . . .

*Wait! Yes, they do.*

Every obstacle they encountered and step they took, while I took them for granted, were actually decisions they were making on their own, without the use of something like Enchant. *How?*

The question set off a chain of explosions in my mind.

Imbue specifically said I imparted a small fraction of my will to my automatons. That made some sense, but how did my ammo find their way back to me? They didn't have eyes or nerves or even the equipment needed to develop a sense. If they were truly thinking on their own, they had no way to do what they did.

There was something I was missing—a piece of the puzzle I couldn't see, but it was integral to the whole design. Magical dark matter. My method worked, though, and, so far, worked without fail.

If I was imparting some of my will when I automated things, that took out a whole lot of legwork normal programmers had to do to get their stuff up and running. What if . . . *Holy shit.* What if I automated more than just my ammo? I could make a smartgun with smart ammo. Hell, with some trial and error I could probably make smart ammo that made *more* smart ammo. Swarms of it. Giants mechs. Magical nanobots.

Wow, I needed sleep.

More than that, I needed time, materials, and somewhere to experiment, like, right now.

*Okay. Breathe.*

I inhaled deeply and closed my eyes, searching for calm. I missed my workshop. Pity that Barrow's people burned it down and even the ashes were a universe away.

*Still have a choice to make.*

Transmute had been at the bottom of the list for a long time, ever since I first saw it. My mind had been consumed with acquiring iron and Shaping it into equipment at the time, so it made sense. I had zero strong Affinities, and I got the impression converting something like limestone into magnesium would be prohibitively expensive. My Mana Pool would bottom out maybe a second into the process. I had Engine to alleviate that, but I would pretty much be giving myself a migraine over and over and over for minimal gain.

However, Consume and Engine were absolute game-changers here. The more I Consumed of something, the higher my Affinity for said something climbed. Eventually, I had to stop focusing on my immediate situation and start playing the long game. I was going to get more Affinities, and I was going to grow them over time.

If I were to take Transmute, I could conceivably . . . literally . . . turn lead into gold, given I lived that long.

*Wait for Ms. Right or settle for Ms. Right Now?*

| Class Ability: Shape upgraded! (Transmute) |
| --- |

Immediate decisions made, I brought up my sheet to get the full picture of my status.

| Ryan Kotes - Level 9 Animator (Uncommon) | | | | |
| --- | --- | --- | --- | --- |
| **Type:** | Artificer (Common) | **Abilities:** | Shape 5 (Transmute) | Devouring Grasp 4 |
| **Class:** | Animator (Uncommon) | | Consume 4 | Volatility 3 |
| **Core:** | Engine (Unique) | | Iron Grip 3 | Imbue 2 |
| **HP:** | 115/115 | | Trigger 3 | Automate 2 |

| MP: | 75/75 | Skills: | Climbing 6 | Unarmed Combat 1 |
|---|---|---|---|---|
| Body: | 24 | | Running 1 | Stealth 5 (?) |
| Mind: | 21 | | Conduit 3 | Split Mind 6 |
| Spirit: | 33 | | Spear 4 | Deception 4 |
| | | Affinities: | Goblinoid F | Mendau Wood D |
| | | | Iron F | Limestone E |
| Free Attribute points: 0 | | | Magnesium F | |

My eyes closed and almost didn't reopen. I desperately wanted to lie down, but entire planets don't just save themselves.

*So much to do. I should stay up and do . . . something.*

The weariness was creeping up on me fast, but this was the first moment in a long time where I was alone and relatively safe. My belly was full, and I had a door between me and the world. That temporarily covered like half of my physical needs. I'd been working with less for a long time.

I rose from the bed and got down on the floor.

I'd collected a variety of materials to play with here, but not all of them were feasible tonight . . . or this morning, rather. Much of my pure iron was already Shaped into my pistol and my ammo worms. I couldn't work with those right now, considering I was in a confined space, and all the best gunfire had the tendency to attract attention.

Melee weapons weren't out of the question, but I kind of had some of those already, courtesy of the goblin ambushers. They were small but wicked things, but I could probably use them in a pinch, whenever my firearm wasn't the right tool for the job. Mr. Grippy would always be at my side, too.

I shook my head. I was rationalizing a choice I'd already made. I wanted to tinker. I just needed to accept that and get the hell on with it.

The Baned were legion, and I was just me. It was time to even those odds.

*Despite lacking eyes, my ammo can find me. I tell it to do something, and it does. Let's play with that. Smart gun? Smart gun.*

One look at the amount of metal I had on me told me that I didn't have enough to make or test anything big. This was going to be a proof of concept more than anything else.

| Shape [4 MP/s] |
|---|

My first victims were five of the goblin hatchets. They were made of something called "baptized bronze" which, as a pleasant surprise, was more than willing to accept mana and do what I wanted. It couldn't be rushed, but compared to what I could do with vanilla iron, I was practically flying through the Shaping process. First, I expanded the holes in the ax-heads to remove their wooden shafts. I'd need those to keep the mana flowing.

> Status gained: Engine [3 MP/s for 1 hour]
> You gain knowledge of material: Mendau Wood [12/1,250]

Next, I went to work hollowing out tubes, just like I'd done with my pistol, but this time, I scaled them down. I wasn't trying to build a fully functioning firearm in a church basement. I just needed to know the limits of my . . . whatever it was.

I made a base for the construct, a simple half-dome that fit in the palm of my hand with a couple of Trigger areas where I could feed mana.

Mounting the barrel on top was fairly simple; it just needed a hole that fit a melded pillar of bronze with just-enough room to turn easily and a ball joint for more range of motion. Additionally, I put a tiny nub of iron on the tip of the barrel and designated it the sight.

The idea would be to get my smartgun to turn so that the sight would be as close to the chosen target as possible and keep it there until told otherwise. Simple in theory, but getting my smartgun to adjust its aim was a little more difficult than I'd anticipated. At first I envisioned gears that would turn to adjust the horizontal position of the barrel, but that required a lot of time Shaping to pull off. I was confident I could do it, but not today.

Instead, I went with what I knew. I gave the base of the barrel and the back of the firing chamber a set of automated, multi-jointed legs that—again, theoretically—would adjust themselves to point the barrel in the right direction. Furthermore, I only allowed the barrel to adjust itself by about sixty degrees in any direction as a safety measure.

The end product was, in a word, ugly. It looked like two mutant spiders using a cannon for a seesaw, but if it worked, I would call the night a success. This was more about pushing Automate beyond what I'd done before.

The final piece, a wafer-thin plate of bronze—the "smart" part of my smartgun—I inserted into the base of the barrel housing where all the component parts would have at least some contact with it. I spent an entire pool of mana and some change automating it.

*When you are Triggered, feed mana into the aiming arms. Bring the sight as close to your target as possible. Feed a small burst of mana into the firing Trigger. Repeat.*

The process took it out of me and felt like blenders under my skin, but it was worth it.

The System agreed.

> Automate is now Level 3.

With everything in their general place, I went about Shape-welding the pieces together, connecting the legs and firing mechanism to the brain housing and placing Triggers where mana could be fed into the different automated bits to activate and deactivate them.

"Okay, here we go," I breathed, picking up the construct and eyeballing all the components. The base sat comfortably on my hand, heavy but not so much that 24 Body couldn't hold it steady.

Up on my feet for the first time in hours, I set the remains of my plate in the corner of the room as a makeshift target. I eyeballed it, shifting my palm so that the smartgun was pointed slightly off to the right, so it would need to make an adjustment to fulfill its programming.

Rubbing the sleep out of my eyes, I reached up and fed mana into the base's Trigger.

Nothing happened. Not a damned thing.

Grumbling, I Shaped it again, diving into the component parts and checking for what went wrong.

Everything that needed to move was getting mana. Nothing was stuck on anything else. The brain was humming, the legs were tensed and awaiting instructions. Why were they just—

*Oh. I'm an idiot.*

I'd not designated a target. I'd just given it a general idea of "targets" when I'd Automated it. Maybe I needed to be more specific, perhaps keeping possible targets in mind when creating the instructions? Furthermore, I also did not give myself a way to designate a target after full assembly. Holy hell, was I tired.

One more ax-shaft Consumed and a full pool of mana later, I was one migraine richer and down to just hoping to see *something* happen. I was starting to fall asleep on my feet, and I knew I was making mistakes. I just couldn't drop it.

*When you are triggered, feed mana into the aiming arms. Bring the sight as close to the ceramic target as possible. Feed a small burst of mana into the firing trigger. Repeat.*

Shape [4 MP/s]

Once the brain housing was sealed again, I fed mana into the activation trigger.

What happened was fast.

The construct jerked itself to the side so suddenly, it nearly leapt off my palm. My reflexes weren't fast after an entire sleepless night blasting mana into delicate machinery, so I didn't catch it. It toppled from my hand even as the programming took control.

*THAP! THAP! THAP! THAP! THAP!*

Tiny balls of bronze, fired at a rate of approximately three per second, pelted the ceramic plate in the corner. The first hit it dead center, shattering the plate into three pieces, one of which, by some fluke of physics, flew up and into the air. The four follow-up shots from the smartgun chased that particular piece, stippling miniature gunfire over the target, blasting it into smaller and smaller bits.

Bronze BBs and ceramic shrapnel hurled themselves around the room, pinging off hard surfaces and raking my skin, a hailstorm of stinging debris. All I could think to do was cover my face and let it happen.

Out of ammo but still trying to fire, my smartgun hit the ground barrel-first and bounced, its brain telling it to destroy all the ceramics in the room but without being properly upright, all it could do was flop on the floor like a fish. It clanked and clattered, its barrel snapping impotently from one of the scattered pieces of plate to the next.

I brought my arms down and checked myself over. There was blood on my chest, but the wound had already closed. Otherwise, I was fine.

I bent down and carefully snatched the little murder machine up, then fed mana into the "off" Trigger.

Now that I thought about it, there really was no reason to give the smartgun actual ammo for the test. That was dumb.

Still. Success!

Regardless, I considered my time well-spent. Again, the System seemed to agree.

You have created: Toy Auto-Turret
You have been awarded 550 Experience points. [650 base, -100 quality]

*Hell yeah, System. I've made a tiny turret!*

I was exhausted, physically and mentally. Clustered ideas ground against each other in my mind—abstract, delirious, wild, exciting, terrifying. My head felt like it was an egg, and a terrifying, roided-up baby chick wearing a red bandana was about to burst forth from my skull.

Flopping down on the bed, I closed my eyes. This was nice. I could stay here for a few minutes, until the migraine passed, anyway.

Then I was dreaming of a rocky beach next to a black ocean.

In front of me was a scattered pile of driftwood, perhaps the shattered remnants of a once-impressive ship or maybe an old hut. It didn't matter. I just needed to leave, and soon. I lashed the disparate pieces together with what little rope I could find in hopes of making a raft, but no matter what design I tried, I kept coming up with doorframes. On the horizon, through the haze of humid ocean air, a great wall of water was rushing closer by the second.

# CHAPTER TWENTY-EIGHT

# Disguise My Intentions

I awoke to a polite tapping on my door. It wasn't easy. The bed, though probably hard and uncomfortable by my old life's standards, was the pinnacle of luxury now that I'd had the humbling experience of sleeping on a cave floor. I opened my eyes, instantly regretting doing so. The overhead light was still on. Apparently, I hadn't bothered to turn it off after Science Time—not that I knew how, anyway. There were no switches on the walls or a chain to pull.

I groaned, sitting up, my eyes bleary and swollen. I put my head in my hands and let my weight slump down until I was nearly doubled over and a quiet sigh slid from my dry lips. The bed creaked under the strain of my shifting weight.

The tapping came again.

*That's not going to go away, is it?*

It did not, in fact, go away. It waited for about a minute, when I was just beginning to become hopeful, then the tapping returned.

Reluctantly, I rose from the bed, made my way over to the door, disengaged the slide lock, and yanked the door open more forcefully than I intended.

The hallway was empty.

"Ah. Good morning, Brother Ryan! I brought you breakfast."

The hallway was not empty. I just hadn't looked down.

There, holding a tray of some kind of glazed pastry stacked in a little pyramid, was Yik'i'trix, his little black eyes staring up at me expectantly. The sleeves and hem of his robe looked like they'd been dusted with flour.

"Uh. Hi," I said, staring at the little vulpa blankly, the speech center in my brain not allowing for much more. After a few seconds of silence, I realized that maybe I should say something else. I'd never been a morning person. "How long did I sleep?"

Yik'i'trix did his full body shudder again, all the way from the tail to the tip of his nose. "Nearly fourteen hours, Brother."

"Fourteen?"

"Yes, Brother," the tiny monk said, nodding gravely. "I did try to wake you, but you must have needed some time to yourself after such a long journey."

I blinked as my mind made a few connections. "Wait. How long have you been out here?"

Yik'i'trix got even smaller than he already was. "Since earlier today, Brother Ryan," he answered evasively.

"How long?" I pressed.

"Oh. I didn't really keep—"

"Please."

"Eleven hours." He said the words so quickly, like he was anxious to rush through them to have them out and be done with them. I'd bet that without the System, I might have had to make the little guy repeat himself, but they came through loud and clear.

"You've been waiting on me for eleven hours? Why?" Constance, how did I kill so much time? I had a whole planet to save.

"I convinced the bishop to let me be your guide. I've heard tales of the Rising Suns, how your bodies are disciplined to need very little rest, and I thought I would wait, lest you need to leave early. It's actually been quite pleasant, not having to do my regular duties around the church. Half a day alone to meditate is practically a luxury."

I brought my hand up to my eyes to rub them. Could I get conventional headaches anymore? I was probably about to find out.

"Ah, I see. Please don't do that on my account, Yik—uh, do you have a nick-name or something shorter?"

"Trix, Brother Ryan."

"Trix," I said, letting the name roll off my tongue and reminding myself that no matter how I perceived it, I wasn't speaking English.

Curious, I wanted to try something.

"People call you Tricks?" I asked experimentally, consciously thinking about communicating the meaning of the English word instead of the literal phonetic sounds. What came out of my mouth didn't sound like English at all.

"Oh, no, Brother. I would never deceive you," Trix assured me. His ears deflated like triangular balloons and his gaze slid down to the floor. "I am not like that." The little guy looked genuinely hurt.

*Apparently, intent is what matters in the translation. Names are different from words. Noted. Kinda feel like a jerk now, though.*

"I'm sorry, Trix. Really," I said as I squatted down to get closer to his height. "Your name sounds like something else in my mother tongue, and I was just— Well, I don't know. I'm sorry."

"No offense taken, Brother," he replied. I knew it was a polite lie, though. Sore subject, maybe?

"Anyway," I said, clapping my hands together. It made a sort of ringing, flesh-on-metal sound these days, but it worked to break the tension at least. "Let's go hit the town. Next time, please don't wait for me like that. I might keep a weird schedule."

He shuffled his feet nervously. "Well, it is my duty to be at your side whenever you need. I took the room across the hall, just in case," Trix replied, indicating the door by turning around and pointing his nose at it.

Of course he did.

I ran a hand down my face, imagining all the trouble this was going to cause me. "Wonderful," I said. "How thoughtful."

Trix drew up straighter at that. "So, what is the plan today, Brother Ryan?"

"Just 'Ryan,' please."

"Oh, no. I don't think so, Brother." He did that full-body-shudder thing again, the pastries getting the worst of the kinetic energy, sometimes leaving the tray entirely, only to land back on top of their pyramid. With that, I realized I still hadn't taken the breakfast Trix had offered. I reached down and grabbed the platter to take the burden off the little guy.

It seemed like a lot of food for one man, but it smelled delicious, sweet and savory at the same time, multiple layers of scents rolling over one another. Maybe there was meat in the middle or something. Before I took a bite, I held one out to my new guide.

"Did you want one, Trix?" I asked.

Trix shook his head, rubbing his front paws together. "Oh, no. Baked goods don't really agree with us vulpa, though I hear they are delicious. I already had my fill at lunch. What's the plan today, Brother Ryan?" he asked again.

I sighed. If we were going to be attached at the hip, that would get old fast. However, I could use a little bit of orientation, and he'd volunteered for just that. "I need to know everything, and I'm not just talking about the plague."

"Everything?"

"Yep. Trix, you are my local expert on everything Eclipse. Pretend I know nothing."

He shuffled his feet some more, unsure of himself. "Would you like to start on a specific topic, Brother Ryan?"

I rubbed my jaw as I thought about that. The root of everyone's problems right now, other than my mere existence, was the Scourge-Touched. They chased the goblins and beasts out. They brought the plague. They were attacking people outside the city. How could I dig at that problem?

*If you're going to dig, you'll need a shovel.*

"Trix, we're going shopping. How good is the Church's credit?"

Yik'i'trix's whiskers trembled slightly. "I—I didn't ask."

"Never mind. Wishful thinking. So, I have a list of things I'll need, and I need you to keep an open mind."

> Skill Unlocked: Disguise
> Your current Skill Level is 1.

"I just don't see why you would want to cover your holy raiment with . . . that," Trix said as we stepped out into the daylight once again, having to lean to the side to allow two elderly women to enter the building behind us. I tipped my hat to the two of them as they passed by, but neither of them took any notice of the courtesy. Maybe that was Gray Man working.

> Gray Man: Stealth now receives bonus efficacy from your Deception Skill. While you are attempting to hide, others are less likely to notice you, and those that do are more likely to disregard your presence. [Passive]

It wasn't the sexiest choice on my list when Stealth hit Level 5, and I still wasn't sure it was the right one. All of the Skills were situationally useful, but after focusing on the long game with my Shape upgrade, I'd felt the need to balance that with something that would be useful to me right now.

My Deception Skill was getting a workout while I was living undercover, and I spent a lot of my time hiding in plain sight. Gray Man made the most sense there, and I couldn't discount that I might find another way to use it in the future.

So far, it had been hard to detect if it was working, like with the women entering the shop. Maybe the women didn't respond because they disregarded my presence, or maybe hat-tipping wasn't a thing here.

*A man buys his first cool hat and can't even tip it? Tragic.*

My hat had a wide brim and a pointed top that reminded me of the old kung-fu films my dad used to play on movie nights. I'd gotten the thing for cheap after buying a full set of local clothes and a pair of shoes to go with it.

Trix didn't complain about the clothes, since he'd picked them out: a simple pair of brown trousers, a long sleeve white shirt, and some light boots. I thought he was going to have a seizure when I proposed taking off my orange head-wrap, though. Thus, the hat was added to the tally, despite Trix's frequent objections. The old tailor had been enthusiastic to sell it to me, almost like he wanted to be rid of the thing.

"What? I can't go around looking like a lit candle the whole time, right?" I asked, straightening the woven straw hat so that it sat properly on my head. It had a tendency to slowly slip down to cover my face.

The vulpa winced. "Brother, please. You share too generously."

He didn't like it when I spoke in public, either. Apparently, my order took vows of silence except in extreme necessity, and I was having a hard time respecting that, especially since I was feeling almost human again. I had a full belly, clothes that fit, real shoes, and I wasn't locked away or fighting for my life.

*Remember where you are, Ryan.*

The Eastern Gate Market was absolutely packed with people, so much the press obscured the surface of the street itself. The sides of the road were mostly pedestrian traffic that flowed in a river that you had to fight against if you wanted to break off and climb one of the stoops like the one where we stood. So many faces, so many eyes moving over me. How long would it take for them to notice the stranger in their midst?

The sheer variety of sentient species and how they lived together was astounding and surprisingly natural. Short folk with broad faces and pointed eyebrows rolled their litter of boisterous kids in padded carts through a gaggle of what I could only describe as burly, walking mushrooms with bright yellow caps atop squint-eyed faces. Tall, spindly-legged creatures wrapped in bandages waded through the throng, gingerly stepping over others at times, patiently waiting for the crowd to surge forward at others. An eight-foot-tall pile of gravel rumbled down the street under its own power, and, though most of the people gave it the appropriate amount of space, the amorphous creature stopped to form a thick pseudopod to gently nudge its way through the crowd every once in a while as well.

The majority of the traffic, however, was made up of the horned folk with sharp features like Jassin. They all had the look of merchants or middle class, judging by the quality of their clothes and the way they walked, as if they were always on their way to somewhere. Serious. Purposeful.

I held out my hand and allowed Trix to clamber up onto my shoulder. He'd protested about this at first, earlier in the day, insisting that he just follow in my wake as we fought the crowds and went about our business, but when I'd pointed out that he needed to guide me everywhere, he'd relented and allowed for a semi-dignified ride on my shoulder.

Once he was next to my ear, Trix was a little more talkative, as long as I didn't raise my voice and break my vows.

"I just feel like covering the thing that singles you out as a member of such a prestigious order of the Church militant would make your mission harder, Brother. The sleeves on your shirt also mask your Dominion sign, so no one will know you are a practitioner, either," Trix whispered.

"You think I'm inviting more trouble by trying to blend in?" I asked quietly, stepping down off the stoop and merging with the part of the crowd streaming deeper into the city.

"Yes, Brother. I'm afraid we might attract the wrong sort of attention if we go around asking questions without some sign of office, and those we do question will not appreciate the deception."

"You may be right," I admitted, but I left it at that. The thing was, I didn't want to be singled out by anyone, even if it made my life easier. I wanted to blend in and tackle the city on my terms, not throw my cover story in people's faces. People tended to believe something more readily if they discovered it on their own, and I wanted to use that to my advantage. Let them believe my status as a Rising Sun was my only secret. Plus, if I were to wear the label proudly, the order's reputation would taint every interaction I had with people, and I required a much lower profile, especially if I was using my own money to buy metal.

It turned out that the amount of gold I had wasn't a particularly hefty sum. Sure, it was enough to buy a set of local clothes and shoes, but after that, I needed to watch my spending. The people the goblins killed weren't wealthy, and the coins the mockvine left me upon its untimely death weren't legal tender. The tailor hadn't even recognized the thick, stamped ovals until Trix started oohing and ahhing over them.

Apparently, they were coins minted ages ago, right after the Purge. Everything always seemed to be framed around the Purge, so much so that I was afraid to ask for clarification on what it was. It sounded like something that was such common knowledge, I'd out myself if I asked the wrong questions. Better to pick it up from context clues.

"If you wanted to look for a collector to take those coins off your hands, we will need to go more toward the center of the city," Trix ventured. "I think that will make it easier to get the rest of the items on your list."

"Okay, do I just head toward the observatory, then?" I asked.

Eclipse, the walled parts of it anyway, was built in a half-circle around the observatory. It was the oldest structure in the city, there in the beginning when the Dark Lord built it, and still there even after the city's newest occupants made themselves at home. No matter where you were in the city, you could spot the observatory—even through the riot of color and motion that was the sky within the market districts—a black tower of glossy stone that stabbed up into the atmosphere higher than even the tallest Mendau, its smooth surface unbroken for hundreds of feet until it terminated suddenly in a jagged diagonal slash, like someone had forgotten to finish construction or a giant had hacked at it with an ax.

Of course, if you were looking up it would be impossible to miss the backdrop of the moon. It loomed overhead—huge, brilliant white, shot through with spiderwebs of gray as clouds of glowing gas flowed around its edges and shifted slowly from one color to the next, while the sky was a vibrant teal broken up by feathery wisps of cloud.

"No, Brother. That way butts up against Riverside, and trouble may find us if we venture too close, not that someone like you would be worried about that, of course."

Riverside was supposedly one of the rougher parts of town, best avoided unless you had business there, and only around noon. It was, unsurprisingly, the part of the city that dealt with trade coming in from the river, but it also had the misfortune of being an area that sank down below water level a few more inches a year.

As Trix told it, when the Dark Lord had originally built his city, the Shenau River wasn't quite so far south or quite so wide. Now, a thousand years later or so, the river was a constant headache for city planners and architects, claiming more of the northernmost part of Eclipse year by year. A couple of centuries ago, a huge swath of Riverside suddenly collapsed upon itself, sinking below the waterline in a matter of seconds, entire neighborhoods vanishing into the depths below.

Now the place was the home for folks down on their luck, treasure seekers of dubious moral character, leather-skinned boatmen on shore leave, or criminals, and one did not need to pick just one category to belong to.

I nodded in agreement. "I did say we're trying to not attract attention. Getting robbed qualifies. Good thinking."

Trix's full body shudders were even more disturbing when he was riding on my shoulder. It was almost contagious. I had to fight not to give in to the tingle as well.

"Where should we go then?" I asked.

"That way," he said, pointing leftward. "This route will take us past the Plague Ward. I assumed you would want to see it before the day is out."

Ah, yes. The supposed scene of my future massacre of innocent people. A must-see, for sure.

"Right. I'll . . . definitely need to see that. Lead on, then," I told my guide. I kept my face neutral, but, inside, I felt queasy. Obviously, I didn't plan on gunning down a bunch of sick folks, ever, but something inside me recoiled at even being in proximity with my hypothetical victims, as if by entertaining the idea I was betraying myself. The System decided to kick me while I was down as well.

Deception is now Level 5.

Upgrade Paths available:

Cloak of Vagary

Compartmentalize

Charming Presence

*Splendid. Can't wait to choose the most effective lying power.*

"So, the Plague Ward is near the center of the city? Doesn't that put people at risk if they stumble into the wrong part of town or if there's a breakout?" I asked.

Trix's head tilted to the side, and he leaned over to look me in the eyes like he was trying to determine whether I was messing with him. "No, Brother Ryan, not at all. Our route takes us deep into the Undercity. No one gets there by accident."

# CHAPTER TWENTY-NINE

# Know My Enemy

Trix had me follow the flow of traffic and make my way over to the other side of the street, a difficult feat if we were at all concerned about being run down by a cart full of grain or accosted by caravan guards. There was an art to it, namely sliding in next to something larger than yourself and using its wake to make your way to the next.

Eventually, we reached a point where we could break off from the main thoroughfare and turn onto a wide street where the pace was much more sedate. People stood and talked to each other here, some sitting on stoops or on the edges of plain stone fountains. The street ended in a cul-de-sac that encircled a squat structure of plain stone in the shape of a blocky pyramid. On each side was an arch with stairs that led down.

And that's where we went, down multiple landings that connected to each other at strange angles. At times, we'd reach a landing that practically had us going straight on to the next set of stairs, and at the other extreme, sometimes the stairs would make a sharp turn and double back on themselves, thinning out until only one person could go at a time. There were few-enough people now that Trix felt comfortable walking again, taking the stairs in bounding, four-legged leaps that would carry him down a flight in less than a second before he would stand up again and wait for me at the bottom. His long, low-to-the-ground frame seemed built for this.

The temperature dropped several degrees, and the humidity spiked. Cool, wet air ruffled my clothes and caressed my skin. More of those little light orbs hung from the walls of every landing, offering some dim illumination and pulsing in time, like the city was breathing.

We went down fourteen flights of stairs before we leveled out. Then we were in a curved tunnel with a vaulted ceiling and intricate stonework featuring lots of strange angles and asymmetrical shapes that confused the eye and distorted the echoes of our footfalls.

Everything was made of dark stone fixed with mortar, except, strangely, where the light orbs shone. Those appeared to be relatively new additions, with rougher-hewn bricks spackled in to hold the light in place. Our tunnel was only wide enough to fit a few people side by side, and it wasn't entirely level, either. The floor would gently rise and fall over time, seemingly at random. Meanwhile, the bricks fit together so neatly, the place must have been designed like this. Why not just build the floor level if you're going to build one at all?

According to Trix, the Undercity—its shape, at least—was part of the Dark Lord's original design. When I asked about some of its stranger aspects, however, he just shrugged and said, "It's mad, but the Dark Lord made it this way for a reason. Most people think it was part of the first Dominion ritual, but we can only speculate. We've simply learned to live with it . . . or above it, rather."

Additional archways yawned at us from the sides, sometimes leading to another tunnel that traveled perpendicular to ours, other times terminating directly in a stairwell or what looked like a railed water well complete with buckets and pulleys.

Every once in a while, we'd enter a significant intersection, a stack of wooden signs hanging down from the ceiling with helpful labels and arrows pointing toward side tunnels or telling us to watch our step. They mostly held street names, but some of the bolder signs said things like "Library," "University Ward," or "Egress." Those were always painted in bright yellow.

Trix was right about it being lighter on traffic down here. People were a rare sight, and even when we did see them, no one was talking. The densest foot traffic was at a wagon-wheel-shaped intersection of eleven different tunnel systems in a big circular hall lit by dozens of those luminous fibers like the ones in Jassin's carriage, high up in the ceiling, swaying like stalks of seaweed in an upside-down ocean.

Clusters of people in black robes or flowing gray half-cloaks gathered and spoke in quiet, intimate tones as they loitered around a cluster of wooden stalls surrounded by tall tables and chairs. The stalls themselves were set up like a pub, with kegs and bottles lined up on the back wall while they served customers from a chest-high bar with stools in front. A lively string-and-drum tune played over all of it, loud enough to be heard but quiet enough for people to still be able to converse over it.

We deviated from our initial tunnel system at one of these unmarked intersections and pushed on until it was pitch black.

"Yik'i'trix?" I asked, groping around and shuffling my feet.

"Yes, Brother?"

"I can't see."

"Oh, yes. Sorry. I hadn't realized. Reach out with your right hand and feel along the wall. There is a rail there for you to hold. We'll be through shortly."

I put my hand out as he asked and found the wall, cold and slick with moisture. So cold, it scraped my nerves raw.

"Is this quellstone?" I asked.

"What? Oh. Yes, I suppose some people used to call it that. Your knowledge base is as old as the coins you brought. Most of the Undercity is still the Dark Lord's design," Yik'i'trix explained. "He used the quellstone for much of his city."

"Why are there no lights?"

"Out of respect, Brother. This is a Returned neighborhood."

I found the railing at about chest height, smooth and cool but not cold like the quellstone.

"And you can see?" I asked.

"Yes, Brother. We vulpa prefer the dark, in fact. It's easier on the eyes."

I walked forward cautiously, sliding my hand on the railing, trying not to trip.

"There is an intersection here. Just follow my voice, and we'll get to the railing on the other s—," he said just before there was a sort of thump, followed by a tiny, pained yelp.

"Oh. I'm so sorry. I did not realize you were there," Trix yipped apologetically to someone out there.

There was a pause and then a slow, rasping intake of breath. It reminded me of a leaky bellows opening wide to draw in air.

"Is fine. Are you lost?" It was a woman's voice, slurred and strangely hollow-sounding. It wheezed with every vowel, like wind over hollow reeds.

"No. We're not lost. We're just passing through. I was so busy leading my friend that I wasn't watching where I was going. Again, I apologize, Miss."

"No worry. Live people visit the Down, and it's good."

"If you are alright, then we'll be on our way. Have a good day," said Trix. I heard Trix's front claws clicking on stone in preparation to get moving again.

"I know you?" the woman's voice asked.

"Uh. I don't think we've met, Miss," replied Trix.

"No. Him. Do I know him?"

"I— I—" Trix stuttered, probably pondering a way to answer without saying I was part of the Order of Dawn. "No, I don't think so. My friend is new in town."

"Someone knows him," the unseen woman declared matter-of-factly.

"That . . . could be," said Trix with some hesitation. "Everyone knows someone."

"Someone knows him. I hear it. It hurts." It was almost an accusation, her tone growing surer, harsher, like Trix had offended her somehow.

There was a pause. I imagined Trix blinking a couple of times and rubbing his paws, thinking of something appropriate to say to that. "Yes. Well. We'll be getting on our way," was all he came up with.

"Wait. I do know him. I do," she said, her voice breaking in the middle as if she were on the verge of tears.

"I really don't think you do, Miss. You're confused."

For a handful of heartbeats, all I heard was my own breathing and Trix's paws shuffling on stone. I wished I could see.

"Maybe," she breathed, drawing the word out weakly. "I do get confused sometimes."

---

Stealth (Gray Man) is now Level 6.
Disguise is now Level 2.

---

There it went again.

*What? What am I hiding from? I don't understand.*

"So do we all, Miss. What is your name?" asked Trix.

"Magtha."

"Have a good day, Magtha."

Then a little vulpa paw was in my hand, and I found myself being dragged swiftly along, nearly doubled-over, until the ambient light in the tunnel started to show my companion in outline. By the time we were in the light, we were both breathing hard.

"What was that about?" I huffed. Crouch-running wasn't something meant to be done over that distance.

Trix shook his head. "I don't know. She was acting strangely—more strangely than the Returned usually act, at least, but they all have their eccentricities."

"That was a Returned?"

"Yes, but she was . . . I don't know. I felt like her attention was elsewhere, too. Strange. I hope she's okay."

If not for my cover, this was when I would have asked what a Returned was, but alas . . .

I guessed I'd figure it out soon, anyway. My money was on zombies or swamp monsters.

"Come, Brother," Trix called. "We're almost there."

Trix led me forward again. It was an easier trek this time. There was enough light to see here, but not because the wall lamps were back. Instead, we were catching ambient light from something bright up ahead.

We entered through an arch into a pentagonal room about the size of my old barn workshop back home, maybe a little bigger, large enough to fit a couple of sizable haulers side by side, at least.

Three metal-clad figures stood vigil—two striking women with bright blue skin and amber eyes next to one of the hairy, lion-maned men like the dead one I'd seen on the road, though this one was much bulkier, barrel-chested and thick in the limbs.

They all stood in front of a set of heavy, wooden doors that took up the entirety of what looked like a grander version of the Undercity's regular archways, fifteen feet high and maybe eight across. A massive, heavy beam had been set across the double doors and latched in place with metal braces that were newer than the rest of the material. Several shields leaned against the wall next to the door, and a dirty pile of tarps lay several feet to the side.

This was the most well-lit I'd seen the Undercity so far. Several metal tripods were set up around the room with long telescoping necks ending in a metal cage that held bright, industrial versions of the light orbs I'd seen everywhere else. They cast the entire room in stark relief and multiplied everyone's shadows.

Yik'i'trix bounded up to the group and stood at his full height to get their attention. "Greetings, Brothers and Sisters. How goes the watch?"

"I know you, don't I?" the taller of the blue women asked, doing a bad job of snapping her gauntleted fingers as she tried to jog her memory. "You have duties at the church. The kitchens?"

"Yes. Yik'i'trix," the vulpa replied, making the little triangle sign on his head.

"Right! Yes. Well, I'm afraid we don't need any of your services today, Brother," she said sadly. "The door is sealed up for the day. We had an incident, and we're letting the infected calm down."

"Oh? Well, I am not here to offer my services. I'm here to offer ours." He gestured to me, and I took that as my cue to step forward.

"Is he a doctor or something?" the other, darker blue woman asked with a tilt of her head. She was smaller than her compatriot, more athletic in frame, but the way her face resembled the other, they could have been related. The way the light hit her skin was odd; if I squinted, I could almost make out rounded, textured lines of shadow and gloss.

*Scales.*

"Take off the hat. Take off the hat," Trix mumbled from the side of his mouth, just loud enough for me to hear.

I resisted the urge to say "Ta-da!" when I flashed them my very important orange rag. It didn't get the reaction I thought it would.

The taller armored woman's expression flashed a kaleidoscope of emotion, rotating through shock, fear, mild disgust, anger, and something like relief.

"Oh, I . . . see," she said with some hesitation. "I hadn't realized it had come to that."

With a growl, the bulky, hairy guardsman marched over to me, shoulders squared, chest out, and mane bristling. He towered over me, steely eyes sizing me up like a deli slicer would a ham. His hand reached out and clasped my own, his meaty paw practically swallowing mine. "It's about time," he said with a dutiful frown. "None of us like to talk about it, but there comes a time where we can no longer sit by. It's gotten bad in there, and it's only going to get worse unless we do something."

I was feeling more uncomfortable by the second. Everyone just saw me and assumed I was here to kill plague victims, and they were just going to let it happen. This guy seemed entirely on board, at least.

Yik'i'trix spoke for me again, looking proud at how my presence, and by proximity, his, got their attention. "The brother is not quite ready to commit to a plan of action yet. Today we are still gathering information. Is there anything you can tell us?"

"We've had to seal the south gate. They always try to get out there. The plague has them violent and unreasonable. We're usually a team of four, but one of our number was injured earlier today when that one attacked us." The guardsman gestured with his head to indicate the pile of tarps. Now that I was looking more closely, they did look like they were covering something vaguely human-shaped.

I nodded to them all, letting go of the big guy's hand and ignoring how sore mine now was. This guy must have been born with Iron Grip. I gestured Trix over to the tarps with me, and we crouched down together. For my part, I got ready to see what I was dealing with.

Pulling the cloth back revealed a ragged, pale head with milky white eyes, clumps of stringy hair, and jagged, rotten teeth.

*Well, Ryan, when you're right you're right. Zombies.*

Suture marks crisscrossed all over the creature's skin, purple like a bruise, while the rest of the flesh there, although pale, was all *different* shades of pale. Black blood oozed out of its mismatched eyes, mangled nose, and mouth. It had no visible ears, but I assumed it could hear somehow.

On a hunch, I reached out experimentally, touching the corpse's shoulder.

Loot Scourge-Touched Undead? Y/N

It was worse than I'd feared.

The Scourge-Touched weren't *coming* for me. They were already here.

# CHAPTER THIRTY

# Incite a Riot

Scourge-Touched.

My problems had followed me here, or, more accurately, beat me here. From the moment I was dropped onto Ralqir, these things had been dogging my footsteps. Now it seemed they'd gotten ahead of me.

*Okay. What does this guy being Scourge-Touched tell me?*

*One: The Church called this a plague. Bishop Kolash specifically said that it was a "most-vexing" one that they can't cure. He also said that only the Returned were carriers so far. So is being Scourge-Touched a plague? Does it spread like one?*

I looked over my shoulder to make sure no one was within earshot so that I could speak with Trix with some privacy.

"When did you first start seeing this again?" I asked in a whisper.

"Three months or so, give or take," the little fox whispered. "I can't say for certain, because none of us can. No one was looking out for sickness among the Returned because of what they are."

"Dead."

Trix's ears flattened out on his head, and he glanced around as if making sure no one had overheard me. "Technically, yes, but it's not said in polite company, Brother. Just call them Returned."

"Okay. My mistake," I apologized. The Returned seemed to be treated as both a potential danger and a vulnerable class at the same time. I would need to tread carefully. "What are your observations here? Give me everything."

"Really?" Trix asked, standing up straight and nervously rubbing his front paws together. "You want me to help with that?"

I nodded. "Yes. You're my resident expert, right? Give me the facts."

"Uh, the facts. Right," the vulpa said, nodding to himself before another full body shiver took him. I'd need to ask Bishop Kolash exactly what that meant when I saw him again. This was becoming all-too frequent, and I needed to know if I was upsetting him, exciting him, or something else.

"Let me see," he mumbled, getting down on all fours again and circling around the corpse, leaning in to examine the odd mark or piece of fabric, lifting up the tarp, even going so far as to sniff under the fingernails. "Well, he is wearing male clothing. That's generally how we gauge their preferences in that arena. They have no opinions either way on the matter, most of the time. He appears to have been built from multiple sources of . . . uh . . ."

"You mean more than one body," I guessed. That would explain the stitch marks. The use of the word "built" caught my attention, though. It implied that the Returned weren't a natural occurrence— that they were *made* instead of propagated on their own.

*Two: Hunty mentioned that the Baned weren't entirely a natural occurrence, either. He'd said something about them debasing themselves, making deals with demons, whatever that meant after hundreds of years of oral history, and it took away their ability to reproduce, which is something all life is supposed to be able to do. A tenuous connection, but I'd do well to keep it in mind.*

"Yes, that's right," Trix replied without looking at me, instead spreading the creature's long fingers wide and running his claws over the joints. "Of course, the Dark Lord didn't have much care for these creatures' lives outside of serving him, so it's very common for them to be from multiple sources, even different species. It causes great difficulty for them and for those who care for them. This one was relatively lucky . . . until the plague took him, of course."

He hesitated, glancing at me nervously to gauge my reaction. "Please remember, I'm not trying to insult you, Brother Ryan. I'm just trying to give you everything, like you asked."

I waved away his concern as convincingly as I could and tried to pretend that I wasn't snatching up bits of Ralqir's history like a starving man snatching at breadcrumbs.

I gave him my best encouraging nod. "No. You're doing great. Go on."

Again, Trix was racked with shivers from tail to nose. Then he went on like it never happened. Did he know he was doing it? He had to know.

"He was killed by a blow to the head. There's no other place on his body that looks like a wound, and the plague doesn't actually kill its victims." He paused to stand up and point to the corpse's eyes and the oily discharge that ran down its skin. "Black blood from the eyes, nose, and ears. That's consistent with what we've been seeing in advanced infections, too. When they get to this point they're either unable or unwilling to communicate, and they become quite combative."

*Three: The Baned and the infected Returned don't speak, and they're both irrationally violent. Trix and I were just talking to a Returned a few minutes ago, so they aren't naturally like that.*

"What color is Returned blood normally?" I asked without thinking, regretting it immediately, based on Trix's reaction.

He tilted his head to peer at me incredulously. "Is this a test?"

I raised my eyebrows and shrugged. "Again, I want everything."

He paused for two slow blinks, whiskers twitching, but then was back to being helpful. "Right, then. Uh, Returned have no conventional blood. They just have to keep enough fluid inside of them, or the magic that animates them cannot flow properly. They could replace all the water in their bodies with ale, and they wouldn't feel the difference."

I contemplated that. "But um—the plagued Returned's blood is uniformly black?"

"That's what I hear."

I frowned as I thought, staring into the corpse's blank eyes.

The "Scourge-Touched" status was certainly acting like a plague, one that only affected you if—what? Didn't fit into the natural order? That didn't make sense. How did the first Baned get infected, then? They were supposed to be regular goblins at one time, corrupted and made into monsters. I would have asked the Stone Hearts for more details if I'd thought the "how" of things was going to be so relevant.

*Nali said something to me a while back at the tutorial facility. What was it? She only reverted to her previous save state in the case of some kind of corruption? Tampering?*

There was something there, I could feel it. The disparate ideas were part of a circuit that I hadn't closed yet.

"Message from up top. You're not going to like it," the shorter blue-scaled guard said. She was holding a tiny notebook up to the light and frowning at something on its pages.

The other guardswoman groaned, running a gauntleted hand down her face. "Probably not. Give it to us anyway."

"The captain is sending down another group."

"Dammit. Really? He knows the gate's sealed up. Why's he sending more of them down here? Is he thick? Because I'm starting to think so. We're down a man, and we're not due for relief for hours." She paced back and forth nervously, her hand gripping the leather of her sword scabbard.

"Another thing, Sissa," the shorter guard said as she pocketed her notebook. "They're sending Bole."

Sissa stopped mid-stride, frozen on the knife edge between panic and outrage, eyes wide, her mouth twisting up into a snarl. Her muscles were tensed like she was contemplating either an attack or the safest direction to bolt.

After several heartbeats, the spell broke, and she was right back in charge.

"Alright, we have an incoming group of infected, and we're gonna need to handle this as smoothly as possible. Geddon, put your ear up to that door and tell me if you can hear anything. Samila, get the lights."

She turned to us as she ratcheted the straps on her forearm. "Brothers, I know this isn't why you came down here, but we're down a man. We could use your help. Nothing hard or—" She hesitated when she looked at me, her mouth scrunched-up like she was trying and failing to hide a scowl. "Nothing violent. We just need to get these people into the ward swiftly and without incident."

I nodded and stood up, stopping momentarily to put the tarp back over the corpse's face. If my theory held true, these infected undead would be in the process of being converted or "Touched," an intermediate state between "normal" and "bloodthirsty horde." This might be the only time I'd be able to see one up-close without it having a good shot at killing me.

Trix was all for it. "We're ready to assist you in whatever you need, Sergeant. Duty and mercy."

"Duty and mercy," Sissa answered.

"Not hearing anything in there. They might still be hanging around, though, waiting for us to open the door," Geddon rumbled, his voice low as if he didn't want the sound to carry.

Sissa nodded to the big guy. "Alright. Good enough for now. With any luck, all the ones that are too far gone will be banging on the south gate anyway. It's always the south."

The shorter guardswoman, Samila, waddled over to the rest of us, lugging two of the tripod light stands in either hand, setting them down dead center, then angling the heads to direct the light at the big Plague Ward doors.

"Alright," Sissa said as she bent down to pick up a round shield. She swung the shield up and over her shoulder, looping an attached strap diagonally over her torso to affix it to her back. "Full protective gear. That means collars, too, Geddon."

Geddon growled, rubbing the side of his neck. "They issued me a Miur collar, I swear."

Sissa scoffed. "It's the right size, Geddon. You're just a baby. As soon as we see our new arrivals, you get the door, and we'll shuffle them on in. I don't want that door open for more than thirty seconds, got it?"

"Got it," the lion man grumbled as he buckled a leather collar across his throat. Then he rolled his neck and shoulders like a powerlifter about to do a set.

Sissa turned to us then. "Brothers, you stand there and try to look impressive. If any of the Returned get confused, just direct them over to the door. If any fighting breaks out, well . . . any other day, I'd say let us handle it, but that's how Fran earned a trip to the healer. Just do what you can and try not to hurt anyone." She looked pointedly at me at the end.

All I could do was shrug and try to look more confident than I felt.

I put on my best stoic frown and took up position in the center of the room by the spotlights. Trix skittered over next to me and stood up on his hind legs, bobbing up and down excitedly, so fast he was generating a static charge against my trousers.

"Calm down," I muttered to him.

"Yes, Brother. Of course. Sorry. Duty and mercy. Warriors of Light." Trix said it like a mantra, shuddering, then seemed to force himself to relax with deep, purposeful breaths.

It didn't take long for the promised excitement to arrive.

The acoustics in the Undercity were such that we heard them coming long before we saw them. The jangling clank of chains, short exchanges of indistinct speech, and the occasional bark of laughter echoed down to us from the far archway, the next one over from where Trix and I had entered.

I peered into the black. There was a glint of something out there, a floating pair of orbs in the dark, followed by another, and another—a gaggle of reflective eyes just coming into range of our lights. Then two dark silhouettes resolved into a pair of armored guardsmen who stepped into the chamber holding the leads of long chains in their hands. Their black breastplates marked them as a different unit than the ones guarding the door down here, and their kit was subtly different as well.

While the Church guards were armored up with plate and chain and carried swords with wide cross guards along with shields on their backs. These guys had thin short swords on their hips and a wooden truncheon dangling from a loop on their belts while their armor was thin leather on the legs and banded mail on the top. If I remembered correctly, some of the gate guards had a similar getup.

Attached to the length of chain at regular intervals was a line of filthy, ragged creatures of all different shapes and sizes, ranging from a tall and reedy figure with mismatched arms to a stocky, pear-shaped man who waddled stiffly, toddler-like, on legs with too few joints. Their clothes were universally ripped and soiled.

All of them had pale, sallow skin that made the dark stitch marks on their faces and exposed limbs stick out like ink on paper. Their hair was uniformly long and thin, sometimes draping down in front of their faces, and their milky eyes stared blankly straight ahead.

The lead guard—a shorter man with five o'clock stubble and watery blue eyes that shone through the shadows of his helm—yanked on the chain, forcing his prisoners to stumble and then come up short so as not to collide with his back. Smiling, the guard halted stiffly and raised his arm up and away from his body until it formed a ninety-degree angle, like he was trying to get his hand as far from his sword as possible. A ceremonial gesture, maybe.

"Hail to the Watch. Also, lovely to see you again, Sissa," he called with a smile that bordered on sneering territory.

Sissa strode forward haltingly, looking like she just swallowed something disgusting. "Hail, Corporal Bole. I wish I could say the same," the scaled Church guard said, not returning the raised hand gesture. She looked like she wanted to spit out something foul.

The chains rattled as Corporal Bole spread his arms wide and tilted his head, the leering smile never leaving his face. "Sissa, darling, my fire goddess. Still haven't moved on, have you? A shame," he cooed before turning to his right. "Oh, yes. This is my man, Private Beedy. Say hello, Beedy."

The lanky guard who had been carrying the chain leads with Bole hung his head and shifted uncomfortably, not meeting anyone's eyes.

Corporal Bole didn't seem to mind his sullen silence, enjoying the spotlight for himself. He grinned, flashing bright white teeth before looking back over his shoulder at the Returned he had in chains. None of them paid any of us mind, content to just stare at the stonework or rock back and forth mumbling or chewing on their fingernails.

"So, the captain is down to using men like you, is he? *Thief.*" Sissa literally hissed the last word in another language. I was starting to get good at spotting when the System was doing the translation thing. I mouthed the word to myself, testing out the sounds and feeling for the meaning. It felt vile, venomous, like it was a grave insult reserved for the most loathed, but that was all I got.

"Oh. I love it when your tongue gets going like that, Sissa darling. Reminds me of old times," Bole sneered, licking his lips and raising a thin eyebrow. If he knew what the term actually meant, he didn't show it.

Samila stepped in front of Sissa, a protective hand raised subtly to shield the other woman. "They're down to the dregs if they've got you running around unsupervised, Bole," she stated flatly.

Bole laughed at that, then slowly, purposefully ran his eyes down Samila's body in a way that made *me* feel uncomfortable, and I was over on the other side of the room.

"That's the funny thing about hard times, yeah? One day you're all high and mighty, then, before you even know it, you're down to using your best man again, when you finally remember the ends are what really matter." Bole jangled the chains in his hand and handed them to his silent partner, Beedy. "Anyway, here you go, Sissa darling. Eight guests, now officially in your care. Hand them over to the nice Church people, will you, Beedy?"

Beedy turned to look back at his eight charges. He mumbled something I couldn't hear that got them moving. He didn't have to pull on the chains; the Returned all seemed to take the suggestion in stride and just followed him over, drifting dreamily over in his wake. The private led them across the room and handed them over to Samila. Without saying a word, she took the lead and kept the train rolling toward the doors, but as she passed us, she rolled her eyes and stuck out a long, forked tongue, subtly gesturing backward with her head.

"Thank you, Beedy. Now I wish you all a good evening, prayers, and all that. Maybe I'll see you later, Sissa," Bole said as he turned on his heel and made for the archway.

The procession of Returned followed Samila past me, none of them bothering to look my way. Each one's arms were bound in heavy metal bands attached to their necks by a secondary chain and collar that didn't allow them to fully relax their arms.

Then, without warning, one of the Returned stopped as if she'd hit a wall, causing a pile-up behind her.

It was a woman, or it had been in life, at least, with a long face and greasy raven hair that hung down to her lower back. Her lips were cracked and too small to cover her mouth fully, and her nose didn't appear to match the rest of her, darker and longer than the rest of her face. She sniffed the air, nodding her head to do the same to her chest, then turned, inhaling heavily until the gesture drew her eye-to-eye with me. She blinked several times, working her mouth and running her tongue over jagged teeth.

As she stood there, swaying, I could almost make out words, but she wasn't using her vocal cords. It was just air playing over her tongue. The rest of the Returned grouped up behind her, and the chain at her hands went taut as the rest of the line tried to pull her on. She didn't allow herself to be pulled, however.

"The keys, Corporal Bole," Sissa ordered. "You brought them in here manacled and chained. They can't live like that in there."

Bole, almost back out of the archway now, snapped his fingers in an exaggerated manner and turned around to leer back at Sissa. "Oh, yes, I'd nearly forgotten. We're still pretending they're alive. Sorry, love." He gestured with his hand, showman-like, to reveal the ring of gray iron keys already looped around his middle finger. "Here you go," he said as he jangled them next to his face.

"Give them to me," Sissa ordered, a scowl on her face and her hands tightening into fists. She took the barest hint of a step forward but stopped herself.

"They're right here, love. Come hither," the corporal replied. Meanwhile, Beedy was already almost all the way down the hall, doing the smart thing and getting himself out of this situation.

"I—" the undead woman in front of me whispered, her breath a wheeze in her throat. Her head twitched on her shoulders, jerking to the side like she'd just been struck. It happened once, twice. "I know you," she breathed. The smell of her reminded me of moldering old clothes.

Still playing the part of the tough monk, I shook my head and tried to look stern.

Trix spoke up for me, of course, helpful fox that he was. "Miss, I think you are mistaken," he said, placing a hand on my leg for emphasis. "Brother Ryan just arrived in our city, and he doesn't know anyone yet."

On the other side of the room, grunting, hulking Geddon lifted the heavy crossbeam from the door and onto his shoulders. The wooden slab scraped against the iron fittings as it slid up and out, and the big doors groaned as they shifted into a new, less-encumbered position. Dust fell down from old hinges. Geddon puffed as he took a few short steps, slowly walking the beam over to the wall and letting one side carefully slide to the floor with a bang.

Volcanic rage shone in Sissa's eyes, her blue scales darkening slightly around their edges, and her lips curling into a snarl. "I will not come hither. These are your chains, and we have no need of them. There are no prisoners here, just sick people. Unlock them and be gone, *Corporal*." She emphasized the last word, as if it was a private barb I didn't have context for.

"I know you," the Returned woman said, louder now. Samila had doubled back to check on the hold-up, and she stood next to the confused undead woman. The petite blue guard gave me a questioning look, but all I could do was shrug.

"I know you." The Returned's eyes widened. Her hollow breaths came in shaky gasps. Her top lip crawled up higher and higher like it was being stretched by invisible strings until they exposed her blackened gums.

"That one giving you trouble, mate?" Bole asked, his question light and mocking. I didn't respond. I was too busy trying to look not like me while the Returned panted in my face.

Whistling casually, Bole brushed past Sissa, close enough to rub shoulders, wearing a smile that felt oily and cruel. "Don't let 'em get in your face," he chided. "Just cuff 'em on the back of the head and they straighten right up. Don't feel a thing."

Bole was next to us now, but he wasn't the only one. The rest of the Returned had somehow gathered close around us, too close, looking on. I felt like they were all staring directly at me. The woman in my face, the ones around me— their bodies spasmed, muscles tensing and going slack seemingly at random, marionettes to a palsied puppeteer.

"What's this now?" Bole shouted derisively in the Returned woman's ear. "Leave the nice monk alone and get back in line!"

The blow was fast, practiced, a cruel backhand swung from down low out of the dead woman's line of sight, meant to catch its target unaware and inflict pain and humiliation.

In my previous life, I might not have even seen it coming nor had the opportunity to intervene.

I wasn't that person anymore, however. I was one of the Exotics, the System's Chosen.

It wasn't conscious. Out of the corner of my eye I saw the strike. I saw the satisfaction in Bole's eyes, the way the corner of his mouth quirked up to reveal his perfect, gleaming teeth.

Reflex guided my hand, the metal one. With a *CLANG!*, Bole's knuckle-guard met my prosthetic forearm, intercepted before it could strike home, while my other fist caught him in the jaw. With a crack, my knuckles met his face, and his eyes widened in disbelief as he staggered backward.

To his credit, Bole didn't give much ground, only a couple of steps. He shook his head, spat, and reached up to feel his jaw. The smile quickly spread its way back across his face, but I saw what it had replaced. Fear. Uncertainty.

"Now you've done it, Monk," he declared as he straightened to his full height, a promise of violence in every movement.

"I—I know you! D-D-Dph—!" the Returned woman stuttered. She either didn't notice or didn't care about what had just happened. She was shouting now. She reached up with her manacled hands to clutch at her head, and her fingers dug furrows in her skin. The other Returned gathered closer around, twitching that way they did, reaching up to grasp at their own scalps.

"Defiled!" The Returned woman ripped at her head, dirty black hair coming off in her hand.

"Defiler! Defiler!" The Returned were starting to join in like a chorus of dead cheerleaders.

"Defiler! Defiled! Defiler!" The woman's shouts crescendoed, breaking, morphing, warping into an inhuman scream, one that opened her jaw impossibly wide and let loose a primal cry of desperate hatred I could feel in my soul.

The rest of the Returned echoed her, lost to whatever force they'd been fighting for control of their own minds.

It may have come from different voices in a different place, echoed off different stones, but I recognized that sound.

The wordless, burning, tormented hatred. The terrible, thoughtless call to violence.

I'd heard it under the mountain. In my cell.

Muffled, muted, but irrefutably audible, more voices took up the call from behind the heavy Plague Ward door with such fervor their screams transcended the physical. I might have just imagined it, but I felt like the walls themselves shook as if they, too, had taken notice of me, and they, too, were baying for my blood.

Then, as one, the Scourge-Touched creatures surged forward to rip me apart.

# CHAPTER THIRTY-ONE

# Contain the Swarm

They came on from all around me, their eyes burning with insanity, their mouths open to shriek their hatred. Long, bony fingers grasped at my limbs, my head and neck, attempting to wrench my body into unnatural angles. Dirty fingernails dug into my exposed skin and ripped at my clothes.

The Returned woman who had spoken to me lunged for my face, reaching out and grasping the sides of my head with her manacled hands and snapping at me with jagged, stained teeth while the chains that bound her ground against the bridge of my nose. I got my arm up in time, wedging my forearm across her throat so she couldn't bite me, but the others were more than willing to take her place.

Scourge-Touched Undead attacks you for 3 Damage.
Status gained: Bleeding [0.3 HP/sec]

Pain lanced through my back as one of the Scourge-Touched latched on to my flesh and thrashed its head like a dog with a rabbit. Others attempted to rip off my arms at the shoulder, but that wasn't quite as worrying. While painful, I was made of tougher stuff now that my Body Stat had climbed into the twenties. Thank Constance for that.

All the while, if their mouths weren't full of me, they were howling in that familiar, mindless way that reminded me of my old cell.

"Stop! Stop!" Trix shouted uselessly over the din. I could feel him down next to my shins, darting in and out, attempting to do something to get control of the situation, but the Undead weren't listening. Trix huffed, attempting to push at the Undead's shins, but they and I had much more mass than he did. He'd be hard-pressed to even shift our weight, much less wrestle anyone off me.

I grunted, trying to free my prosthetic from the press of bodies by curling it like you would a dumbbell, but someone had a tight hold of the wrist. The desire to shift my feet and get more power into the move was there, but I instinctively knew if I lost contact with the ground for one moment, I'd be down on the floor and in a lot more trouble.

The scuffle carried on for a handful of seconds like that, me trying not to die, the Returned screeching and ripping at me, while my vulpa guide tried to talk the rabid Undead down. It was odd—surreal, even—to be in a crowd of capable people but essentially alone fighting for my life.

Eventually, though, the Church guards stopped gawking and jumped in.

A mailed arm snaked around the Returned lady's neck and pulled her back. She still had a hold of my head and tried to pull me with her, but one of the great things about temporary baldness was that there wasn't much to hold on to. The woman's nails raked over my temples and past my eyes, but then she was off me, now wrestling with Sissa.

The chain that connected all of the Returned wouldn't let the two go far, however. Sissa, though seemingly stronger than her opponent, couldn't drag the woman farther away than a few feet before they ran out of slack and were now fighting the weight of the rest of the Undead.

Sissa had given me space to take a swing at the creature holding on to my metal arm, though. My clenched fist crashed down on the Returned's forehead over and over, not the greatest of spots to focus on, but I was working with what I could get.

Scourge-Touched Undead takes 1 Damage. (Bludgeoning)
Scourge-Touched Undead takes 1 Damage. (Bludgeoning)
Scourge-Touched Undead takes 2 Damage. (Bludgeoning)
Scourge-Touched Undead takes 1 Damage. (Bludgeoning)
Scourge-Touched Undead is stunned.

The angle wasn't good, robbing my blows of a lot of their strength, but after the fourth or fifth strike, the steely grip on my arm loosened, allowing me to have use of my entire upper body.

Sissa and Samila were both grappling with a Returned now. Sissa was still working on the woman in front of me, pinning the snarling Undead down with some kind of technique that twisted the limbs and pinned them under her body-weight, while Samila was to my right on the floor with the tall, lanky Returned that had bitten into my back. That one's long, oddly jointed arms were wrapped around Samila's shoulders like ropy tentacles, bringing her in close so it could bite at her neck, but the guard looked more disgusted than anything, her face scrunching up like she smelled something awful. Her armor was holding up well against the teeth, but she wasn't exactly winning her fight, either.

You take 2 Bleeding Damage.
Corporal Fidus Bole attacks you for 4 Damage.

Something hard slammed into my stomach, driving the air out of my lungs, toppling me and the remaining six or so Returned baying for my blood backward and onto the floor, exactly where I didn't want to be. I heard the crunch of bone as our combined weight came down on whatever unlucky Undead was behind me. Then my vision flashed white as my head made contact with the stone floor.

Status gained: Stunned

"Next time, watch who you sucker punch, Monk."

I blinked, looking up from the dog pile to see Bole standing over me, a cruel smirk tugging at the side of his mouth, made even less appealing since his lip was starting to swell.

*Oh, yeah. I did just deck this guy, didn't I?*

"They really don't like you, do they?" He shouted over the insane howls of the Undead. He waggled his eyebrows cheekily at me as he wound up for another kick like the one that had bowled me over.

Despite his proximity, the Returned didn't give a damn about Bole. They scrambled past his legs and over me to get at my torso to bite and claw. Their weight pinned my legs and fouled up any attempt I made to soften the incoming blow.

Corporal Fidus Bole attacks you for 5 Damage.

Bole's kick caught me full-on in the side of the ribs. If I hadn't already been out of breath, I would have groaned.

*BAM!* From the other side of the room, something slammed up against the heavy wooden doors that led to the Plague Ward. The noise, despite the chaos, drew every living eye. The doors shifted on their hinges, groaning slightly and parting the tiniest bit in the middle.

"What the hell?" Geddon bellowed from beside the arch. "Sissa! They're charging the door!"

That old, familiar chorus of innumerable, wordless howls shook the walls of the chamber.

Status lost: Stunned

*They're all Scourge-Touched. All of them.*

I curled in on myself to protect my ribs, then kicked out to get some space, sending the two Undead on my legs backward until the chain arrested their falls. I gasped for breath, as my diaphragm kickstarted my breathing process once again, and I snapped an elbow into the nose of one of the Returned attempting to hold on to my prosthetic.

Scourge-Touched Undead takes 3 Damage. (Bludgeoning)
Scourge-Touched Undead is stunned.
Unarmed Combat is now Level 3.

The two I kicked off were undeterred. There was just a half second of freedom before they were back in the game, crawling up my legs to get at my face.

Bole jumped onto their backs, straddling me and my assailants, crouching down until his weight pinned the Undead on top of me. A flash of metal caught my eye as he drew a tiny hooked knife from his sleeve that was small enough to be concealed in his palm. He struck like a snake, lunging for my face.

Corporal Fidus Bole attacks you for 2 Damage.
Status gained: Bleeding [2 HP/sec]

I got a hand up to intercept the blade before it could strike home, the blade carving a neat line down my wrist. Either the adrenaline in my system or the razor-sharpness of the blade kept the pain from being debilitating.

Wearing a sadistic grin, Bole leaned into his blade arm, putting more and more weight behind it, forcing my blocking hand down toward my cheek. He leaned forward, close enough to speak with only me, a little intimate conversation in the middle of a dogpile. The tendons in his neck flexed and strained at the effort he was having to put into it. I had to imagine I looked the same.

"Nothing personal, Monk," he said. "Blood for blood."

I was starting to understand why Sissa didn't like this guy.

Setting myself, I pushed up with all my might, forcing the knife back. "You don't think you're overreacting, just a little?" I asked through gritted teeth.

"Mmf! Geddon, hold the door!" Sissa called out from somewhere. "They've gone mad! Don't let them out!"

"What do you think I'm doing?!" he roared. "I can't reach the bar! I'm having to hold it myself!"

I bucked at the waist, trying to shift Bole's weight, but he and the feral Undead were too heavy.

Suddenly, something brown and wearing robes shot out of the dark and stuck to Bole's face like a furry pie. The smiling bastard made a noise, something short and muffled, while he violently shook his head to try and dislodge Trix, but the vulpa was stuck fast.

"Don't worry, Brother Ryan! I've got him!" Trix shouted as he held on for dear life with his claws.

Bole tried to say something like, "Mmmph bfff morglmf," but I couldn't make it out. I'm sure it was pithy.

I needed an out, something that could change the equation here.

Bole's partner, Beedy, turned out to be just what I needed. He slammed into the pile of people on top of me, toppling Bole and Trix and bringing the two Returned along for the ride. The man must have shoulder-tackled us at full speed.

Suddenly, I had no one weighing me down.

That gave me the chance to wrest myself from the pile. I twisted at the waist and tore myself out of the grasp of the rest of the Returned, having to give up parts of my shirt to get free, but it was a cost I paid gladly. Sissa and Samila were still busy restraining a few of them, but the Undead seemed to feel no pain. They fought hard to get at me, even if they had to go through the women who were just doing their jobs. Those not currently engaged tugged at their bonds but weren't strong enough to drag their chained fellows with them to follow me at least, so there was that.

Something slammed up against the doors to the Plague Ward again. Geddon, currently bracing the doors with his body, grunted as he was pushed forward. Then the muscles in his legs bulged as he heaved backward, shoving the doors closed once more. "Someone help me! Get the bar!"

If more of the Scourge-Touched joined the fight we were screwed.

I started staggering backward toward the door, sparing a glance for the pile of bodies where Bole, Trix, and Beedy went down. I couldn't see Trix, and that worried me. Even so, the doors needed to stay closed, or we were going to be neck deep in Undead.

*BAM!*

The doors jerked forward while dust sprinkled down from above to land on Geddon's neck and shoulders. His boots scraped the stonework as the force shifted him. He snarled as he found his traction again and shoved back hard. The door didn't slam home this time. The Undead behind the door had Geddon matched for strength with their numbers.

I hit the rightmost door at full sprint, slamming my shoulder into it. Something snapped—close, wet—and the doors slammed closed again. I looked down to see a pale arm, long and sinewy with black spiderweb veins just underneath the paper-thin skin. It was mangled at the base where the doors had crushed it. Black blood oozed from the narrow gap. The wood bucked again, even as I braced against it.

Geddon grunted, spreading his arms and flexing his shoulders to get more leverage. "The bar. Get the bar!" he snarled through clenched teeth.

I nodded, looking to my right to find the beam leaning against the stone of the arch. It was . . . sizable, easily nine feet long and as wide as my waist. When I laid my hand on it, I could instantly tell it was dense, too, as if there was almost no hollow space, even among the fibers.

I set my feet and wrapped my arms around the middle.

*Come on, 24 Body. Don't let me down.*

The muscles in my legs, back, and shoulders bulged, my neck went tight, and my diaphragm tensed to the point where I was no longer breathing. Blood roared in my ears.

Nothing.

Well, not *nothing.* The top of the beam, which had been resting on the stone, shifted slightly and its angle altered. The bottom of the beam, however, did not move. It was much too heavy for me.

Then someone else was there. Gloved hands grasped the beam above mine. They weren't lifting, though. They were pushing. The wooden slab started to shift, leaning toward me, over me.

*No. No. Have to get it up. Up!*

"Move!" Bole's voice sounded out right next to me, breaking my concentration. I opened my eyes. The man's face was right there, bleeding from claw marks on his cheeks. His watery eyes tightened at the edges as he strained. "Bloody move!" he commanded again.

The beam toppled toward me. I disengaged myself from my hold and wrenched my body to the side. The weight of the thing forced my shoulder down painfully, nearly doubling me over as the angle changed. Its trajectory was . . .

*Oh, shit.*

"Geddon!" I called, turning to face the hulking lion man. He was in a bad way, sweat dripping from his face, knees trembling, about to buckle. Upon hearing his name, his eyes shot open and refocused, like a man coming out of a trance. The beam was picking up speed.

"Move!" I commanded him, putting every ounce of fake authority into my voice that I could.

It worked. Geddon, a military man at heart, followed the command without hesitation, diving forward as the beam crashed down in front of the door. It hit with a deafening *BOOM!*, kicking up dust and shaking the floor enough for me to feel it through the soles of my boots.

Before the beam had even settled, the doors to the Plague Ward slammed up against it, hard. The wood rattled and cracked as what I could only assume was a multitude of bodies surged forward to escape. The beam only slid forward a few inches before Bole was upon it, crawling down beside it and bracing it with his feet.

The damage was done, though. The doors were open—not all the way, but now there was a foot-wide gap between them. Pale faces with milky-white eyes, deformed and mangled hands, and black tongues burst from the breach like maggots from a bloated corpse, crowding in to be the first through, the first out.

The faces howled and bayed like dogs when they saw me, their white eyes only for me.

Bole saw what was coming before anyone else. He cursed, kicking at the heavy beam one last time before reaching into his cuff again to pull out his hooked knife, the one he'd tried to use on me. Then he jammed it into the bricks at his feet directly abutting the beam, a makeshift wedge to keep the barrier in place.

He jumped to his feet, backpedaling swiftly away from the tide.

Already, bloody ragged figures were slipping from the narrow gap in the door. They squeezed themselves through the slit. They left flesh behind, cracked rib cages, bled black globs of stinking slime too thick to be rightfully called blood.

The Plague Ward was birthing a host of horrors.

"Run!" someone cried.

# CHAPTER THIRTY-TWO

# Get Them Out

Run, you daft pricks!" Bole shouted. He was already on his feet, practicing what he preached.

Geddon scrambled to pick up his shield. It looked small in his hand, more like a buckler. He was breathing hard already, and his legs shook. I couldn't really blame him, since he'd single-handedly held back a tide of the Undead. Regardless, he gave no ground.

I stood next to him, watching the bodies pile up in the gap between the doors, their snarling faces attempting to press through. If these things acted like the Scourge-Touched I knew, we wouldn't be able to beat them back, not without killing them all, and I didn't even have a way to do that.

The memory of my first fight on Ralqir surfaced in my mind, how the goblin essentially killed itself trying to get at me. The mindless determination they displayed in the cave had reinforced that impression.

The Scourge-Touched wouldn't stop. They'd flow into the room. They'd bury us under a flood of bodies. I hated to admit it, but Bole was right.

"We have to move," I said.

The lion-maned giant shook his head, baring his teeth. "You move, then. I can hold them here."

"Brother Ryan!" Trix's voice surfaced above the noise.

I turned. Two of the Returned were down, slumped on the floor and unmoving. The rest were fighting with the guards, who'd come together to form a sort of shield wall, Sissa and Samila in the front, Beedy behind, taking half-hearted swings with his truncheon over the shorter Samila's shoulders. It was a stalemate of sorts, the Undead bound by chains, the guards bound by their so-called duty and mercy. Trix, for his part, was behind the line, an arm slung in the ties of his robe and one eye closed from swelling.

A cold, wrathful shudder ran through my body. Who had done this to Trix? The Returned, I could understand if not forgive, but Bole . . . "Trix! Are you alright?"

"I'm fine," he wheezed as he attempted to stand up straight. He was favoring one of his sides. "I'll rub a little dirt on it."

"We need to get these people out of here," I said as I limped toward him. Questions could wait for later.

He looked from me to the door to the guards, confusion evident in his swollen eye, giving him a deranged look.

"We can't!" Geddon bellowed as he swung his undersized shield in the face of the first Undead to get out of the ward, snapping the creature's head back and sending it end over end to the floor. "If they get out, they'll infect the whole Undercity!"

The wall of bodies writhed on the other side of the doors.

*One sufficiently charged grenade could do . . . what? Buy time? Probably not.*

It was no good. I'd kill a lot of them, but their bodies would still be in the doorway keeping us from closing it. Then their buddies would already be in our faces, and we'd be right back to square one. Besides, this problem was bigger than this door. I was starting to realize just how big.

"It's too late for that," I said, locking eyes meaningfully with Trix.

He tilted his head and perked up his ears as if he were waiting for me to explain further, but the little vulpa was sharp. Slowly, over the course of several seconds, realization seemed to come to him, and his pained expression gave way to horror.

"It's already out," he gasped, blinking a couple of times as his mind came to grips with the implications. "It's already out! We met an Infected on the way here!"

"That doesn't mean anythi—Back, you!" Sissa called as she and Samila shoved the gaggle of Undead off their shields. She'd positioned herself between the chain gang and me, and they only seemed to be paying attention to what was in their way when it actively hindered them. "If they didn't attack you, how would you know? You're not a healer."

"She spoke like one of them," I said as I bent down to pick up Trix and put him on my shoulder again. He winced slightly as I got my hand around his midsection but didn't complain, choosing instead to lean on my neck and use his good arm to hold on tight. Something told me that if I asked him about who'd hurt him, he wouldn't tell me.

"You're not a healer! We have it contained here!" Sissa protested. Her voice had a desperate edge to it.

"What are the odds, Sergeant, that the one Returned we ran into on the way here was infected?" Trix asked. "I'm not a gambler, but a chance encounter seems unlikely unless the plague has already spread wide."

I glanced over my shoulder to check on Geddon, only to see him throw an Undead back toward the open doors. It smacked into the writhing mass, forcing the pale faces to duck slightly but otherwise not hindering them. There were six of them in the room with us now. Two circled around Geddon to get at his sides as the other two got back to their feet. The hulking guard was slowing down. His chest was heaving, and his arms hung at his sides.

Other Undead poured into the room like a liquid, pooling in tangled piles of pale, fumbling limbs before they resolved into individual, screaming berserkers.

"Weapons free, Sergeant?" Geddon panted as he manhandled the next of the circling Returned to come within reach, spinning it around and launching it at the others.

Sissa shook her head, clenching her jaw.

As it was, this room was going to fill with hostile Returned in minutes, and, even if we were willing to kill them all, the Scourge-Touched would wear everyone down and run through the Undercity unchecked anyway. The guards needed to decide now or they would die.

"Unless you've got backup on the way, it's only a matter of time," I predicted. "Make a decision or it'll be made for you."

Sissa's dam of indecision broke, and she let out a frustrated growl as she shoved another of her assailants to the ground. "Dammit. Private . . . Whatever Your Name Is, reach into Samila's pouch and send the signal. Blue."

Beedy was on the ball. He was moving even before the guard sergeant had finished her sentence, crouching down behind Samila. He reached up to rip a tightly bound leather flap off the back of Samila's belt.

"Hey, watch the hands, Private," said Samila. Her voice was awfully calm, considering everything. She was the most put-together of any of us, going through the motions of controlling the crowd without losing herself to uncertainty or exertion. She even had a little determined smile on her face as she jammed her shield up under an Undead's jaw and laid it out flat on the cobblestones. "You ready to run, Big Guy?" she called over her shoulder.

"No! *Gyaa!* No biting!" Geddon shouted. He knocked one of the Undead attempting to chew on his calf down to the ground hard with an open-hand slap that I felt from a dozen feet away. "I'm not built for running!"

Beedy had something in his hand now, a blue slip of paper. He cupped it in his palm and used his free hand to strike the metal plate on his wrist. There was a flash, and the blue paper burst into equally blue flame, sparking and flashing like a cheap firework.

"He's got it! Everyone good? Alright, people, we are leaving! Move!" Sissa shouted.

As one, Sissa and Samila charged at the battered Undead, shields first, bowling them over. Geddon disengaged as well, with a whirling swipe of his shield and a quick hook from his meaty fist that sent one of the infected Returned down to the ground out cold. Then he was moving, too, in sync with his squad. They formed up quickly, practiced and professional as they jogged together.

They didn't wait for me, and I didn't expect them to. They took flight toward the archway I'd seen Bole use.

I broke into a run, taking a slight detour toward the center of the room. I reached out and plucked the pair of tripod spotlights off the floor. Samila hadn't been faking it before. They were heavy.

*Would be a shame to leave this to the Scourge-Touched.*

I didn't allow myself to break stride.

Transfer Entangled Lantern to Spatial Storage? Y/N
Consume Entangled Lantern? Y/N

I chose "yes" to both.

You gain knowledge of material: Steel [3/10]
You gain knowledge of material: Link Glass [1/10]
You gain knowledge of material: Link Glass [2/10]
You gain knowledge of material: Steel [4/10]
You gain knowledge of material: Steel [5/10]
. . .
You gain knowledge of material: Steel [10/10]
Affinity Type: Steel is now Grade F.
Steel Mana Conductivity increased. [10%]
Component material: Iron: Affinity found.
Iron and Steel Affinity gain rate increased.

"What was that?" Trix yelped from my shoulder.

"Practitioner stuff. I told you I need metal. May come in handy later," I said. I would have rather put them both in Spatial Storage, but they were really heavy. Seconds were going to count here. Plus, I finally got a steel affinity at Grade F, so it wasn't a total loss on the second one.

Trix didn't press the issue. He just held on for dear life.

The chained Undead on the floor reached for me as I passed, jumping to their feet to lunge at me as I skirted around them. Half of their number were unconscious on the floor, however, and it slowed them down, allowing me to skirt around.

The Scourge-Touched now trickling out of the gap in the doors had no such hindrance. They tore through the opening and plopped to the floor to give chase, not even pausing on impact. They didn't seem to feel any pain. They didn't even need to breathe. They only filled their lungs with air to scream after me as they poured over one another to be the first to get a taste of the human.

I sprinted through the archway and up the gentle incline of quellstone, easily catching up to the others since I wasn't wearing armor or weapons like the rest of them, and Trix hardly weighed anything. Geddon was true to his word on how terrible a runner he was. We'd gone maybe a hundred yards and he was already flagging badly.

Meanwhile, the Undead were hot on our heels. They weren't overly fast but they came on with singular focus.

I stayed behind Geddon, bringing up the rear of the group, trying to assess how quickly we'd be caught. Too soon, by my reckoning. I summoned my pistol with a flash. Then I stopped and steadied myself on the wall to take careful aim. I targeted the frontrunner—a tall Returned with long, even legs that gave it an advantage over its less carefully constructed comrades.

Breathing out, I carefully drew a bead on his head and tightened my finger on the trigger.

*POP!*

---

Scourge-Touched Undead takes 11 Damage. (Piercing)

---

Trix flinched on my shoulder, reaching up to cover his ears.
I racked another round.
*POP!*

---

Scourge-Touched Undead takes 15 Damage. (Piercing)
Pistols is now Level 2.

---

The Undead I'd been aiming for went down hard, his legs giving out underneath him while his arms reached out to steady himself, tripping up his friends and creating an impressive pileup. I'd aimed for where I estimated his pelvis was, and with how heavy my ammo worms were, it must have done the job at shattering the bones. If he were human, he'd be in agony.

It bought us precious seconds at least.

I ran to catch up with the others.

It wouldn't be long before the chase was back in full swing. If we were equally matched in the speed department, we needed to put something between us.

"We need another door!" I called toward the front of the group.

Sissa was far ahead up the curling slope, looking down at us and urging us forward. "Any heavy doors would be at the next ward, and if they're following protocol, they'll be shut."

"Then . . . where are we . . . oh, Light's mercy . . . going?" Geddon gasped. He was leaning on the walls for support every couple of strides now.

Sissa waited for us to close the gap between us to answer. "The closest hub. Smaller openings. Materials to maybe block the arch."

"We can't secure one of those, Sis. We'll just be setting up a buffet," Samila cautioned.

"I know! I know! Just go!" Sissa groaned as she waved us past. Then she got under Geddon's arm to help him keep moving.

I remained at the rear.

Soon the Infected were nipping at our heels again, just around the last bend. Their howls echoed off the walls around us. Every time I looked ahead, I half-expected a pale hand to grab my ankle and drag me into the sea of flesh and teeth.

"There!" Samila shouted, her voice husky from the extra exertion of bearing some of Geddon's weight.

We were on a straightaway leading up an incline until it leveled out somewhere up ahead where dim light played over the bricks.

I got under Geddon's other arm, exchanging a look with Sissa around the big man's breastplate, and the both of us surged forward, practically carrying the exhausted giant up the hill. I was huffing and puffing now, too. My calves burned like I'd been running all day.

The light got brighter and brighter, the apex of the slope coming closer. The Undead's voices sounded close. My mind conjured images of sharp claws tearing into my flesh, vivid enough to be felt.

Then we were up and barreling through a bright archway. The light blinded me, but we kept moving. Something crashed into my shins.

*CRACK!*

Wood shattered and splintered as we charged directly into a shoddily constructed barricade. Geddon's mass turned the three of us into a battering ram of sorts, one that easily broke through the barrier, the inertia carrying us irresistibly forward. Exhausted, Geddon toppled as he tripped over something near our ankles, and I came along for the ride, watching the quellstone floor come up to meet me. My face ground painfully into the stones.

"Hey!"

"Get that back up! Now!"

The big man just laid there, heaving for breath, his arms searching for the best way to get upright again but failing.

I disentangled myself from the Geddon pile, shaking my head and reaching up to wipe blood off my mouth.

We were in one of the big hub rooms: a pub, it seemed. A big wooden structure stood in the middle of the room, a sort of self-contained bar with shelves stocked with bottles, glassware, and little casks stacked up on their sides. Tables and stools were scattered all over, many of them in the middle of being knocked over or picked up.

A crowd of people hurried around the room, running with various bits of furniture in their arms. Some brought pairs of stools. A group of three carried a long wooden table, while a huddle of other folks was crouched next to the bar, grunting as they attempted to loosen the heavy top. Frightened people carried their disparate pieces of wood over to the archway we'd just burst through and piled them up to block the opening. Others sat huddled on the floor, nursing wounds that bled through ripped clothes. One woman had missing fingers, and someone was bandaging the wound with what looked like a towel.

"Oh, no. Seriously. When I said 'run,' I didn't mean *with me*! You're going to get us all dead!"

# CHAPTER THIRTY-THREE

# Pick a Lock

A familiar voice split the relative calm. Bole, the man himself, sneered at us from behind the bar. He had his sword clutched in his upraised hand and a bottle in the other. There was a wild look in his eye, too, exacerbated by the bleeding scratches from Trix's claws.

Samila, cool as always, sighed and shook her head, turning back to get to work on reinforcing the barricade the others were constructing, taking a stool from an old woman and running to throw it onto the pile. Beedy was already working, hoisting a rounded table up onto his shoulders and bringing it to the archway.

"Shut up, Bole!" Sissa snarled. "You're lucky I don't stab you for what you pulled back there!"

"If you ever find the spine, Princess," Bole shot back. "Your man was about to lose it. If I hadn't done what I did, you'd be in their bellies by now instead of running. Now, if you'll excuse me." He ducked down behind the bar, out of sight, and I could hear metal ringing on stone.

Sissa fumed, clenching her gauntleted fists and turning around to take in the room, her anger seeming to melt back into uncertainty. She stopped when her eyes met mine and seemed to remember who I was. The scales around her eyes darkened slightly. "Get him off the floor. The stones will sap him further," she said.

I nodded, bending to get a hand under Geddon's shoulder. Trix hopped down to help, too. He couldn't do much, but the gesture was nice.

"Any practitioners here?" Samila called out. The barricade was quickly stacking up to the top of the archway now, and they were working on making it denser. Mercifully, the Undead were just trickling in and jumping onto the ramshackle construction, weighing the pieces down and making the (un?)lives of the other Scourge-Touched more difficult in turn. Some of them ripped at table legs or clawed at the wood, howling all the while. It wouldn't hold in the long term, but we had a brief reprieve.

I got Geddon to an upright chair next to the barricade. Maybe his weight would help it stay in place, or he could take a swing at the first Undead face that pushed its way through. Either way, I was sure this was where he would want to be. I slapped him on the shoulder and nodded to him when I caught his eye. He was too out of breath to do anything other than nod back.

"Practitioners!" Samila yelled again. "Get over here and help with this barricade!"

Trix pulled on the now-ragged leg of my trousers.

"Brother Ryan?" Trix asked without asking.

I shook my head. "Not that kind of practitioner."

"You at least the useful kind, Monk? Could use a hand." Bole had damned good ears if he could hear me from back there.

Curious, I staggered over to look over the bar top.

I found Bole crouched down on the ground next to an open cabinet, the contents of which seemed to have been hastily extracted and left on the floor while the cabinet's bottom had been splintered and ripped out. Next to Bole was a man in dark gray robes that had the look of a uniform to them. Bole had his sword jammed into the gaps between the quellstones, and he was using it as a pry bar, while the robed man tried to help.

"You see anything?" Bole asked his robed companion.

The man bent down and put his hand on the quellstone, nodding. "There's something down there, for sure. Empty." The guy sounded young—younger than me, maybe.

"Can you pry it up?" Bole asked.

The robed guy shook his head. "No, I can't. It's the darkstone."

"Fuck!" Bole shouted, winding up and jamming the tip of his sword into one of the gaps between the bricks.

Sissa came up behind me, sword drawn. "We're about to have to fight to hold this position. Tell me you had a plan when you scurried up here, Bole."

"Oh, I planned to run until I saw moonlight, but someone triggered the lockdown before I could get to the egress. It's shut up tighter than a Miur sphincter."

Sissa scoffed. "You're stuck down here with the consequences of your actions. I guess there is justice in this world."

Bole ignored her, turning to me. "Monk, you got something that'll help us open this?"

"What is it?" I asked. I felt Trix shudder at the fact that I was speaking to the man, but we didn't have time to worry about that now.

"A locked door," he said vaguely. "Goes somewhere other than here. Can you help?"

"Why do you want to get down here and not through another of the tunnels?" I asked.

"It's locked down. Every tunnel leads further in or to a barred door. We'll be trapped down here if we try to take the normal ways out."

I looked to Sissa, who just stared at the two men trying to pry stones from the floor, a pensive frown on her face. I tilted my head to try to catch her eye.

"Sergeant?"

"I'm thinking," she said, holding up a finger to forestall me. "You're talking about the smugglers' tunnels then."

"Aw. You do remember the old days," Bole replied.

Sissa shook her head, incredulous. "They filled those in."

"Sure they did." Bole's tone was mocking.

"You're saying there's one down there?" the sergeant asked with narrowed eyes.

Bole slammed the pommel of his sword down on the unyielding quellstone cobbles and grunted with displeasure. "Yeah. Normally, if one were to . . . hypothetically . . . engage in illegal activity, you'd be issued a key, and the door would open up, no problem."

I shook my head. "We don't have a key."

"Or the tools to break in," Bole added, slapping the flat of his sword contemptuously.

"If we break containment, we could be putting the rest of the city at risk, Bole," Sissa warned.

"Darling, I think containment's already good and broke. You listen to some of them poor bastards been trickling in here, the ones with bites all over 'em. Deadheads are going feral all over. The match's been struck."

"They're called Returned, Bole."

"Sure. Whatever. If I can get this thing open, I'm getting out of here. Help me or fuck off."

Hopping over the bar, I shouldered Bole aside and used Iron Grip and a slight twist to wrest the short sword from his hand. He took in a breath to object but seemed to think better of it when he saw the look on my face.

Bole and I would square up later about Trix. I had some serious questions.

I saw what he'd been doing here. The brickwork was not only clogged up with what had to have been years' worth of dirt and sediment which Bole had been chipping away, but the stones were separated by no more than a millimeter of space.

*Hard to get between, for sure.*

Experimentally, I wiggled the sword tip around in the crack between the quellstone cobbles. No joy.

I looked to the guy in the robes. Now that I could see his face, I noticed he was, indeed, young—no older than a teenager. His sharp, hawkish features were angular and smooth like a polished river rock, marred only by cracked, jagged stone that seemed to stab into the skin around one of his eyes and travel up toward his temple until it vanished into the dark of his hood. The affected eye was a burning coal of orange.

"It's my Dominion sign," he said flatly, not meeting my eyes. "Don't worry about it. It doesn't hurt."

"Right," I said, clearing my throat. "This is the edge, then?"

He nodded passively. "It goes down about a handspan, then it's open space. I can't do anything with it, because it's darkstone. He says it's magic. No hinges. The bricks just peel back," he explained, seeming to shrink in on himself, bringing his hands into the sleeves of his robes. "I'm sorry I can't help," he added.

*Less a door. More magical in nature. I don't know a damned thing about magic, and I'm too pressed to learn right now.*

I'd just have to brute-force it.

"Sergeant Sissa, I'm going to need a minute," I said, wrapping my fingers around Bole's blade. I needed to get under the trapdoor.

Shape [12 MP/sec]

My MP rushed out of me in a torrent, so fast it surprised me.

*What the hell?*

That was . . . expensive. I checked the log, asking it for more detailed information

Shape [12 MP/sec, 4 MP/sec base, +8 MP/sec external drain]

*The quellstone.*

It was affecting my Shape.

There was no getting around it, though. I spent my entire pool saturating the blade but only *just*. I could feel the mana draining out of the metal like water through a sieve. I . . . some part of me . . . was being drained away and extinguished every second I did this.

I gasped for breath, tapped out before I'd even done anything.

"What, that's it?" Bole spat next to my ear.

I didn't want to stop Shaping the thing. My grip on the metal was tenuous, ephemeral as if my mana were smoke being carried away by the wind. Re-saturating it would take even more of me.

"I need something to burn," I said, shutting my eyes to distractions and holding out my metal hand like a craftsman asking for a tool.

"They're breaking through!" A desperate shout came from elsewhere. I couldn't focus on it. I was busy being sucked dry by evil rocks.

Geddon roared.

"Weapons free, warriors of the Light! Kill only those you must! Duty and Mercy!" Sissa's voice buzzed, distorted and echoing strangely in my mind. Something about the tone felt bright, steely. The issued command filled the chamber, drowning out the howls of the dead until they were just background noise. Warmth spread to my fingers and toes; my pulse fluttered, and my face flushed.

Then, to us, she spoke quietly, her words teasing with that same power. "You better be right about this." With that, she was gone to help the others.

"Wow." The robed guy breathed.

"I know, right?" Bole had lowered his voice to a whisper. "You think it's great now, kid, court one sometime."

I panted as my power left me and bled into the stones. The sword was elongating, stretching its material down into them, bleeding between the tiny cracks and into the space below like candle wax.

Meanwhile, I was being ripped away. It hurt. It hurt so much. I shut my eyes against it as it drained me dry.

"Something to burn! Now!" I ground out. "I need something that—" Something heavy, smooth, and cold slapped into my prosthetic hand.

Consume Mansekind Molasses? Y/N

The message was barely on my screen before I chose "Y". *FWOOM!*

"What the fuck, Monk?!" Bole shrieked before going into a coughing fit.

I felt the heat on my face, sticky hot syrup splattering over the skin of my legs and neck. Hands slapped at me, but I couldn't take the time to worry about that.

Status gained: Burning [4 HP/sec]
Status gained: Engine [26 MP/sec for 10 seconds]
You gain knowledge of material: Mansekind Molasses [1/10]
You gain knowledge of material: Mansekind Molasses [2/10]
Status gained: Mana Overflow
Conduit is now Level 4.
Status lost: Burning
HP 45/105

I Shaped the blade. More like I loosened the molecules, allowed them to flow with gravity, nudging them to surge between the cracks in the quellstone like the world's slowest-flowing liquid. Once I felt the empty space underneath, I curled upward, disparate strands of liquid metal swinging in empty space, meeting together, intertwining, melding.

*Good.*

I spread further, between more of the cobblestones, filling in the gaps in the brick with steel. The more stones I touched, the greater the drain on my mana.

Shape [20 MP/sec]
Shape is now Level 6.
Status lost: Engine
Shape is now Level 7.

"More," I grunted, holding my hand out for another bottle.

"You sure?"

"More!"

"Just wait for me to get aw—" *FWOOSH!* Bole started to say as he slapped another bottle in my hand, but I'd Consumed it before the liquid even had a chance to settle. "Fuck, Monk! Seriously!"

Status gained: Engine [24 MP/sec for 12 seconds]
You gain knowledge of material: Fungal Bourbon [1/10]

I was on fire again. I didn't feel it as much this time. Again, the hands slapped at my clothes and skin to put the fire out.

Volatility [15 MP/sec, 1 MP/sec base, 14 MP/sec external drain]

I poured the power in. I let it burst out of my body. The wild mana, happy to oblige, soaked into the steel, engorging the molecules with frenetic energy.

After a seeming eternity, I opened my eyes to find Bole and the stone-eyed practitioner staring at me in horror, their mouths open. Parts of their clothes were charred, and the side of Bole's face was an angry shade of red. I didn't have the mental bandwidth to take any pleasure in that. What used to be Bole's short sword was a glowing, vibrating lump of purple death on the floor, the only recognizable part being the pommel that I still clutched in my shaking hand.

"Up. Out," I ground out between my teeth, every ounce of command I could muster going into those two words. Either the look in my eye or the tone of my voice communicated the urgency of my request, because the two of them didn't need to be told twice. They were up and over the bar before I was even on my feet.

"Get everyone back!" Bole yelled.

I leaped over the bar, nearly toppling. My vision swam as I staggered away from the bomb I'd just made. The room was a swirling mess of motion and sound, like everything was smudged paint on a canvas. Was I drunk? I'd never been drunk before.

"Mouths open, everyone!" I shouted. "Deep breath!" I didn't look back. Cool guys never looked back at explosions.

I snapped my fingers. I didn't know why. I was feeling a little showy. Maybe I *was* drunk. A drunken monk. Haha.

*BOOM!*

I came to on the floor again, face-up this time. Above, the partially charred stalks of luminescent filament swayed in the unseen breeze. Something sharp clawed at the bottom of my eye.

[HP 81/105]
Status gained: Underfed (-1 Mind, -1 Body)

"He's awake!" Trix shouted. "Come on, Brother. Time to go!"

I was up on my feet, though I couldn't feel much of my body anymore. Smoke stung my eyes and nose.

A crowd of people were gathered around where the bar used to be. Shredded, wooden debris lay strewn about, so thick it could have doubled as a carpet. One by one, the people filed down to disappear into the floor.

I stole a glance back at the barricade. It was still there. Geddon was hacking at any of the pale limbs that reached through. Bodies of the fallen formed the mortar that held a large part of the barricade together.

Grim but functional . . . for now.

"Come on, Brother. It's our turn," Trix said.

I shook my head painfully.

"You need to get down there now. You're weakened, Brother. You need time to recover."

I shook my head again, getting some more of my sense back. The mana wasn't messing with my head anymore, at least. My Engine buff was gone, too.

"Get them down. I'm fine."

Trix only hesitated a second. Then he hopped down and began to usher more people down into the hole.

I spotted the nearest intact pile of debris and made for it. The feeling in my body was starting to come back, and, strangely enough, my stomach felt hollow, growling loud enough for me to hear. The pastries hadn't gone too far, I guessed.

Geddon was the last one to the trapdoor aside from, surprisingly, Bole. I would have figured he would be the first out.

"Alright, Monk. Get in," Bole commanded.

When I didn't move, the sneer returned to his face. It looked ridiculous with the swelling. "You're not making a heroic sacrifice here, Monk. Just get in, and we can all get out alive."

I felt the familiar weight of Trix climbing up my leg and clawing his way up my back to rest on my shoulder.

"I blew up your door," I stated. "They're just going to follow us down."

Bole ran a hand down his face. "You're going to fight them off, are you? That's stupid. You're stupid."

"I volunteer to fight them off, too!" Geddon piped up. He stood up straighter and puffed out his chest with a huge, canine-exposing grin. I could practically see him getting his second wind right in front of me.

"No, you will not! You're helping me get these people out!" Sissa's voice, muffled from filtering through the brickwork, doused Geddon's dreams instantaneously.

"Not going to fight," I argued. "I'm going to draw them off."

"They do seem to be fixated on Brother Ryan," Trix opined.

"That's why you're getting in the hole, too, Trix," I said.

The vulpa shook his head and clung tightly to my shirt as if he were afraid I was going to throw him in. "No, Brother Ryan. I know my way around, and I can see in the dark. You need me."

"Of course you are! You always do!" one of the blue women exclaimed angrily from down in the hole, the tail end of an argument we hadn't been privy to. I couldn't tell which of them was upset, but I was leaning toward Sissa.

Then Bole was shoved aside, making room for Samila to climb out, followed by Sissa, the latter looking grievously upset, her jaw clenched and nostrils flared.

*Well, crap. Now I have to live through this, don't I?*

Sissa glared at us all, daring us to say something, but when none of us took the bait, she let out a resigned sigh. "If you're staying behind to draw them off, we're staying, too. We'll gather more survivors. You do the baiting, we'll do the saving."

"Yes!" Geddon was practically bouncing on his toes. "Weapons free still, Sarge?"

Sissa didn't answer.

Bole shot a look over the bar toward the barricade. Wood cracked as more of it was ripped away. He blew a frustrated puff of air through his lips and spat a pink glob of something on the quellstone floor.

"Fine. Get yourselves dead. See this?" he asked, holding up a shattered wedge of stone, the face of which was painted in bright yellow. "It's a piece of the trapdoor. There's a lot of these under the hubs. If you find one, you can get in. Yellow means it's safe. Follow the arrows. Don't deviate if you want to live."

I cast about for a larger piece of the former bar, found it, and dragged the wood over to the crater that used to be a magical door as Bole ducked down inside.

"Bole," I called, just as I was about to lose sight of him.

He stopped and came back, looking up at me expectantly.

I reached out, offering my hand.

Bole seemed surprised at first, flinching slightly like I was going to strike him, but once he realized what this was, he smiled that formerly perfect, oily smile of his and grasped my hand.

Iron Grip [1 MP/sec]

It was my fleshy, human hand, so it wasn't up to the stone-crushing standards of my prosthetic, but 24 Body and a multiplicative bonus went a long way.

The bones in Bole's hands creaked. I felt a series of satisfying pops, loud enough to hear over the howls of the Scourge-Touched, and the man's face briefly contorted into a mask of outrage and pain. It warmed the darkest parts of my heart.

I pulled him up until we were close enough to whisper.

"They all get out, Bole. All of them."

He didn't reply. He didn't make a sound. I could see the strain on his face as he fought the urge to cry out.

"Nod if you understand."

Bole's breathing was rapid, frantic whistles through his nose, and sweat poured down his face. He was mastering himself now, though. He was thinking again, despite the pain. I could almost see the gears turning, the scales being filled and measured, pride warring with pragmatism.

He nodded.

I let him go.

Dragging my makeshift camouflage over the hole, I arranged it to best hide the opening for as long as possible. There was just enough left of the bar to sort of conceal what I was doing, but the Undead would eventually find it if they knew to look. I just needed to have their attention long enough to give the innocents a head start.

So, we got moving. I started at a jog, then broke into a sprint, going past the barricade and choosing an archway at random. Trix rode on my shoulder. The guards followed, shields fixed and swords out.

I gave the Scourge-Touched a little wave on the way past to make sure they saw. They didn't like that.

The howls of the dead echoed off the stones—some close, some impossibly far away.

# CHAPTER THIRTY-FOUR

# Do It Better

Stealth (Gray Man) is now Level 9.

**S**pots danced in my vision as I held my breath and forced my body to slow down. Tired, oxygen-starved muscles threatened to cramp, thanks to the awkward position I was maintaining, lying on my side and curled up, but if they did seize, I would have to bear it in silence. The walls of the cupboard where we hid were made of cheap, thin wood that conducted the sound of even the slightest of movements with extreme efficiency. It was like hiding in a cardboard box where every errant twitch sounded like an alarm.

The problem with Scourge-Touched Undead was that they could be absolutely silent if they wanted to. Apparently, their bodies didn't run off oxygen so they didn't need to breathe, and when they weren't howling at the top of their lungs, they didn't feel the need to communicate with each other. Whether they didn't need to or chose not to, I didn't know.

Once they saw me, though, they were like hounds after a deer, baying and snarling up a storm.

I waited and listened. Trix was tucked in behind my head, and I could hear his tiny heartbeat, quick and light.

Detect Magnesium was giving me little hits outside of my wooden box—a wisp of movement here, a flash there. It wasn't much to go on, but we were definitely not alone.

Detect Iron, I'd discovered, wasn't particularly useful at seeing the Undead, since they didn't have hemoglobin like living people did. Sure, I would get a hit once in a while, but the chances of it being something that wanted to eat me came down to a coin flip. Magnesium, though . . . they had that in their bones just like us—not a lot of it, but it was there. Impressions. Glints. It was like trying to see a shadow on a black wall.

*Shhs.*

Something dragged over the counter above our heads. I could almost make out the shape of something humanoid running its hands over the countertop, probing with too many oddly jointed fingers.

*CRASH!*

Glass shattered on the surface of the counter. Liquid trickled down and slapped the pavers outside. Then there was silence. I couldn't be sure, but I thought I heard a whisper of a footfall, far away.

We stayed there another half hour before I decided to slide the door open to check our immediate surroundings.

Nothing. No pale-fleshed legs or milky-white eyes, at least not behind the counter where we hid. I slowly unfolded myself, careful not to brush the fabric of my clothes over the wood any more than I needed to.

Trix was out faster than I could be, scrambling over my body and bounding to the floor. He knew the drill by now. We needed his eyes and ears. Absolutely silent, he snuck over to the side of the counter and peeked around to get a good look at the room. Then he crept back to my side as I was massaging my left calf to work out some of the soreness.

"They're gone, Brother Ryan," he whispered in my ear. "I'll keep listening."

I nodded, sitting upright and stretching my upper half, my neck especially.

The intersection where we'd set up was much bigger than the last one but oddly shaped, a sort of asymmetrical octagon that someone had bashed with a hammer until it was functionally two separate areas.

Small, single-proprietor shop stalls were built against the walls, angles set to snugly match the odd geometry of the room. Whatever logic Ralqir's Dark Lord had used to make this place, I couldn't help but think this intersection was an oversight, a kind of slapdash solution that just needed to be there to make the rest of the more-important parts of the design fit. Maybe it was like a leftover screw at the end of a big project where you just throw up your hands and hope for the best. Then again, what did I know?

"Base camp" or the stall with the best hiding place, rather, was a wooden box built a bit like I imagined a street vendor would want. It was large enough to fit a few people behind the counter, but the front was solid enough to withstand some punishment, and, at one time, it had big shutters that could be locked from the inside. On the wall behind me were various bottles of cheap liquor and sweet water as well as a few local publications that I hadn't had a chance to read. A freshly broken bottle bled sticky red liquid that still dribbled off the countertop and down into the floor, the smell of which reminded me of rice pudding.

*Back to work, then.*

It had taken us a few tries to find another hub with a magical trapdoor again. First, it was about finding another hub, one free of undead. Then we had to lead the Scourge-Touched away from said area long enough for me to conduct a search. Geddon hated that part. The guy was getting more cardio over the past few days than he probably had in years. However, it kept the guards moving and searching for those they could save, so his complaints were more in jest than annoyance.

We had the system down pretty well now.

In the early hours of our little crisis, it was relatively easy to avoid the Returned. They made enough noise to not be able to hear us, and they tended to clump up into little swarms that left all sorts of space for stealth. What it wasn't easy to do was to avoid seeing what they'd done. Not everyone had made it out before the lockdown. There were signs.

We'd gotten turned around in the side tunnels once and came across a market of some kind, one constructed from Mendau, the floor carpeted with mats of beige wood and string with flimsy, ramshackle booths everywhere. Unlike the quellstone, that place displayed exactly how much carnage had happened. Everything was stained with the blood of the living, the mats still sticky and wet.

No bodies, though. There were never any bodies.

That had been a wake-up call for all of us, especially Sissa. The sight of the massacre had affected her the most. During our time in that place, she withdrew, listlessly going through the motions of searching through the market but not allowing herself to really be present.

I could sympathize. She was the ranking guard down here, and she was being presented with terrible choices, given two paths to choose from where both led to a bad end. The market was one of those ends. If she needed to put down her burden for a while and check out, I wasn't going to judge. It was only after we found our first pair of survivors an hour later—a little boy and his grandmother—that Sissa came back, and she came back hard. If anyone made it out of this place alive, it would be those two. Sissa would make sure.

For my part, I dealt with things differently. People were dead. It was my fault. I didn't like that.

So I worked the problem. The exit problem.

I'd learned a lot since my last bout with quellstone. The more surface area my metal made contact with, the bigger the drain on my Mana Pool. So I'd Shaped off a piece of Baptized Bronze about the size of my finger and used it as my probe. I thinned it out, elongating it until I had a hair-thin bit of bronze wire which I would then use to feel around underneath the quellstone, looking for empty space. It was still a drain on my mana, but it was only enough to add a couple of points to the MP/sec. It helped that I was much more practiced now and was able to probe a spot in the floor in about thirty seconds, thanks to the Baptized Bronze's willingness to comply.

Well, we were done with that part. Now it was about getting in. I was not about to blow up a whole other room to get into the tunnels this time. Less mess. Less noise. The acoustics down here were such that the sound carried for ridiculous distances. We needed something more specialized, and I had just the thing in mind.

I summoned my hybrid steel tube I'd salvaged from my stolen lamp stand. I use the term "tube" loosely, because that implies a rounded shape. Now this one was a sort-of hollow V with a round top and pointed legs. Then I'd salvaged the rest of the Baptized Bronze to form the inside wall of the V. The whole thing was about as long as my arm and had enough space inside to fit my pinky.

"Brother Ryan, I don't mean to question . . ." Trix didn't finish his sentence. He was up on the counter now, ears perked up, head tilted. He took his job as the lookout very seriously.

"We're going to get out of here," I said, summoning the sister tube of steel from my Spatial Storage to begin Shaping it to fit inside the other tube's cavity. "But we're doing it right this time."

We'd talked about going back to Bole's already-open tunnel and getting the civilians out that way, but we'd decided against it. If Bole was half as clever as Sissa said he was, he would have found a way to block up the exit on the other side. If we were discovered in the tunnels, we'd be sandwiched between a blocked exit and a horde of Scourge-Touched, and I wasn't confident that I would be able to blow open an exit in a confined space and not kill us all in the process.

"So, you don't have to set yourself on fire?"

"Hm," I grunted, saturating the steel and beginning the slow process of thinning it to fit into the cavity. "And this is, theoretically, going to be quieter."

"I had assumed self-immolation was part of your method."

"Side effect," I said. "Did not enjoy it."

"How do you feel, by the way?" Trix asked. Ever since Trix had healed me, I'd not been feeling myself. I felt hollow, like I was missing something.

"Still weak. Everything feels sore."

"I'm sorry. It's a side effect of our . . . my magic."

Trix was cagey about his mojo, and I didn't begrudge him his secrets. I had plenty of my own. I knew I wasn't doing well back when I'd blown up the pub room. My HP was low, and I was unconscious. When I came to, however, Trix was right there, and my HP had ticked up despite being laid out on a quellstone floor. Whenever I asked him about it, all he would say was that he healed me, but there had been a cost.

"Whatever you did, it worked," I said. "No need to apologize."

Trix didn't seem convinced. "You need to eat. Your body needs nutrients."

"I ate back at the market," I lied. I used my Spatial Storage to stash the food I'd found there. I'd been slipping it to the civilians we'd found, especially the kid. I hadn't had much of an appetite after seeing the market anyway.

"Yes, but you need more. It's why you feel the way you do. I'd cook for you, but I'm afraid it might attract attention with the smell."

He was probably right. If the others came back with food tonight, I'd have a little, but right now, we had a small window to get this done. The Scourge-Touched had spread out, and they patrolled constantly. Once one of them saw you, they'd do that howl thing, and the rest would swarm. Then it was a running battle to get clear.

Trix was right to say that I needed him down here. His knowledge of the Undercity helped us lose pursuit multiple times when I was sure we were screwed.

I worked in silence for a few minutes before Trix wanted to talk again.

"Are you making another . . . uh . . . what was the word you used? Firement?"

"Firearm? No. This is something else."

"Oh," he said, hesitating, rubbing his paws together that way he did. "Either way, I have been meaning to ask you about it. Are they common in the Order? I've never seen one."

"They're common where I'm from. They're one of the most popular means of warfare."

"It's not like a crossbow. Crossbows are big and heavy and they take real strength to load."

I nodded. "Back home, a long time ago, they called guns the great equalizer. You don't need a lot of physical might or special talent to use one."

"You don't need to be a Rising Sun?" Out of the corner of my eye, I saw Trix racked with one of his trembling fits again.

"No," I answered. "You just need to have hands, and even then, that's negotiable. It's a tool, one that's been refined to make it accessible to as many people as possible."

The vulpa paused briefly to consider the concept, only answering with an "I see."

I finished thinning the steel out and slipped the rod all the way inside.

"Do you think they made it out, Brother Ryan?" he asked quietly.

"The people from the pub?"

"Yes."

"I hope so."

"I hope so, too. It would be better if we managed to at least save someone."

He was thinking about the market again, and he was about to make me think about the market again. I didn't have time for that.

I cleared my throat uncomfortably and steered us away from that subject. "If we do this right, we'll save at least three more."

"I know," Trix said. "It's just becoming harder to imagine anything good coming of this. I keep imagining all those people coming to an evil end."

*No time for that. Do it later.*

I shut my eyes and became the steel. I thinned out, molded to fit the cavity.

*Do it right. Think about it later.*

After another period of silence, when I'd nearly filled the center of the hollow with my next piece of steel, Trix spoke up again. "How does your technique work, Brother?"

"In general or just this?" My tone was flat. I was having to split my attention between Shaping and conversation, so something had to suffer.

"Either."

"It's a hollow," I explained. "A V-shaped pipe. Strong, thick metal on the outside edge, softer metal on the inside. The explosive force I can put out will deform the soft metal, compress it, blast it out of the bottom. With some luck, it'll cut right through the door."

"This is part of your Dominion then?"

I felt myself shrug slightly. "It's physics."

"And you've done this before?"

I coughed, nearly losing my grip on the metal. "Uh, yeah. For sure."

I'd seen this done to split rocks and demo old concrete from a distance. I knew how it worked, though. Sort of.

---

Shape is now Level 8.
You have created: Crude Shaped Charge
You have been awarded 70 Experience points. [100 base, -30 quality]

---

*Don't you judge me, System. I'm working with what I've got.*

"Will the Infected Returned not come when you use your technique?" Trix asked.

"It's a possibility."

The little vulpa was doing the math, though. "If we make another egress, won't the Returned follow us? Even more will die if we let them out, Returned and the living alike."

"I've been brainstorming that problem, too, and I think I have something. The good part of a plan, at least. That's why I've been sucking up every little piece of metal we've come across."

"And the alcohol."

I grimaced, remembering the sensation of self-immolation. "Yeah. That, too."

"You want to set yourself on fire again."

*"Want* is a strong word."

Automate [20 MP/sec]

*When you are Triggered, feed mana into the aiming arms. Bring the sight as close to the nearest intact and moving Scourge-Touched target as possible. Feed mana into the retention pin Trigger. Feed a small burst of mana into the firing trigger. Wait for the bolt to come back into contact with you. Repeat.*

I breathed out, keeping hold of the concept I was trying to imbue into the thing, making sure I didn't miss anything.

*Don't shoot friendlies. Don't shoot* through *friendlies, either.*

Automate is now Level 4.

Someone cleared their throat from elsewhere in the room. The others were watching. I knew that. I made it a point not to look at them, though.

I wiped sweat out of my eyes and Consumed another table leg to get my Mana Pool back into the double digits again. Then I carefully inserted the targeting card into the brain housing of my newest creation.

This was the final piece. It had taken an entire day, but we'd finally cobbled together enough material to get up and running.

I dove inside to Shape-weld all the parts together and eliminate any uneven surfaces and previously unseen air pockets. There wasn't a lot, but when I was done, everything fit together smoothly, down to the micrometer, and the welds were no longer welds; they were a singular piece, bonded at the molecular level.

I'd scaled up my Bronze prototype and made some improvements starting with using harder materials like steel to make the firing chamber, barrel, and the aiming arms. Those were going to have the most heat and stress with repeated use, so having a high melting point was crucial. The legs, however, were made of whatever junk metal I had lying around, a combination of tin, brass, and aluminum, all scrounged from cookware we'd found in the now-abandoned parts of the Undercity. Whatever alloy I'd made when I fused them all together, I was sure would make any self-respecting smith break out in hives.

I needed the new model to be reliable so I took the extra time to give the bolt and firing chamber a spring action that loaded from the magazine when the spring was depressed, and fired when the bolt slammed forward on the retention pin.

The magazine was still a gravity-fed hopper like my pistol, which I wasn't happy with, but I didn't have the time to create a feeding system that was both accommodating of large amounts of ammo and reliable enough to trust. So, instead, I relied on good old Isaac Newton. For now, I was using a tin funnel with its own Automated stirring system near the stem that massaged the ammo down into the tube with the use of a few different Triggers.

The gun part was a bulky three inches around at the chamber, with a barrel that tapered off to be long and skinny at the end. I didn't have any rifling on the inside of the barrel, so I wanted the length to give the shots some accuracy. The tripod had a wide stance for maximum stability but was tall enough to see over moderately high obstacles. When I had the whole thing put together, it came up to my waist.

> Shape [22 MP/sec]

Satisfied with all that, I dove into the tripod, focusing on the feet and melt-Shaping them into the cracks between the quellstone. This was the really expensive part, and it hurt. I was starting to really hate quellstone. The pain was necessary, though. Without a solid footing, my new weapon would just knock itself over before it did us any good.

The spring I'd used to slap the bolt back into place after each shot was a relatively weak one by necessity, since I couldn't run a lot of tests to get the exact strength needed. That meant that every time my new gun fired a round, the bolt slammed up against the rear wall of the tube hard, and the one test round I'd put through the gun design had a significant, unpleasant recoil that I wouldn't wish on anyone living.

Therefore, my tripod had to be melded to the floor or the gun would just breakdance on the cobblestones as it tried to kill things.

> You have created: Junk Auto-Turret
> You have been awarded 1,345 Experience points. [1,800 base, -455 quality]

*Okay, System, now you're just being mean.*

With a satisfied sigh, I took my hand off the tripod leg and brushed nonexistent dust off my hands.

Despite what descriptor the System used, I was pretty proud of my work, especially considering this was all scrapped material.

I turned to the others.

Sissa, Samila, Geddon, Trix, and our three survivors all looked at me and my new superweapon with some variation of confusion or concern. I'd promised them a miracle, but the miracle wasn't in the form they'd expected, with the additional drawback of having taken an inordinate amount of time to make.

The silence was too much.

"Ta-da," I said, with a wave of my hand encompassing the entirety of my handiwork.

The kid, a Miur boy we'd found hiding in the market, no more than eight years old, started clapping, but his grandmother shushed him.

Sissa was the first to voice her concern. "That's it? What is it?"

I couldn't help but grin. "I'm glad you asked, Sergeant," I said, rubbing my hands together. I couldn't help it. Despite everything, I loved building stuff. Even more, I loved solving problems, especially if the solution was mechanical.

I put my hands behind my back and took in a deep breath, a primer on the Laws of Motion on the tip of my tongue. It felt, briefly, like I was back in my workshop explaining engines to Vince instead of buried alive with flesh-eating monsters.

But Samila interrupted before I could begin. "It solves our Geddon problem."

"Aw, really?" Geddon deflated, shoulders slumped, his gaze falling to the floor. He looked legitimately disappointed.

"Our Geddon problem?" Trix asked, looking to each of us in hopes we'd share.

"It was a question of time," Sissa explained. "Brother Ryan's method for getting us into the tunnels draws a lot of attention, and we'd never escape in time without a buffer. It meant that someone would need to stay behind to buy us all time to get to the surface."

I cleared my throat uncomfortably. I could feel the wind rushing out of my sails. Someday someone would let me crow a little bit when I'd done something cool.

"Um. I was calling it our 'Heroic Sacrifice' problem, but . . . yes. This is meant to solve it," I said with a lot less energy than I'd been feeling before.

"We'd already talked about it, and I was going to have that honor." Geddon sighed wistfully.

Sissa slapped Geddon on the shoulder, hard. "No. We talked about it, and I said we'd find another way."

"But you had a look in your eye," Geddon insisted.

Sissa glared at him reproachfully. "The answer is still no, Geddon."

"Go. All of you," Geddon said, placing his hand over his eyes dramatically. "You may thank me by living full, meaningful lives."

"Shut up, meatslab. Die a heroic death on your own time," Samila chided.

"I would rather see you live through this ordeal, Brother Geddon," Trix said.

I waved them all down. "Hey! I just said no one is staying behind. This—" I slapped the hopper of the turret, feeling the tripod legs wiggle slightly. I'd need to tighten those up. "—this baby will make the sacrifice for us."

"Does it explode?" Sissa asked, tilting her head to look at the turret.

"No . . . Ma—" I sputtered. "Yes, but in a good way."

"You really were making a firearm," Trix said.

Geddon saved me by asking the right question. "How does it help us?"

"This is—Well . . . Okay, think of it like a crossbow or a slingshot that fires itself. I'm going to blow the door off the tunnel. Then we're all going to hurry inside while this turret covers us," I said.

Sissa leaned forward, interested now. "It can do that? How long can it hold them off? Won't it run out of bolts?"

"Trix?" I called upon my assistant.

Trix blinked, confused, but then he remembered his role. "Ah, yes."

Then he scampered behind the bar and came back dragging a heavy sack of ball bearings behind him.

"Are they all cleaned up? No debris or dirt?" I asked.

"None, Brother Ryan."

"Okay," I said, taking the sack from him and pouring it into the hopper as quietly as I could. It sounded like gravel on a tin roof.

He handed me another.

There was a particular type of rotating table that was popular down here, one that used the little metal balls to facilitate motion. I'd found them when I was poking around with Detect Iron in a different neighborhood. The stem of every table lit up like little beacons, and breaking one open got us fifty or so little ball bearings. Once we knew what we were looking for, it was fairly easy to find them, and I'd tasked everyone with cracking said tables open and bringing me the proceeds. They weren't all iron, but they were roughly the same size. I'd made my barrel and chamber accommodating for them all.

"These are the ammunition," I said. "Hopefully, I'll have the hole all patched up before the turret runs dry."

I'd saved a good chunk of metal just for that purpose. It was going to be another "touch all the quellstone and try not to get sucked dry" situation, but I didn't see a way around it this time.

"He's going to set himself on fire again," Trix added.

"I like this plan more and more," Sissa said dryly. I tried not to take offense.

"And if he can't plug the hole, his burning corpse will deter pursuit for a little while at least," said Samila. "Smart."

I shifted uncomfortably at the thought. "Yeah. Well, that's the backup-backup plan."

"Why does he get to go out in a blaze of glory, and I don't?" Geddon complained. He was smiling though, like he could smell a good fight just over the horizon.

# CHAPTER THIRTY-FIVE

# Pay the Price

**W**e huddled in the archway as far from the detonation zone as possible. I was at the front, closest to freedom but also closest to what would be the blast. Geddon stood behind me, a wall of armored muscle upon which my insides would be tastefully splattered if I'd done this wrong. The giant's role would be to clear any debris my explosion might leave behind while everyone else got the survivors down into the hole and then themselves.

Geddon was also the tallest among us and now served as Trix's new perch, where he stood upright, ears perked all the way up and whiskers twitching. He'd tell us if there were any Undead near.

Behind them, the three survivors huddled close together, the old woman and the boy as well as the sweaty, round shopkeeper. Sissa and Samila brought up the rear, Sissa with her eyes on me, Samila looking into the darkness behind.

I looked up at Trix, waiting. I didn't speak, though. I needed his sharp hearing just now. The vulpa's ears turned like twin satellite dishes following a moving signal.

After a tense moment, Trix gave me the signal, which was just a hand wave. They didn't seem to use thumbs-up on Ralqir, and I'd been looked upon as a bumpkin for having to have it explained to me. How was I supposed to know not every species had thumbs?

I nodded, starting the countdown on my fingers. The others covered their ears.

Three . . .

Two . . .

One . . .

I blew out a long, slow breath. This needed to be flawless.

*PHOW!*

It wasn't the earth-shattering explosion I'd done for Bole and his group. This was more of a high-pitched, tinnitus-inducing peal of miniature thunder that, if I wasn't an Exotic nowadays, would have probably affected my enjoyment of certain types of music later in life. Dust and wood splinters flew up in a vertical plume, nearly to the ceiling twenty feet above.

I was moving before gravity had a chance to let any of the particulates settle, bounding into the hub at a sprint. I spared a glance for my turret that was on the far edge of the room to my left, overlooking the trapdoor and the approach from four separate archways.

My breath caught in my throat as I looked down the barrel, my life flashing before my eyes in the two steps it took to get past, but then the moment was behind me as I hurried on. The barrel didn't track me. The auto-turret just stood there—a spider, poised, silently watching for prey that entered its web.

I knew it wouldn't shoot me. I'd tested it earlier. However, I couldn't bring myself to trust my Automation process completely . . . not just yet. Maybe that said something about how much I trusted myself.

Over the ringing in my ears, I heard the distant, echoing howls of the Scourge-Touched. They began just as I arrived at the blast site at a full sprint, sliding to a stop next to the heavy wooden countertop we'd laid over the charge to somewhat muffle the sound. It was in a few triangular pieces now.

The calls of the Undead were faint.

*Doesn't sound too close. We might just have time.*

Geddon got there right behind me. With a grunt, he flung the pieces aside to reveal the damage I'd done.

My heart, such as it was, stilled.

"What is it? Why have we stopped?" Sissa asked. The sound of her sword leaving her sheath grated across my already-tender eardrums.

The Shaped charge just laid there across the quellstone bricks, all of them fully intact.

*Impossible.*

Disbelief flooded my mind. I shook my head and reached down to pick it up.

| Transfer Spent Shaped Charge to Spatial Storage? Y/N |
| --- |

I felt numb. This should have worked. I'd done it right, hadn't I? Or did I just get all these people killed?

I chose "Yes."

The band of warm metal disappeared with a dim flash.

Sissa pushed to the front of the group, holding her sword above her head. "What are we doing? Someone say something. They're coming!"

I squinted at the . . .

*Oh.*

There, in a neat, arm-length line about two inches wide, the quellstone bricks were simply gone. My Shaped charge had done its job so well, had sheared the trapdoor so neatly, that the magic was the only thing keeping it together.

"It's not open! It is, indeed, a good day to die!" Geddon bellowed. Did he have to sound so excited about it?

"Oh, Light's mercy, please," the old woman sobbed, falling down to her knees next to me.

"Dammit. Circle up, warriors. Put the civilians in the center," Sissa ordered.

*Well, shit.*

"Duty and mercy! Duty and mercy!" Sissa chanted, that strange, bright power infusing her words. It ran through my blood, charged my muscles, and brightened the dark corners of my psyche.

There . . . There was a gap in the stones. I'd made a gap. I could work with this.

I started breathing again.

"I'm going to need a minute, Sergeant!" I declared, crouching down on the stones to check for any amount of give. Nothing.

"Not like we have a choice, Monk," she growled. "Work quickly."

Forcing my breathing to slow, I stuck my prosthetic fingers inside the gap.

Iron Grip [1MP/sec]

Bracing my feet, I pulled, flexing my back and extending my legs. I heaved with all my might.

It didn't give in the slightest. It was like they were still part of a floor. Whatever magic this was, it was solid. I was working with an unknown here.

"Here they come!" Trix yipped from somewhere.

I looked up, still straining to get the quellstone to move, even just to jiggle. I was lucky enough to look at the right archway as the first pale figure shot into the light, using its arms and legs to run like an ape, bare feet and palms slapping on the cobblestones, filthy, ragged clothes flapping against its body. As it charged forward, its dead eyes widened at the sight of me, and its mouth yawned to broadcast its special brand of hatred to the world.

With strength I hadn't realized the Returned possessed, it bent its knees and leapt high into the air to bypass the guards and get straight to me.

Samila, the shield on that side of the circle, shuffled to the right and tensed her body to receive the charge. I saw her knees bending slightly, boots angled to absorb the kinetic energy. She didn't get the chance, however.

From the corner of my eye, I saw the barrel of the auto-turret, impossibly fast, jerk to life, a spider seizing upon unaware prey. It snapped its aim dead-center on its target, just like it was programmed to do.

*FWUP! FWUP! FWUP! FWUP! FWUP!*

The metal walls of the firing chamber were thick, and the barrel was precisely built, so the sound of the tiny explosions were muted. Most of the sound came from the hypersonic ball bearings ringing through the barrel and the snapping of collapsing air pockets in the rounds' wakes. Superfluous propellant energy bled from the action and the barrel with every ignition, a dangerous violet cloud of extra explosive potential, the brightness of which left floating spots in my vision.

The turret scored three hits, even as the pale Returned flew toward us. The first two rounds hit it in the side of the rib cage right under the creature's armpit. Bones cracked, the significant force applied by the spherical projectiles setting the Undead's body into a spin while black blood blossomed from pulverized meat. The final round caught it under the jaw where the throat connected to the head. Splintered bone and pulverized brain matter blew out of the top of the creature's skull, and the light went out of its eyes.

The body flopped limply at Samila's feet, sliding to a stop, not quite having the inertia to hit her shield anymore.

Scourge-Touched Undead defeated.

You have been awarded 3 Experience points. [16 base (-2 Level, +2 nemesis, -13 non-combat Class)]

*FWUP! FWUP!*

The turret put a couple of more rounds into the Scourge-Touched's body for good measure. Perhaps it had detected an errant twitch in the creature's nervous system, or my programming was shoddy. Hard to tell.

Everyone just kind of paused at that moment, staring at the broken body.

Judging by the looks on everyone's faces, they were shocked, terrified, hopeful . . . Geddon barked out a laugh.

For my part, I was relieved that it had worked at all.

All eyes slowly drifted to me, and I pretended to be very engrossed in getting the door open. The old woman was still weeping, holding her grandson close, maybe for multiple reasons now. The shopkeeper wiped his handkerchief nervously over his sweating brow but avoided looking directly my way.

It was oddly quiet among the living. The howls were growing closer, but I could still feel the eyes on me. I glanced up to see Samila assessing me, a strange, hungry look on her face. "I want one, Sis," she declared matter-of-factly.

I felt my cheeks flush. I couldn't articulate why.

"Same," Geddon shot back with a vicious laugh.

"Get your own, meatshield."

"He can make more."

"That's n—"

Sissa hissed to quiet them. "Shut up and watch your angles. Monk, where are we on the door?"

I shook my head and went back to work in earnest, stealing one last glance at Samila.

*Did she just wink at me?*

I put it out of my mind. There wasn't time for that. I reached down and took hold of the magical bricks yet again. I'd been avoiding this, but other than triggering another huge explosion with no guarantee of success, I was out of ideas.

Trix heard them before we saw them. "Here they come! Watch out!"

---

Devouring Grasp [5 MP/sec]
You gain knowledge of material: Quellstone [1/10]

---

With a crack, the two bits of stone within my palm gave way, and disintegrated into a cloud of black motes.

Cold fingers wrapped themselves around my Core, my lungs, my stomach, my brainstem, and they squeezed. Spots danced in my vision. The blood in my veins thickened to a sludge. I felt slow. Lethargic. Like I was encased in ice and my body was giving in to hypothermia.

A terrible, agonized groan ripped its way out of me, and I slumped to the floor.

Gibbering. Howling. Snarling. Cries of rage.

Someone roared.

*FWUP! FWUP! FWUP! FWUP! FWUP! FWUP!*

---

Scourge-Touched Undead defeated.
You have been awarded 35 Experience points. [16 base (-2 Level, +2 nemesis, +16 group, + 16 chain, -13 non-combat Class)]
Scourge-Touched Undead defeated.
You have been awarded 35 Experience points. [16 base (-2 Level, +2 nemesis, +16 group, + 16 chain, -13 non-combat Class)]

---

I came back to life in the middle of dying.

"Brother Ryan!" Trix was there, his clawed fingers on the sides of my face. I felt hollow, and my head throbbed.

---

HP [92/105]
MP [0/75]

> Status lost: Mana Sap
> Status gained: Underfed [-2 mind, -2 body]

The world was a swirling vortex of violence.

The unhealthy white of the Scourge-Touched streamed in from the archways. Long limbs and snarling faces bathed in pale light from the glow lamps above. I watched as three blurry Undead swarmed over one another to charge the gray smudge that was Geddon before their bodies were torn apart by a swarm of angry supersonic impacts.

To my right, a pack of Returned was bearing down on Sissa. The leader of their group took an unfortunate round in the arm that snapped the bone in half just as it put its full weight on it, causing the creature to tumble forward and trip those behind it. They piled up for only a second, but that was all it took for my auto-turret to decimate their numbers. The pile of creatures became a sagging mound of pulped meat as ball bearings zipped in from the right and cut through multiple bodies before continuing on to ruin someone else's day.

*FWUP! FWUP! FWUP! FWUP! FWUP! FWUP!*

> Scourge-Touched Undead defeated.
> You have been awarded 35 Experience points. [16 base (-2 Level, +2 nemesis, +16 group, + 16 chain, -13 non-combat Class)]
> Scourge-Touched Undead defeated.
> You have been awarded 35 Experience points. [16 base (-2 Level, +2 nemesis, +16 group, + 16 chain, -13 non-combat Class)]
> . . .
> Scourge-Touched Undead defeated.
> You have been awarded 35 Experience points. [16 base (-2 Level, +2 nemesis, +16 group, + 16 chain, -13 non-combat Class)]

Geddon roared in the Scourge-Touched's faces, hacking at those unlucky enough to get into range. Sissa and Samila were slightly more measured, choosing to take a blow on their shields and to then follow up with a riposte that slipped between ribs or sliced throats.

"He's okay!" Trix shouted. "Come on, Brother. On your feet."

"Ugh," I said as I pushed myself up into a sitting position. My MP was gone, and my head pounded. I summoned a piece of scrapped furniture wood and Consumed it.

> You gain knowledge of material: Mendau Wood [61/1,250]
> Status gained: Engine [3 MP/sec for 30 minutes]

I wanted to vomit. I might have.

"Are you back with us, Brother Ryan?" Trix asked with evident concern.

"I'm here. Just . . . *damn*."

<hr>

Consume Mendau Wood? Y/N
Status gained: Engine [3 MP/sec for 60 minutes]

<hr>

"What are we going to do? Can we get through?" Trix asked.

"Hold them off, Trix," I croaked. "I'm gonna need time." I summoned my pistol and a handful of ammo worms, holding them out for Trix to take. "Remember what I said."

The vulpa looked down at the weapon with trepidation and shuddered. "Uh. Point and shoot. Right?"

"Right. Save it for when you need it."

Mercifully, the Returned were still streaming in, not coming in overwhelming numbers as of yet. We couldn't count on that to continue, though.

All the while, the sound of the turret never ceased.

*FWUP! FWUP! FWUP! FWUP!*

<hr>

Scourge-Touched Undead defeated.
You have been awarded 35 Experience points. [16 base (-2 Level, +2 nemesis, +16 group, + 16 chain, -13 non-combat Class)]
Scourge-Touched Undead defeated.
You have been awarded 35 Experience points. [16 base (-2 Level, +2 nemesis, +16 group, + 16 chain, -13 non-combat Class)]
MP [58/75]

<hr>

More often than not, as one of the guards engaged with a feral Undead, their opponent would be cut down by a hail of fire from the turret, dropping it before swords had a chance to strike. Bodies with black, weeping holes were piling up around our protective circle while our group of survivors huddled next to me, not daring to look at the battle unfolding. I saw the kid trying to take a couple of peeks, but he didn't like what he saw, burying his head on his grandmother's shoulder.

I reached out and took hold of another stone.

"Oh, no. You can't," Trix said, reaching out to stop me, but he was too late.

<hr>

Devouring Grasp [5 MP/sec]
You gain knowledge of material: Quellstone [2/10]
Status lost: Engine

<hr>

I did vomit this time. Engine guttered and died, and my MP ticked down five points at a time. My lungs seized inside of me.

Status gained: Mana Sap
Consume Mendau Wood? Y/N
Consume Mendau Wood? Y/N
Consume Mendau Wood? Y/N

It took three more pieces of wood to get my Engine humming again before I bottomed out my MP. I shivered and wiped sweat from my face.

I felt like hammered shit.

*Do it again.*

I summoned another few handfuls of wood to get ready for the next round.

Devouring Grasp [5 MP/sec]
You gain knowledge of material: Quellstone [3/10]
Status lost: Engine
Consume Mendau Wood? Y/N

It went on like that. Every time I would Consume another bit of quellstone, it would *kill* my mana. I wasn't sure how else to put it. One moment I was humming along—precious, vital blue energy flowing through me—then the quellstone did *something*. It blackened what it touched. Withered it. Extinguished it.

I'm not sure how long I rode that rollercoaster of pain. Minutes, probably. It felt like a lifetime.

The Undead were turning from a stream into a full-blown flood, too many to count, not from down on the floor like I was. The stink of their blood dominated my senses.

*THWOK! THWOK! THWOK! THWOK! THWOK!*

It was hard to hear the bark of the action on the turret now above the screams of the Undead and the wall of corpses between me and my construct. What did reach me was the disturbing slap of metal on flesh and splintering of bone as the piercing projectiles did their gruesome work.

I tried not to think about how these were all people.

*Get them out. Get them out, then you can think about it.*

I used what I had to get us out of here. I killed. I Consumed. I killed the Dark Lord's creations. Consumed the Dark Lord's legacy.

And it cost me.

My body and soul withered before my eyes. The veins under my skin were dark, spiderwebbing roots that burned every time I reignited my Engine, every time they came back from whatever brink I'd pushed them to.

Affinity Type: Quellstone is now Grade F.
Core Ability gained: Detect Quellstone [Radius: 10 feet]
Resistance to Mana Sap increased. [ERROR:M_Type_&#%R^_AuthorityNotFound]
Resolving . . .
You gain knowledge of material: Quellstone [1/50]
Status lost: Engine
Consume Mendau Wood? Y/N
You gain knowledge of material: Quellstone [2/50]
Consume Mendau Wood? Y/N

. . .

You gain knowledge of material: Quellstone [26/50]
ERROR:M_Type_&#%R^_AuthorityNotFound resolved:
Core Ability gained: Tempered Channels

Something happened at that point. Whatever mojo that kept the stones together finally fell apart. Something ceased, like the power being cut from an electromagnet, and the rest of the bricks blocking our escape tunnel collapsed under me. I found myself tumbling painfully down a new set of stairs, along with a pile of quellstone rubble.

"He's got it!" Trix yelled triumphantly on my behalf.

Sissa didn't waste any time. "Everyone, inside!"

# CHAPTER THIRTY-SIX

# Stick the Landing

It was dark down here. The light from the hub room above couldn't quite reach the bottom of these stairs, and none of the glow lamps I'd come to expect from the populous parts of the Undercity were anywhere in sight, either.

That was okay. The dark was a nice change.

The stones where I laid felt good against my skin, a smooth caress of comforting coolness after I'd essentially just gone on a mana-killing bender. These rocks weren't quellstone, though some of that had certainly tumbled down here with me.

[HP 19/105]
[MP 1/75]
Status lost: Mana Sap

My eyelids fluttered, and my vision drifted in the dark. I got the impression the room would have been spinning if I were able to see anything. Sweat beaded on my skin, instantly cold, and I felt that cold acutely. Inside, though, I was burning. Everything ached. Disembodied voices jabbered meaninglessly in the darkness.

"I can't! He almost killed himself getting us down here!"

"If you don't, all of us are dead!"

"I literally can't! Look at him! He'll die!"

Status lost: Fever (Severe)

Scourge-Touched Undead defeated.
You have been awarded 35 Experience points. [16 base (-2 Level, +2 nemesis, +16 group, + 16 chain, -13 non-combat Class)]

I tried to shake my head, only having the strength and coordination to twitch slightly, but a tiny new part of my face was now resting on the cool stones. That was nice.

My muscles, the ones I'd tried to move so far at least, seemed to have checked out for the day, and my brain didn't mind terribly much that it couldn't muster up any activity.

When had I closed my eyes again? It didn't matter. Lying down was good. It was right.

If only things weren't so noisy. An unnatural, discordant choir sang unpleasant songs that shook the air and scoured my tender nerves.

"It's a tide of them up there! He would want you to do it!" That was Sissa's voice, strained, fearful.

What she said made me feel discomforted. It wasn't anywhere close to a clear, logical thought, but the kernel was there, a burning coal, hissing and stinging under my blanket of peaceful ignorance. I tried to ignore it, tried to smother it with thoughts of rest.

"Don't say that! You don't know him!" shouted Trix.

"Neither do you!" Sissa shot back.

I still had something to do, didn't I? That little thought gave my coal of consciousness a puff of oxygen, and soon there was a gratifying spark of real consciousness.

*I have things to do.*

My prosthetic moved first. I curled its fingers, then bent it at the elbow until my metal hand was up near my face. I watched the fingers flex delicately, one by one. That first, conscious motion was a crack in an already overflowing dam.

*I'm not done.*

My body seemed to remember how to interpret sensory input again. It was decidedly unpleasant. Living razors had grown inside my muscle tissue, and they busied themselves slithering along under my skin. At least that's how it felt. I was damaged. Leaky. The sensation cascaded outward from my Core until it was everywhere.

Scourge-Touched Undead defeated.
You have been awarded 35 Experience points. [16 base (-2 Level, +2 nemesis, +16 group, + 16 chain, -13 non-combat Class)]
Scourge-Touched Undead defeated.
You have been awarded 35 experience points. [16 base (-2 Level, +2 nemesis,

+16 group, + 16 chain, -13 non-combat Class)]

"He's coming around," Samila observed from close by.

The other two didn't hear her.

"Get him up on his feet. That's an order!"

"As I'm constantly being reminded, I'm not a warrior. You can't order me to kill him."

"Everyone's a warrior today, Brother Yik'i'trix. Do it."

A gentle but strong hand slipped across my chest and helped me get to my knees. My trembling limbs betrayed me, nearly bringing me down again, but the other person held me tightly until I could master myself. Things slowly got easier.

"He's strong, Fuzzball," Samila said as she loosened her hold on me and slipped around to my front to look into my eyes, a knowing smirk on her face. "And we need him."

I checked my HP.

HP [21/105]

"I'm fine," I coughed, and something gritty welled up in the back of my mouth. My stomach spasmed, and I vomited. What came out was hot and foul, splattering on the floor between Samila's knees. She didn't flinch, just placing her hands on my shoulders to keep me from keeling over.

"What the hells is that?" Sissa cried, putting a hand over her mouth and nose.

"Brother Ryan? Are you . . . Light, it smells. What—" Trix sounded like he wanted to throw up as well. I couldn't blame him, though I would argue I had it significantly worse. The aftertaste was something I could tell was going to linger.

Geddon roared his defiance at unseen foes up above.

The XP messages just kept rolling in.

Scourge-Touched Undead defeated.
You have been awarded 35 Experience points. [16 base (-2 Level, +2 nemesis, +16 group, + 16 chain, -13 non-combat Class)]
Scourge-Touched Undead defeated.
You have been awarded 35 Experience points. [16 base (-2 Level, +2 nemesis, +16 group, + 16 chain, -13 non-combat Class)]
Scourge-Touched Undead defeated.
You have been awarded 35 Experience points. [16 base (-2 Level, +2 nemesis, +16 group, + 16 chain, -13 non-combat Class)]

"I'm fine," I said again. I spit a chunky remnant of the hell-vomit onto the floor.

I had shit to do.

"Trix, let's go," I growled. I don't know where the determination in my voice came from. Yeah, the situation was dire, but I sounded so sure of myself. Maybe I was too tired to overthink things.

"Brother Ryan?"

I staggered to my feet. Samila didn't follow, choosing instead to watch me, head tilted curiously.

I turned to the stairs. Upon reaching the first step up, my knees gave out briefly, and I had to catch myself against the wall to stay upright. That wouldn't do.

"Heal me," I said, reaching down to my side where the vulpa's voice was coming from.

"Brother Ryan, you . . . no. If you could see yourself—it's bad."

"I know," I replied wearily. For an instant, my head spun, and I nearly toppled backward. I stopped myself before I could, though. I hoped Trix didn't notice.

"It will hurt you, Brother," Trix whimpered. "There's a cost. You need food. Water. Rest."

"I need HP."

"What?" he asked.

I shook my head. "Sorry. I need healing."

We were close enough to the entrance now to catch Geddon's silhouette against the glow of the lights. He fought savagely, sword in hand, hacking at ill-defined foes around his knees. His shield was gone.

"For the last time, it's not . . . It's not real, Brother Ryan! How can you people not understand this?!" Trix yelled.

With monumental effort, I turned my whole body to look down next to me. Trix's teeth were bared, and his ears bent back until they were flat on his head.

"It's real enough," I replied. "And we need it now."

"Nothing a vulpa does is real! It's mirrors and mind games!" he cried. His voice cracked, and I sensed a deep wound being torn open.

Then anger gave way to shame. He shrank away, turning to hide his eyes. "I fool your body into healing your wounds quickly. With every spell, your body cannibalizes itself," he pleaded. "I am killing you every time I heal you."

I didn't have the energy to do this right now. I tried to keep my tone flat but sure. "Objection noted. Still need it."

"You could die. Don't make me do it." He was pleading with me now, acknowledging that he could, indeed, do it. Good.

"Trix, listen to me," I began, out of breath even before I started speaking. "No one else is dying here. Not him." I pointed weakly up the stairs at Geddon, my foot already on the next step up. "Not them." I pointed behind us, over my shoulder with my thumb. "And not you," I said, reaching down to put my hand on his shoulder.

"I'm the only one who can do this. I need to do this," I insisted. Everyone needed to live, and I could do that for them.

I'd never been so sure of anything in my life, and time was wasting.

"I don't—"

"Heal me!" It burst out of me; the roughness in my throat made it come out harsher than I wanted, but my words filled the stairwell so completely, they left no oxygen for any more objections. A little more of an Outers accent, and I would've sounded exactly like my dad. That felt strange.

Trix's tiny hand snapped up to dig its claws into the skin on my wrist, hard enough to draw blood.

HP [78/105]

Status gained: Underfed (Severe) [-3 mind, -3 body]

The stairs blurred, and I felt myself beginning to topple forward. I braced myself against the wall to keep upright.

I summoned a piece of wood from my Spatial Storage and Consumed it.

Status gained: Engine [3 MP/sec for 30 minutes]

It would have to do.

I approached the top of the stairs. Much like the last entrance to the secret tunnels, the way out was a rounded portal. While I'd blown the last one wide open and destroyed a good bit of brickwork before, this one's door had simply collapsed inside, leaving a perfect circle with smooth edges that transitioned from empty air to quellstone as it had been designed to do.

*Thwup! Thwup! Thwup! Thwup!*

Scourge-Touched Undead defeated.

You have been awarded 35 Experience points. [16 base (-2 Level, +2 nemesis, +16 group, +16 chain, -13 non-combat Class)]

The turret was still active. It couldn't have much more ammo left, though I'd lost my sense of time somewhere between Consuming my first evil rock and now.

Now that I had a bit more HP and was on the move again, I was feeling relatively well. "Geddon! Down!" I yelled as loudly as I could. As forcefully as I could.

After a handful of heartbeats where I thought he hadn't heard me, suddenly he was there. There was empty air, and then the big man flew down through the doorway like a bullet, sure-footed, at exactly the right angle so that his momentum carried him down as far from the entrance with as little effort as possible.

Geddon's armor, slick with black blood, came and went by. His wide shoulders scraped along the stone walls, slammed into me, and nearly brought me along for the ride, but I was able to squeeze to the side as the big man's angle changed.

I felt like I'd almost been run down by a truck.

"Waste no time," he barked at me from lower on the stairs. His colossal chest rose and fell with every ragged breath. "Even now, they are entering the circle."

I reached up until my hand barely crested the edge of the hole and summoned the sheet of iron I'd been saving for this. It was a disk of flat metal, about an eighth of an inch thick, big enough to fit over the entire door and then some. It appeared in a flash of light, the handle I'd Shape-welded onto my side of the surface right next to my hand. The weight of it settled to rest over—

*BONSH!*

Something heavy slammed into the top, forcing the makeshift lid closed and nearly dislocating my shoulder. Whatever it was that hit me glanced off the metal sheet, and my soon-to-be door rebounded slightly and shifted to the side before I could catch it, turning a nearly perfect seal into an imperfect one with a small gap on the edge.

"Augh!" I grunted, clutching my shoulder, but the pain only rattled me for a moment. I reached up with my prosthetic and took hold of the handle just as bloody, cracked fingernails wormed their way into the new breach. I held on tight, attempting to shift the weight and get a more perfect fit, but something or multiple somethings had already settled on it.

---

Iron Grip [1 MP/sec]
Iron Grip is now Level 4.

---

"They're on top of it!" I shouted. Slapping palms, scratching nails, exposed bone grating upon the iron—all of it conducted perfectly through the metal.

"They leap down from the wall of corpses your turret built for us." Geddon panted. "It was shoulder-height when last I looked. A glorious redoubt made of slain foes. Perfect for a final stand."

I was barely listening. Geddon's wish for a glorious death might still be granted if I didn't do this right. I summoned my three bottles of booze and placed them at my feet. Then I reached up and touched the iron lid to begin the process.

---

Shape [22 MP/sec]

---

The metal was already touching so much of the quellstone. My breath was stolen from me as I tried to saturate it all.

It took all of four seconds for my mana to go dry. My Iron Grip faltered. I didn't have the spare mana to give to it. My body felt like it was being shredded from the inside, the way my mana was being ripped out of me. What's more, my prosthetic was tied up with trying to keep the disk in place.

I was going to lose it if I didn't dip into the booze. It had become a mathematical certainty.

"Help!" was all I could manage, all the brain power I could spare.

A catcher's-mitt-sized hand closed around mine, around the handle, and a bulky presence crowded onto the stairs next to me.

"Hang on!" Geddon yelled in my ear.

He was doing something . . . No. Someone else was there. Claws scraped over my knuckles, and something long and thin was passed through the metal loop next to my fingers.

"It's on!" Trix announced. "Pull!"

Then Geddon was out of my personal space. The leather cord they'd fastened tightened around my hand.

"Let go, Brother Ryan!"

I did. The lid shifted slightly as the angle of force being applied to it changed, but otherwise, it held.

There was no time to waste. I was barely holding on to Shape. With my metal hand, I reached down and grabbed a bottle of booze.

"Get back as far as you can!" I ordered them.

> Consume Mirebold Whisky? Y/N
> Status gained: Engine [29 MP/sec for 15 sec]

Liquid fire ran through my veins, and my mana flowed in bright rivers through my channels, as the System put it. It forcefully rejuvenated me. I felt like a man who had just been given his first drink of water in days, and it was through a firehose.

> Split Mind is now Level 6.
> Status gained: Burning [5 HP/sec]

*Hello, Burning, my old friend.*

"Put him out! Put him out!" Geddon shrieked. Was he afraid of a little fire? For some reason, that amused me.

I had to trust them to tend to my body. What these people needed was a closed door, and I had to deliver.

The iron had to flow, had to bind to the floor. Seamless. Immovable.

The metal deformed, elongated, melted like candle wax under my will into the minute cracks in the Dark Lord's perfectly laid floors. There was a setback when the disk bucked an inch into the air, stretching and shattering my tenuous bonds. Apparently, something had been able to get its bony fingers into the gap, but Geddon heaved it back into place with a grunt, severing more than one set of dead appendages.

*CRUNCH!*

All the while, the Returned kept dying.

---

Scourge-Touched Undead defeated.
You have been awarded 35 Experience points. [16 base (-2 Level, +2 nemesis, +16 group, + 16 chain, -13 non-combat Class)]

---

Meanwhile, I burned. I melted. I dripped into the floor. I coated the brickwork, wound my way through the empty spaces and filled them with myself while the world tried to snuff me out.

---

Consume Mirebold Whisky? Y/N
Status gained: Engine [29 MP/sec for 15 sec]
Status gained: Burning [5 HP/sec]
Status lost: Burning

---

Trix tended to me sometime during this.

---

Status gained: Underfed (Severe) [-6 body, -6 mind]

---

I wrapped around the bricks, flowed into all the space. I became a puddle on the floor, one so smooth and natural, the Scourge-Touched could never think to dislodge me.

My body gave out before I was truly satisfied, however. One moment, I was iron, rigid and in control. The next, I was a heap on the stairs, a desiccated pile of useless bones.

I'd done it, though. That door was good and sealed. No drooling Scourge-Touched was getting through that—not for a while.

"Brother Ryan?! Stay awake! Do not go to sleep!"

I didn't feel like listening, though. I was bone-tired, and things kept flashing in my vision, too fast to comprehend.

---

Scourge-Touched Undead defeated.
You have been awarded 35 Experience points. [16 base (-2 Level, +2 nemesis, +16 group, + 16 chain, -13 non-combat Class)]
Scourge-Touched Undead defeated.
You have been awarded 35 Experience points. [16 base (-2 Level, +2 nemesis,

+16 group, + 16 chain, -13 non-combat Class)]
Scourge-Touched Undead defeated.
You have been awarded 35 Experience points. [16 base (-2 Level, +2 nemesis,
+16 group, + 16 chain, -13 non-combat Class)]

Level Up!
You are now Level 10.
Max HP +10
Max MP +10
+1 Attribute point.
+1 Focus point.

Achievements awarded this Level:
Spirit of the Warrior: You gained 51% of your Experience this Level from
defeated foes as a non-combat Class. [+3 spirit]
Big Spender: You have spent 10,420% of your total Mana Pool this level.
[+1% Mana Regeneration per second.]
Doing Your Part: Some of your creations have been used against agents of the
Scourge. [+200% Experience awarded for new designs next Level]
Inventor: You have created at least five new designs this Level. [+1 Mind]
Boss Killer: You have defeated a foe far above you in Level. [+2 to all Attributes]

Allocate focus point to increase depth? Y/N
Status lost: Underfed (Severe)
Status gained: Starvation [-7 mind, -7 body, -0.1 HP/sec]

It was too much. I wanted to sleep. Someone slapped me . . . Repeatedly.
"Whyyyyyyy?" I groaned.
"He's alive. Gods of old, by all rights he shouldn't be. Hold him still."
It was all so tiresome. I was done, wasn't I? I'd done what they needed.

Quest Update: ???

??? (Continued): Become worthy.

# CHAPTER THIRTY-SEVEN

# Forward, Not Back

Despite what they asked of me, I did nod off a couple of times. I couldn't help it. We finally had a wall between us and the horde of flesh-eating monsters, and my part was done. Plus, if you were to believe the System, I was starving to death, so a lack of energy made sense.

If only they'd just let me be.

"Strip everything off. I need to see."

"Why are we stripping the monk, Vulpa?"

"I need to make sure he's not bleeding or burned somewhere I can't see. We have to treat it conventionally if that's the case. I dare not use my magic again."

"It worked fine last time."

"You call *this* fine?"

"No . . . Sorry."

I could feel myself being turned around, the remains of my clothes being peeled away, even my stupid orange hat. Funny that it had survived so long. Was it made of some kind of special material? It would have to be flame-retardant if nothing else.

"Looks like the arm is part of his Dominion sign, after all," someone murmured. "I thought it might have been another one of his inventions, but look here. It's grafted right into the skin."

Delicate fingers played over my scalp. "He's not Miur."

"Who could possibly care, Sam?"

"Well, I'd guessed that he was a Miur with how he talks, but he's not. Don't judge me, he always had the thing on."

A weight settled on my chest—light, warm. "Who has food? Give it to me. This is dry. Going to need water, too."

I was slapped again. When had I nodded off?

"Drink it, Brother Ryan."

A vessel was pressed to my lips, and a cold, lumpy porridge was poured into my mouth. I didn't take it well. I coughed and gagged, but they were quite insistent that I finish it all. I got as much into me as I could, but the process was slow and infuriating when I'd much rather have been passed out on the floor.

> Status lost: Starvation
> Status gained: Underfed (severe)

By the time the torture was done, everyone had quieted down, and most had gone to get their own types of rest now that they knew I wasn't about to die.

Trix and Samila propped me up against one of the stone walls and pushed a cup with more of the porridge into my hand, though I didn't feel like eating. My HP was ticking up again, now that Starvation was gone, but I still felt hollow and weak. I did have enough mana to reach up and gently charge a cobblestone above my head with Volatility just enough to give off a gentle glow, though, enough to at least be able to see.

The tunnel we'd escaped into was pretty tight, the floor maybe five feet wide while the walls went straight up, then gently curved into a basic arch maybe eight feet high at its apex. The masonry was a smooth, irregular white stone, affixed with moldy, crumbling mortar. To my right, nearer to the staircase to the Undercity, I saw a recessed part of the wall, a little alcove where I imagined someone might set a lantern.

It was almost depressingly utilitarian after the strange eccentricities of the Undercity.

Samila was to my side, close enough that I might find myself leaning on her if I were to pass out again. The blue woman's eyes were closed, head resting against the stones of the wall, but I couldn't tell if she was sleeping or not. She seemed smaller like this, relaxed to the point that her armor was the only thing keeping her upright, an exoskeleton that only allowed for a certain level of rest.

For his part, Trix sat across from me, his fur in disarray, his head and shoulders slumped forward like he didn't have the energy to raise them just now. My little pistol sat between his outstretched feet. His breathing was rhythmic and slow, but his eyes were shut tight, ears laid flat on his head.

Not everyone was at rest, however.

The clomp of boots from my left, further down the hall, preceded Sissa stepping into my makeshift wall lamp's light. She looked tired but a little more herself now that the immediate danger was done.

"You're looking much better, Mo—Brother Ryan," she said. She actually used my name. That was new, though my fake title did sour the moment somewhat. Sissa crouched down next to her sister and ran her hand gently over the other woman's cheek, wiping off a smudge of grime. Then she turned back to me, squinting.

"If I didn't know any better, I'd say you were getting healthy right in front of my eyes."

This was the part where I was supposed to allay suspicion, come up with some explanation that would fit, but nothing came. I just opened and closed my mouth a couple of times, then ate my cold porridge.

"That is, indeed, what is happening," Trix interjected flatly, not bothering to open his eyes. "His burns are disappearing, his veins are lighter, and he's actually gained muscle mass—more than a ration of gruel could possibly provide. I've never seen anything like it. I would be astonished, if I had the energy just now."

Sissa raised an eyebrow and let out a little whistle. "You're made of deceptively tough stuff, Brother Ryan. Sam, you have my blessing to marry this one. With his Dominion, your kids wouldn't even need supervision to live to adulthood."

I sputtered.

"See, this is why I thought he was Miur, Sis. He scares easily," Samila replied, fully awake now and grinning wickedly at me along with her sister.

I really didn't know what to say to that. Nothing in my entire lexicon seemed to fit the situation. Being the Clan pariah hadn't done much for my social skills, and I hadn't done much to rectify that by spending the majority of my time alone.

Sissa only let me suffer for half a minute before she was back to business. "Well, I'm sorry to have disturbed you all, but it seems we've traded one problem for another," she said matter-of-factly.

"What's going on, Sergeant? What new horror has the darkness conjured to test us?" Trix asked, leaning his head back to thump it off the stone of the wall over and over.

I squinted, trying to interpret his expression. I'd only known him a little while, but Trix didn't seem to be himself.

Sissa must have shared my concern. She gave the little vulpa a look, but Trix didn't feel the need to elaborate.

"I've gone further down the tunnel," Sissa continued, "and sifted through the rubble we have down here. Bole's yellow arrows, the ones that keep us on the safe path, there are none."

Now this was a subject I was more comfortable with. Put me in front of a wall of snarling death or above a bottomless pit, as long as I don't have to answer personal questions.

I was in such a hurry to dive into the subject, I think I overdid it. "How—

*BLAPFT!*" I choked. Then I was beset by a coughing fit that brought up something unpleasant. The smell and taste reminded me of the vomit from earlier. Apparently, some of it was still stuck to my vocal cords. Wonderful.

"How do we navigate without them then?" I rasped.

Sissa shook her head. "I don't know."

"The way Corporal Bole spoke, he implied you had some knowledge of the smugglers' tunnels, Sergeant," Trix recalled. He didn't bother opening his eyes.

The guardswoman's expression hardened at the mention of the man, and her hand drifted to her sword hilt. She made no move to draw it, however.

Samila spoke up for her. "Sissa wasn't a part of that world. Bole's a thief and a liar."

Sissa put her hand out and shook her head. "I just socialized in those circles for a time. I never did anything illegal, and, because of that, I was never fully brought into their trust. What I know of the smugglers' tunnels are just stories passed down from drunk blowhards who couldn't shut up around female company."

"What can you tell us then?" I asked.

Sissa ran a hand over her face and rubbed at her eyes with an ungloved hand. "It's probably not accurate. Conjecture from dishonest and disreputable people, more liable to bias us against what we'll encounter than inform."

"We need to know at least the outlines of the problem, Sergeant," I added, a bit more strength in my voice now. "I'd take an exaggerated account over nothing right now."

Seemingly resigned, she took a step to the side to put her back against the wall, then slid down next to her sister, sighing as she did.

"Based on the stories I've heard, we've gone from certain death to death for certain," she said. "These tunnels were made alongside the Undercity for the Dark Lord's personal use. Secret—or, at least, restricted—access tunnels. Supposedly, they go everywhere, every part of the city, but no one's ever mapped them all out before."

I tentatively raised a hand. "Sorry. I'm not from here. Isn't this city extremely old? Why has no one explored them? If I had a network of secret tunnels underneath my house, I would be down there all the time until I knew what I was dealing with."

"Then you're the type who would venture into them and never return, Brother Ryan," Sissa said with a shrug. "You think no one has tried? There's a whole industry built on it, selling gear to foolish tourists in Bogtown who want to make a name for themselves."

She shook her head disdainfully. "Before the Crusaders liberated the entirety of Eclipse and cut down the Dark Lord in his observatory, where do you think they suffered the majority of their losses? It wasn't at the hands of the Returned, I'll tell you that."

I noticed Trix perk up at the mention of this. He'd opened his eyes and leaned forward, ears up to catch every bit of the story. His expression was still pained, but he was actively listening now.

Sissa continued.

"After a month of frustrated stalemate trying to batter down the doors to the Dark Lord's sanctum, the sappers found one of these entrances by chance. 'Finally,' they thought. Maybe it wasn't progress, per se, but it was *something*, some direction to go. So they sent in teams of scouts to find out where the tunnels went. They didn't come back. Well, you've probably read what the Crusaders were like. If something struck them, they made sure to smear that something's insides over several city blocks. Some of their people were dead, so that warranted a full-scale invasion, full kits and blessings. They sent an entire battalion inside, tasked with killing whatever beasts they found and mapping a route of ingress to the observatory. They succeeded but at great cost. Only a handful out of a thousand lived to report back. They cut their way through the Dark Lord's pets, smashed the traps they could find, and blazed their way into the sanctum. That's still the safest part of the smugglers' tunnels. Ever hear of Gnima's Corridor? That's what they're talking about."

"So we are in an unmapped part of the tunnels," I inferred.

"Probably. I'm not saying no one's ever been down here, but they either didn't bother to mark things or they're dead."

"We can't go back," Trix said.

"No, we can't, Brother Trix," Sissa replied. "We are down to three capable fighters now that Brother Ryan is—"

"I'll be fine," I objected. Probably better than fine, once I got more of my HP back and a little more food in me. I'd Leveled, after all. Now that my mind was engaged again, I wanted to sit down and make some choices.

"Apologies," Sissa said with a little nod in my direction. "We still can't go back there, though. The only way is forward."

"In that case, I say we push on as soon as possible." Geddon loomed into the light from the stairwell. His posture was hunched now that he was in close quarters with us all, but that didn't stop him from absolutely filling the hall. "The entrance is good and sealed. The Returned are still attempting to claw their way inside, but the barrier hasn't budged even slightly."

Sissa nodded. "I agree. We can't stay here, and we can't go back. We'll need to brave the unknown and hope to cross the smugglers' ways. We'll get some rest, then it'll be time to move again."

I absentmindedly took a bite of my fourth cup of cold porridge as I stared at the text on my screen, contemplating my next move. I'd volunteered to take watch, since I'd gotten some sleep and had a chance to eat.

With everyone still and, presumably, unconscious, our tunnel's ambient noise level dropped to tomb-quiet. The loudest snorers of the group were the shopkeeper and, surprisingly, Sissa. When that woman decided to rest, she rested hard.

While everyone else slept, I had a choice to make.

---

Allocate Focus Point to increase Depth? Y/N

---

I focused on the word Depth.

---

Depth: Degree of intensity, measured in Focus Points. Investing Focus Points in an aspect of your being produces a qualitative difference in the aspect's strength, growth, and potential. Every level of Depth allows for greater awareness and mastery of yourself as related to the affected aspect.

---

*And here we have another layer of the System. Am I going to keep stumbling upon these for the rest of my life?*

The language being used here was interesting. I'd thought of the System's numerical values as a concrete thing, standardized and categorized for every Exotic. Someone with 100 Body would be able to lift more than someone with 80. Now, though, it was telling me that by adding one of these Focus Points, I'd alter the formula somehow. It would be a qualitative difference where points with Depth meant more than points without.

If I were able to look at other Exotics' Status Screens, did my numbers stack up with theirs? Did we even use the same scale?

Of course, I had to do it. No mentor was going to pop out of the walls to tell me what was going on, and I needed all the edge I could get.

The only question was where I'd put the point.

I chose "Yes." Then I examined my Status Screen again.

| Ryan Kotes - Level 10 Animator (Uncommon) | | | | |
|---|---|---|---|---|
| **Type:** | Artificer (Common) | **Abilities:** | Shape 8 (Transmute) | Devouring Grasp 4 |
| **Class:** | Animator (Uncommon) | | Consume 4 | Volatility 3 |
| **Core:** | Engine (Unique) | | Iron Grip 3 | Imbue 3 |
| **HP:** | 130/130 | | Trigger 4 | Automate 4 |
| **MP:** | 113/113 | | Tempered Channels 1 | |
| **Body:** | 26 | **Skills:** | Climbing 5 | Unarmed Combat 3 |

| Mind: | 24 | | | Running 4 | Stealth (Gray Man) 9 |
|---|---|---|---|---|---|
| Spirit: | 38 | | | Conduit 3 | Split Mind 6 |
| | | | | Spear 4 | Deception 5 (?) |
| | | | Affinities: | Goblinoid F | Mendau Wood D |
| | | | | Iron F + | Limestone E |
| Free Attribute Points: 1 | | | | Steel F + | |
| Free Focus Points: 1 | | | | Magnesium F | |

*Okay. So, what do I do?*

Experimentally, I honed in on the Body Attribute.

Allocate Focus Point to Body? Y/N

So it was as simple as that. No information. No fanfare.

Of the three Attributes I'd been using since I received my Exotic status, I wasn't overly sure which one would be the most valuable.

Body literally kept me alive, which I found incredibly useful. Making the Stat better wouldn't be a bad idea.

Mind governed my mana and a fair number of Abilities and Skills. Not only that, but it affected my mental acuity. What would a point of depth do there?

Meanwhile, Spirit was far and away my highest Stat and accomplished its fair share. Putting a Focus Point in that would, in theory, make all those points mean more. I'd get the most bang for my buck if I chose that one, at least immediately.

I blinked. Was I thinking about this correctly?

Again, I focused on a different part of my Status Screen.

Allocate Focus Point to Shape (Transmute)? Y/N

*Oh. That's interesting.*

I tried something else.

Allocate Focus Point to Spear? Y/N

I swallowed the lump that had suddenly appeared in my throat. It was an option any number of the people in my Clan would have chosen. Maybe not the Spear Skill. They'd choose the Skill that matched their heirloom weapons, of course.

Just having the opportunity was . . . It hurt.

What I wouldn't have given to have this chance back on Proxis. I would have given everything, especially if I had had the Sword Skill. My father would have been so proud.

Then the moment passed.

I wasn't that person anymore, obviously.

*Okay, Ryan. Think. The System says that you'll gain awareness and mastery in all things related to where you put this point. What do you need?*

I needed everything. I was inadequate in lots of ways. My Class was meant for building, not fighting. My HP and MP were constantly being taxed to their limits. My combat skills were severely lacking, too.

*What sets you apart?*

Engine. The error messages.

I'd concluded long ago that Engine wasn't something I was meant to have. By some wildly improbable chance, I'd been integrated while being run through with a spooky sword, and the System had compensated by rearranging things so that I could live. It was the first thing in my new life that wasn't what it was supposed to be.

Then there was Volatility. I'd received it through an error in the System, when I'd earned an achievement meant for a different Class. It was still a significant factor of my success. The fact that it never Leveled left it out of the running, though.

There was another one, too . . .

I checked my Status Screen again. There it was. I'd nearly forgotten.

Tempered Channels: By channeling multiple volatile, opposing Mana Types through your body, you have forced your body and spirit to adapt. Your Mana Pathways are permanently scarred. Sensitivity to and control of foreign Mana Types moderately decreased. Strength and control of personal Mana Type greatly increased. Personal Mana Type altered.

That was, in a word, frightening. Apparently, not everything we Exotics did could be healed over time. I'd done something to scar myself, and while it came with benefits, it had limited me somehow. Putting points into Tempered Channels would undoubtedly be interesting, but I knew nothing about the Ability yet.

That left Automate. It was an attractive option, since it encompassed a lot of different things. It used my highest Attribute, I wouldn't have had it if not for an error in the System, and it would be prohibitively expensive for any other Animator to use. My unique situation gave me the chance to not only acquire the Ability but to use it enough to Level it up. I also had to admit that I had a special affection for Automate, as it was an ability I earned on my own instead of having it handed to me by the System. I even got a special achievement for it.

Plus, I was a mechanic at heart. I liked making things that worked.

Allocate focus point to Automate? Y/N

Focus Point allocated.

Depth increasing. Stand by . . .

# CHAPTER THIRTY-EIGHT

# Change the Equation

Depth increasing. Stand by . . .

I absentmindedly took another swallow from my lumpy porridge cup as I stared at the message, but my depth remained frustratingly un-increased. With how much buildup there had been before my choice, I had expected a bit more of an immediate payoff. Instead I was being asked to be patient . . .

Which was the word of the day.

We'd been down here for an indeterminate amount of time, and things were looking exactly the same. Hours of walking past identical-looking bricks, identically grimy mortar, and identically empty lantern alcoves proved to be a different test to everyone's mettle. At least I had my System Interface to look at, but there was only so much that could be done in there. I had the Combat Log pretty much how I wanted it now, but that had only killed a couple of hours.

That didn't stop me from scrolling, however. It was either that or stare at the shopkeeper's back. I practically knew the sweat stains on his clothes by heart by this point, the positioning of his hand on the wall to keep his balance. The rest of the civilians were in front of him, in the middle of our formation.

Behind me was Trix, followed by Samila, who would be dutifully keeping an eye on our rear, a tiny lantern affixed to her belt to give her plenty of light to see by now that the locals needed it. Geddon had a similar one up at the front.

"Intersection. Bearing left," Sissa's voice chimed in a sing-song sort of way meant to sound light and just a touch bored—her way of telling us she was just as affected by the situation as the rest of us. I could hear the indecision in her voice, though. She, as the ranking guard, was responsible for us all, and the passages were giving us nothing to go on. With every decision we were further from what we knew.

The intersection was like all the others, perfectly right-angled with four arches meeting in the middle to form a point, a lantern alcove for each hallway.

The group paused to allow Trix to scratch a set of arrows on the stones to indicate where we'd gone, just to make sure we weren't going in circles.

I took the opportunity to have some more tasteless gruel. My Underfed debuff was gone, but Trix insisted I get more food in me, presumably fattening me up for when he needed to heal me again.

In light of recent events, I couldn't argue with that logic.

I sighed. We were walking single-file through the most banal death trap ever conceived. Of course, maybe that's how it got you, lulling you into a false sense of confidence, then dropping the floor away when you least expected it. I shook my head and tried to focus.

The kid didn't seem to feel the tension that the grownups felt and started to act like a kid again. It had been a long time coming. Honestly, I was surprised at just how quiet his grandmother was able to keep him in the Undercity when we were being hunted. Now, in defiance of the oppressively boring environment, he bobbed and weaved through the group, ran his hands over the brickwork, played little jumping games where he'd only step on the odd-shaped stones . . . Kid stuff.

It was during one of his little skips that he changed things for us. His foot landed badly, and he reached out to steady himself on the wall.

"Ow!" The kid's shout echoed off the hard surfaces of the tunnel and broke the plodding time-spell we'd all been under. He winced and pulled his hand away from the wall, sucking air through his teeth.

A dam broke. Suddenly, everyone was engaged.

"I told you not to act a fool," his grandmother chided, already wrapping the boy up in her arms. "Twist your ankle and one of these people will have to carry you. We are all still in grave danger, and you mustn't make it worse."

"No. It's not that, Ma. It cut me," the boy argued.

Trix was moving straight away. He bounded up to the boy and stood to his full height to take his hand and give it a look.

"It's alright. Let me see," Trix said, leaning in close.

"I told you, boy. I told you not to act a fool. When I speak of this to your father, he'll get an earful," the grandmother continued.

Trix let out a displeased hiss. "Please, Miss. Calm yourself and get out of my light." He poked at the cut and pulled out a bandage from somewhere, wrapping it around. He turned to me with an uncertain look. "This isn't from a stone."

Taking the cue, I bent down to the kid's level and examined the wall, running my fingers along it, over the imperfections in the rock, through the rough grooves between. Then I felt a prick on my fingertip. Something was protruding from the mortar, about a millimeter long and wire-thin, very sharp. Sharp enough to get a bead of blood out of my finger before the System closed it back up.

"Looks like you are coming away from your adventure with a scar, young man, and what a story you'll have behind it," Trix said encouragingly, finishing his binding on the wound. "Your friends will be very impressed."

I rested my fingers on the little barb and probed it with Shape, letting my mana flow over it and map its contours. It was shocking just how fast I could do this now. I probably had Tempered Channels to thank for that.

*One point in the positive column.*

I still wasn't sure if I was happy with acquiring Tempered Channels. What little testing I'd done concerned the hell out of me. Any ability that involved Volatility felt different now than what I remembered. I could still direct it, giving it a path to leave my body, but I didn't feel in control of the power as acutely as I once did. In fact, the experience had grown unpleasant, biting, like I was spooling barbed wire in the cold with numb hands.

Using Shape and my own personal mana, on the other hand, felt like second nature to me. What's more, the mana itself was more forceful, more elegant, irresistible. I felt it twist and weave between the molecules of the thing in the wall, stretching on further and further. I felt the metal, sensing the matter and how it was bound together even before it was saturated.

"It's metal," I announced as I channeled myself into it. The thing was long and thin like a wire but also had barbs and cutting razors at regular intervals that hooked into the mortar like hagbrush roots. I wasn't able to saturate it yet due to its size, but I could tell the general direction my mana flowed. It went on and on.

"Is it some kind of trap?" Sissa asked.

I shook my head. "Not sure. It's a wire . . . a weird one. Wait!" I paused, blinking. My mana had reached the end, and I'd reached full saturation. Slowly, I Shaped a finger-length piece of the stuff out of the wall and thinned out the middle until I could snap it off with my prosthetic. What came away in my hand was a silvery stick.

---

Consume Tendril? Y/N
You gain knowledge of material: Cobalt [1/10]
You gain knowledge of material: Nickel [1/10]
You gain knowledge of material: Deep Lead [1/10]

---

"The end is that way," I said, pointing in the direction we were going. "Don't know what it's for, but it's something."

Sissa looked through me, lost in thought. "The question is whether to follow it or get away from it."

"I say we follow it. If it is connected to a trap, the architect of this place will have believed it is worth defending," Geddon said from the front of the group.

Sissa nodded. "Better than running around down here for the rest of time. Let's go."

Just as my Shaping had told me, the wire ended after about ten minutes or so of walking forward. It wasn't connected to anything other than the stone, which Sissa appreciated.

What had cut the wire, however, wasn't what we expected. Geddon held up a hand for us to halt and called us all up to have a look at what he saw.

Our hallway, which had been level and mostly straight, solid and dry, ceased to be all of those things right where Geddon crouched. It was as if a giant had stepped on our little tube and snapped it like a twig. The hallway continued, but . . . lower. The route had been severed, the way forward now several feet down from the one we currently used. Broken stones and loose earth packed in around the sides of the tunnel here, and the archway above our heads had crumbled until it resembled a cave ceiling rather than something that had been constructed.

Sissa had to crouch to enter the new, broken hallway, and her feet hit the ground with a splash.

After a quick look around, she turned back to us, only her upper torso and head visible. "Looks like a collapse. Judging by the water, we've either gone north or are in a tunnel connected to one that goes that way."

"Is that good?" I asked.

She shrugged. "Are you a good swimmer?"

No. No, I wasn't, but I compensated for it in other ways.

"Rest up, everyone," Sissa commanded with a grin. She finally had something in front of her she could assess. "This will be the last time we'll be dry for a while."


"You have the look of a man at the end of a bender," Samila commented the next morning as she strapped her shield to her back. "Should I assume you built something last night, and that's why you never woke any of us for the next watch?"

I rubbed my face tiredly, then shook my head. "It's complicated. You'll all need to hear this." My voice sounded raspy, and my mouth was dry. It had been a long night.

The first thing I'd done once everyone had bedded down was go looking for the severed ends of the wire and Shaping a manageable amount of it out of its hole, having to take time to smooth the barbs out and thin the wire enough so it could be pulled.

It cost me a fair bit of scrap furniture wood to keep Engine going, but in the end, I got about eighty pounds of Weird Cobalt Alloy (my working name for it) from my work and an F-Grade Affinity for the stuff.

Then Detect Cobalt found me half a dozen more strands, some leading down into the next part of our hallway.

That's where things got interesting.

"See here?" I asked, pointing to a particular strand of metal. "It's another one of those wires, probably the continuation of the one we found."

"How far does it go?" Sissa questioned.

I shook my head. "Don't know. I can't saturate it."

"I don't know what that means. Is that normal?"

"If something is too big or if it's a material I can't Shape, yes, but this is metal. I can definitely work with the stuff. The problem is that I can't even connect with it. Here," I said, reaching out and putting a finger on the end of the wire. I let my mana flow out of me, pooling at the tip of the metal and pressing at the barrier of the matter, but that's as far as I got.

The wire *recoiled*.

Like a living thing, it shrank away from me and curled in on itself.

Geddon was the first to comment. "That's new. It doesn't seem to like you."

"He's an acquired taste," Samila chirped from behind me.

Sissa just rolled her eyes.

I cleared my throat uncomfortably and rushed to explain more of what I found.

"Not just that." I grabbed the wire and attempted to hold it still for the Shaping. This time, the metal tendril reacted violently. It whipped back like a snake while several tiny barbs appeared down its length. I let go before it could do more than superficial harm.

I turned to the rest of the group. "Something else is in there," I declared.

The metal was alive. I couldn't really explain it otherwise. When I'd used Devouring Grasp on it last night, it had almost looked like it was in pain the way it writhed and retreated. Meanwhile, I couldn't for the life of me saturate it or get it to accept my mana in any way.

"Someone or something with a similar domain perhaps?" Trix asked. "A member of the Order?"

I blinked.

"Uh. No. Probably not," I answered.

If it was someone with powers like mine, they'd have to be controlling the metal constantly and—considering there were lots of these wires—expending an ocean of mana every second they did so.

Sissa nodded and stood up to address everyone. "This tunnel is the best lead we've had so far. Let's move quietly and keep an eye out for markings. No one touches any creepy living metal until I say so."

* * *

We saw our first yellow arrow a little farther down the partially flooded tunnel. The water was up to our shins, but it never got higher than that, though the floor was more uneven now and turned ankles were more a danger with every passing moment. Trix spent most of his time riding on my shoulder again, but he was largely silent and brooding.

I could sympathize. We all needed real rest and some natural light. Every problem we solved seemed to turn into another one, and that beat our morale down until it was in the mud.

That changed with the spotting of our first yellow arrow. Sort of.

It was on the left side of a four-way intersection, pointing in that direction. However, it was old and faded, and someone had made another, only slightly-more-recent slash through the middle of it. That wasn't what we wanted to see.

"I say we follow it anyway," Geddon opined, one hand on his chin and staring at the yellowed brick. "Even if the mark means that the way is no longer safe, the fact that it is here means this passage at least leads somewhere the smugglers wanted to go."

"I don't think they would have given up on a route easily if it were profitable to them. They likely saw something they couldn't handle and cut their losses," Sissa rebutted.

Geddon looked unconvinced. "Thieves and crooks are generally cowards. What they saw might not be as much of a threat to us."

"We've got civilians with us, Big Guy," Samila said quietly, reaching up to pat his shoulder. "Maybe we could handle it, but if it's a running fight we can't keep them safe."

"I'm leaning toward trying a different passage. We have a one-in-two chance of taking the route the smugglers took to get here. From there, we just follow the arrows back until we get to a safe passage," Sissa mused.

I thought about the problem. We'd been down in this lower passage for hours now, and the tunnels seemed to be as big as the city itself. Only the shopkeeper and Samila carried packs, and they were getting lighter by the hour. I still had a bit of food in my Spatial Storage, but clean water was a problem. I scooped up a handful of the water down at my feet and smelled it.

*Nope. Dysentery would be a hell of a way to die.*

We wouldn't be able to run around down here without direction, and the physical activity was sucking our supplies away.

The kid was listening with rapt attention. His grandmother simply looked tired. She leaned heavily on the boy now, her aging body unable to keep up with this kind of stress over such an extended time.

I felt around in my Storage. I had a good bit of Weird Cobalt Alloy, a dwindling pile of scrapped furniture, food, and some of my weird loot from the mockvine. I could do something here.

"We should make camp," I announced as authoritatively as I could.

The Church guards turned around as one to stare at me, Geddon with a frustrated grimace and the two sisters with looks of equal parts curiosity and incredulity.

I cleared my throat. "People are worn out, and this is a decision that will need time to make."

"Time isn't something we have in abundance," Sissa replied. "What's more, we shouldn't sleep in this muck. One or more of us could catch our death. Brother Trix should only use his Dom—"

"It is *not* my Dominion," Trix corrected with a hiss.

"Okay, sorry. He shouldn't use his healing magic—" Sissa paused to see if there was an objection to that one, but Trix simply looked sullen.

"If he does, our dwindling supplies will be depleted further," she continued.

I nodded. "I get that. I have a stack of wood in my Storage that we can use to keep fairly dry, and I have a plan for the water situation."

"That's not all, is it, Brother Ryan?" Trix asked in my ear. His little black eyes were hard.

"Yeah. I'm going to scout ahead," I replied, attempting to sound sure.

Sissa's refusal was a given. "No. We stay together, and we'll get out together."

"We have a choice of three ways," I explained, turning to speak to everyone. "Two of them lead to our deaths—one by the mystery monster, the other by starvation or dehydration. We need to be damn sure of the way we take. I can eliminate one of them, removing the ambiguity."

"It's still time wasted," Sissa argued.

"Hold on, Sis. He's got that look in his eye. He's going to build something," Samila said with a little smirk. "Right?"

I couldn't keep myself from grinning. "I'm going to build something."

# CHAPTER THIRTY-NINE

# Go Monster Slaying

I ended up cannibalizing some of my gold coin collection to help with the water problem. One good thing about gold is just how conductive it is for heat, and it made for a pretty good boiler. Add to that a bronze tube that fit perfectly on top and another container to catch the condensation, and they would probably be able to get a couple of gallons of drinkable water out of it before I got back. It took some of the pressure off our supplies, at least.

Trix handed me my pistol as I was leaving.

"I'd much rather you came back alive than have a weapon in hand while I watch the mold grow. I still haven't fired it," he said.

I nodded to him in thanks and handed him a glowing purple rock. "I'll be back with it soon enough, and, if you're lucky, with a big monster you can shoot."

He took the stone and rolled it around in his paw curiously. "Please do not do that on my account. What is this?"

"If that stone, uh, explodes or suddenly stops glowing, it means I've found something bad. I'll do my best to get back to you if it's safe after that."

Trix raised an eyebrow and set the stone down carefully on the pile of stones we'd cobbled together in the middle of the intersection. "Perhaps it's best I not keep it in my pocket, then."

Choosing the tunnel that led in the opposite direction of the marked-out smugglers' arrow, I set off at a jog, water splashing around my shins. I kept a finger-sized rod of the cobalt alloy in my hand for light. The light was weak, but I didn't need overly much, thanks to the tunnel being so small and the water reflecting a good bit of it. At every intersection, I marked the way I went by scratching an arrow on the brick at about shoulder height.

Detect Cobalt was going nuts.

When I started out, only two of the wires ran through the mortar of the brickwork, but that changed quickly. At each intersection there was always a clearly-more-densely wired passage to take, a place where the strands seemed to flow together. While my passage had two, they would knot up with others in the ceiling of an intersection, then continue through another tunnel. It was as good as anything to follow.

Soon the tunnel I was in practically glowed to my extra sense. The wires were a twisting nest of barbed weirdness running on into forever, channeled by the mortar highways they'd chosen as their habitat.

I was so focused on Detect Cobalt that I almost missed the slow change in the environment. I didn't realize there was light or that the water was practically a puddle on the floor now, going from splashing under my feet to simply being slippery.

Then the smell hit me.

It wasn't just rot—though that was certainly a way that I could describe it. It was subtly different, however, the air thick with stagnation, stillness, and stale death, as if something had putrefied—but then microbial life whose entire purpose was to break down the dead and dying wouldn't touch this. It repulsed me in a way I'd not felt before.

Once I realized something was wrong, I crouched down and stowed my light in my Spatial Storage. Then I listened for a solid minute. Air moved through the tunnel oddly at the best of times, blowing against my face one moment, at my back another. The slow trickle of water down the slimy walls was almost ubiquitous. Underneath that, I heard a sputtering hiss so quiet, I might have mistaken it for my own breathing.

Stealth is now Level 10.
Upgrade Paths available:
Subtle Casting
Blur
Knife in the Dark

Well, that confirmed that I wasn't alone, but it also confirmed that Stealth was working on something.

I took that as an opportunity to stop and listen more. I had a choice to make.

Subtle Casting: Your Abilities are much harder to detect through means magical and mundane.
Blur: Your outline is blurred to even the most observant onlooker, as long as they are not aware of your precise location. Once detected, Blur is removed until line of sight is broken.

> Knife in the Dark: Opponents that are not paying direct attention to you take X additional Damage from your attacks and Abilities where X = Stealth/5.

All of them looked useful in the short and long terms. However, Knife in the Dark held an opportunity. As Nali had said, I channeled myself into the objects I Shaped. Was that because of the type of mana I used, the "me"-type?

If that were the case, I used "me"-type mana in everything I did, with the exception of Volatility. Would something like my Turret Construct get the damage bonus? How much "me"-ness did my mana retain? Choosing Knife in the Dark would answer these questions, and that would be worth missing out on the others if only to know how it worked in the future.

The worst that could happen if I took the Ability would be if it ended up being a straight-up flanking skill, and even then that would be legitimately useful.

I made the choice.

Back in the moment, slowly, carefully, I set one foot in front of the other. The light coming from up ahead didn't strike me as daylight or the gentle glow of the filament stuff they used in the Undercity. It was a sluggish, red hue that turned the world into a blood-soaked blur, that is until there was a spark, then a flash, sudden and violent, that pulsed down the tunnel, bright enough to hurt my eyes and leave little spots in my vision. I found it easier to look down at the water and my feet instead of directly ahead or to pay attention to Detect. The tunnel was absolutely riddled with wires here, and the concentration grew thicker by the foot.

I continued until I found myself at an intersection unlike the ones I'd seen before. It was bigger—no, *grander*—than the others. It was a circular cavern-type room with many different archways to tunnels that intersected this one. A deep-red crystal hung from the high, vaulted ceiling, which was maybe fifty feet up. Being this close to the thing didn't help the visibility problem much. Everything still appeared dreamlike in my vision, indistinct and shifting.

Detect Cobalt told me that all the wires were headed up that way just like the other intersections, until I lost them at the edge of the Ability's radius, but I could make out naked silver further up the walls. Maybe there just wasn't space in all the mortar for the concentration of tendrils in this room.

Then there was an explosion of sorts: a gout of white flame and an incandescent shower of sparks that trickled down to the floor to reveal a—

*What the hell is that?*

It was a creature of some kind, splayed on its back underneath the crystal. It was huge—longer than it was thick, maybe the size of a couple of train cars, vaguely reptilian or maybe amphibian with mottled, yellow-pink skin. The body was wider than it was tall, and its mouth gaped wide open to expose multiple rows of finger-sized teeth.

The thing's eyes were closed, and it looked like it was enjoying itself. It stretched languidly under the crystal's blinding light and burning sparks like a cat in a sunbeam. Its multitude of long, muscled legs that all ended in two-toed claws curled and flexed with pleasure, and its muscled tail slithered back and forth as it basked in the presumed warmth.

The sparks gave me a better view of the room as well. There was a gap in the floor in my tunnel's threshold as it fed into the room, wide enough for me to fit inside. Flaps of pale translucent material hung from quite a few of the naked wires running through the open air. Piles and piles of vaguely organic refuse were scattered about the room, and though it was hard to estimate their size, I suspected they would do much to block my view if I were to try to sneak among them.

I'd seen enough. It looked like I'd chosen the wrong way. The only saving grace here was that the creature seemed too big to fit into our tunnel, so I would need to count that blessing once I was far, far from this place.

Even as I backed away, I reached out with my will and, hopefully, set off Trix's stone. I'd never tried it from so far away before, but, if it worked, it would make for a good data point on how the Ability worked.

However, as soon as I sent the mental command, the creature froze mid-slither, so still it looked more like a corpse than a living thing.

I froze, too.

Had it heard me? Had it heard Trix's rock? That shouldn't have been louder than a pop, and it was so far away. I had to imagine the party's footfalls and voices would have carried farther than that.

I stared at the thing, unblinking, afraid to move.

Stealth is now Level 11.

With sudden, explosive force, the creature was upright and moving fast, its dozens of powerful legs carrying it smoothly over the cavern floor, between the piles of refuse and up onto the walls where it circled erratically, sniffing, turning its head this way and that. The motion was so quick, the thing had already almost made a lap around the room before I even had a chance to take a breath. It never made even a whisper of a sound.

The creature didn't seem to have eyes, though it did have some sort of vestigial sockets whose hollow appearance made me uncomfortable whenever they turned my way.

*Nope. Time to go.*

I took a step back, slowly so as not to disturb the puddles on the floor, and I was about to turn away when my eyes brushed over a marking on the wall, a full arrow that was pointed down my tunnel.

My magic metal heart sank.

I'd chosen the right way after all, but our assumptions had been wrong.

*Possible danger in front, definite danger behind.*

My mind conjured the image of a group of men carrying packs through the dark, a routine trip for them, transporting illegal goods from here to there, but as they reached this room, they found themselves set upon by a huge salamander thing.

Would they have stuck around to cross out their yellow arrows near the creature's den? Probably not. Instead they probably marked passages as unsafe where they could.

*Definite danger here, but . . .*

This creature was so large—too large to fit into my tunnel—and the way out was definitely this way.

Lucky me, I knew someone that specialized in ranged combat.

Remote ranged combat.

I backed down the tunnel at a glacier's pace, not daring to disturb the water nor make a sound until I was well out of sight and out of the red light.

Once I was out, it was time to build.


*When you are Triggered, feed mana into the aiming arms. Bring the sight as close to your target as possible. Feed a small burst of mana into the firing Trigger. Repeat.*

*Do not shoot at or through me.*

Automate Depth increasing [2 of 3]

So the System had been waiting for me to use Automation to start increasing its Depth. Good to know. If my brain hadn't been entirely engaged in the design process just now, I might have been frustrated.

I inserted the little Automated wafer into the brain housing on my new turret and Shape-sealed it shut, running through the final checks to make sure everything was running smoothly. Where my junk turret that fired ball bearings was long and slender, this monster was a bulky, squat sort of death machine with chunky legs, a barrel thick enough to swallow my hand, and a low center of gravity that would keep it from toppling over when it fired its substantial payload.

*Speaking of which . . .*

I grabbed the three pieces of my prototype shell casing, one that would break apart once it left the barrel and expose the real shot. Then I carefully began to pack the ammo inside. In this case, the ammo was thirty-four wickedly sharp cobalt-nickel darts wrapped around a foot-long cobalt-nickel alloy spike, the tip of which I was touching now.

*When you are struck, feed mana into your Trigger and burrow into anything softer than yourself. Do not burrow into me.*

Thirty-four times I'd had to give that command and channel that mana. It had used the last of my stored scrap wood, but if this paid off, it would be worth it. I wanted to end this fight in one blow, a surprise attack from the dark that would guarantee death or retreat from the creature. I didn't want it to surprise me with a ranged attack or go hide somewhere and wait for me to come into its lair.

I wanted a one-and-done.

The entire thing, loaded and ready to go, had to weigh as much as a full-grown man and then some . . . maybe more since my scale of physical fitness was out of whack now that I'd put points into Body. Cobalt was heavy stuff, and I'd made the whole thing to last after scavenging a lot of wire from the tunnel walls. Unfortunately, it was too massive to put into my Spatial Storage, so that had me lugging the whole thing back up the tunnel to the creature's den a good mile away.

By the time I was back in the red light, my back hurt, and my heart was humming away as if it had something to prove. I couldn't allow myself to breathe like I wanted to, and that had me seeing spots in my vision.

Once I got close enough, I heaved my new turret off my shoulders and gently set it down on the stones with the barrel angled toward the mouth of the tunnel behind me.

Then I sent mana into the Trigger to key the activation.

Now it would just be a matter of luring the—

"You have returned."

The voice—low and sonorous, smooth like sandy silt at the bottom of a river—spoke to me. The force and will behind it were staggeringly huge. It scrambled my thought processes and shook my insides simultaneously.

Hot, fetid breath tickled the small hairs on my neck. Then the smell, the turgid stagnant rot, flooded my nostrils.

Slowly, I turned around until I was face to face with the creature.

Its mouth, wide enough to stretch from wall to wall of my tunnel, was open, its jaw relaxed enough to display rows and rows of teeth in the gap.

Nothing happened to me physically, but I had the sensation of my ears popping. Then, suddenly, I could hear the creature's breath, its tongue slapping wetly against the roof of its mouth, the scratching of its claws on the stone, and the distinctive sound of bones snapping as it wriggled another inch into my tunnel.

The creature literally filled the hallway. It was packed from wall to wall as if it was a liquid.

"What strange-tasting magic you are," it said. The sound came from its mouth, but the mouth didn't move. "It fooled me once, but now that you have troubled my home for the second time, I have you. If not for my many centuries in the dark, my senses might have slipped over you and never been the wiser, little ape. My mind slides from yours so easily, as one might slide from a mossy rock into a grotto. My mind is drawn to the water, the air, the light, the stone, the other . . . never you. So familiar, so known, yet mysterious."

I didn't know what to say, so I simply shrugged, doing my best not to look back at the turret I'd just activated. A step to the side, and it would have a clear shot.

"Do not run, little ape. That path has availed no one thus far," it said.

I cleared my throat and attempted to call some moisture back into my dry mouth. "I had thought about it," I said. I kept my posture open and my movements slow, lest my host take sudden movements as an insult, or worse, get us right to the eating part of this encounter.

"They all do, but it all ends the same. Very tedious. If only they knew who they flee. My name means nothing to transient beings such as yourself but know this, the beasts of this world build shrines to me when food is scarce and starvation drives them to desperation. If you force me to chase you down, I will indulge my baser instincts only sapient prey can satisfy."

# CHAPTER FORTY

# Tell the Truth

I—I certainly don't want that," I replied, careful to keep my voice neutral and my body still. No need to antagonize it.

Besides, I was standing in front of the barrel of the turret after giving it explicit instructions not to shoot through me. If I moved, this party would kick off early when I was in prime biting range.

"Few do," it replied and fell back into silence. Its eyeless stare and motionless body gave me nothing to go on. It didn't even breathe.

"So, what do we do now?" I asked haltingly.

"A pressing question, but it is not the right one. Your life grows shorter with every tedious, superfluous flapping of your mouth." While superficially pleasant, I could feel its voice in my bones and my head like tiny insects chirping from inside me.

"You haven't eaten me," I observed. I felt like the eating should already have begun, but, instead, this thing wanted to have a word. "And I also haven't run. Uh—Why am I still alive?"

Its expression stayed that cold, neutral mask, but its tone grew hot. "A second tedious question, little ape. I will not bear a third."

*This thing could have eaten me as it snuck up on me. Instead it chose to speak. It claims it could chase me down no problem, but it asks me not to run. I'm not necessarily food . . . yet.*

"What do you want?"

"Ah," it breathed, its breath noxious like rotten eggs and charred meat. Its slightly open mouth pulled back to reveal more of its teeth. "We've finally come to the correct question, little ape. You are slow but teachable. Even so, I will expect more of you if this conversation is to continue."

"I'll do my best." I didn't want to ask another question the creature would consider superfluous. Instead, I limited myself to statements. "You just want to talk."

"No. You frame this interaction as you would a moment between mortals. This is an insult and a grave error. A dragon such as I never wants just one thing from any moment in our lives. Small thinking such as this is what keeps mortals weak and afraid their entire lives."

It just laid the word "dragon" on me, and I wasn't sure how I felt about that. This thing looked and smelled like it lived in a sewer; that wasn't how dragons had been described to me.

The multiverse was big, though. It probably had room for weird, gross, fleshy dragons, at least somewhere.

Didn't Sissa and Samila say they were offspring of dragons? I couldn't imagine a creature like this producing children like them.

I tried to make sure not to show my disbelief on my face. Instead, I thought things through, since it didn't seem to mind long gaps in the conversation.

What did I have that this dragon could possibly want?

"You want something from me, and it's not necessarily food," I said.

"Essentially correct, though you and all that are like you will forever be food for dragons. We take what we want until we cannot. That is the way of things. However, in this instance, what I propose is an exchange of truths. If you sufficiently entertain me, you will live, and, if you ask the right questions, you may more fully understand the danger that shadows you and yours."

Bones popped and claws dragged along the brickwork as the creature backed away a few feet to give me some breathing room. Then its head tilted slightly to the side as it waited for my response.

Its word choice gave me pause. I turned inward again. For a moment the creature ceased to exist for me, and I turned the words over in my head—the danger it had mentioned.

"You aren't talking about yourself, are you?" I asked.

"The right question, but we aren't playing the game yet. You have no reason to trust my words. Come fully into my home, and the exchange can begin."

It might have been a ploy to get me fully into its lair. It painted a gruesome picture of what would happen if I ran or fought. Then it gave me an out that happened to bring me into its domain. Carrot and stick. It even baited me by teasing a greater danger lurking out there somewhere to sweeten things.

I didn't like being kept in the dark, and I didn't like being trapped. This felt like it was doing both. I tensed, calculating how much force it would take to jump to the side and what kind of moves I would have to make to rebound off the wall and take off down the tunnel.

*Then again, what if it's telling the truth?*

Ever since I'd come to Ralqir I'd been hunted. Scourge-Touched didn't seem to need a reason to kill and destroy. They simply *did*. Did I really need a dragon to tell me why?

Curiosity, as it always did, was going to get me killed.

"I will agree to your exchange of truths on one condition. I will be completely safe as long as we are playing the game."

"Done," it barked. Then came a sickening chorus of cracks and pops, and the creature was gone and slithering around the cavernous room, too fast to track. It moved so suddenly, so quickly, the vacuum left in its wake made me stumble forward a step.

The red light was back now that the dragon wasn't filling my entire tunnel.

I inched forward stiffly, putting one foot in front of the other like a man approaching the gallows he'd just built for himself. I had the presence of mind to keep my body between the turret and the creature, so the programming wouldn't fire. Not yet, at least.

The mouth of the cavern grew wider and taller until I finally stepped over the water-filled gap that made up the threshold and into the full light. The smell was worse here, thick and suffocating. My head spun with the intensity of it.

The red crystal flashed again and sparks shot through the room. I held up my hand to shield my eyes.

"Beautiful, isn't it?" the dragon asked.

"Uh—Yes. It's a lovely shade of red."

The dragon hissed with irritation. "No, not the rock. No more sophisticated than a sump in a The'si icehouse. Watch, ape," it said, motioning upward with its head to direct my attention to the crystal.

The silvery wires, hard to pick out in the thick red hues, crawled up the vaulted ceiling in thick bundles, weaving in and out of the mortar and intertwining with one another to form a woven tapestry dense enough that sightings of the stones were few and far between, except next to the crystal. Very few of the wires ran there, and none touched it.

I strained my eyes to see what the dragon meant. The red light played tricks on my vision, and things seemed to pulse and writhe in my—

Wait. There was movement up there.

One of the wires, more like a creeper vine with all of its multiple barbs and razors that kept it attached to the roof, approached the crystal and reached out to touch.

"It's—Uh . . ."

"Yes. The roots. The Crusader steel. The roots are drawn to the power in the crystal, thirsty fumbling little things. Watch," the dragon insisted.

A flash. Sparks.

The tentacles recoiled like snakes, like they did when I disturbed them with Shape.

My brow furrowed, and I took another step forward. The crystal, now that I was looking closely, wasn't complete. Something had broken it on the half facing me, and there was some kind of dark shape lodged inside.

"What is this?" I asked.

The dragon preened under the shower of sparks that played over its skin and only replied once the last spark was out. "No, little ape. This is my home and my game. I go first. Where are you from?"

"Vistia," I lied before I even had the conscious thought to do so.

"A lie, but that tells me much already. This is not a story you have concocted but one given to you, I think."

I kept my face neutral, but the dragon had me dead to rights.

"This is why I go first, little ape. To train. For each truth you give me, I shall give you another of the same quality. I know many, many truths for I am older than the world you now scurry over."

"And if I entertain you, you'll let me go?" I asked.

Without warning, it surged forward, deathly silent, huge and menacing, only stopping when its mouth took up my entire field of vision. "Of course."

I didn't even have a chance to have a fear response, it happened so fast. Yet, I was still alive.

"Okay." I shuddered. "I will amend my answer. I'm not from Ralqir."

The dragon slithered backward until it returned to the center of the room and curled up to bathe in the light again. "Vague but technically truth. I will amend my answer to match. You are cautious. Continue to be so, and you will be in danger of boring me. To your question: If you give me the stimulation I desire, I will allow you to run."

I breathed out through clenched teeth. I was vague, so he was vague. Nothing in his answer necessarily guaranteed I would live through this. My ace in the hole was right there if I needed it, though—with several pounds of atomically sharp cobalt to help matters.

Still, if I wanted to get any water from this stone, I'd need to do it right.

"Next question," it continued. "Where does your power come from?"

"My home," I replied, pausing and choosing my words carefully before I went on. "I was chosen to wield it, and I am still learning how it works."

"I detect truth in your words this time, though I am unsure if you realize just how much. Delicious."

"My turn, then," I said. "What is happening with the wires and the crystal?"

The dragon bathed in the light of another shower of sparks and made a wet, purring sound in its throat before it finally answered. "It is a dance they have been doing for hundreds of years, through no fault of their own. The power inside the roots yearns to corrupt and assimilate, but the light of the maelstrom is elemental. It will not be changed or tainted. The roots do not understand why they are rebuffed. They cannot. Their mind is ash, the hollow it left behind another sump for a different kind of power. It reaches for the power it craves so desperately and is burned every time."

So, if the rules the dragon laid out were still in effect, its answer was the truth, but I didn't or couldn't realize just how true they were . . . probably?

"Why are you here?" it asked, taking its turn.

This one was easy, since it was a sore spot for me. "I was sent here against my will."

"You are dangerously close to boring me, meat. Do so again, and I shall take offense." The dragon loomed up high on its back end, its multiple arms giving it the appearance of a fleshy centipede. Its mouth opened wide to display its rows of teeth and *multiple* tongues that slapped against its jowls though no sound could be heard.

I tensed in preparation to dive to the side and let the turret fire, but the attack didn't come.

I kept talking.

"Then I'll amend my answer. I was sent here against my will to learn when I was chosen to wield my people's power. I don't know why I was chosen. Things haven't gone as I believe they were supposed to. If I'm being honest, I believe my 'power,' as you put it, isn't working the way it should."

That seemed to placate the dragon somewhat. It slowly lowered itself to the ground, arm by arm until it laid there facing me straight on, only a few feet from my body, as if to say, "I could end this at any time. Don't test me."

I didn't give it a chance to change its mind. "What are these 'roots?'" I asked.

"A symbiote that ultimately killed its host. It draws power from the collectors—or crystals, as you call them—in preparation for a spell that cannot be cast. Where did your people acquire their symbiotes?"

I blinked and turned my head to the side in confusion. "We . . . What? We don't have symbiotes or parasites or whatever."

"Hmmm. Untruth but through mortal ignorance. I will not hold your answer against you, as you know too little to answer truthfully."

"I don't—"

"It is still my question, as you could not answer mine. Will you ever be able to do what it does?" the dragon said, again gesturing up to the silvery wires with its foremost leg.

I shook my head. "I . . . don't know a lot about them."

"It," the dragon corrected. "The other. A singular organism. A singular mind."

"I don't know," I answered with a shrug.

"A lie."

"No, it's not."

"It is an untruth through self-enforced ignorance, a thing for which I have little tolerance."

"If I were to try—um—using the metal like that, at the scale it does, I would have to expend so much mana I have no idea where I would get it all. Additionally, the way it moves is way beyond what I can do, and I have no idea if I ever will be able to."

"So, it is possible, but you limit yourself in the scale of your thinking. Continue to do so, and this conversation will end, meat."

"My turn," I growled. I was just about done being insulted by a puffed-up salamander with delusions of being a dragon. "You said something about danger shadowing me. What did you mean?"

"The things from between. Void given form by breach of natural law, a sin against the very spirit of reality. It is the same danger that one brought to my world," it said as it reached up to pluck at one of the wires like a guitar string. "It, like you, was willfully ignorant of the damage you do when you visit us. You taint us. Take from us. Bring us low." The dragon's tone grew more heated with every word as if giving voice to its truths fanned the glowing embers of its hatred, and fire was imminent.

"I haven't done anything to you," I protested.

"Characteristically small thinking, yet again, meat. You are not simply yourself but the avatar of your species, a title inherited when you took up their tainted power. You have done and you will continue to do to us as long as you live. At what point does your power destroy you?"

"I—What?"

"Your symbiote, ape! Your dark passenger!" It boomed as it rose up to its full height, towering over me. "It will, someday, overtake you as it does all it touches, as it did the other. At what point in your growth does this happen? How powerful are your Elders?"

Accusations and burning questions. The veneer of civility was quickly peeling back. I was about to be out of time.

"I don't understand. We live for—"

I fell silent.

Our Elders back home did have a soft limit on their power. They called it the Wandering Threshold. At a certain point, elite, high-level Exotics tended to take off one day and rarely, if ever, came back. It had happened maybe a handful of times in our history, but it was a noted phenomenon.

It took centuries and a ridiculous amount of experience to reach that level of power, but once you did, you tended to drift away. People generally attributed this to age and power that slowly untethered Exotics from the concerns of mortal beings and made them desirous of greener pastures, much to the relief of some.

But how could a jumped-up lizard from another universe know this?

"You do not comprehend because you haven't asked the right questions of yourself, and you willfully refuse to be better. Weak. Detestable. Useless," the dragon boomed inside my skull.

This was about as south as this conversation could go. I needed to wrest control back somehow, if only to get more answers.

"I don't know what you want from me," I shot back. "I can't give you answers I don't have."

It stood still, looking down at me from high above. Sparks played over its flesh, but it no longer reacted to their touch. "Final question, and make it a good answer, human. You become metal as it does. Can you drink from the Collectors as it does?"

"No . . . Maybe."

"Could you replace it?" The dragon slammed down to the floor, an act I could feel through my feet but not hear. Then it surged forward, its tongues dripping foul saliva on the floor inches from my body. Desperation oozed from its pores, and its voice grew higher and shriller.

"I care not for your Scourge or your pitiful slave existence. I have been too long below, little ape. I want to see my sun again."

Replace it? Why would I replace this "other?" What did it actually want me to do?

Something clicked into place. The dragon called the thing in the crystal Crusader's Steel. Brightsteel. It's the term the System used so long ago in its description of the broken blade in my Spatial Storage. The brightsteel reacted badly to the tendrils when they touched but not to the crystal with all the mana.

The tendrils weren't just being used by a Dominion similar to mine. They were being Shaped . . . by an Animator.

*Brightsteel reacts badly to our mana.*

"Wait—"

I didn't get a chance to say anymore. The dragon was done waiting for answers.

It was so fast. It picked me up with surprisingly warm, slimy claws. I struggled to free myself as the mouth loomed closer, the tongues writhing like eels.

"Worry not. I will not end your life today. We have much to do, you and I, but I must leave to eat those you came with. You will not need to walk, not anymore."

It lifted me up into the air, rearing up on its back legs higher and higher while bringing its teeth down on my shins. Teeth sank into my flesh and grated against my bones. I screamed.

*BOOM!*

The Damage messages scrolled through my log too quickly to track. The turret's initial volley would have been thirty-five projectiles, but I waved the log away before it became too distracting.

Ancient Wretchwyrm takes 21 Damage. (19 base, 2 Knife in the Dark bonus) (Piercing)
Ancient Wretchwyrm is bleeding.

Ancient Wretchwyrm takes 17 Damage. (15 base, 2 Knife in the Dark bonus) (Piercing)
Ancient Wretchwyrm is bleeding.

Ancient Wretchwyrm takes 50 Damage. (48 base, 2 Knife in the Dark bonus) (Piercing)
Ancient Wretchwyrm is bleeding.
Ancient Wretchwyrm takes 21 Damage. (19 base, 2 Knife in the Dark bonus) (Piercing)
Ancient Wretchwyrm is bleeding.
. . .

I could feel the impact even through the creature's claws and its mouth. Big as it was, great amounts of energy were just transferred to its soft underbelly all at once.

You are poisoned. [numbing]

I fell to the ground with a thud. Feeling nothing from the bleeding messes that were my legs, I got my arms underneath me and levered myself upright until I could see.

The dragon writhed on the floor, its tail whipping back and forth, arms twitching and clutching at its skin, ripping at its own innards.

That meant my ace in the hole was performing its secondary attack . . . or attacks. I'd first gotten the idea from my ammo worms and speculating what they would have to do to get back to me if they'd been lodged in a target—what damage they might do. I'd simply taken the idea to the next level, thanks to the barbs and razors the cobalt tendrils liked to use.

Right now, the needles had deployed their razor spines, sharpened their heads, and grown a multitude of hook-tipped arms inside the dragon. What's more, the spines would be vibrating and sawing back and forth as the rounds burrowed their way deeper and deeper into their target. It used a lot of energy, but I only needed to use them once before they were out of juice.

It was a hell of a way to die—not something I would have wished on anyone, but I couldn't afford to take chances.

The dragon flailed. It slashed at the air and at itself. It only remembered me after I'd already dragged myself halfway to the tunnel from where I'd come.

The creature gurgled something unintelligible, followed by a deep, echoing "NO!" that rattled my brain against my skull.

Blood poured from the monster's mouth to drench the floor, as it came on like a freight train, having given up on extracting the rounds from its flesh and probably hoping to bring me down with it. If I had been crawling into the tunnel to escape that might have happened.

Instead, though, I dragged myself forward toward my real goal even as the numbing poison worked its way up my body, now to my thighs and stomach.

As the dragon reached for me, its claws only found air as I slipped my body into the gap between the floor and the tunnel and into the foul water below. Claws scrambled into the gap to find me, but I was already deep inside and sinking deeper, an aluminum diving tank appearing in my hand and Shape-opening the aperture for me.

# CHAPTER FORTY-ONE

# Break and Enter

You have been awarded 34,557 Experience points. [84,322 base (+8,690 Level, +9,002 camp, -67,457 non-combat Class)]

I waited until I received the Experience notification before I thought about resurfacing. The poison had worn off sometime in the past hour or so, but my limbs still felt weak and tingly despite the System telling me I was fine. The Level-Up process helped with that somewhat, the euphoric feeling chasing away some of the cobwebs and bringing life to my stiff muscles.

Level Up!
You are now Level 11.
Max HP +10
Max MP +10
+1 Attribute point.

My Achievements window was about how I expected it to be, giving me Boss Killer, Doing Your Part, and Spirit of the Warrior yet again. Though nice in that they gave me lots of Stats, I looked forward to the days where my Levels came from making stuff instead of . . . this.

The crevice down below wasn't particularly deep—maybe about twenty or thirty feet—but the water was, in a word, nasty. The brickwork down here was no better, having a thick film of slime that sloughed off in my fingers, which even my prosthetic struggled with. The only saving grace was that long years underwater had loosened things up somewhat, and the walls were an uneven mess. That left me handholds to pull myself to the surface and get my prosthetic up to the lip where I'd entered the pool. The climb up to the top was made easier by the extra points in Body from Boss Killer, which I was thankful for.

Climbing is now Level 7.

When my head crested the water, I spit out my diving tank and finally took a big lungful of un-canned air.

I immediately wished I hadn't. The cavernous room was repulsive before, but whatever had happened while I was down in the water had pushed the smell into biblical-plague territory. My eyes watered, and I fought my gag reflex as I pulled myself up onto solid ground to come to rest on the floor with a wet plop.

Fireworks—or, more accurately, brightsteel sparks—heralded my return to life above water level and lit up the room. Above me, flaps of translucent organic material hung in tatters from the web of cobalt wires. Charming.

"Oh, Light and gods of old, it's him!"

A big, gauntleted hand seized my neck and hauled me roughly up to a standing position. I thought about struggling, but the deed was done before I could get a hand up.

I looked up to see Geddon there, his broad face plastered with a toothy grin. The furry giant twitched slightly, seeming to be waffling between going in for a manly hug or staying at arm's length, but he chose the latter with a wrinkling of his nose. He awkwardly slapped me on both my shoulders instead.

"We thought you'd gone down fighting the beast, Brother Ryan, but I guess you're holding out for a more heroic death, eh?" Geddon turned to shout. "Brother Trix, he needs healing again!"

"No. Don't." I spat, trying to get the unique taste of the water out of my mouth, but it didn't help. "I'm fine, Geddon. Really."

"Of course you are," he replied with a sly wink. "I just want to share this— uh—olfactory adventure with another man before it passes us by."

I gave myself a sniff. Maybe it wasn't the room itself that smelled terrible.

Trix was there a second later, yelling my name. "Brother Ryan! Brother Ryan!" The vulpa's claws scrambled over the bricks and around the piles of filth the dragon had kept around itself. He came on full-bore before skidding to a stop a dozen feet from me, a pained expression on his face. He reached up to put a paw on his nose.

"Oh, Brother Ryan. I am—" He was beset by a series of gags that doubled him over. Worried, I took a step forward to do something for him, but Geddon stopped me with a hand on my shoulder. A second later he let go with a grimace and surreptitiously wiped his hand on his already-soiled tunic.

I looked down at myself, then back to him. Yeah, I wouldn't want to touch me, either.

"No. No. Please," Trix said after half a minute of looking like he wanted to be sick. "I apologize, Brother. I have a very developed sense of smell. I just can't— *Mff . . .* express how good it is to see you alive."

"You smell like a musk-eel spawning pool crossed with a slaughteryard," Geddon explained, reaching up to cover his nose. However, he made the mistake of using the hand he'd just used to touch me. I could see his gorge rising even under his armor. He tried to hide it, but I could tell.

"Oh," I said, trying to look sympathetic to their plight but failing. "Pardon me. As I look back on how I slew a monster of legend with one attack, there are some things I'd do differently if only to spare your delicate senses."

Geddon started to laugh but what was supposed to be a mirthful outburst seemed to morph into something else halfway through. He made a dash to the tunnel mouth to throw up.

"Where are the others?" I asked as Geddon did his thing. "And why are you here? The plan was for you to wait for me when the rock popped."

Trix looked apologetic but only *just*. "Sorry, Brother. The stone had been fading for some time while you were gone until it was hard to detect light from it at all unless I took it down the tunnel for some distance into the true darkness. The last time I took the stone into the dark to check it, it was entirely out of light, and I couldn't shake the feeling that it happened too abruptly."

"You came looking for me," I said reproachfully. "Trix, you knew that was a terrible idea. What if I'd found something dangerous?"

"That's precisely why we came, Brother," Trix argued.

"Not just us," Geddon interjected as he returned to stand near me like nothing had happened. "We all came. Now let's go. The dragonkin sisters will have another reason to admire you after this."

"Uh." My brain's speech center sparked and caught fire. "What?"

Geddon turned back to give me a wink as he led the way into the maze of dragon refuse. "One more than the other. You'll have a reprieve for now, but once we get you topside and into a bath, you're going to have your hands full."

Some kind of filmy residue squished under my boots, but after what I'd just taken a swim in, my disgust level just wasn't going anywhere above a four. What Geddon was saying left no room to dwell on it, anyway.

The big guy's steps faltered for a moment, as if he'd just tripped on something. Then he turned back to whisper to me. "Don't tell them I told you. I just thought you needed a warning."

"Uh huh," I said, paragon of wit that I was.

We turned a corner around a pile of unmentionable things, and the full body came into view just as a shower of sparks played over its jaundiced pink skin as they did in life. The ancient wretchwyrm died in the exact center of the room under the crystal where the red light was strongest. The flesh on the dragon's underbelly was in tatters, falling in strips and ribbons and sagging down to the floor. The multitude of palsied limbs were all bent at strange angles, and the creature's jaw laid slack. Long tri-forked tongues spilled out of the mouth onto the blood-soaked floor.

"Hell of a way to go," was all that came to mind, not for the first time. There had to be some kind of law back home against the kind of weapons I'd created. If not, maybe I'd have to lobby for one since I was an Exotic now. Even so, I was glad the creature was dead and not doing to me what it hinted it would.

The civilians stood huddled together far from the dragon's corpse, the grandmother clutching the boy close and shielding his eyes, while the shopkeeper gave us a respectful nod as we walked by, smiling slightly at seeing me alive but then turning away suddenly when the smell hit him.

Sissa and Samila were both standing in front of the dragon's corpse, near the head, Sissa with her sword in her hand and Samila crouched down to examine the beast's face.

"Anyone know a good taxidermist?" I said in an attempt to break the tension.

The both of them turned, Samila with that little, knowing smirk on her face while Sissa turned from me to the dragon and back again, wild-eyed.

Samila spoke first. "I knew a guy who could mount anything, but that's probably not what you had in mind."

With a clang, Sissa's sword fell to the ground. Then, with stiff, deceptively quick strides, she'd crossed the distance and wrapped her arms around me, nearly lifting me off the ground with how fiercely she was embracing me. She even laid her head against my shoulder despite how wet I was.

I didn't handle it well. Paralyzed for a full second, I just stood there while she gave me a spinal adjustment. When my brain finally caught up to what was happening, I did an awkward, arms-out, air-hug thing where I wasn't sure if I wanted to slime her more than she was already doing to herself but I also knew I needed to reciprocate somehow.

"We thought you'd died," she said, not bothering to acknowledge the smell or the horrible substance that soaked my clothes and my newly sprouted hair.

Then, in a sudden reversal, she pulled away and slapped me, hard. So hard, I had to work my jaw to make sure it wasn't broken.

"You're so stupid, you know that? What made you think this was a foe you could fight? Don't try to feed me an excuse. I saw your turret machine. You didn't get caught. You planned this. Do you have any idea how lucky you are? How can you be so godsdamned ready to kill yourself?" She was at shouting volume just a few words in, and, by the third or fourth question, I started to catch on that all of them were rhetorical.

She went on a tirade, a good minute and a half of increasingly outlandish insults to my mental faculties before she paused to catch her breath, and I felt it was probably incumbent on me to respond. I had nothing, though.

"Uh," I began, stalling for time, but I'd just gone through exchanging truths with the dead thing in the middle of the room. I wasn't sure if I had the answers Sissa wanted.

Sissa had simply been waiting for me to try to answer to say more. "You jump on every sword blade, step in front of every arrow. Who asked you to be everyone's shield? Who appointed you? Huh? You are *my* responsibility while we are down here, and no one gets to fucking die unless I say so. Do you understand, *Brother?*"

In another strange turn, the guard sergeant began to laugh maniacally. That swiftly turned into sobs, tears beginning to flow down her blue cheeks as the scales under her eyes darkened in tone until they were navy blue.

Everyone else just looked on in some form of shock, unable to figure out what they should do. None of us got a chance to react, though. Sissa swiftly turned on her heel and marched back toward the dragon to pick up her sword.

I had the urge to reach out and . . . I don't know . . . do *anything*, but I was woefully incapable of reading this encounter.

Samila, as always, came to her sister's rescue. "We were all worried about you, Monk, and when we saw this," she said, gesturing behind her to the dead wretchwyrm. Then she shrugged. "It's a lot."

"Ancient enemies," Geddon said from my right, nodding as if the two words said it all.

"My people will give you a title for this," Samila continued. "Or burn you at the stake. Depends on which ones you tell."

I shook my head. "Listen, I don't know what this is about. I . . ." I hesitated. What could I tell them?

"Listen, I don't know Ralqir. Not the way you people do, at least," I began.

Samila rolled her eyes. "Obviously."

"Yes. Everyone is in agreement that you are woefully ignorant of the wider world," Trix agreed. "We've all noticed."

I nodded. "Thank you, Trix."

"And your knowledge of peoples and history is also far short of any school worth its accreditation," the vulpa continued.

"You're the dumbest smart person I know," Geddon added helpfully.

"Right, well—"

"We've talked it over, and we think you ride that line between bravery and being too stupid to realize what you're doing," Samila stated flatly.

"Listen, all of you," I pleaded, pausing to choose my words as best I could. "Where I come from, things are very different. Everything is small. I had a family and a people. That was all there was, all I aspired to have, even when I did things that I thought were bigger than myself. Now that I'm here, there's all this history and culture and people that I know precious little about, and so many things I've never learned."

Being so vague with my party—my friends—felt wrong, especially after having to be so candid with the man-eating wretchwyrm thing. The words felt hollow leaving my mouth, but, at the same time, it was safer for everyone involved.

"Since I came here, I've been on the run or on the attack. I've nearly died a few times." My voice dropped to a whisper, my mouth suddenly dry. "I've had to kill people. Someday I'll have to stop and think about that."

"Brother?" Trix questioned, but I ignored him.

"I'm out of my depth here, but the only thing I am absolutely sure of is that you are all worth whatever sacrifice I need to make—not that I'm keen on dying in the process. I'm just not willing to see anyone else die for me or instead of me. In the grand calculus of things, I feel like there are worse ways to live."

I paused, looking up from the blood-slime pool I'd begun to stare into and catching Sissa rejoining the group, fully composed again. I cleared my throat and forced a smile onto my face.

"I'm also probably only alive and sane because I don't know exactly what I should and shouldn't be afraid of. So, please, tell me what the deal is with big, pink, and squishy over there."

Sissa grasped onto the question like it was a lifeline, going right into the good stuff. "When Ralqir was thrown into the maelstrom, the planet was awash in the maelstrom's light. It scoured the surface of our planet and forced us all underground. That was the Purge. You know that much, yes?"

I nodded. I'd pieced something like that together so far, but I was happy for the confirmation.

"Well, dragons were no exception. They were the gods of our planet since the beginning, but even they couldn't stand in the light for more than a few hours at a time. Even then, displaced from their rightful seat in the cosmos as they were, their power was too great. The world could not sustain them anymore. So, for all our sakes, they chose to sleep."

At that point, Samila took up the story. "Our sire is one of those. A blue. Not all of the dragons were content to hibernate and place themselves into obscurity, though."

"Yes. Some of them, such as this one, took the wound the Purge dealt them and let it fester," Sissa said, sparing a glance for the hulking, slimy corpse over her shoulder, like she was making sure it was still dead.

"They became evil, corrupting creatures. Dragons were the holiest, most powerful beings on Ralqir before the Purge, but not all of them were good or wise. These . . . the wretchwyrms, instead of letting their era pass in peace, chose to diminish themselves, go underground and gnaw at the fabric of reality out of spite."

I peered over at the dragon's face, the empty eyes and gaping mouth. "An evil god, huh? Am I going to have . . . I don't know, like a cult or something out for my blood for doing this?"

Samila spat and her eyes hardened. "No. Don't say that. It wasn't a god, not even an evil one. It was one, eons ago, but godhood is in what you are and what you do. This thing gave that up to become something else—lesser in every way."

"Did you—uh—talk to it?" Sissa asked haltingly.

I nodded.

Her expression grew concerned. "What did it say?"

I took a deep breath before answering. "A lot of things, mostly about me and my home. It talked about crystals and Collectors and spells and symbiotes and—" I began, my mind wandering back to the half-revelations it had used to pry information out of me. "It was angry, maybe not at me but at my people. It seemed to know a lot, but everything it said was frustratingly vague and riddled with contradictions."

"Believe nothing it said," Sissa said with absolute conviction. "They only exist to corrupt. Whatever it told you was to hurt you."

"It wanted to exchange truths," I explained. It knew, or maybe guessed, about so much. My origins, the Wandering Threshold, the System. It could tell, despite having never been to my universe. What did that mean? What did it mean by symbiotes? Did it mean the System? Maybe. The System didn't seem to have any influence over my mind in the way the dragon seemed to think it did. Would that happen as I grew in power? Then there was the presence of another Animator here on Ralqir. They had to be old and extraordinarily powerful if they controlled all this. How long had they been here?

I blinked, coming out of my spiraling thoughts and gave a little, half-hearted shrug. "It gave as good as it got. That's all."

Why did the brightsteel react so badly to me? To *us*, I guessed. I watched as the tendrils tried to connect with the crystal again, the violent outburst of sparks that hurt to watch directly.

Sissa reached out and grabbed my hand, giving it a squeeze. Her grasp was warm and gentle but firm. When had someone last taken my hand like that?

She looked into my eyes, a pained look on her face like I had been the one doing the crying just a minute ago instead of the other way around. "Listen, Brother Ryan, you can't trust anything it said. Even the truths you thought you heard are probably not what you think they are. These creatures are incapable of doing anything good, even simple things like telling the truth."

That struck me as only partially true, maybe some kind of cultural bias. What it had said fit so well with certain parts of my life. Then again, maybe I had been taken in by the thing's riddles and vague hints, filling in the gaps so the dragon never had to.

I still felt like there was something there I needed to think over.

*Brightsteel. Why does it do that?*

Whatever the wretchwyrm had said about them, I was almost entirely sure another Animator was here on Ralqir, and they'd been reduced to what I was seeing here, a husk that only knew to Shape and to grow, to collect mana for something. A slave to some kind of design.

It sounded like torture and mutilation to me.

Something stank on Ralqir, and it wasn't just me.

I mentally added another person to my list of those who would need to be saved.

I had to take apart my fat cobalt turret before we left, which meant everyone had to stand around waiting for me while I did it. I wasn't about to give up good material, though, not after it saved my life and could be used to do it again. I was able to save the smart card, but its connections to the rest of the Triggers and such would need to be reconnected once I brought the whole thing out of Spatial Storage.

There was one other thing, too.

---

Loot Ancient Wretchwyrm? Y/N?

---

Corrupted Dragon Bone x 18: Bones of an ancient wretchwyrm of the planet Ralqir. Bodies of magical beings such as dragons are a product of their terrible will and these bones reflect that. This wretchwyrm chose a life of filth and loathing over a dignified hibernation after its world underwent a great upheaval. The bones are pitted and brittle but emanate a strong presence closely tied to hunger, desperation, and darkness. One would do well to use these bones with care.

---

The smugglers' arrows, crossed out as they were, still led back further into the tunnels. We were cautious in our approach but less so than we were before. The dragonkin ladies insisted the wretchwyrm wouldn't have left anything else alive down here for miles, but I wasn't convinced. I didn't want to have come this far only to trip over the finish line.

Eventually, however, we found ourselves at a dead end, facing a black wall with a semicircle painted on it in flaking, faded yellow.

*Hello, quellstone, my old friend.*

Since we didn't have a key, I needed to work some magic. Unfortunately, I was out of wood, so I ended up Consuming the goblin herb pouch I'd looted from the ambushers outside the city. That gave me enough just to get a spike of steel through the gaps in the quellstone. Then I set about expanding the width of the metal, atom by atom, from the inside. Grueling work but not quite as bad as I remembered thanks to my greater control of my mana. I still felt the pull, but it wasn't as irresistible as before. Still painful and alarming, for sure, but more manageable.

It probably helped that I wasn't charging it to blow—not in this confined space at least, especially given how we'd come across quite a few collapses.

The tedious process of thickening the steel rod took about an hour, but, eventually, I was rewarded with a sharp crack as the weaker of the quellstone bricks gave way, crumbling to the ground as it lost its shape.

An alarming amount of light blasted out of the hole I made. Real, actual light.

There was a voice, too.

"Stop what you're doing!" came a muffled shout from the other side. "Stand back and make no sudden moves!"

We all looked at each other, all hearing the exact same thing but not quite believing it. For the first time in forever, we'd heard a voice that didn't belong to the eight of us.

"Stand back!" the mystery voice commanded.

We did. What else were we going to do?

Then the bricks seemed to peel back, rearranging themselves in a folding pattern. They seemed to collapse into each other, then into the wall on the other side, click-clacking until we were looking at a smooth, arched entryway into . . .

Someone's bedroom.

Two beds on either side of a nightstand were pressed up against our threshold. A bookshelf hung on the wall on the opposite side of the room, filled with bound papers and expensive-looking leather tomes held up by metal bookends. Some kind of banner hung over the door, black with silver trim, and sporting a white bird on an equally white branch.

There were also several armed guards with crossbows pointed our way. Their grim, unblinking expressions gave them a professional air, their fingers wrapped tightly around the crossbows' triggers.

Their commander, an unshaven Miur with some kind of insignia on his shoulder and a red-blotted bandage over one eye, addressed us.

"Lay down your weapons and get inside, lest this breach be the death of us all."

# CHAPTER FORTY-TWO

# Retake the Initiative

Tensions were high.

The Church contingent wasn't particularly keen on surrendering their weapons after so long in the dark, and it took some negotiation to come up with a way to do it. The guard commander wouldn't let anyone take a step without full disarmament and removal of armor. Sissa didn't like having her squad shown such disrespect, and she wasn't backing down. Meanwhile, Geddon and Samila stood at Sissa's side with their hands ready to draw.

Trix and I, on the other hand, had no weapons to drop as far as the guards knew, so we stood with the civilians, though they did eye my metal arm with some concern. One by one, all the quarrels slowly drifted over to point at me, and the commander had some probing questions about what I could do.

"He is a Brother of the Order of Dawn, and he's as trustworthy as any of us, you pillock," Sissa argued in my defense. "And I'd wager he's done more to save innocents in the past week than you and your band of bullies have your entire lives."

It was a bit much, but, as I said, tensions were high.

Sissa's words didn't go over well. The commander's face turned red, and a prominent vein popped out of his forehead. "I very much doubt that, young miss. You're lucky I don't just have you shot, then seal this tunnel back up. Would be a lot less trouble for us, and we could go back to our posts."

"I might be the first shot, but I won't be the first to die," Geddon rumbled, stepping forward before Sissa stopped him with an outstretched hand.

"We have civilians with us, sir," I said, hoping to appeal to his sense of duty or humani—Miurity? "Seal us in if you have to, but they don't belong down here."

The man's eyes shot over to me, then to the civilians, calculating. Then his gaze came to rest on the kid.

That took the wind out of his sails. He calmed, taking a big breath and relaxing his shoulders, closing his good eye for a good five seconds.

"Alright, all of you come inside, and we'll get this sealed up. Weapons sheathed and no sudden movements. You'll all then be taken to quarantine until you can be examined for plague. Is that acceptable, Sergeant?" he finally asked Sissa, putting a significant pause between his question and her rank.

It was a start.

Sissa turned back to look us all over and gauge everyone's feelings, then nodded. "That is acceptable, but I won't stand for my people being treated badly."

"Neither would I." The guard commander sighed. "And I'm protecting my people by confining you. You've had too much contact with the plagued to not be regarded with some caution."

"Fine," Sissa agreed tersely, sheathing her sword and stepping to the side to allow the civilians to come through.

The grandmother was weeping; the shopkeeper remained stoic. The kid, however, looked shell-shocked, more than I'd seen from him even in the Undercity. Maybe seeing the adults at each other's throats removed a layer of comfort he'd been able to cling to prior. Hard to tell.

After that, the guards took us in while the commander removed a ring of little dangly charms from his belt and waved it at the portal to the smugglers' tunnels, which prompted it to close.

All but one conspicuously missing brick of course. I wondered what the going rate for magical quellstone door replacements was.

The guards gave me a wide berth once they got a whiff of me. Trix, with his filthy Church robes and small stature was treated with the most deference, surprisingly, with guards apologizing to him for their treatment and asking if there was anything they could do for him.

Trix, for his part, seemed to deal with the attention by trying to hide behind whoever was closest at hand, Geddon ideally, Samila as a backup.

I caught Samila's eye and raised an eyebrow in question. She leaned in to whisper in my ear: "Always be nice to the healer."

"I heard that," Trix said. "Just to clarify, I'm not a healer, Commander. I can ward off death for a time, but it's not true healing."

"We'll take anything we can get right now, Brother Yik'i'trix," the guard commander declared grimly. "Even as you are, you are most welcome inside these walls."

"Not to sound unappreciative, but whose walls are we inside?" I asked.

"You've broken into the Spire, sir," one of the guards said hoarsely, a young man with a dirty bandage wrapped around his throat. "Specifically the Black University, if the banners and colors didn't clue you in."

"Now if you'll come with us, you've all been assigned an escort, and they'll take you to accommodations. Fennel!" the commander called to a young, lupine-looking guard with sharp features and facial hair everywhere but his eyes. "A bath for this one, then off to the quarantine."

I was separated from the group and escorted down a series of long, straight hallways of smooth, white walls and regularly spaced pairs of doors. My eyes were still getting used to how bright it was in here, and the white certainly didn't help things, my eyes tending to water and blur when I looked directly at anything.

Were they overcompensating for just how dark the underground typically was elsewhere? Had to be.

Our route took us past all the white, then through a large room with multiple soft couches and tables that were set up for some kind of social occasion with softer light coming from golden lamps and flickering sconces. Books laid strewn on most of the tables along with playing cards and dice. I recognized the general setup, even if I'd not been to university myself.

*A common room. We came in through a dormitory.*

The only people we encountered were after two flights of stairs where we passed a pair of women that, upon seeing us, retreated into one of the doorways, quietly engaging the lock with a click. Understandable considering how I looked and smelled but disquieting nonetheless.

Any misgivings I had for my situation vanished, however, once Fennel showed me to an honest-to-Constance bathroom with running water, scalding hot and absolutely glorious. The bath was a big, group-sized bowl, more like a shallow, steaming pool than a personal tub, but I had the place all to myself.

On the wall were brushes, mirrors, and towels along with a bucket of white flakes that smelled like soap and worked into a lather when I experimentally rubbed them between my fingers.

Slipping into the water, I felt the first warmth I'd experienced in a long, long time that wasn't the result of self-immolation.

I didn't know quite how to react to it. It felt wonderful, like a return home to civilized life but wrong somehow, like this moment of comfort was not what I should have been doing, not what I deserved.

Soon the questions were rolling in.

Where were the others? Were they getting the same treatment I was? What had the dragon wanted to do with me? How was I supposed to "send them home?" Would I need to send the people of Ralqir home to save them? Was that a good thing? How would I do that?

How would I find the other Animator on Ralqir? What would I do when I found them?

What was happening outside right now?

What was I going to do about it?

It was all so big, and I'd just gotten to the point where I couldn't count my Levels on my fingers. The pleasure I should have felt during my first touch of civilization was gone, replaced by a hollow feeling of smallness.

I hurried to be done, cleaning myself as deeply as I could, scrubbing hard until my skin turned red and I started to get Damage notifications if I lingered too long on one spot.

Fennel had clothes for me when I stepped out, simple black robes and undergarments. He told me to leave the old ones. He'd come dispose of them later—probably burn them. The man was in a hurry, nervously dancing around with his crossbow on his hip like he had somewhere to be, but he was tight-lipped when I asked him what was going on.

He wasted no time in getting me to "quarantine."

Quarantine turned out to be someone's office—a very small office no bigger than a broom closet where the desk took up the majority of the room with only enough space to fit a chair on one side of it and a chair on the other for visitors. The rest of it was decked in papers and books.

*Real page-turners.*

*Treatise on the Formation of Isolationist Groups in Western Imperial Provinces* and *Variance of Dominion Signs in Tribal Societies and Social Implications* were two of my favorites. I almost got through the opening paragraphs of those.

The same feeling I'd experienced in the bath was still there in my mind. I felt like I should be doing something. I had the urge to be somewhere.

To know what I'd set into motion.

The guards that had come to get us all had injuries. Fresh ones, too. Did that mean there had been fighting? They wouldn't say one way or the other, too concerned that we would be amongst the Plagued soon if we'd made contact with infected people.

The office had no windows, so I couldn't look outside.

Reading wasn't diverting my mind. The walls were too close, the air too still. I imagined the Undead scratching at the ground beneath my feet, chipping away at the foundations of the city until I was back down there with them in the dark.

*I can't stay here.*

The door, of course, was locked. The lock, however, was metal.

One Shaping session later, I had the front cover off the locking mechanism and the tumblers exposed. They were actually quite complicated from a mechanical standpoint, small and intricate with metal and rubbery bits jumbled together in some kind of knot. I didn't know much about locks. Engines were more my thing.

So, I simply touched each tumbler one by one and Shaped it until I could just extract it from the lock as a whole. Then the scrap metal went into my Spatial Storage. Soon I was just looking at a rectangular hole where the lock used to be, and the door opened with a click.

I smiled, stepping out into the hallway, feeling pretty pleased with myself for not resorting to explosives this time.

That feeling left me two feet from the door when I bumped into a terrified-looking Miur in black robes. The guy had to be about my age, maybe a little older, with long, brown hair, short, two-pronged antlers, and big doe eyes. He was standing, mouth agape and staring at me, his bent glasses hanging down on his mouth like he'd forgotten he had them on.

"Uh. Hello," I ventured, giving him a little wave.

In a move that seemed more like a socially ingrained reflex than anything, the Miur boy returned my wave and mouthed something akin to a greeting.

I cleared my throat and continued. "Sorry about the—uh—sorry about the lock. I think it engaged by mistake. Was thinking about going for a walk."

The young Miur shook his head, his prominent antlers banging into the doorframe across the hall and bringing him up short. He didn't seem to notice, though. "You—You're supposed to stay in quarantine until—"

"Hey, I know. I really do. But I've been in there for a while. Look at me. I'm obviously not infected."

"We've sent for the headmaster." The words came off like assurance. He wanted to let me know that someone was coming to help, but there was an undertone of warning as well, as if the mention of the headmaster should have kept me in line. I was too ignorant to be cowed by that, however. There were some advantages to being an outsider.

I shrugged. "Okay. Great. He can come find me when he gets here, then."

The robed Miur looked left and right down the long hall and pushed his glasses back up to his eyes. "You have to be in quarantine. The guards—"

I changed tacks. "Listen, friend. What's your name?"

"Angol," he replied after some hesitation.

"Angol, I've been underground for a long time, and I'm tired of it," I admitted. "And I want to know what's going on."

Angol shook his head vigorously. "I'm sorry, but you can't wander around. You could infect others. You have to get back in the room."

"No, I don't think so, and I promise you I'm not infected. I would know," I assured him. "I'm pretty sure the plague only works on certain types of things. I'm not one of them."

Angol swallowed, looking like he wished desperately to have someone else here to back him up, but, despite his wishes, no one materialized. "The guards said we need to be sure," he pleaded. "People can't see you out and about."

So now it was about who saw us instead of him actually considering me a threat. That was progress.

"Well, I'm out now, and you've made contact with me, Angol. Wouldn't you have to quarantine, too, if you followed the guards' orders?"

"I—" He paused, thinking. "I don't know. Maybe. Probably n—"

"Looks like we're stuck together, then."

"That's not how that works," Angol said, some conviction seeping into his words now.

"We'll have to find another room," he continued. "And we'll inform the guards. We can bring you food, too, if you cooperate."

He was thinking now, at least, meaning I could reason with him.

I stood my ground, channeling my inner Samila. "I'm not getting into another room, Angol, and you and I both know no one is here to make me. I want to walk, maybe see the daylight. I'm sure you have better things to do than babysitting me."

"You can't," Angol declared with finality.

I pulled out my trump card. "I have to poop."

"You must be joking."

"Kind of," I admitted. "I'm just pointing out that this whole thing hasn't been well thought-out. Tell you what. Maybe you can come with me. Show me around. Keep me away from others. It'll be just like quarantine, but with fewer broken doors and soiled undergarments."

His expression grew calculating, and he looked down to the floor for a moment to consider. "You wanted to see daylight?"

I nodded.

"Okay. If I do what you ask, will you go to quarantine after?"

I shrugged. "Depends on what I see."

Angol frowned, not liking the answer. "Just don't talk to anyone or touch anyone. Also, don't be seen by anyone."

"Total Gray Man. Deal."


We went upstairs. Lots and lots of stairs.

I'm not going to say I was tired by the time I started to see daylight, but I knew that without my enhanced Body, I would have had to take several breaks.

Angol, on the other hand, took it like a champ. Maybe Miur were descended from mountain goats instead of deer like I'd assumed. The guy was always quick to lead me up further and further, peering into hallways on each landing to make sure the coast was clear before we continued upward.

The glimpses I caught of each landing definitely had the feel of a school to them. We left the dormitory section after a few floors and entered classroom territory. Grand lecture halls with wide-open double doors would be right next to the stairwell while honeycombed cubicles and lab equipment were on other landings.

We encountered very few people, but the times we did were strange. Everyone looked on edge. Many were armed, and not just a sword on a hip here or there but full-on naked steel clutched in white-knuckled hands. We gave them a wide berth.

At one point, Angol had a tense, whispered exchange with a handful of students who had formed a checkpoint of sorts on one of the floors using turned-over desks and stacked chairs, but they let us by unopposed once they saw my arm. The knives they carried looked sharp and their faces hard, but apparently they weren't ready to tangle with someone they perceived as being a practitioner.

"Charming people. I can see why folks are clamoring to get in," I joked.

I had no idea how popular the Black University was, but the whole thing felt wrong. Even if Angol had spoken just to correct me, it would be better than all the nervous silence.

Angol let out a high, strained laugh, painful to hear and probably more painful to do. "Oh, they are clamoring to get in, alright, now more than ever. That's the problem."

"How so?" I asked.

"We've had to bar the doors." He said it so matter-of-factly, it took a handful of seconds to sink in.

"The Returned?" I guessed.

Angol nodded, not bothering to look at me, climbing another flight of stairs. When he spoke, he sounded tired.

"Everyone with a Dominion or combat experience has been conscripted by the prefect. That just leaves a handful of us."

"Conscripted?" I asked. I knew what the word meant, but my clan had never been the type to make people fight against their will. If you didn't volunteer for a fight, there was something wrong with you by Constance's standards.

"Yes. She called for faculty and staff as soon as the walls were threatened and then for qualified students shortly after," he said as he waited for me on the next landing. "Since then, there have been no more public announcements."

"They have students manning the walls?" I asked, incredulous. "Can they do that?"

"No," Angol replied with a shake of his head before he added, "Well, some took up posts on the wall originally, I guess, but I don't know where they are now. Like I said, it's all the students with Dominions and military experience. It's not unheard of. We're an Imperial school. It's just not been done in recent history. Lucky us, I guess."

"So, it's just you and others who didn't meet the criteria?"

"Yes," he said, his shoulders stiffening. "We're still here, doing our best. This is our floor. Come."

Angol took me away from the stairs and to another landing with big double doors that stood closed, but I could see daylight streaming in from between them and under the sweeps.

The lanky Miur pushed the two doors open with a hard shove to reveal a wide observation deck, or, upon closer inspection, an outdoor amphitheater. We were up high where the seats were arranged in a semicircle that went down step by step to face a podium with its back to open air . . .

. . . and the city below.

What I saw down there froze my breath in my lungs.

I'd never seen the city from above before, but I could tell things were all wrong. Smoke billowed from several different places where buildings laid collapsed in ash, the black columns casting huge shadows over entire neighborhoods in the golden evening sun. Two of the gates I could see had either collapsed on their hinges or been thrown open. Screams echoed up from the ground below, faint and indistinct from such a distance but harrowing—scenes of lives being ended, made somehow more real by how small they seemed from up here. Flashes of something from the eastern gate preceded a sharp crack that came half a second later. Black shapes poured over the battlements of the walls and over the roofs of buildings, through the streets and out of doorways.

Shouts and the clash of steel alongside wild, animalistic snarling merged into a tapestry of background sound that I would not soon forget.

"You said you've been underground for a long time, right?" Angol asked me.

I nodded, dumbfounded by the picture in front of me.

I was going to save *this*? How?

Despite looking down on the scene like a giant, I felt so small.

Angol didn't come to the railing as I had. He stood behind me, but turned away so that he couldn't see.

"All the Returned in the city went mad all at once. That was bad enough. Then the beasts from the wilds came. The guards and the staff were called away, then some of the students. We were told to barricade the doors and lock ourselves inside. That's spared us much of the violence so far. I was up here when Queenshall fell. That's our sister school. I—I saw the Returned take them below," Angol stated in a brittle voice.

He paused to let me take it in, or maybe he was lost in his own thoughts. "I just thought you should know what's going on if you're so eager to break quarantine and risk us all."

I worked my tongue around to try to get my dry mouth working again. "So, everyone that was in charge is gone, and you've been left to your own devices?"

Angol's slumping shoulders lifted slightly in a half-hearted shrug. "We have the guards, but they are busy repelling the enemy down in the library. They were able to seal up the entrances to all but two of the Undercity arches," he informed me grimly. "They tell us what's happening sometimes, but it's mostly the wounded that come up to rest. Even then, I think they are trying not to tell us much, so we don't panic. My classmates and I—We formed a group that helped keep people fed and calm, and that's all we've been able to do."

"I see."

"So, if you could just get back in quarantine, and not give me another thing I need to worry about, that would help me greatly," he said, taking his glasses off for a vigorous cleaning to give his shaking hands something to do.

I thought for a moment, looking down at the chaos of the city—the carnage. Black shapes swarmed through the streets. Limp bodies were being carried indoors while others were being ripped apart.

"Angol?" I asked.

"Yes?"

"When you said you sent for the headmaster . . . he's not actually coming is he?"

Angol's eye twitched. His jaw clenched. He looked like he wanted to deny it, but he couldn't bring himself to do it. After a handful of heartbeats, he shook his head in confirmation.

"He's out there somewhere, isn't he?" I guessed.

"They all are," Angol whispered. "We're alone."

I swallowed and drew myself up straight, turning to put my hands on both of his shoulders like Geddon had done with me. I hoped I was doing this right.

"Angol, you've done a great job," I began, putting as much force behind the words as I knew how. "I mean that. I can tell you care."

"I'm just doing what anyone would do," he muttered, looking away uncomfortably.

"Maybe so," I conceded, angling my head to meet his gaze and hold it there. "But, as alone as you feel right now, you're not. You have us. Were you told who I came with?"

"Some Church guards and a healer?"

"Right. I have a proposition for you."


"Here I was hoping for some time to take my boots off," Sissa said breathily as she leaned on the railing overlooking the besieged city.

Could I even call it besieged anymore? Didn't that require the enemy to be outside the walls? I didn't know. Maybe I'd ask later.

I nodded. "Yeah, I thought maybe that was in the cards, too, but even with a bath, I couldn't sit still until—"

"Until there was no more work to do. No more arrows to jump in front of."

I didn't answer, but she'd hit it on the head.

She shuddered, crossing her arms in front of her chest and rubbing warmth into her shoulders. "It would have been nice if things had been handled after we did what we did. No more civilians to save. I was quietly hoping someone topside who knew what they were doing would have received our distress call and had this under control by now, someone with gray hair and ink stains on their sleeves. You know the type."

"Yeah," I answered. "I think I do. Someone with a plan."

She sighed, wiping her eyes, stretching her neck, and showing off just how bright her blue scales shone in the sun, a contrast to her black borrowed robes that practically drowned her. Down in the Undercity, I knew on an intellectual level that she was shorter than me, slighter in frame, but this was the first time I'd realized just how small and fragile-looking.

I knew better than to believe that, however.

Slowly, Sissa straightened, her shoulders flared out, and her back went straight, going from zero to soldier right before my eyes. Her mouth turned down, and her eyes hardened until she was staring down at Eclipse as a different person, namely the sergeant.

"The way I see it," she said with the force and confidence of her rank again, "with the streets taken by the enemy, supplies and healers can't reach our fighters out in the field. See that? How the pockets of fighting are clumped so far apart? That means they are going to lose sooner or later. The enemy can afford to bring fresh troops in and fight even as they die by the hundreds. Meanwhile, every loss on our side can't be replenished. Every drop of sweat or blood is another mark against us. They've been fighting like this for a week, you say?" She turned to Angol who stood off away from the railing, taking great care not to look over the edge.

He nodded in answer. "More or less, ma'am. There used to be larger and more numerous battles happening down below, but they've gone now."

"We have to assume they were overrun," Sissa said quietly to herself, biting her lip.

"Angol, you said that you've been feeding everyone since this kicked off," I reiterated. "How much food and supplies does the university have access to?"

He blinked rapidly as he did some calculations in his head. "Our stores are supposed to feed a full stock of students and faculty, I think, with some things coming in daily from the market, but we have plenty if we ration, not the most appetizing stuff but edible."

"Do you happen to have a med school? Doctors? Surgeons in training? Medical supplies?" I asked, fleshing out my half-formed plan.

"Uh. Yes, but no healers," he replied. "I'm actually on the medical track but I don't have my Dominion yet. We can only provide the basics."

"What's that over there?" I asked, gesturing toward one of the gates where the sea of bodies surged and flashes of magical power zipped around the area like angry hornets.

Angol turned to follow my pointed finger. "That's the southern gatehouse and refugee area. They've held out the best so far."

Sissa nodded as if that wasn't a surprise. "They had a lot of guards stationed there when the goblins started to come to us for help. Goblins tend to cause trouble, so more guards were dispatched to keep the peace. I guess that's worked to their advantage."

I experienced a pang of worry for the Stone Hearts who were probably housed there, but there was more to think about just now. Now it was time to lead the conversation to where I wanted it to go.

"Okay. If you were to set about rescuing one of these groups, how would you go about it?" I asked with a raised voice meant to include the others.

Geddon didn't disappoint. "Overwhelming force, collect the survivors, charge back to a safe zone. Stop for nothing. Take heavy losses but gain capable fighters," he boomed from the second row of seats, his giant feet up on the row in front of him. "Not much else to do."

Samila seemed to agree, coming in to stand on my right, opposite her sister. "The big guy's not wrong about the situation needing a heroic charge for once. You have to be effective enough to relieve pressure on the group, enough to let them move safely, then have a corridor for retreat to a position of strength."

"Well, we have one of those," I said, slapping the railing with my natural hand. "The Spire is holding out pretty well. That just leaves overwhelming force and a safe corridor."

"Don't forget the ability to relieve the pressure," Sissa cautioned. "It won't do any good to get there and ask them to move if they've already got one arm in the creatures' mouths."

"Okay. Fine. I'll move it further up the list," I said.

"What are you proposing, Brother Ryan?" Trix asked from Samila's shoulder. He couldn't see over the railing without some assistance, but he refused to climb *on* the railing. Maybe he just liked riding people now.

I looked down at the rooftops, the straight streets with long lines of sight, the lack of civilians that might end up as collateral damage. With enough material, it could work.

"Brother Ryan?" Trix asked again, bringing me back to the moment.

Blinking, I turned back to the rest of them, the plan cementing in my head . . . kind of.

"He's going to build more of those things." Samila sighed. "And we'll be on scavenging duty until he's done."

"Hey, give me some credit!" I protested. "I was going to take on some interns."

Samila grinned wickedly. "We *are* at a school."

# CHAPTER FORTY-THREE

# Plumb My Depth

Not for the first time, I jolted awake before my hand could slip off my new project, the beginnings of a mana headache starting to flare behind my eyes. In fact, that was probably the thing that woke me in the first place. I reached over to the left side of my workbench to my stash of flammable materials and Consumed something.

I shook my head and concentrated. The mana levels in the construct were looking pretty good, positively overflowing with me-juice— Urgh, I needed better phrasing. Me-mana? Me-flavor? No, that sounded like a sports drink. Could I sell a me-flavored sports drink back home? Maybe. I really didn't want to be known as the sports drink Exotic, though.

My mind was wandering.

*Stop it. Focus. Just a little longer.*

I kept the mana flowing, intent clear in my mind, with an emphasis on what part of me to use.

For the thousandth time, I went over the messages again, calling up the section I wanted from last evening.

You have created: Magazine-Fed Auto-Turret
You have been awarded 2,500 Experience points. [2,500 base]

Automate Depth increasing. [3 of 3]
Automate Depth increased.

> Automate+: Program your creations with simple instructions and empower them to be extensions of your will. Strength, amount, and complexity of Abilities are dependent on your Spirit.

It went without saying that I'd not been blown away by my "Depth" increase when it happened. I'd just put the smart card in my fourth auto-turret when the message appeared in my vision in one of the weird pop-ups that I thought I'd eliminated a while back. On the surface, the Ability looked the same, did the same things, but I couldn't shake the feeling that I'd missed something.

The feeling lasted until I pulled up the original description of Automate from before. How long had it been? Months?

*Not important. Right. Focus time.*

The previous description read differently:

> Automate: Program your creations with simple instructions and empower them to carry out your orders independently. Strength, amount, and complexity of instructions are dependent on your Spirit.

The difference in verbiage wasn't huge, but it *was* different.

> Split Mind is now Level 7.

*Thanks, System. I know.*

I gave the bowl I was holding another full mana bar, practically having to force my eyes to stay open. I couldn't afford to have this fail because of a lack of mana. This really, really needed to work. I'd spent too much time on it already, and if I was wrong about this, the cost we would pay would be in time—time we didn't have.

The four turrets I'd already made over the past couple of days stood sentry against the far wall, watching me, judging me and silently saying: "You gambled and lost. Move on."

The new designs looked otherworldly, like predatory insects with their new fan-shaped magazines and wide-stanced, segmented legs.

Then again, everything looked otherworldly in here. When I'd told Angol about what I needed to get to work, he'd led me to what was, from how he described it, a practice room for newly minted practitioners.

It was, essentially, a barn-sized cube made of seamless, glossy, white glass, or perhaps a cousin of glass that had done hard time. It was tough stuff, tougher than anything I could throw at it at least, with steel-reinforced barriers set up symmetrically on either side of the room meant to shield from blasts or errant projectiles.

The lighting was what made everything seem weird, though. There was no source. The light simply *was*, everywhere and from every angle. Nothing had a shadow, giving everything a uniformly sinister dose of the uncanny.

Reluctantly, I let go of the metal bowl that had been the source of all my troubles for the past few hours.

*There. Screw it. If you don't have enough mana to do your job now, you're useless anyway.*

You have created: Prototype Casting Bowl
You have been awarded 2,400 Experience points. [800 base, +1,600 Doing Your Part bonus]

Well, at least the System recognized what I was doing.

I got up from my stool and walked over to the pile of scrap metal my interns had acquired for me. None of them majored in metallurgy, so the pile was generally sorted by color, with brass and bronze on one side while darker metals tended to make up the bulk of the middle. Then there were the shiny metals that merited their own pile to the side.

For my experiment, I chose something from the dark metals, taking a loose handful of the smaller bits and walking back over to the workbench from which I selected a furniture nail, smaller than the tip of my finger.

Then I threw it into the bowl and waited.

Nothing happened.

*Yay. Success.*

Nothing was supposed to happen, or, at least, nothing *visible* was supposed to happen, not with that amount of material. Sure, it would have been nice to have some kind of visual indicator of whether or not it was really working, but I was on iteration 0.1 here.

I added a handful of other metal scraps to the bowl, mixing them around with my hand before returning to watching and waiting.

This was the real test, do or die time.

"Come on. Please," I whispered.

"You've been alone too long if you've started talking to your Dominion, Monk," something behind me said.

My heart seized in my chest, and I immediately went into some kind of fight-or-flight mode.

I think my lizard brain wanted me to whip around and get into a fighting stance or maybe grab something and beat whatever had startled me over the head, but what actually ended up happening was I did all of those things out of order. I did the grabbing first—of my workbench, specifically. Then my body tried to whirl around to do the beating, but I was holding on to the surface of a table heavier than I was at the time, so, given my prosthetic's grip strength, I had no chance to dislodge it, and I didn't have the wherewithal to realize that.

The result was a pathetic flailing of my legs as my upper half jerked the workbench up off the ground and nearly tipped it over, my stool skittered across the floor to crash into the blast barrier behind me, and several loose tools I'd left next to my legs tripped me up and sent me down to the ground.

Sissa was there in the doorway, a plate of food in her hand, a cup of something steaming hot in the other, and on her face, the look of someone unsure if they should run in to help or just run away.

The dragonkin sergeant, brave as she was, chose the former option, but she did it slowly, gingerly stepping around the bits of wood and metal that littered my workshop floor to approach me like I was a wild animal.

She put down the food next to my hitherto-unused cot, then sat down on the edge, folding her hands to look me up and down appraisingly.

Her frown was not one of approval.

"Am I to assume your work is proceeding apace?" she asked dangerously.

I used my secure grip on the workbench to haul myself up, taking a second to smooth out my sweaty shirt and dress pants, all borrowed.

"Uh. Yes. Kind of. You know how it is, building superweapons in a school basement. It's got its highs and lows," I hedged, moving to position myself shamefully in front of the bowl.

"You know it's morning," Sissa said, her tone icy.

"I'd guessed something like that," I replied cautiously. "I've made some progress."

"The third morning."

"Oh," was all I could say.

"'Oh' is right," she replied.

That long. Why hadn't I requested a clock or an hourglass or something?

"I'm sorry. I'm working as fast as I can. The university didn't have everything I needed in the way of ammo, and I'm having to find a workaround. I'm so close, though," I explained, the words spilling out of me like liquid as surely as if I'd tipped Sissa's drink onto the floor.

Then I was babbling. "First, it was about making the turrets. That went fine, but then I was doing the math, and I had the students check for the rotating tables with the ball bearings, but I guess they aren't as popular in an academic setting with no need for stupid spinning coffee tables, so I had them taking apart anything that moved but all we came up with was nails and hooks, which don't work worth a damn especially with no manufacturing base on this stupid planet and nothing being the same size unless it's from the same artisan. Would it kill any of you guys to have a standard set of sizes? It would be so much easier if we had an assembly line or interchangeable parts. We'll have to invent that later. Whatever. So, here I am, having to skip the whole industrialization part of civilization, so that I can save it, and I've got to do it all before zero hour. I don't know. Maybe it'll work. Maybe it won't. I just know this is the way forward, but I don't know if we have the time for it to begin with."

I took a breath, ready to go on, but Sissa's face shut me up. She didn't look angry anymore. She looked worried. She leaned forward, one hand tentatively reaching out, but she hesitated and, instead, bent down to pick up the cup.

"Ryan," she began. No title. That was kind of nice. It was nice to be Just Ryan again. Then she went and ruined it. "You need to eat and sleep."

"Uh. Yeah. Of course," I said. I did know. Eating and sleeping were both on my list, just not at the top.

She raised a disbelieving eyebrow. "So, you realize how . . . stretched you seem?"

"Of course. I just have this little problem to solve before I sleep. Please tell me that's coffee. I'll run down to the cafeteria and buy them out now if that's coffee." I knew I was speaking too fast, probably sounding like I was overcompensating. It didn't matter, though. *Was* that coffee?

"What is coffee?" Sissa asked.

A long, disappointed, mournful sigh escaped my mouth. "Something I miss," I lamented. "My mom liked it, and I got a taste for it. It's fine, though. I just have this one thing to do, and then I'll get some sleep."

"Your helpers talk, and the stories aren't flattering. You're going to fall asleep on your feet or have a heart attack if you continue like this."

Could I have a heart attack anymore? Probably not. That part of me was a magical mystery machine now. If anything were to happen to it, I'd probably just explode or catch fire.

My mouth kept moving despite my brain not being fully engaged. "Okay. Fine. Thanks for the concern, but I can sleep when I'm dead. Seriously, I know what this looks like. I just don't think I could rest until I know."

"Know what?" she asked.

"If I've made the right decision, Sergeant Sissa."

She made a placating motion with her hand. "Just Sissa, please."

No titles for her, either. Also nice.

"Sorry, uh—Sissa. I can't stop working until I've solved a big problem. If I don't solve it, the plan is scrapped."

"It also won't get solved if you work yourself to death, Ryan." The fire was back in her voice. She wasn't particularly pleased with how I was treating myself, and on an intellectual level I understood that. I just couldn't afford to do this any differently. Not with the stakes as they were.

"I'm not sure if that's possible anymore. I need to know if this works. It's the only way. If it doesn't, it's going to . . . I'm going to—"

"*We'll* just be back in the same situation *we* started in and come up with a new plan," she said forcefully. "You don't have to carry the weight of the entire world on your shoulders, Ryan."

Her face grew pensive, her eyes staring at something far away. "Light and gods of old, listen to me. I sound like my sister. Listen. I get it. You have a part to play, and it's life or death. You pick up the responsibility and you can't put it down. Then you pick up more. But soon, if you're not careful, you'll be holding it all, even if it's not yours to hold."

To hear someone else describe it like that . . . To understand what I'm going through . . . To say I wasn't alone . . . It both warmed my heart and saddened me profoundly. It wasn't lost on me that she offered no advice on how to do it right. Maybe we were both figuring things out as we went along.

Then a wave of exhaustion hit me.

I took a deep, shuddering breath, closing my eyes deliberately for the first time in recent memory. They almost didn't open again.

"So," Sissa began, softening her tone somewhat as she got up and leaned companionably on the table right next to me. "What problem are we solving?"

"The ammunition problem," I replied with a shake of my head. "You guys have no standardized parts for anything. It's all handmade. If we're going to get the most bang for our buck, all the ammunition needs to be alike."

She bit her lip as she considered the problem I was posing. "I follow you so far. Arrowheads are the same way. The guard tries to have them made uniformly, though they vary slightly depending on where you get them."

"Exactly," I said, tilting my head to indicate the bowl on the table. "What I'm trying to do here is make a—"

I spun around to face the bowl and stopped speaking. I even stopped breathing.

Then I started laughing maniacally.

Sissa spun around as well, her hand drifting to her sword, scanning the table for what had clearly broken my sanity. "What? What is it?"

I was still laughing. While I'd been talking to the nice blue girl with the golden eyes and fierce protective instincts, my new creation had been working unobserved.

There, in the bottom of the bowl, two identically shaped conical bullets wobbled against one another while little blobs of excess metal laid off to the side.

*My constructs can use my Abilities! Hot damn.*

The words burst out of me like an alien parasite. "This motherfucker can SHAPE!" I shrieked excitedly.

"I don't understand. Ryan, are you okay?" she asked, grabbing my shoulders and trying to get me to meet her eyes. My mind was going a mile a minute.

My stuff could make stuff! My stuff could make stuff that could make stuff!

I wasn't Magneto so much as I was . . . I couldn't conjure up any appropriate supervillains to reference. Dr. Robotnik? No, he put animals in machines. That was a level of weird I wasn't interested in exploring. Although . . .

*No. Just no.*

Now it was all about how much I could Automate before we needed to move on my plan. The more ammo we had, the better, but the people of Eclipse wouldn't hold out much longer.

I hadn't overpromised as I'd feared. I could still do this.

Relief washed over me, so intense my eyes stung with tears. I turned away so Sissa couldn't see.

"Ryan, talk to me. What's going on?" she asked as she finally caught my eye.

"We just automated ammo production, Sissa," I said shakily, my excitement bubbling up from within. "The equation just changed again."

"That's great, I guess!" she exclaimed, picking up on my feelings but not entirely able to understand.

It *was* great. Better than great.

I don't know why I did it. I was feeling giddy and drunk on victory with no sleep or food in Constance knew how long.

It was stupid and inappropriate, but I wasn't thinking.

I bent down, grabbed the dragon woman around the waist, and spun us both around like I'd seen people do at dances back home. She felt lighter than I expected. Delicate. I held her up high and twirled. We went around once, twice before we stopped, her borrowed robes flowing down over my arms and brushing my cheek.

I held her up in the air for a half-second that seemed to stretch into forever.

She stared down at me, her yellow eyes frighteningly large, her lips slightly parted, her body tensed for . . . something, like she wasn't sure if she wanted to claw out my eyes or go around again.

Then my brain caught up with my body and I put her down, remembering to breathe again and meticulously fixing my already fixed shirt. My eyes were drawn to everything in the workshop except for her.

"Yeah. Um. Sorry. Anyway. Now that I know it works, I can make ammo in my sleep. It's a—uh—it's kind of a big deal for me. Maybe for everyone."

Sissa stood statue-still, silent. I could see it from the corner of my eye, sense it somehow: I'd done something wrong.

I did my best to straighten up my work area, getting the alignment of my tin snips exactly right-angled to the edge of the table. You've got to align your tin snips properly, or the entire setup collapses into chaos. Chaos was a mechanic's natural enemy.

I didn't see her leave, but her retreating footsteps sounded stiff and robotic, echoing against the practice room walls.

Once she was gone, I ran my nails roughly through my new hair.

Why did I do that, especially to someone who valued being in control as much as Sissa did?

Well, I certainly wasn't going to sleep now. I grabbed another cooking bowl and began work on Casting Bowl number two.

I woke to the sound of hard rain—intermittent, staccato plops and snaps of fat drops slapping metal. It was a familiar sound, reminding me of my family's hab, when the whipping ice and airborne pebbles of Proxis's winds popped and panged off the walls.

I rolled out of my cot, reaching down to the floor to grab my grimy shirt, but before I could put it on, I realized why I'd awakened.

A blue dragonkin woman was perched atop my stool, but not the one I'd feared it would be.

Samila sat there, a plate of food next to her on my workbench, another one of those steaming cups of tea next to it.

"Good morning!" she shouted over the noise. The rain was far too loud to converse any other way.

I shook my head, pulled myself into an upright position, and rubbed the sleep out of my eyes.

*No, not rain.*

I looked to my left.

Along the wall, on a shelf I'd had my interns bring in last night sat five casting bowls, set snuggly into the wood in freshly cut circular holes. Heaping piles of metal debris, from nails to dresser handles to curtain rods, were piled on top of the bowls to the point that I worried the shelf might collapse under the weight.

As I watched, one by one, the bottom of each bowl formed an opening through which a newly Shaped bullet fell through to land on a canted sheet of tin with an ear grating *clack*. The bowed tin sheet, angled as it was, funneled the fresh, rolling nubs of metal ammunition downward until they tumbled into a wooden rain barrel, which was now full to the brim and then some. The trickle of bullets hit the top of the pile before rolling off and clattering to the floor.

I really needed to empty that out.

*Next on the list, get the interns to load the magazines and get a second barrel.*

I looked back to Samila, a self-satisfied smile playing across my face. Ralqir just got its first factory.

She didn't look impressed. She said . . . something, maybe asked a question, which was hard to hear over everything else.

What was on the agenda next? Tightening fittings for the deployable turrets, for sure. Definitely needed to fix the janky tracking on the big guns. Both important. Both dangerous if unaddressed.

Motion . . . Oh, yes. *Samila.*

The dragonkin hopped down from the stool and held out the food and drink. The tea smelled like the bitter stuff I'd had yesterday—effective but so far from the coffee I craved, it practically made me weep.

She said something else, but I lost it to the combination of white noise and full brain. I tried to smile and nod, but she wasn't buying it. Instead, she crouched down in front of me, plate and cup in hand, tilting her head as if she expected a real response.

I did have the wherewithal to accept the food and put it down on the cot next to me, finally taking the time to find the correct orientation for my shirt to slip it over my head.

But then my shirt was gone.

Samila, quick as a snake, had snatched it away and was yards from me before I could even react. Reflexively, I tried to dive after her and make a grab for the shirt, but she held it out so that I couldn't grasp it without going through her. My reach was longer than hers, though, and I ended up with a hand on the prize, fighting for control.

Then the encounter changed gears. Samila's posture changed. She leaned in, one hand against my chest, the other behind her, slowly bending her arm to bring my shirt and—through our connection—my hand to the small of her back. Then she was up against me, close, her face nearly touching mine, the contested shirt and my arm firmly affixed to her waist.

I froze. I imagine I came across as quite deerlike in that moment, more so than any Miur I'd met so far.

She was still wearing that little smile she favored—the one that told you she knew something you didn't.

Samila's hand slowly slid up from my chest to wrap around the back of my neck. She drew me close and put her lips next to my ear.

"Can you hear me now?" she said in a low voice. My hair, such as it was, stood on end.

I simply nodded, slowly, afraid to move more than that.

"Good," she purred with some satisfaction. "You look like hell. You need a shower and a change of clothes. Take your food with you."

And just like that, the room had oxygen again.

I pulled back. I had the shirt now, possession fully established. Samila was already sauntering away, somehow making her oversized robes *sway* with her hips. It was her turn to have a self-satisfied smile on her face.

Then my train of thought finally pulled into the station. What had she said?

I brought the shirt to my nose for a sniff test and immediately regretted it. My body, I was just noticing, wasn't much better.

"Monk!" Samila shouted from the doorway.

I looked up. She was leaning on the doorjamb. This time, her smile was conspicuously absent.

"Tomorrow morning! Clean and well-rested!"

That was it. There was nothing else to be done.

I was out of time.

# CHAPTER FORTY-FOUR

# Alter the Plan

I still don't understand why we aren't going together," Trix complained from his perch atop the speaker's lectern as the guards and I strapped on our armor. "We have faced danger such as this before, and we work well as a group. There's no reason we should be split up."

I struggled with the strap to one of my oversized leg guards. It was tough, dark leather stuff, thick and unbending, the straps a horrible combination of tri-way buckles, ties, and other weirdness I couldn't wrap my brain around. The young Leori I'd borrowed the set from said she'd never worn it, but her father insisted she have it in case she met a "good hunting mate" while she was away at university. She actually seemed pretty happy to get rid of it.

Geddon seemed to think it was good stuff, at least, saying he had one like it tucked away somewhere. Apparently, lots of sets such as this were passed to Leori kids when they went out on their own.

"For one," I began as I tried to cinch a couple of more inches of play out of the straps, "this plan is a Hail Mary, a big, stupid ploy for a similarly big, stupid situation. It's got a lot of moving parts, and it requires more than one group to get done."

"We could ask willing students for their help," Geddon suggested, but it was half-hearted.

I shook my head.

We'd exhausted this topic long ago.

The students had their parts to play, but it wouldn't be out there. They'd been left behind for a reason and a good one. None of them had fought before, much less under life-threatening pressure. I tried not to remind myself that, before a few months ago, I would have been one of them. On some significant level I still was.

We were lucky enough to have some of the students on our side here. The few guards we saw aboveground wanted us quarantined, and that was the only word they were willing to give before they went back down below and made us someone else's problem. Most of the student body were content to follow their orders, but Angol's contingent knew the score better than most, choosing to cover for us in hopes we'd change things for the better.

Trix looked unconvinced. He sprang from his perch, bounded over to the first row of seats on the observation deck and stood to his full height to look me in the eye. "I could go with you, Brother Ryan. I can be your eyes and ears again, and I can help us avoid undue attention. You know I can. We can put Angol here at my post."

"I need you here, Trix," I insisted. "You're going to be our ace in the hole. Once things start to move, and we get into trouble, you're going to be the one to bail us out. Just remem—"

"Yes. Yes, I know. You've told me many times now. Flip the switch on the turret up here once our people get into the square."

I made a "go on" gesture with my hand. Apparently those were universal whereas thumbs-up were not. Ralqir was a silly place.

Trix hesitated, thinking, but then he recalled the rest. "And have my helpers constantly load the magazines and feed the turret ammunition."

"Good," I replied with a nod. "One correction. It's a gun emplacement, not a turret."

"Semantics. What concerns me is that you are leaving me behind and yourself exposed for no good reason. You'll understand if I interpret this as you keeping me out of the real fight, Brother," Trix said bitterly. "Because it does exactly that."

"It's not like that, buddy," I insisted. "I need a real person doing the aiming this time. I'm afraid the targeting logic on these things isn't really up to life-or-death decision-making, especially when you're giving cover to a big group of friendlies. You're the brain on this one, Trix. You can make the tough decisions. We *need* you up here."

"Not all fighting is done with a sword and shield, Brother Trix. You are our position of strength. Do not forget," Sissa added earnestly. She was already strapped and helping her sister into her set, but she was paying great attention to everyone else. Her game face was on.

Defeated, Trix made a show of standing a little taller. "Very well then. I'll just have to do my best and hope I'm not right."

"Did I ever tell you the story of how I once fired a ballista by hand? It was only through my prodigious strength and steady hand that I—" Geddon began. We all knew this story. He knew we all knew this story. He was just trying to lighten the mood, and we knew that, too.

My eyes shot over to the gun emplacement, a double-barreled monster I'd cobbled together out of piping I'd appropriated from the school's irrigation network. I'd reinforced them, thickening them until the action was about as wide as my wrist, while the barrels were longer than I was tall.

A wheelbarrow-sized seat (because I'd made it from a wheelbarrow) was welded to the side of the joint housing with a crude pilot's stick jammed in the middle that sent signals to the aiming arms when it was moved.

"Just watch where you aim the thing," I warned him. "It's got lots of firepower and very little precision at this distance." My recoil suppression system was the opposite of sophisticated, just a locking pin that kept the ball joints still when the trigger was depressed. Another reason I didn't trust the aiming system to not do its thing once the action kicked off. Better to have someone cautious like Trix than trust the cold logic my turrets used.

"Angol, is your door team ready?" I asked.

The young Miur nodded, turning to his friends behind him. There were around a dozen of them, many looking decidedly wrung-out. I'd had them up a lot of the night loading magazines and feeding scrap to my casting bowls, not that I'd been fully spared that myself. I had to get up a couple of times during the night to recharge the things.

"Yes. When I get the signal, we'll start clearing the door and getting ready to receive people," Angol declared.

"Good. Rescue team? How are you doing?"

"Worry about your own part in this, Monk," Samila grunted as she hefted a webbing backpack up onto her shoulders. The barrel of the turret inside stuck diagonally past her shoulder and above her head. "Could you have made them any heavier? Hrmf. Or more awkward? I have a metal knob up against my kidney."

"Uh. Yeah. Sorry. Still working on that kind of thing. Maybe in the next version."

"Easy for you to say that when you can just magic stuff out of thin air," she growled.

"Not too bad for me," Geddon quipped with a cheeky grin, hefting his pack up onto his shoulders with a single hand. "As long as I don't have to run, I'll gladly carry five of these."

Sissa looked at me and frowned. "You could come with us, you know."

I was tempted. I really was. It would be nice to have some backup out there, someone I could trust. It wasn't possible, though. "Too risky. If they recognize me, I'll bring down all sorts of hell upon myself. Easier for me to skulk around for the setup. Don't worry. I'll be around."

"You better be," Sissa replied with a simultaneous slap on my chest. Her gauntlet rang off the metal where my heart should be. "Like I said. No one gets to die without my say-so."

We moved in the darkness of the early morning, not that it was ever truly dark in Eclipse. The moon, huge and wreathed in flaring auroras as it was, always shed some light on the city. Today was close enough, though. Cloud cover smothered the moon in gray, while brilliant shafts of otherworldly color stabbed down through the thinnest parts of the fog to illuminate the odd block or part of the glade outside the walls.

The Returned could see in the dark better than any of us, other than maybe Trix, but, as we'd observed from the Spire, the Undead didn't make up the entirety of the Scourge-Touched swarm. Maybe a few of them had crappy night vision like me or even worse. Sissa was counting on it being a factor, at least.

We lowered ourselves down on a rope from the Spire's north side, a balcony built on top of one of the big gates they'd added to the building's architecture to make the place more welcoming to people that wanted to visit the observatory. It was the lowest, safest spot on the Spire, but that didn't mean it was that low. We still had to be lowered about fifty feet before we had the ground safely beneath us.

I was the last to go, by necessity. I was wearing a hood and a cloth face mask, but I didn't really know how the Scourge-Touched recognized their prey. If I went down there before it was time and tripped the alarm, the whole game would be over before it began.

"Good luck," Angol whispered to me as he nodded to the others on the rope line. Then they started to lower me down.

As my feet hit the pavers, Geddon helped me out of the harness. Then we tugged on the rope to get Angol and his people to pull the thing up again.

From this point, we were on our own.

The rescue team and I nodded to each other before going our separate ways. Sissa and Samila looked cold, stern, and professional, while Geddon just grinned like . . . well, *Geddon*.

For my part, my stomach was doing backflips and handstands. This was my plan, my gear, my friends on the line.

Suddenly, now that I was down here, I didn't feel so sure anymore.

What the hell was I doing? Six months ago, I had been fixing wheels on farm equipment. I hadn't been a warrior or even a monk or even a fighter. If not for my fake title, nobody would even give my ideas the time of day. I was going to get these people killed.

It was too late to back out, though. Sissa, Samila, and Geddon were already moving, loping to the far edge of the square, staying low and in shadow.

The square around the Spire was big and open, like no one really wanted to build anywhere near the footprint of the thing, leaving the University practitioners to do their thing while the normal folks just got on with their lives elsewhere. That left anyone wandering around in the square exposed. That worked both ways, however.

I saw dark shapes out there sniffing the air and pawing at loose debris. There weren't a lot of them—just enough to make you realize you weren't truly alone, a thin-enough crowd to avoid being within spitting distance. Not all of them were the lanky, misshapen forms of the Returned. I could also see packs of smaller shapes skittering over the square on all fours, gibbering that way I was so familiar with. It had been a while, but I recognized the Baned easily. We'd been roommates for a while, after all.

I crouched low and started toward the edge of the square to the east, aiming for where I saw the fewest roaming figures. Quick and quiet, I crept from pile of debris to pile of debris, stopping to watch and listen before setting out again. Nothing saw me or paid me any mind. Was this Gray Man at work? Impossible to know.

The edge of the square was tantalizingly close when I suffered my first setback. I slid behind a row of stone planters in front of the building I was aiming for when I heard something chewing. At least that's what I thought it was. Wet, ripping sounds assaulted my ears, followed by crunches and the smacking of lips, slow and methodical.

I was forced to double back and try a different way.

Stealth is now Level 12.

Upon leaving the square, I went west, crossing one of the canal bridges to come to the correct street, another one of the combination market/residential strips where the buildings were built too close together and signs clogged up the sky.

We chose this particular street for our plan thanks to how wide it was and its generally long sightlines. None of the streets in Eclipse were truly straight, but the city planners had some kind of vision when they paved this one. For its entire length running all the way to the western gates, it had all of two turns, both under thirty degrees or so. What's more, the Western Gate was noticeably higher in altitude than the rest of the city, giving the road a general slope that led it down through multiple neighborhoods, over three canals, and all the way to the Spire.

I chose one of the shops at random, one of the four-story ones whose door hung off its hinges. As with the other shops I'd been inside, the stairs were right next to the entrance.

*   *   *

Hopping from roof to roof was slow and physically taxing, made more so since I was concerned about noise. So, it took me half an hour to get to the first turn where the two straight parts of the road met at a corner. One last jump and I was on top of a tavern, the roof of which was a seating area with big circular tables, a miniature bar, and a wooden awning overhead covered in ivy that kept the whole place in perpetual shade. It looked posh, like people would come up here to sip on expensive cocktails and stare imperiously down at the crowd below.

*Perfect.*

I squatted down in the shadows and listened for a full minute before I got to work.

Snarls in the distance. Swords clattering. A howl from somewhere to the north. None of it was near me.

I summoned my first turret of the night in pieces, barrel first, then the action, then the legs.

Quietly as I could, I slipped the action onto the leg housing, then the barrel into the action before Shape-welding them together. Last, I summoned one of my new, fan-shaped magazines. The "fan" was pretty much a row of separate three-foot-long, spring-loaded tubes that shoved my manufactured bullets into the bolt with such force I wasn't comfortable handling the springs barehanded. I'd Shaped them inside the tube instead.

The idea was that, once one tube was out of bullets, a charged plate at the bottom of the magazine would touch the action, which would then rotate itself clockwise to align with the next tube's opening with little or no downtime. The entire fan held about nine hundred rounds.

Next, I secured the turret's legs to the floor of the building's deck with sandbags, again summoned from my Spatial Storage. The legs were wide and heavy, but I was still worried about the recoil moving the whole turret around during the fight. Better safe than sorry.

When I was done, my predatory insect automaton was staring over the wide street, covering two separate lines of sight, one directly to the Spire, the other going as far down the road as the next canal.

*One down.*

I repeated the process three more times, focusing most of my firepower on the corners of the street where the turret could cover multiple angles at once. The only exception was the bridge that connected this neighborhood to the gate district. That bridge *needed* to stay clear. My final emplacement was set up there, its field of fire concentrated so that it could aim only at or directly around the bridge.

*Four. Phase One done.*

I checked the sky. I needed to hurry.

Sissa would probably murder me for what I had planned for Phase Two.

*Time to step in front of another arrow.*

* * *

I arrived on the roof of a marble building on the edge of Spire Square, nearly back where I'd started, except I was to the north of the Spire this time, on top of some kind of administration building. It was grand in size but almost brutally utilitarian in construction, with great marble blocks holding up great marble columns holding up a great big marble slab that made up the roof, the only access to which was a stairway secured by a singular storm door I'd Shaped open to get up here.

Tilting my head and holding up my thumb, I looked up to the observation deck where Trix would be sitting in his gunner's seat. The deck was still in shadow, but I thought I could almost make out the big barrels jutting out of the side of the railing. I wanted to wave to see if he was watching and that he remembered what we'd discussed, but I didn't dare.

It didn't matter anyway. What mattered was that he was able to see me from where he was. He was the only other who knew this part of the plan.

The way I imagined it, the rescue team would be arriving at the Western Gate right about now. There would be a sea of Scourge-Touched there, surrounding a knot of beleaguered and wounded soldiers and guards, tired from days of non-stop fighting. Samila and Geddon would set up their turrets, get themselves ready, and pull the levers to begin the assault. The guns would fire up, the guards would cut the enemy down, and the two forces would meet.

From there, I could see it playing out in my mind:

They try to get everyone moving, but the soldiers won't leave without their wounded. The wounded have to be helped or carried.

Everyone is already tired. The line bogs down. The turrets either run dry on ammo or are destroyed. Then they are all trapped together, but now they've taken more losses. The end is inevitable.

A handful of pop guns wasn't going to turn the tide in the way everyone hoped.

But me. I could do that.

I plopped down on the southernmost part of the roof, closest to the Spire, and summoned the rest of my turrets, three of them. Then I went through the process of assembling them and anchoring them in a wide triangular formation around myself.

The roof had a sort of lip that was maybe a foot tall, preventing the turrets from seeing down below and into Spire Square.

That sucked. I hadn't seen the lip from up above. That meant my turrets couldn't get a good angle on targets as they approached the building and would need to engage as the baddies climbed up onto the roof. Dangerously close stuff. I'd just have to roll with it.

I summoned my extra magazines, laying them out in a line.

Then I looked to the horizon—to the west this time, where my friends should be. They should have engaged by now.

*Trust.*

I summoned my emergency pile of wood, pungent with the oil I'd soaked it in.

I summoned my pistol, checked to make sure it was loaded and ready before sticking it in my belt.

Finally, I summoned my sword.

My stupid, weak, fleshy hand trembled as it gripped the hilt.

The sword was a simple thing—a blade of Shaped steel with a handle of wrapped leather cords, long enough to be held with one or two hands, pointy at the end, sharp as could be on the edges.

Holding it, though, wasn't so simple for me. I'd not held one of these since I was a kid, before the accident. Before I'd been broken and cast aside by nearly everyone I knew.

If Dad saw this, he'd probably be ecstatic. His Exotic son was taking up the sword again. "By a miracle of Constance, the System fixed my boy," the Clan chief would say in his heart of hearts.

He wouldn't cry. He was too stoic for that. He would just see it as the world going back to the way it was supposed to be, his son back to being a proper warrior of Constance.

How nice that would have been for him. He could pretend like the accident never happened.

*Like I'd never been broken. Like Mom had died alone.*

The thought of throwing the sword over the rail flashed through my mind.

If it all went well, I wouldn't even have to use it anyway. I could get by without. I didn't need to be their perfect warrior. I *never* needed to be perfect. I'd done so much already without their precious rules and traditions, without their help or training and despite their scorn.

It took everything I had not to at least put the sword away where I didn't have to see it. I couldn't get rid of a tool like this, though. Not now. That would be foolish, and too many people depended on me. I had to bring everything to this fight.

My new life didn't afford me the luxury of casting aside my past. Whether I accepted it or not, the accident happened, my exile happened, and despite what the Clan thought, that didn't make me any less worthy to carry on my family's legacy.

Becoming an Exotic didn't *fix* me.

*Say it. Mean it.*

"I'm not broken," I proclaimed. The words, long in my heart but never spoken aloud, felt right. The chord they struck resonated within me. My heart thrummed. My trembling hand gripped my weapon tightly.

Somewhere, far to the west, distinct eruptions of gunfire—too rapid and numerous to count—began to echo over the roofs of the city. There was no slow ramping up to full intensity, no hesitation. The turrets were going, immediately, full-bore.

Scourge-Touched Goblin defeated.
You have been awarded 10 Experience points. [10 base (-4 Level, +2 nemesis, +10 group, -8 non-combat Class)]
Scourge-Touched Goblin defeated.
You have been awarded 12 Experience points. [10 base (-4 Level, +2 nemesis, +10 group,+2 chain, -8 non-combat Class)]
Scourge-Touched Undead defeated.
You have been awarded 25 Experience points. [16 base (-2 Level, +2 nemesis, +16 group, +6 chain, -13 non-combat Class)]

. . .

It had begun.

"I was *never* broken," I whispered softly but firmly.

I closed my eyes and took a deep, cleansing breath. I forced myself to relax, to concentrate, to bring the entirety of my being into the present where I was needed. I brought my surroundings and myself kicking and screaming into hyper focus.

My enemy didn't know it yet, but I was done being hunted. Done hiding. Today, I was the predator, and I was going to exact a cost for everything they'd done.

Mentally, I flicked the Volatility detonation switch I'd been holding in my mind. The three turrets on my roof jerked to life, their barrels standing at attention and scanning for targets. Far away, on the westbound street and next to the canal bridge, my other turrets simultaneously powered on and immediately added to the crackling peels of thunder in little fits and starts as they set about clearing the way for my friends.

I gripped my sword and made my way over to the lip of the roof, placing one defiant foot up on the rail and standing tall. Strangely, the dark shapes down below seemed to pause all at once, hesitant, one by one turning their heads to look my way as I ripped off my hood and mask.

I filled my lungs with the cold morning air, lifted my chin and roared:

"Come on, you little shits! I'm right here!"

# CHAPTER FORTY-FIVE

# Turret Mage

The entire city howled.

It wasn't just in my immediate area, though the distinctive, mindless scream of the Scourge-Touched did come through clearest from nearby. No, this was *everywhere*. It was like a demonic choir conductor had just swiped his baton. Every creature in every part of the city contributed to the chord, perfectly in sync, baying for my blood.

I fought to not let the unease I was feeling show.

This wasn't quite what I expected. I'd expected the howling, maybe a chain of them starting from ground zero where I was and making its way outward and around the city eventually, but this . . .

The Scourge-Touched went into a fit at exactly the same time.

Then it hit me. That's why I'd never seen them communicate.

*A hive mind? Maybe something like it?*

If that was the case, I'd just given every Scourge-Touched in the city (maybe the world) my exact location. I'd counted on getting a lot of attention, but I'd hoped the horde of flesh-eating monsters would at least have to ask for directions before they got here.

I stepped back from the marble lip and walked into the middle of my triangular turret perimeter, my sword clenched tightly in my hand.

*Well, the idea was to create a distraction. Well, done there.*

I didn't have to wait long.

Soon enough, claws raked across the inside of the metal stairwell doors. A single Scourge-Touched wasn't going to get those open, though. I'd Shape-welded them shut in multiple places, even freezing the hinges.

The murderous bastards would have to come up the fun way if they wanted to turn my face into a loincloth.

My first lucky customer on this fine gray morning was a Scourge-Touched goblin who'd elected to climb the building's facade instead of taking the stairs. Sharp, grasping claws preceded a dark, leering face with owlish eyes and a demonic grin as it pulled itself up into view, eager to be the first to take a bite out of this world's only human.

It was barely able to get its shoulders above the lip of my roof before—
*BRRAP!*

---

Scourge-Touched Goblin defeated.
You have been awarded 20 Experience points. [10 base (-4 Level, +2 nemesis, +10 group,+10 chain, -8 non-combat Class)]

---

For being the first, it was rewarded with a quick death. The turret on my left tracked almost too quickly for the naked eye and put two, maybe three rounds into the monster's face. Then said face was gone as quickly as it had appeared. If not for the leftover chunks of skull still sailing backward in sedate parabolas down into Spire Square, I might have thought I'd imagined the whole thing.

Then they came in little fits and starts. Two or three creatures (not always goblins, but they were the most prevalent) would climb up the sides of the roof at the same time only to be cut down in a hail of gunfire.

*BRAP! BRAP!*

The targeting on the turrets was flawless, if I do say so myself. With actual rifling on the inside of their barrels and properly shaped projectiles, their accuracy was a thing to behold. Nothing survived the first volley, and sometimes a burst of fire would take out two or three targets at once. The monsters skittered forward and were cut down within seconds, their bodies becoming new obstacles for their comrades to overcome.

Meanwhile, the doors to the stairwell were quickly becoming popular. They groaned under the pressure of the growing number of bodies pressing against them all at once. Claws raked over their insides and powerful blows rained down on wherever the creatures could reach. I was under no illusions that the doors could hold forever, though. In minutes I'd probably have lots of company.

The Experience points were flowing in too quickly to keep track, the group and chain bonuses to Experience already at their max. Individually, these monsters were worth a pittance, but together, as a horde, they were going to put me through Exotic University, if that was a thing.

Not all of the messages were coming from my rooftop, either. The gunfire on the wind had ceased to be discernible as separate emplacements as various locations found and engaged targets. Judging by the sound, it was a storm of lead over there across town. I silently hoped my people were doing alright.

The relative calm on my end didn't last. I was busy supervising my turrets as they cut down the steady trickle of climbers and watching the Experience notifications roll in when the turret directly behind me—the hitherto-silent one that was supposed to cover the stairwell doors—let loose with a long peel of thunder.

I whipped my head around. Somehow, the creatures had found a way onto the roof that wasn't within the turret's line of fire. They'd come up behind the boxy stairwell housing, using it as cover to gather and build up sufficient numbers for a charge.

By the time I was aware of the problem, the turret had already cut down a handful of them, its withering fire reducing their bodies to mewling, broken piles of flesh and bone, but there were still five able-bodied Baned left, coming on at full speed.

My turret raked its fire across the line of them. Two of them went down with multiple holes in their sternums and a third caught an unlucky round on the crown of its skull, splitting it open while the creature tumbled forward to dash what was left of its brain on the dusty marble of the roof.

The other two took to the air, doing that grasshopper jump thing that almost ended me on my first day as an Exotic. They sailed over the turret as their comrades died, already past where the gun was programmed to track.

I didn't really have time to think. Before they had a chance to land, I found myself rushing forward to meet them, a silent war cry on my lips. The tip of my sword took the first goblin right above the collar bone, sliding inside with a nearly inaudible pop as the blade broke the skin.

There was absolutely no resistance. I'd made the edge sharp at the molecular level. The sword entered the creature at a near-vertical angle, going down through the soft flesh and into the lungs. The creature's momentum dragged my blade down, but Dad had taught me well. I flexed at the knees and sprang back to disengage, my weapon retracting before the goblin's body weight could bind the blade up.

On instinct, I brought my sword around in a quick slash to counter the attack I suspected was coming from my left, and the Baned that had just been about to cut my hamstring lost two fingers. It reeled back, not out of fear or pain but to tense its legs and go for another jump.

I advanced before it could right itself, however, reaching in with my prosthetic left hand and wrapping my fingers around the thing's face so that when its legs finally received the proper nerve signals to make the jump, all they did was push my stupidly heavy, enhanced body back an inch or so. I saw its black eyes widen through my metal fingers. Its feet kicked at me, and its claws dug into the sleeve of my armor.

Devouring Grasp [5 MP/sec]
Status gained: Engine [+2 MP/sec for 5 min]
You gain knowledge of material: Goblin Bone [19/50]

I let the ruined monster drop to my feet, feeling a cold wash of adrenaline run through me. My grip on the sword was shaky once more.

Skill Unlocked: Sword
Your current Skill Level is 1.

The three turrets around me were tracking targets every couple of seconds now. Packs of snarling faces would pop up from the lip of the roof—some attempting to sprint toward my position, some electing to leap as their more successful fellows had. Not many of them made the trip intact, but they were making it.

*So many.*

And this was just the beginning.

I was already seeing spots, and my heart was going a mile a minute. I had to force myself to move, force my legs to take me where I needed to go. The sword knew what it was about, though. Those Scourge-Touched that ended up inside my perimeter died as quickly as I could reach them.

*Their fault for not bringing their own swords, really.*

You are now Level 12.
Max HP +10
Max MP +10
+1 Attribute point.

Achievements awarded this Level:
S—

I killed the Combat Log. I didn't have time to read it. There was too much going on, too much at stake.

The three turrets barked.

*BRRRRRRAP! BRAP! BRAP!*

The Scourge-Touched never stopped. They died by the dozens, but not all of them charged in mindlessly.

Clumps of them were forming on the lip of the roof now, hanging from the side with their sharp claws, peeking over their cover from time to time to tempt the turrets. The targeting logic wasn't handling that particularly well.

*BRRRRRRRRRAP!*

Chunks of marble spun off into the morning air as the turrets tried to engage with all they saw, but maybe one in three bullets found flesh.

The Baned were adapting. They weren't just coming straight on anymore. They were clumping together and getting ready for a charge.

They were starting to *think*.

*No. We can't have that.*

I sheathed my sword and summoned a nicely shaped throwing rock from my Spatial Storage.

---

Volatility [1 MP/sec]

---

One. Two. Three. Four. Five . . .

I'd need to time this.

That's when the doors to the stairwell finally failed, and not at the welds as I'd expected. The hinges gave way with sharp, individual cracks that sent dust pluming out into the air. Then the doors blew off their hinges and slammed onto the marble floor with a muffled clang.

Snarling, pale Returned bodies spilled out from the now-open doorway, while more of them bubbled up from underneath, shoving their way into the open through a sea of flesh.

They'd been stacked like cordwood in there.

Just as the Returned contingent joined the fight, the goblins made their move as if they'd planned it this way. With their long, powerful arms and muscular legs they sprung up from their perches on the roof's lip, and suddenly I was facing a towering wave of howling monsters.

The turrets opened up on full blast. Sound lost all meaning for me. My world was the ceaseless peel-crack of the guns. The air shook with the violence of it.

I hadn't counted on this. I didn't expect them to change tactics. I was going to need my sword, but here I was holding an exploding purple rock.

After a short, preparatory roll of my shoulder, I chucked said rock into the roiling cauldron of the Undead, as far into the stairwell as I could.

*BOOM!*

Bright purple flashed from within; the walls that once housed the doors cracked and then buckled as what my explosion had started, the weight of the Returned's bodies finished. The stairwell housing collapsed like a tiny building undergoing demolition.

I stopped. Blinked. I hadn't expected that to work so well.

Sure, it wouldn't hold them forever, but it would keep them back for a moment or two.

Meanwhile, the Scourge-Touched made their move. They loped along the ground, bounded into the air, scrambled over their fellows: a tide of black eyes, sharp teeth, and wicked claws.

The barrels of my turrets spewed death. There was no gap between volleys anymore. An unending torrent of lead (and a few other heavy metals) tore into the wall of monsters, pierced them and tore open their backs, then entered those unlucky enough to be directly behind.

BRRRRRP! BRRP! *BRRRP!*

Black aerosolized blood or whatever the Scourge had in its place misted against my face, filled my nostrils and coated the back of my throat. I fought not to gag.

The turrets, arguably, had it worse—the blood mist sizzled against the super-heated metal of the barrels, while chunks of pulverized meat and bone slapped against their legs as they engaged the horde at close range.

Yet, the Scourge came on. Too many.

Perimeter breaches quickly became the norm.

The sword was out again, whatever finesse I'd remembered to employ when I was fresh was quickly forgotten due to the sheer amount of things that needed to die.

My feet carried me from one breach to the next. My opponents didn't all arrive healthy and whole, but they had to be put down regardless. They didn't stop trying to kill me until they were utterly dead.

You are now Level 13.
Sword is now Level 2.
Sword is now Level 3.

I slashed at their faces. I chopped at their necks. Stabbed their hearts.

The bodies piled up around my machines and me.

As fatigue loomed, I switched my sword to my metal hand. It wasn't nearly as adept at this kind of thing as my natural one since it had no nerve endings, but it was the best solution I had.

I summoned another rock to throw, but the Scourge-Touched wouldn't let me breathe. I was always moving, always chopping.

*No time.*

*Screw it. Please let this work.*

I summoned more stones, a handful of them at a time, and began to channel. Knives of ice threatened to erupt from my splitting head.

Volatility [1 MP/sec]
Volatility [1 MP/sec]
Volatility [1 MP/sec]
Volatility [1 MP/sec]
Volatility [1 MP/sec]
Split Mind is now Level 8.

*BRRRRAP! BRRRRRRRRRRRRRRRRRR!*

It was a constant. The turrets had so much to shoot at. So many hateful faces. I needed space. I needed it now.

I channeled Volatility into the rocks in my hand as long as I dared until the splitting feeling became unbearable, then I cocked my arm back and let fly with a side-armed pitch Vince would have been proud of, a throw that released all of my glowing stones at a different point in the arc.

The stones fanned outward, past the stairwell turret and into the line of monsters.

*BOOM!BOOM!BOOM!BOOM!BOOM!*

You are now Level 14.

The world went quiet.

Status gained: Deafened [1 min]

Breathing hard and feeling a full mana migraine flaring behind my eyes, I staggered over the broken, perforated forms of my enemies and to my pile of oiled wood.

Status gained: Engine [14 MP/sec for 10 min]
You gain knowledge of material: Mendau Wood [1,092/1,250]
You gain knowledge of material: Pex Oil [1/10]

I got my feet under me. The roof spun in place as my ears wept blood, and I fought to stay upright.

"Come on! Come on!" I shouted at their faces, spinning around to make sure they all saw I was fine and unafraid. "You wanted me! I'm still here!"

Of course, the multiverse being what it was, that was when the first turret ran dry.

# CHAPTER FORTY-SIX

# Just Hold On

The turret facing the stairwell—the one that had been hardest pressed up until this point—just went dead.

*Oh, shit.*

All things considered, I was lucky to have seen it happen. As deaf as I was just now, it could have taken me a long time to notice, and then I'd have been drowning in monsters and not knowing why all the way up until they ripped me apart.

The Scourge-Touched within the blast zone were slow to get up, their crumpled bodies and shell-shocked neural tissues making them sluggish and clumsy. They were tenacious, though. Some of the more-robust specimens were already pulling themselves forward using whatever limbs they still had, snarling and burbling silently as they advanced on my position.

They had no fear, no response to pain or loss, and fresh, grinning faces. I had maybe a few seconds before the tide would be lapping at my feet again.

I wobbled to where my stash of spare magazines were supposed to be and used my foot to roll the good part of a Returned corpse off them (where the rest of it was I didn't know), revealing the slimy but still-functional row of spare ammo fans.

Drunkenly and with considerable effort, I bent over and snagged one of the magazines without falling to the ground to join them. The world was spinning around me, and it was all I could do not to lie down and wait for it to stop. My ears really couldn't heal fast enough.

My salvation in hand, I turned and stumble-sprinted over to the dry turret, smacking the release lever with the hilt of my sword to disengage the empty magazine.

*Stuck.*

Not thinking, concussed, or maybe a combination of both, I then made the obvious mistake of using my fingers to work the lever.

I snatched my hand away with a frustrated growl, one I couldn't hear but I could most certainly feel. Even through the leather of the gloves, the extreme temperature of the turret's action cooked my flesh within half a second.

To say that my turret design had heat issues would have been a gross under-statement. I filed this flaw away in my mental "To Address If I Live" folder.

*Hot metal bad. Do not touch.*

My metal hand was much more able to work the thing, but the time I'd wasted flash-frying my pointer and middle finger came back to haunt me immediately.

I was just disengaging the spent magazine when I caught swift movement out of the corner of my eye, and I pulled back from the turret just in time to get my sword up.

Something hot and wet slapped against my sword arm, my chest, and the bottom of my face. The surprise, coupled with the weight and force of it, made me take a reflexive step back, but I was disoriented and dizzy. I went down to the ground, hard.

Now on my back and covered in . . . something, I struggled and kicked my legs, grunting with the effort—though, again, I couldn't hear myself, and not just because I was deafened. My mouth, like a large part of my upper half, was covered in some kind of yellow, oily sheet that smelled of rotten lemons, and the grip it had on me was getting progressively stronger. It seemed to slide over me, expanding its surface area like spilled liquid over a table.

Bending my neck, I struggled to look down at my feet to see what I was dealing with.

Yes. I was wrapped in something yellow, slimy, and vaguely organic. Most of me was covered in whatever it was, and the rapidly vanishing parts of my body that weren't bound up in pus-colored bedsheet were quickly being smothered in the stuff as well. My sword was the only thing free after having punctured its way through the slick membrane by sheer luck or old reflexes from training I barely remembered.

Near my navel, a thick . . . proboscis?... tentacle?... struggled against me, forc-ing me down on the marble roof and holding me still. It was a tube of similarly slimy yellow that bloated and pulsed to a beat I couldn't hear. Meanwhile, my fleshy prison expanded to cover more and more surface area. By now, it was fully wrapped around my back and was working its way up my neck.

My eyes tracked to the end of said fleshy tube and saw something along the lines of a giant snake. A fat, giant snake. At least that's how my mind cat-egorized it at a glance. Its head was at least shaped like a snake's, but after that, Earth biology became less and less helpful. The body, though longer than it was wide, was only just so, and a plume of yellow spines grew down its back like a mohawk.

This monster, like the other Touched beings, looked worse for wear, with rheumy white eyes and patches of missing scales, but it certainly had all of its teeth—rows of them.

The thing's body was as wide as the entire stairwell, and, as it wriggled its way onto the roof, I could see other, less fortunate Scourge-Touched crushed against the sides of the marble walls.

Where a snake was long and generally fit for slithering, this one seemed to locomote more like a worm, except for a prominent, overdeveloped rib cage that started a few feet below its head, the sides of which were pumping like bellows, flapping in and out, stretching the creature's grayish-green skin, then sharply contracting over and over. When its body contracted, the tube attached to my prison expanded noticeably and the yellow flesh tarp tightened around me.

Muscles contracted in the snake's throat, and the tube that connected us shortened visibly with every second.

It may have been struggling to make it all the way onto the roof, but it was getting ever-closer to eating me. It was reeling me in, its inwardly curved teeth ready to grab and never let go.

What's more:

Status gained: Necrosis [2 HP/sec]

I was being digested. This was the second time in my new life something had tried to digest me without doing the polite thing of killing me first.

Ralqir was a silly place.

Just then, my hearing came back, a whine at first, and then things resolved into something akin to normal, in time to experience the sound of the creature *HORF!*-ing as it pumped biological mystery juice into my yellow flesh sac. It sounded like a giant cat trying to hack up a hairball, except far more sinister, which was a feat and a half based on the cats I'd met.

Well, if it was going to do the eating now and the killing later, I was well within my rights to do the killing now and the dying later.

I groaned against the slimy tissue, flexed my sword hand at the wrist, and made use of my enhanced Body score.

The supernaturally sharpened blade did most of the work cutting through the membrane, and soon my arm burst from it with a slurping sound I would probably have nightmares about later. The scent of sour fluids and half-cooked armor and skin permeated the air.

*Think about it later. Think about it* much *later.*

Then my blade arced over to the proboscis and severed it with two short chops. Clear fluid spewed from both ends of the tube, and the creature shrieked indignantly.

Instantly, the pressure around my body ceased, and the yellow sac seemed to shrivel and bunch up around my chest until it flopped to the ground next to me, a wrinkly pile of goo and fibrous muscle more like a tongue than whatever shape it had taken before.

The creature yowled, but it didn't stop advancing. As it wriggled closer, it slurped its remaining tubage up like a meaty piece of spaghetti. That nearly did me in.

*Do. Not. Vomit.*

Thankfully, the monster wasn't fast—probably an ambush predator, or maybe it was just dumber and slower after falling to the Scourge plague. As it finally freed itself from the stairwell, it trundled forward at the speed of a chubby toddler, albeit one with a taste for human flesh. I had to force myself to look away from all the slowly approaching teeth and fumble for my magazine.

Finally, I slapped the new bullet fan home and engaged the locking lever.

Instantaneously, the turret was back to dispensing death with a deafening volley of shots into the creature's face. Flesh and bone were quickly parted from the rest of the body, the fresh stream of bullets so intensely kinetic, they sawed through the fat snake's insides, splitting it down the middle until the turret found something vital or the creature just stopped moving.

---

You have defeated Scourge-Touched Joroba.
You have been awarded 360 Experience points. [150 base (+30 nemesis, +150 group, +150 chain, -120 non-combat Class)]

---

I forced myself to breathe again.

*Peachy. The Scourge has gotten to the wildlife, too.*

Then the auto-turret was on to the smaller targets, and just in time. The Scourge-Touched Undead and goblins had fresh bodies to throw at me now that the stairwell was unobstructed again, and they were already too many and too close for my liking.

I staggered back to the center of the triangle.

My skin felt like it was on fire. When I moved, I could feel the tender parts of my flesh rubbing together painfully, weeping sores coating the insides of my clothes. Whatever poison or acid the joroba had used was still active in some way, or it just hadn't gotten to my nerve endings yet.

I couldn't stop moving, though. The Scourge-Touched were already back inside the perimeter.

Then I was back to hacking and stabbing everything that moved. What I couldn't kill with my sword, I crushed with my metal arm, either with Devouring

Grasp or through the sheer blunt force of a closed fist and amplified . . . what was my Body score now?

*Not now. Check later.*

The lip of the roof was just gone, the courtyard beyond, too, their memories replaced by a wall of sagging meat. The dead became the walls of my fortress, and their comrades clambered over them only to die and add to the mass.

They never stopped coming.

I waded through the lucky ones that breached the perimeter, dispatching the fresh enemies first and the wounded ones when I could spare a second, but I took stinging wounds to my legs, my arms, and my hands. For each enemy I ended, another was right there to make me pay a price for it with claws or teeth.

Nothing I did came for free.

The north-facing gun went silent next, as I'd feared it would. I just didn't know what I could do about it, I was so pressed.

The monsters, seeming to collectively sense their opportunity to end it, boiled up from the corpse wall with renewed vigor for their final charge. I pulled my pistol out of my belt.

Faces appeared before me and were cut down. I hardly had to aim, I was so close to my targets. My fat ammo worms punched ragged, gaping holes in whatever they hit.

Slash. Fire. Slash. Stab. Fire. Fire. Slash.

With every downed foe, I couldn't help but look up to watch more enemies piling over the north wall. They'd figured things out quickly.

And I was drowning in monsters.

My world was steadily reduced to a desperate, bloody struggle just to stay alive. Hands reached for me. Mouths shrieked as they snapped at my face.

Hack. Slash. Stab. Fire. Slash.

They were too many, too close. Their claws raked me even as they died. Their teeth gnawed at my legs.

Gulping for oxygen, blood trickling down into my right eye and painting my world red, my sword arm hanging limply at my side, I looked up one last time.

The Baned leapt down from the overrun battlements, something akin to glee on their expressions as they rushed to be the first to rip me open. They howled in unison, in anticipation of their triumph . . .

. . . only to be obliterated from above.

Too fast to perceive as anything other than streaming gray streaks of force and mass, a volley of projectiles slammed down upon the monsters' shoulders, backs, and heads. Supersonic wasps of iron and lead broke limbs, shattered skulls and spines. The multitude of corpses the monsters had used for handholds quickly turned to mulch.

*THWUP! THWUP! THWUP! THWUP!*

I let out a long, shaky sigh of relief.

Slowly, my blurring vision traced the stream of death up, up from my grim redoubt to the Spire, to Trix's position on the observation deck. Strobing purple-white muzzle flashes bloomed from the ends of the twin barrels of his gun emplacement, and the lead fell like rain.

Trix was scratching my back.

That meant two things. Firstly, I had the little vulpa's attention, which was nice. It felt good to not be alone. Secondly, the fight had been going on longer than I'd realized. Trix wasn't supposed to reveal his position until all of our friendlies were at least inside Spire Square.

My heart thrummed at that thought. They were here, I was alive, and I wasn't alone.

The hand that had been tightening around my chest seemed to loosen its grip, slightly.

I used the breathing room Trix gave me to grab two more magazines. I replaced the one on the dry gun and then preemptively refreshed the other, less-pressed turret. It would have run out soon anyway.

Once I was back in business and my guns were active, Trix seemed to take the hint and turned his fire elsewhere.

That was okay. If someone else needed him, I'd hold. The longer I held, the longer I was doing my job, and the longer the rescue team had to run to the Spire.

You are now Level 15.

It wasn't even a question. HP was a resource that I needed right now. I slapped all of my available points into Body and felt myself begin to knit together instantly, my tired muscles feeling that much fresher, and my breathing becoming that much smoother.

*Just a little longer. Hold on just a little longer.*

# CHAPTER FORTY-SEVEN

# Follow the Light

The breathing room Trix gave me didn't last. That was the problem with opponents with no instinct for self-preservation. They were perfectly fine throwing themselves at me and being reduced to a puddle of goo if there were even a remote chance of said puddle of goo making my footing slightly more tenuous.

I did use the window of relative calm to charge up another handful of stones, though, if only to give my body a rest.

Split Mind is now Level 9.
Conduit is now Level 5.

I was glad at least someone appreciated how difficult the trick was. That biting, cold feeling I experienced when using foreign mana types (thanks, Tempered Channels) ripped at the edges of my concentration every time I pulled this little maneuver, and I knew I was tempting fate with every additional rock I added.

This time I made sure to be well away from the blast zone before I launched rocks toward the growing mound of corpses that used to be the stairwell. I aimed for the top of the pile, having the rocks zip over the peak before I triggered the detonations directly on top of the creatures currently climbing over.

A panorama of purple explosions ripped through the rising tide.

*BOOM! BOOM! BOOM! BOOM! BOOM!*

My head absolutely throbbed. I wasn't low on mana—far from it, in fact. My oiled wood technique seemed to be working beautifully in keeping me topped up. However, the constant bottoming-out of my mana pool and subsequent drink-through-a-firehose recharge was starting to do something to me that was decidedly unpleasant. I felt empty yet brimming with energy, like I'd gone two days eating nothing but coffee grounds. Maybe, more accurately, I felt like I was a pass-through for all of this mana instead of in control of it like I should have been.

The stairwell side suppressed for now, I turned my attention to the rest of my defense. The turrets barked as the flow of Scourge gradually grew from a trickle back to a roar.

I slapped a new magazine into the stairwell side turret and got it back in business. By this point I wasn't as worried about the stairwell as I was about the north and east side turrets. The slain monsters, though both a blessing and a curse everywhere else, had begun to choke the stairwell entrance to the point where the press of bodies was keeping the flow of Returned to a steady drip. That didn't stop them from coming up that side of the roof, but without the stairs, it bottlenecked a large part of the enemy host up to where they were manageable.

Everywhere else, the Baned were making my life an absolute nightmare.

They used their dead as cover to climb up onto the roof, grouping up near the top of the corpse walls to come at me in larger numbers. They were starting to do their grasshopper leaps before they even crested the battlements of my ever-growing fortress, and that left the turrets with precious little time to track and kill them all before they were in my face.

What's more, the amount of things on the roof was quickly becoming the biggest problem. Not only were my fortress walls growing in height but, as physics dictated, in width as well. With every downed foe, the base of the wall of dead things crept closer to my perimeter, a noose of my own making that was slowly tightening as the fight wore on.

The Scourge-Touched I'd had to dispatch with my sword laid at my feet, now a thickening carpet of tripping hazards that leaked blood and unmentionable fluids everywhere. They made moving from breach to breach with any speed or technique almost impossible. My now-higher Body score was helping with that, my supernatural balance and grace keeping me upright, but soon I'd be walking on nothing but dead Scourge. At that point, it would only take one stumble to end it all.

I had to keep moving, though. To stop moving meant death.

The Scourge-Touched were starting to adapt to our strange equilibrium. Now, instead of going into a murderous rage every time they saw me, some of them would eschew the direct approach and lunge for the turrets. Usually, that plan would just end with another dead goblin, but about one in five that tried would make it as far as the turret's legs. Fewer still would get a hand on the machine and have a chance to flip it over.

It only took one nearly catastrophic incident to vindicate my practice of killing breaches as they happened. I had a hell of a time flipping the turret back over. It was heavy and awkward, and its programming didn't particularly care whether it was upright or not. I'd never been a livestock guy, but if I had to create a metaphor for the situation, it would involve trying to lift a pissed-off, three-legged, mechanical murder bull. Oh, and the bull's shoulders and head were hot enough to ignite fibers and fry skin.

Yes, after that, I was very attentive to breaches.

Movement was key. I had to be everywhere, protecting the turrets so they could protect me.

I had to imagine my ammo worms were having a hell of a time trying to fulfill their programming by returning to me, or maybe they already had but I hadn't noticed in all the chaos.

The focus and technique Dad drilled into me was doing me some good when I had a chance to use it, but Dad didn't teach me fighting like this—the mad scramble for survival amid hundreds of tiny threats that would stop at nothing to draw just a little of my blood.

This was butchery. Mass slaughter.

I had no room for a proper parry or riposte, my feet couldn't turn or slide the way I'd been taught, and there was a massive qualitative difference between a duel between armed opponents and a swarm of monsters that just threw themselves at you without regard for their own lives. The best I could do was jump at opportunities for free hits and swing for the fences.

*Just a little longer.*

---

Sword is now Level 4.
You are now Level 16.

---

The arc of my swing connected with the Undead's neck, the creature's spine stubbornly halting my swing before the blade could cleave all the way through, and I felt the muted impact in my chest even through the metal of my arm. The Scourge-Touched, unfazed at the sword embedded in its neck, grasped the sides of my cuirass and used its unnatural strength to pull itself closer in an attempt at a bite. Growling, I set my pistol hand against the monster's chest and slowly straightened my arm until I had the right amount of space. Then I jerked my blade free to slam it down again and again until the thing finally fell over dead.

Spots danced in my vision, my muscles burned, and my lungs cried constantly for more air untainted by the foul emanations surrounding me. The battlefield was a horrific slurry of broken bodies and gore. The turret barrels sizzled in the polluted air, and the smell was everywhere.

I missed the sword's atomically sharp edge desperately just now, but I had no time to re-Shape it back to what it was. I just had to endure a little longer.

*PHOP! PHOP! PHOP!*

The stairwell turret was getting low on power, and the barrel had a noticeable bow to it now, the heat finally making the steel pliable enough for gravity to warp it in such a way. The gun still tracked and fired, but it was having a hard time. Its individual rounds, with a less than straight path out of the barrel, were more sluggish and less impactful when they hit. I just felt lucky the action's spring was weak enough to keep the feed of lead going.

My right hand hung down at my side, and I could feel the hot rush of blood pumping through torn muscle fibers. Overworked tendons throbbed at my joints. The effort I'd expended to wrestle with that last Returned was all I had left. I could barely even lift the pistol in my hand anymore. My body was tapped out, my prosthetic the only part of me not weak and bleeding.

I slapped my new free point into Body and felt the effects immediately, like I'd just gotten an injection of electrolytes and saline. It wasn't much—just enough to take the edge off—but it was something.

"Come on," I whispered hoarsely against the polluted air. The boom of the guns and the howls of the Scourge-Touched drowned out my voice, but this was for me more than it was for them at this point. "Come on, you little shits."

*Just a little longer.*

Just then, something flashed in the corner of my vision, pale-blue, arc-welder bright. What was this now?

Turning my head, I tracked the intensity of the light up, north, toward the Spire.

A flare. A bright blue flare was floating lazily down from somewhere near Trix's observation deck.

What did that mean? It had been part of my plan . . . My brows knit together in thought. It felt so long ago, and I was so tired.

A scrap of a thought blew lazily through the hollows of my mind, tumbling before finally clipping the edge of another.

Blue meant . . . *safe.* They were safe! Samila. Sissa. Geddon. They'd made it back to the Spire, and they were safe. All of them.

It was time. It was time to move.

*Forward. Move forward.*

I wobbled forward, toward the light. A Baned loomed up to block my view. My body reacted.

Scourge-Touched Goblin defeated.

> You have been awarded 18 Experience points. [10 base (-6 Level, +2 nemesis, +10 group, +10 chain, -8 non-combat Class)]

Stepping over the crumpled form, I followed the light past the northern turret, its rate of fire now in sluggish staccato bursts of *FWUPFWUPFWUP FWUPFWUPFWUP*, a beat I could feel in place of a pulse.

Any other day, I'd hesitate to get in its way, but after spending all this time in a constant state of knife's-edge tension, I had a hard time rising above the level of a two on the fear scale anymore, especially for my own machines. It had my back, just as I'd asked it to when I'd made it.

I pressed forward, my sword hacking at the monsters that presented themselves to me. My sword strokes were weak and slow, only serving to keep my enemies' grasping claws temporarily away from my body. That was okay, though. I just had to keep moving forward.

The turret did what I couldn't. The best the Scourge-Touched could hope for was one, maybe two swipes at the human before they died in a hail of bullets. All I had to do was survive.

When I came to the wall, I climbed. The smell was worse here. It didn't matter.

What mattered was getting over, getting through, getting to the light.

The mound was unsteady. The bodies gave when I stepped on them and slid down when I grasped them—landslides of dead things.

I pushed that grim thought aside for now. Then I was standing at the top.

Before me was a nightmare. The city was swarming. Teeming masses of monsters crawled over rooftops, flooded the streets, choked the doorways. All of them flowed toward me, like I was the drain in a bath. I was a nexus, the black hole where they meant to cast out their lives in the hopes of drowning me under their combined weight. As one, they wordlessly roared their desire to do so.

It turned out I still had room in my mind for fear after all. My legs nearly gave out at the sight of it.

*Holy Constance, preserve us. Holy shit. Holy shit.*

There was only one island of order amid all the chaos.

At the center of the square, beyond the black sea of scourge, ranks of people . . . *soldiers* stood in neat lines, shields and spears leveled and at the ready. They were waiting for me.

That was where I had to go.

The Scourge-Touched were climbing up from down below me, while others were rushing in from my sides.

*Forward. Move. Move now.*

Another handful of rocks appeared in my hand. I needed a few seconds.

*One.*

A claw slashed at my shins, scoring across my armor.

*Two.*

A Baned leapt at my face from the approach to my right. It didn't take much convincing for my legs to give out, collapsing to the floor to allow the monster to sail overhead. Something from within the mass of corpses grabbed my neck from behind, weak but still alive, its broken claws attempting unsuccessfully to tear open my throat.

*Three.*

I sat up and stabbed out with my sword to take one of the Scourge in the stomach. It didn't die, but its lower half gave out, sending it tumbling down the wall and over the lip of the roof.

*Four.*

Something jumped on my back, digging in with its claws, and its teeth sawed into the armor on my shoulder. That felt familiar.

*Five.*

I couldn't wait any longer.

With one final lungful of breath, I screamed as I forced my tired leg muscles to straighten, and leapt from the battlements of my fortress. The sea of black rushed up to meet me.

*BOOM! BOOM! BOOM! BOOM! BOOM! BOOM!*

My charged rocks hit the ground before I did: a carpet of wild, explosive power that pulped the Scourge-Touched down below, as packed in as they were.

From above, hundreds of angry hornets zipped down in blurry gray lines to lay waste to everything they hit. The Scourge-Touched were mowed down like wheat.

*ZUP! ZUP! ZUP! ZUP! ZUP! ZUP!*

I landed badly, among the shell-shocked monsters. I had the sense to tuck and roll, but when I made impact, the air left my body in a *whoosh* and I tumbled forward to hit some of the only exposed paver stones for many yards.

---

Status gained: Broken Bone [Arm]

---

I laid there for a full second, opening and closing my mouth like a fish suddenly pulled from the water, but I knew I had to move. Moving was all I could do if I wanted to live. I got to my feet and stopped, blinked. What happened? I'd lost the Spire. Where was it?

*ZUP! ZUP! ZUP! ZUP! ZUP! ZUP!*

*The blue. The blue light. Where?*

Spinning, I tracked the light, orienting myself. It gleamed off teeth and claws, cast shadows behind individual monsters in the swarm.

Behind.

There. Behind me. The Spire. I had to get to the Spire.

I hobbled forward, following the track Trix's withering fire gave me. He blasted huge swathes of monsters in five-second bursts. Wherever he turned his fire the entire area became a mess of fountaining blood and flying splinters of bone. Then he would shift to my side or to my back.

Crossbow bolts zipped past my ears, one of them inches from my skin before it sank into something behind me with a *thwuk*. The dying breath of whatever it was caressed the hair on the back of my head.

I couldn't think about that, either.

I kept moving forward. Always forward. Trix and the crossbowmen paved my way.

An Undead rose up in front of me, missing an arm, its head listing sideways but not entirely damaged enough for it to stay dead. I tried to swing my sword but found that I'd dropped it somewhere in my landing. So, instead, I reached out and slammed my fist into its face with my prosthetic, then shoulder-charged the creature until it vanished from sight. I didn't bother to finish it off.

I kept moving.

The world narrowed. All I could hear was my own breathing. All I could feel was my burning lungs and pumping legs while the rest of me was just cold.

All I could see was the sliver of light between the gates. Between me and it, the ranks of people—real-live people—gesturing me forward. Cheering.

"Come on! Come on!" they said to me. "Don't stop!"

I kept moving.

My eyes felt heavy. Only one of them could fully open anyway, but for the life of me I didn't know which one. It didn't matter. I knew where I was going. Something heavy battered me from above. A burning line traced down the center of my scalp. I reached up and grabbed, triggering Devouring Grasp, and then it was gone.

*Forward. Forward. No stopping.*

*FWOOM!*

Then the air went still.

With great effort, I opened my eye.

Faces surrounded me. The two closest people, male Miur in ragged robes held up their glowing hands in confusion, severe looks of concentration on their faces, sweat pouring down their brows. That wasn't the light I was following. Mine was blue. The Miur didn't get in my way, though. My feet kept moving.

*Forward.*

Something tried to grab me, but I put a stop to it. No. I was so close. Nothing could stop me. I had to get to the Spire.

The ranks of soldiers, Miur, Leori, and a few species I didn't recognize in their armor, all slowly parted to let me pass. None of them said anything, as if the still air had put a hush spell over them.

My rattling breaths seemed to be the only sounds allowed to bypass said spell. They echoed in my head, accompanied only by the hum of my metal heart.

Up the stairs. That took some time. My leg wasn't working right anymore. No one made a move to stop me.

I reached out for the door.

Then, in a turn I could never have foreseen, a skeletal Miur with ridiculously pronounced cheekbones interposed himself between me and my goal. He bent down, his hawkish face peering into mine with a look of . . . concern? Frustration? It took me a handful of breaths to really get a good bead on it.

He was saying something. His voice was so familiar, but the memory of it was just out of reach. I shook myself, blinked blood out of my eye.

"What?" I heard myself say.

He reached out hesitantly for my arm, his fingers wrapping around my bicep and steadying me. His look of absolute disbelief was amplified by his gaunt features.

"It's alright, Ryan, we'll take it from here." He breathed softly as if he were calming a wild animal. Then he shook his head before adding: "Unbelievable."

Jassin? *What are you doing here?*

I felt myself falling forward, darkness gently slipping over me like a warm, heavy blanket.

It didn't matter. They were safe. I could rest.

| Ryan Kotes - Level 16 (?) Animator (Uncommon) | | | | |
|---|---|---|---|---|
| **Type:** | Artificer (Common) | **Abilities:** | Shape 9 (Transmute) | Devouring Grasp: 5(?) |
| **Class:** | Animator (Uncommon) | | Consume: 5 (?) | Volatility 3 |
| **Core:** | Engine (Unique) | | Iron Grip 4 | Imbue 4 |
| **HP:** | 220/220 | | Trigger 4 | Automate: 4+ |
| **MP:** | 186/186 | | Tempered Channels: 3 | Knife in the Dark: 22 (?) |
| **Body:** | 40 | **Skills:** | Climbing 7 | Unarmed Combat: 5 (?) |
| **Mind:** | 33 | | Running: 5 (?) | Stealth (Gray Man): 11 |
| **Spirit:** | 77 | | Conduit: 5 (?) | Split Mind: 9 |
| | | | Spear 4 | Deception: 5 (?) |
| | | | Disguise: 1 | Sword: 6 (?) |
| | | | Pistol: 4 | |

| | | **Affinities:** | Goblinoid F | Limestone E |
|---|---|---|---|---|
| | | | Iron E | Cobalt E |
| | | | Steel F+ | Deep Lead E |
| Free Attribute points: 0 | | | Magnesium F | Nickel E |
| | | | Mendau Wood D | Copper F |

# Trix

Trix burst from the stairwell and onto the Spire's ground floor, his limbs shaky from so long in the gunner's seat and then the climb down from the observation deck. The place was absolutely full of rough-looking warriors fresh from the field of battle, but putting duty first, as such people always did, many still busy with the business of fortifying the doors, tending the wounded, or organizing the others.

Those who had no immediate task set for them laid on the floor to preserve their energy. Dirty, scarred faces stared off into space, while ready hands were wrapped tightly around their weapons. Trix imagined even the *thought* of letting go of said weapons was far from their minds. They clung to them as drowning men to driftwood.

These people had been fighting for days straight, in constant action, facing horror head-on. It would take some time to convince them they were safe.

The stench of blood and stale fear threatened to overwhelm Trix, but he fought to not let it show. They needed him to be a calming presence, a symbol of sanctuary, if only a minor one. If Trix had been through what they had, he would have taken comfort in a friendly face. He would endeavor to be that for them now.

Through the crowd Trix went, dodging more than a few pairs of legs as their owners hurried to carry out their duties. Dry, rasping voices, too long at the task of combat, echoed in the vestibule.

"Tanker, you old nub, you made it," a Miur with a bandage over where one of his antlers should have been said to another soldier. Then the two embraced briefly, slapping each other on the backs.

"Might have to find religion after this, eh, boy?" the older soldier joked, earning a wet snort from the other.

The younger one chuckled quietly, sparing a look around as if his mirth might be offensive to others. "Better than having it find me, I think, given what I just saw. Never paid Rising Suns' reputation much mind before. Think I will now, though."

"Did you see that?" another unseen voice asked. "He climbed out of a mountain of corpses and swam through a sea of bad."

The old one nodded. "Like seeing a one-man crusade."

"Not sure about all that, but if it's the Church that's responsible for putting a wall between me an' those things, I'll start tithing right now."

In the middle of the room now, Trix was shocked to hear the clear pitch of a small child.

"Can the monsters get in, Mom?" it asked.

"It's alright," its mother soothed. "We're alright now."

A prayer of thanks for the safety of these people passed over Trix's lips. He hoped the light could hear him. What were his prayers compared to all of this?

He looked down at his shaking paws. He could still feel the vibration of the guns, the urgent need to be steady when every twitch, every wasted movement, would cost lives. His heartbeat, though audible to his vulpa ears, sounded all the weaker and less significant compared to the boom of the guns and the terrible, churning storm of combat.

He blinked and shook his head. He was here for a reason.

Sergeant Sissa stood near the fountain that was the central fixture of the room, her armor covered in blood as she spoke to a tall, harsh Miur in immaculate robes. The man looked like he hadn't eaten in a long time given how thin he was.

"I'm afraid I insist," the sergeant said, anger simmering under her otherwise-tired voice. Corporal Samila, at her left elbow as always, looked similarly put out. It was easy to tell their relation when the two of them were in sync like this.

"I assure you he is under the best possible care," the gaunt figure replied dourly.

Sissa worked her jaw and let out a slow breath, the kind she used to calm herself before she said something she regretted. "I am sure he is, Headmaster Jassin. I should know. We set up the triage rooms before we came to rescue you. Angol should have filled you in."

Trix's heart skipped a beat. The headmaster. Had they lucked into rescuing one of the most powerful practitioners in the world? There may be a dawn coming to disperse the night after all.

Headmaster Jassin seemed to take in the dragonkin's words, thoughtfully disassembling them, analyzing them. He paused for a brief second, then allowed the look on his face to soften somewhat. Then he gave a small but incredibly significant bow of acknowledgement of the sister's heroic efforts.

Sergeant Sissa charged into the gap that the headmaster had just opened. "The problem is that he is not in any of the triage rooms. You must understand our concern." Subtle stressors in her voice gave Trix the impression that this was repetition of a previous part of the conversation.

They were talking about Brother Ryan. Trix was sure of it. He'd lost sight of the Rising Sun when he'd passed into the shadow of the Spire and out of the gun emplacement's line of fire, but Trix had been almost entirely sure the monk was safe.

Did that mean the brother's injuries had been severe? Trix's claws clicked together nervously. The thought of using his inherent magic for this purpose again was troubling, but for his brother— No . . . his *friend*, Trix would do it again. Though the fact that Brother Ryan seemed particularly resilient to the terrible side effects helped a bit.

Before he knew it, Trix's paws had carried him over to the group and up onto Samila's shoulder. He ignored the pungent stink of the Returned on the corporal's armor as well as the messy smears of half-dried blood, how it got on his robes and paws as he clambered up. Trix had killed many of these same creatures today from afar. He couldn't let himself be squeamish now. To shrink away would be to disrespect the memory of those he'd slain.

"I volunteer my services to whoever is in need," Trix squeaked before he could reconsider, and the chilly feeling of a promise made passed through his body. "However, if Brother Ryan's wounds are dire, I wish to see him first."

"This is the 'gunner' you mentioned previously?" Headmaster Jassin asked.

"This is Brother Yik'i'trix, without whom none of us would be alive. He was on the tower keeping the infected off our backs." Sissa turned her head and gave Trix a tiny smile. There was something there, in her look—an acknowledgement of some kind. Something like kinship or—

Respect. Sergeant Sissa *respected* him.

"Whoa there, fuzzball. You're going to fall off," Samila chuckled, reaching up to steady him. The gesture wasn't required, of course. Trix's balance was uncanny compared to most of the larger species of Ralqir, but perhaps he had gotten a little close to the edge. He was rather tired.

Still, the sergeant *respected* him. Did she consider him an equal? One of them?

The possibility meant so much to him that he was afraid to believe it was real.

Headmaster Jassin also regarded Trix—not necessarily as a warrior but something else. A curiosity, perhaps, something worth attention, and, from someone of such high station, that was a compliment indeed.

"In that case, I want to extend to you my sincere thanks for your part in rescuing my people, Brother Yik'i'trix. Also, for your organization of the students in the kitchens. My people have been without hot meals for a long time, and this will go a long way toward health and morale," the headmaster intoned formally. He nodded to Trix and his eyes flashed. "Also, if you ever have a moment, I would very much like to talk with you about what being a 'gunner' means."

"You keep talking, but you continue to evade our chief concern. You have one of ours, and we would like him back." Geddon loomed over the headmaster's back like a mountain.

While the others showed clear signs of having been in battle, Geddon was a walking slaughterhouse. Blood and viscera hung from his body, clung to his face, stuck between the seams of his armor. The only clean spots on the Leori were his teeth, which he flashed in a grin that bordered on predatory. If Trix hadn't known any better, he would have thought Geddon was ready to start a conflict with the headmaster just because he wasn't ready to be done fighting for the day.

The headmaster turned only slightly so that he was able to address the entire party at once, then raised his hand in what could be interpreted as a placating gesture. However, Trix's sharp eyes detected the faintest sheen of magic gathered near the fingertips.

"We have all been through much these past days, and I would advise you to direct your ire toward the real enemy we all fought so viciously to be here. Brother Ryan is stable and recovering in a special location due to his unique Dominion. His injuries were severe, but he will make a full recovery under my personal care, I assure you."

"Forgive us, Headmaster, but we hadn't realized your field of study was medicine. Brother Trix would be glad to lend you any assistance you require to care for our brother, as he has served as Brother Ryan's physician for years," Sergeant Sissa bluffed. Trix felt his fur rising, and he fought to keep the distaste for the lie his companion told from his face.

"Has he now?" the headmaster asked, turning to Trix once more. The undeniable pressure from the headmaster's stare forced Trix's eyes to the floor, and his head followed. With effort, he tried his best to disguise his guilt as a bow.

But whatever questioning Trix had feared from Headmaster Jassin never materialized. Instead, the powerful noble grinned.

"Unbelievable," he said. "When I next speak with him, I will be sure to mention how fiercely his friends fought to see him. However, we stand in my house, Sergeant, and my order still stands."

A bit of smugness crept into the headmaster's smile as he leaned in to whisper conspiratorially. "And we all know that man does not need a physician."

# Dad



*Proxis 3: Now*

Myron Kotes sat on a dirty fabric camp chair, staring at a rust-colored stain on the rocky ground, his eyes tiredly blinking away the grit. The winds were mild today and at his back, giving his face a break from the goggles he'd been forced to wear day in and day out for however long he'd been at this. The sand-blasted cliff where the System had seen fit to snatch his boy wasn't the most sheltered of places to set up camp—more exposed than he would have chosen.

He reached up to scratch his beard, resisting the temptation to rub his eyes as well. The skin there was red and raw, and if he got too enthusiastic, his fingers might come away with blood. His scalp itched as well, the dust in it turning his jet-black hair prematurely gray.

Normally, he was an exceedingly well-groomed man, upstanding and respected among his peers. Now he wasn't sure if any of the Clan would recognize him.

A metal thermos of coffee thumped against his shoulder, warm to the touch. The rich, bitter smell of it tantalized him. Worse, it tempted his mind to relive better times.

"Take it," a cold, robotic voice said from behind him.

Myron reached up and took the thermos, using his filthy nails to crack open the top and expose the liquid inside while grimacing at the unpleasant idea of drinking the stuff. Riley had loved coffee, and she'd passed that love along to Ryan. Myron himself had never been a fan He did like the smell, however dangerous it was.

"Thanks," he croaked after a long swig of the near-boiling liquid.

When was the last time he'd spoken?

"This marks thirty days, Mr. Kotes," the man behind him droned in a professional manner, like he was a bureaucrat in an office somewhere instead of camping in a portable hab in the middle of nowhere, waiting for the System to regurgitate its latest Chosen. The tone reminded Myron of the synth voices they used on passenger trains.

"He'll make it," Myron affirmed for himself for the hundredth time. It had become a mantra of sorts, one he now repeated even in his dreams.

He'd begun to speak it ever since they'd come to rescue the boys that fateful morning, when Myron had learned his boy was taken.

*Taken from this very spot.*

The ground was still stained with Ryan's blood, though it was fading in the elements, wind-blasted like all of Proxis 3. Like Myron himself. Myron wouldn't forget where the spot was, though.

"Of course, Mr. Kotes," Mr. White said, punctuating his words with a pair of slow, awkward pats on Myron's shoulder. "Once again, allow me to put you up somewhere while we wait. You can still come out to this location whenever you wish, courtesy of a CRF transport."

"No," Myron replied as he'd done every day now.

Mr. White, the man behind him, was an Exotic, probably an old one. Of that Myron was increasingly sure. The way he moved was too graceful, too deliberate and exact, his presence too domineering even when he was silent. White carried no weapons, wore no protective gear, just a simple coat with buttoned pockets and a wide-brimmed hat that covered his shaved head. Myron was fairly sure the man didn't actually sleep in the portahab he'd set up, either. All of it felt off, like a terrible thing trying to imitate a human instead of being one of them.

Plain, wiry, deadly, White wasn't at all like the Exotics the Colony put on the airwaves. He was a man to be watched closely, a born killer if Myron had ever met one.

"I'll be waiting for him when he gets back, Mr. White," Myron said, fighting not to let his hand stray to his belt where he kept his pistol. "He deserves someone who'll be there for him."

*Someone who* should *have been there.*

"You are a leader among your people, are you not? Do you not need to be there for them as well?"

Myron shook his head, keeping his eyes fixed on Ryan's fading blood. "They'll understand. I'm going to do what's right by my boy."

The Exotic sighed performatively, this time resting a gloved hand on Myron's shoulder and giving it an uncomfortably hard squeeze. "Then he will find us both, I am afraid. This—the waiting—is what I do."

Myron turned and narrowed his eyes at White. "Is it, really? By my recollection, what you claim to do has been a different thing every time it's mentioned. What was it last time? Documentation? Security? What really is your job, Mr. White?" he asked for what must have been the fifth time now.

"To be there for the birth of rogue Exotics. To ensure their safety and to guide them home. To tell them their places in our society," White intoned, his too-pale face moving to sound out the words and no more. Myron might as well have been talking to a moving corpse. Still, it was a longer answer than he'd gotten before. Maybe White was feeling magnanimous today.

"Integration can be traumatic for mortal born Exotics," White continued. "He will need someone here who understands."

"I think I understand my own son, Mr. White," Myron growled, probably showing a bit too much anger than was wise. Secret agenda or not, Myron didn't need to antagonize this creature. Watch, yes. Be ready to shoot, yes. Antagonize, no.

He forced his body to relax and his blood to cool—no small feat while staring into Mr. White's pale dead glare, knowing he might have intentions for his only son.

Perhaps it was time for a more direct approach.

"I know when I'm being fed a line, Mr. White," Myron challenged. "I also know Ryan has been gone too long for it to mean anything good, even considering interversal time differentials. Why did they send someone like you out here to wait on a boy who may never come home?"

Mr. White's mouth twitched upward slightly, the first bit of expression Myron had gotten out of him since the day the Colony Exotic had arrived. He couldn't be sure, but Myron thought he saw something then, in White's eyes—an inky shadow that passed like a cloud over night sky.

Myron suppressed a shiver.

"They send me to all Rogue Exotics, Mr. Kotes. Ones that are chosen as opposed to born. The process of integration is unpredictable and poses significant risk, the mitigation of which I have made my purpose in life."

Unsure if he wanted to know the answer but simultaneously unable to resist posing the question, Myron swallowed. "What kind of risk?" he asked in an unintentional whisper.

The look on Myron's face must have amused the Colony man, because Mr. White slowly peeled back his lips to show his teeth.

"The kind you send someone like me to handle."

# About the Author

J. Drude is the author of the Turret Mage series, originally released on Royal Road. In addition to writer, he has at various times undertaken the roles of cook, computer jockey, soldier, and professional tabletop game master—yes, that last one's a real job; no, it doesn't pay well—but his most challenging and rewarding position to date has been that of a husband and father. J. Drude lives in Texas with his wife, two children, and a menagerie of creatures (only some of which are actually domesticated and at least one of which is most certainly plotting his death).

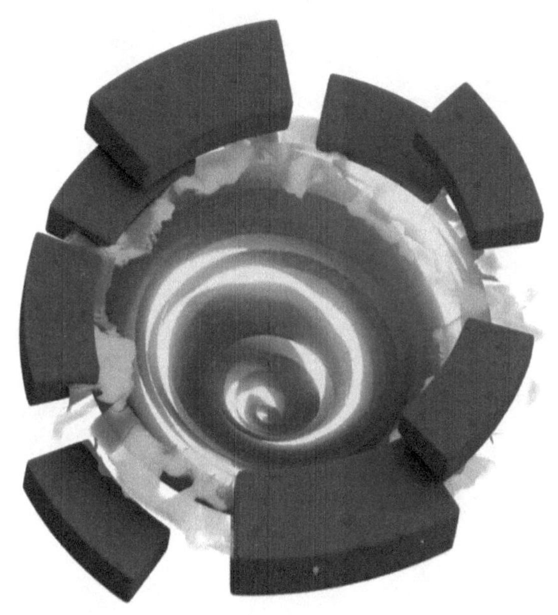

# RESPAWN YOUR CURIOSITY

*follow us on our socials*

 podiumentertainment.com

 @podiumentertainment

 /podiumentertainment

 @podium_ent

 @podiumentertainment

www.ingramcontent.com/pod-product-compliance
Lightning Source LLC
Chambersburg PA
CBHW030923120726
47906CB00002B/455